Pilgrimage

A Novel of the Sovereign Era
The Charters Duology Volume Two
by

Matthew Wayne Selznick

MWS Media

Long Beach, California

Pilgrimage—A Novel of the Sovereign Era

Published by MWS Media

First publication: June, 2013

ISBN-10: 0976942488
ISBN-13: 978-0-9769424-8-1

Cover Art and Design: Neal Von Flue
Developmental Editor: J. C. Hutchins
Copy Editor: Cameron Harris

Find a typo, continuity error, or other mistake? Please contact MWS Media at mwsmedia@gmail.com and let the publisher know about it! We'll confirm it and, if applicable, correct it as quickly as possible. Thanks!

Pilgrimage

A Novel of the Sovereign Era

The Charters Duology Volume Two

Dedication

This is for Carmen, who makes it all happen.

Acknowledgments

This book may never have been written if not for the patient and persistent encouragement and enthusiasm of my community of readers and fans. Their evangelism and support continues to make a meaningful difference in my life and my art.

The following folks were willing and able to materially support the creation of this book through their exceptional, generous patronage:

Chrispian H. Burks
Timothy P. Callahan
J.C. Hutchins
Larry Latouf (xgdfalcon)
James Melzer
Jason Penney
Cassandra Perryman
Jason Rennie
Carmen Whitmer

Author's Note

This story is largely told through the written journal of Nathan Andrew Charters. I have taken some liberties with the source material in the service of clarity and consistency, but I've endeavored to maintain Nate's voice wherever possible, as this is, after all, his story.

The sections presented from the points of view of other characters are an extrapolation based on interviews, court documents and transcriptions, and the public record, and should be considered a storytelling construction.

-- Matthew Wayne Selznick

Sovereign Ability Classes

(Adapted from a joint report of the Donner Institute for Sovereign Studies and the Office of Science and Technology Policy, November 14, 1985.)

The variety of Sovereign metahuman abilities is apparently without limit. However, we recommend the adoption of classification of Sovereign abilities for the purposes of defining and quantifying the Sovereign phenomenon.

Latent

Individuals appear physiologically identical to baseline humans. While psychological or physical stress may cause some individuals to manifest abilities of a different, higher ability class, most live their lives without realizing their potential.

There may be as many as 3,000 latent Sovereigns in the human population.

Nominal

Individuals possess minor psychic or physical abilities outside of the human baseline.

Psychic abilities provide measurable, reproducible results more reliably than could be predicted by statistical chance. Physical abilities are expressed through one to three specific characteristics that fall outside the measured human baseline. Abilities are usually passive in nature and personal in range.

Approximately 35% of all Sovereign belong to the Nominal ability class.

Standard

Individuals possess a "suite" of related psychic and/or physical abilities with a localized range. Physiological adaptations that support the ability suite may also be evident.

Passive and active abilities are found, with range limited to the immediate vicinity and restricted to line-of-sight.

Approximately 3% of Sovereign can be classed as Standard.

Exceptional

Exceptional-class Sovereigns also possess passive and active talent suites, but at a greater power level. Range is limited to a localized area around the individual, and targets (if any) must be in line-of-site.

About 1.5% of all Sovereign can be classified as Exceptional.

Titan

Similarly possessing a talent suite of related physical and psychic abilities with supporting physiological adaptations. Titan-class Sovereigns are vastly more powerful than Exceptional individuals. Range for active abilities is potentially regional and not necessarily limited to line-of-site awareness.

We estimate the existence of no more than two dozen Titan-class Sovereigns.

Paramount

The Paramount class is defined by Sovereigns whose psychic or physical abilities have little or no discernible thematic connection. Paramount class abilities are demonstrably unrestricted in terms of power level or range.

Further, Paramount-class abilities appear to defy the

laws of physics and our definition of reality as currently understood.

At this time, one Paramount-class Sovereign has been identified: Doctor William Karl Donner.

Pilgrimage

The Charters Duology Volume Two

From The Journal Of Nate Charters
One

About a year later, I was a celebrity.

It was stupid.

It was bad enough people would do a double take when they saw me in the grocery store, or passed me on the freeway. I was used to that. It's how it's been my whole life. When you look like me, it's just what happens.

A year after Declaration Day, I was lucky if I didn't see myself as a badly airbrushed artist's rendition on the cover of *The Weekly World News* in the checkout line.

Me and Bat Boy, tabloid superstars. Except he's not real. I don't think.

Hard to know for sure, these days.

On Friday, April 11, 1986, a week before the first anniversary of Declaration Day, the lawyers decided it would be a good idea for me and my mother to be guests on *The Azarrio Show*.

So there I was, Nathan Andrew Charters: household name, boy freak, full-on metahuman and fake Sovereign, roasting under the lights and sweating in a big sticky vinyl chair across the stage from the parents of my childhood rival, who were also trying to sue me and my mother into the poorhouse at best or help the feds throw us in jail at worst.

It was stupid.

My throat clenched as the host, Hank Azarrio, strode across the stage. "Okay, gang… we're back from commercial in thirty seconds." He oozed an oily, gunky stink of hairspray, sweat, makeup like swampy clay, and really terrible cologne. I was the only one in the room bothered by that, of course. Just one of my little gifts. "Everybody all set?"

My mother's "Yes" slipped out of pursed lips. She had righteous indignation to maintain.

Marc Teslowski, doughy and pink, nodded his square head up and down and blinked his piggy eyes. His wife, Jeri, was either terrified or starstruck or maybe both. She smiled with her lips closed and bounced her clenched, knobby little fists in her lap.

Our lawyers straightened their ties and stuck out their chins. The firm had sent Drake Ottman, a young dude with a soap-opera name, to sit in our corner. The name of Teslowski's guy had slipped out of my head a second after I broke off our cold handshake.

What did stick with me was how he'd tried to avoid my fingernails by curving his hand, even after I'd gone to the trouble of clipping and filing them down for the occasion. I scared some folks. This guy was part of that club.

It bugged me, sometimes. Not so much, that day.

The red light over the studio audience blinked. Azarrio ran his hand lightly across his salt-and-pepper-and-cement hair, licked his bushy gross mustache with a thick, pale tongue, and addressed the live camera.

"We're back on *The Azarrio Show* with four people at the center of a controversy directly connected to the story of the century: the remarkable phenomenon of the Sovereigns."

Azarrio indicated me with a wave of his hand that pushed his stench up my sinuses. I suppressed a gag. As much as I didn't want to care, I tried to look cool when one of the cameras zoomed in on my face.

"This young man, despite the fact that he probably

needs no introduction, is Nathan Andrew Charters—your friends call you Nate, though, right?"

All the makeup in the world couldn't hide the acne-scar pockmarks cratering his cheeks. I wondered if that acne had made him a pariah when he was a kid the way my... nature... had made me. I felt the corners of my lips twitch up at the thought of a junior Azarrio having his backpack emptied into a trash can.

"Nathan's fine," I said.

Azarrio's eyes narrowed slightly, but the grin beneath his bushy lip stayed steady.

"Nate, here, is at the center of an ongoing legal battle that has captured the fascination of the entire world. How does it feel to get all that attention, Nate?"

Asshole acted like I was six, not sixteen.

Fine. I was getting really good with confrontation.

Imagining my girlfriend, Lina, in the front row of the studio audience of housewives and unemployed middle-aged twits, I pushed down a little flurry of butterflies in my belly and kept my eyes on Azarrio and off the cameras.

"Are you asking how it feels to know the same people who turned my dad into a crazy freak and then tried to kill him are trying to pin two murders on me and him and my mom?"

Azarrio's eyes glittered. It occurred to me that I was feeding him just what he wanted, but screw it. This whole thing was lame. In for a penny, or whatever.

"I guess it's gonna feel great, once those people end up in prison and PrenticeCambrian and the government cut us a big check and stuff."

Red light for me, green light for Azarrio. He addressed the camera.

"Nate's referring to allegations from PrenticeCambrian —which, by the way, the powers that be want me to mention, is the parent company of some of our affiliate-station sponsors—that his dad, the former scientist Andrew Charters, killed two PrenticeCambrian employees and that Nate himself assaulted a high-ranking executive of PrenticeCambrian subsidiary Tyndale Labs."

My mother's scent drifted on the currents of the studio air-conditioning. It was barbed with tension.

"Call them what they were."

She leaned forward in her chair. I imagined someone in the control room giving the word to put her on camera. "Assassins."

"Alleged assassins, as I'm sure PrenticeCambrian's legal team would want us to note." Azarrio wore a mask of concern and empathy that didn't match his almost-predatory scent.

I wondered if that was what this was for him—if he looked at his guests like prey to corner so he could extract reactions that would bring high ratings for his time slot.

I hoped my mother kept it together, even if I felt my own irritation scratching like bugs multiplying under my skin.

"Ask Marc Teslowski if there's any question on that point." She acted like he wasn't eight feet away from her. Dude was suing us, too, after all. "It's his son those *assassins*," she hissed the word, drawing it out, "nearly gutted in my mother-in-law's driveway."

I don't think Azarrio liked my mother directing his show for him. Instead of turning his attention to Teslowski, he addressed the camera, smooth as sculpted shit.

"Ms. Charters refers to young Byron Teslowski, the teenaged boy hospitalized after the incident at Kirby Lake left two dead under circumstances that are at the heart of the Charters' legal battle with PrenticeCambrian, the government, and, in a related but separate case, the Teslowskis."

Now he faced Marc Teslowski, who held the arms of his chair in a white-knuckled grip. Teslowski didn't look at me in the same way my mother didn't look at him.

So, I made sure to stare, hard, at him.

"Marc and Jeri Teslowski," Azarrio said, "you contend that your son Byron, who the Sovereign claim as one of their own under the controversial Sovereign Compromise, is being illegally held at the Donner Institute for Sovereign Studies near Missoula, Montana."

"That's right." Teslowski spoke through gritted teeth. "Everybody knows that."

"And you hold the Charters—including Nate's father, Andrew Charters, a fugitive and suspect in the killings—responsible. How, exactly?"

Teslowski turned to look at me at last. I let the shit-eating grin I'd been holding back push slowly at the corners of my mouth. I kept my eyes on his.

"That punk helped my kid make a break for it—"

Teslowski's lawyer put his skittish hand on Teslowski's shoulder. "We intend to show that Nathan Charters," he made his voice project, "very likely with the cooperation of his father, and on behalf of the Sovereign, conspired to create an opportunity by which the Donner Institute for Sovereign Studies could apprehend Byron Teslowski."

Our boy Drake spoke up. He had a voice like that DJ on KLOS who plays whole albums on Sunday night: deep and slow. It didn't fit his face. "As our suit brought against PrenticeCambrian and the United States will show, those accusations have no basis in fact."

I looked away from Teslowski to glance at the audience. They were getting into our little circus.

Azarrio acknowledged both attorneys with a nod of his head and turned back to Teslowski. "Marc, you and Jeri also have a civil suit against the Donner Institute for Sovereign Studies to get your son back. Why isn't this a case of criminal kidnapping?"

Teslowski's face darkened. "The goddamned Sovereign Compromise." I imagined someone in the control room hitting the bleep button.

Azarrio shook his head and looked as if he wanted to tut-tut into his microphone. His sympathy didn't reach his eyes.

"Mrs. Teslowski...Jeri..." She went as white as her husband was red. "How long has it been since you've seen your son?"

She swallowed and looked at her hands. My smarmy grin felt a little tired. I didn't have a problem with Byron's mom. She still had to live with her husband.

At least Byron got out.

"It was..." She glanced past me, I guess to my mother. I didn't see any blame in her face. Figured. The Teslowskis might be suing us, but it must be all Marc Teslowski's idea.

"It was May fourth, last year."

Azarrio seemed to actually soften for a second. "That's a

long time."

She nodded, birdlike.

Azarrio turned to me. "What about you, Nate? Byron's a friend of yours...the Donner Institute is assisting you and your mother in your legal battles...have you heard from Byron Teslowski? Maybe chat on the phone?"

"Nope."

I think Azarrio expected me to say something else. When I just looked at him, he ad-libbed, "Do you think he's being held against his will?"

My mother said, "You don't have to answer that— Drake, should he answer—"

"Knowing how things were," I said quickly before Drake could speak up, "I bet Byron's fine."

Marc Teslowski grunted. Azarrio met my eyes like we were partners in his little show.

"Why do you say that?"

Byron Teslowski had made my life hell for years. He somehow made it okay to pick on the weird kid with the odd bone structure and giant eyes when no one would even think of making fun of Tom Harper in his wheelchair or Keri What's-her-name with one leg all bent and shorter than the other one.

We hit high school, and he filled out, and girls liked him, and he kicked ass at every sport he tried. All along, he kept pushing at me, making sure everybody kept thinking I was the weird kid. He ended up with a whole little gang of jocks and cheerleaders in orbit around his smirking face. I could count my friends on one hand and not need my thumb.

Declaration Day changed everything. I learned some

things about Byron. About his dad.

Which is why I helped Byron a year before, but not in the way the Teslowskis thought. It's also why I answered Hank Azarrio the way I did.

"Because his dad's a prick."

A groan of disapproval flowed off the audience. Azarrio, his back to them and fully aware the live camera was on me for the moment, actually gave me a wink. He was quick about it, and made sure he closed his left eye—the one the Teslowskis couldn't see.

Asshole.

He turned his back on me and faced the audience while a different camera put him in frame.

"Strong words from a young man in the eye of the storm." His tone hit perfect notes of concerned disapproval. "When we come back, we'll hear what our audience thinks. After this."

The lights turned red. We had two minutes. Teslowski made the most of it. He flew out of his chair and loomed over me.

"You little shit. Who do you think you are?"

His belly strained beneath his button-down shirt. It was kind of a stupid move, really, putting his gut right in front of a guy whose fingernails can slice through aluminum cans and "still cut tomatoes like this," as they say on the knife commercial.

I fought the urge to see how good a job I'd done blunting my nails. I stayed seated. Fucker wouldn't dare try anything, not with the lawyers all there, not with the studio security guards moving in…not knowing what *I* could do.

"Mister Teslowski, please sit down." Azarrio probably wished Teslowski had waited to perform this little show when the cameras were live.

My mother stood up. "You even think of touching my boy..."

I looked over my shoulder, up at her. "Seriously?"

I saw she was as irritated with me as she was with Teslowski. Great. What had I done, other than say what everyone on our side of the stage all thought?

"Marc..." Jeri Teslowski's protest, if you could call it that, was a little peep.

Teslowski stayed where he was as the seconds ticked away. We looked at each other. The smell of his sweat was thick on my extra-human olfactory glands. He reeked of anger and...yep. There it was.

Fear.

It made my own crawling irritation and frustration with this whole stupid ordeal ratchet tighter. The dense muscles in my thighs bounced with the urge to leap. My peripheral vision blacked as my focus narrowed.

This guy had no idea.

Jeri Teslowski, too quiet for anyone but Marc and my own sensitive ears to hear, said, "Please stop," in a whisper that was way more disgusted than I thought she had the guts for.

Teslowski slumped in his chair, glaring at nothing, and acted like he hadn't heard a thing.

Azarrio moved up into the audience. He was unruffled and ready when the lights changed.

"Welcome back to *The Azarrio Show*, where we're with

two families at the center of a number of legal battles sure to affect relations with the people calling themselves Sovereign for years to come," he said into the camera. "Let's see what the audience thinks of all this."

He found a bald man even softer and fatter than Teslowski. "Hello, sir. What's your name?"

"Frank."

"And what do you do, Frank?"

"I'm a corrections officer."

"A public servant. Good for you." Azarrio put a hand on Frank's shoulder. "Do you have a thought you'd like to share, or a question for our guests?"

Frank's gaze swept past me in the want-to-look-don't-want-to-stare way I'm very, very used to. "My question is for Mister Teslowski..."

We'd been coached on this. Teslowski grumbled, "Hi, Frank."

Frank nodded. He had that weird air of bashful excitement I'd seen on so many television audience members; it was strange to watch it in person.

"Hi. Um...why do the Sovereigns say your son agreed to stay at their...headquarters, or..."

"Institute," Azarrio said helpfully.

"Yeah, their Institute? I mean, if they kidnapped him, what are their demands?"

I almost laughed out loud, which made my mother nudge my chair: a subtle warning for me. How awesome. I couldn't help but wonder if our lawyers had planted this guy.

"Well...Frank..." I watched Teslowski lick his lips and flare his nostrils. "They're not going to come right out and say they kidnapped him. Right?"

Frank scratched the side of his head. "I don't know... I mean, their whole thing is they don't care about our laws, I thought."

Azarrio said, "Perhaps the Sovereign would be reluctant to admit to kidnapping, given the somewhat negative opinion of them held by the majority of Americans, according to one recent poll." He looked at me. "No offense, Nate."

The camera was on me again, ready for a reaction shot. I tensed my legs to keep them from jumping. The butterflies came back.

A memory from almost a year ago popped into my head. My friend Jason, standing up to Byron Teslowski, even though Jason was about a foot and a half shorter and fifty pounds lighter. That helped.

"None taken. Everybody knows I'm not a Sovereign. Hank."

Azarrio had a twinkle in his eye that made me want to rip one out and feel it pop between my teeth.

"That's the assertion of your legal team—funded in part by the Donner Institute for Sovereign Studies itself, we must remember—but doesn't PrenticeCambrian contest that?"

This particular time, I didn't mind my mother speaking up. "I don't think there's a single person in your audience who doesn't know the basics of our legal fight."

Azarrio inclined his head briefly. "You claim there's evidence PrenticeCambrian conducted human experiments that provided Andrew Charters—your husband—with Sovereign-like abilities...and that Nate inherited some of those abilities."

"Conducted, and continue to conduct." My mother's face twisted with disgust. "The assassins they sent after Nathan and Byron had been turned into…monsters."

"These…assassins, as you call them…were killed by Andrew Charters, according to the police report filed by an eyewitness—"

My mother kept her tone firm, but civil, like when she tried explaining why I really, really needed to take the trash out for the good of all mankind. "That's not correct, Mister Azarrio. Andrew killed one of them, in self-defense. The other one died when Lester Brenhurst," she said the name carefully, as if it was a rotten piece of fruit with a pit that threatened to break a tooth if she bit down too hard, "tried to kill my husband."

"Allegedly," Azarrio smiled. He took control of the exchange by turning back to the camera.

"Immediately after the events in question, Andrew Charters disappeared. He remains at large, despite the fact that his testimony could resolve many of the questions at the crux of this drama of corporations, our government, the Sovereigns, and these two families.

"Now, we extended an invitation to both PrenticeCambrian and the Donner Institute to be part of the show today, but their respective representatives declined." Azarrio put his attention on us again. "It makes me wonder, though: have any of you met the leader of the Sovereign and, it's said, the most powerful metahuman known…Dr. William Karl Donner himself?"

As if. I shook my head. I heard my mother exhale with exasperation. To my left, the Teslowskis shook their heads as well.

Azarrio moved to stand near Byron's mom. "Jeri Teslowski, William Donner, quite possibly, has been in daily contact with your son for nearly a year, while you've literally counted the days since the last time you heard Byron's voice. If you could say one thing to William Donner, what would it be?"

I was developing a real healthy hatred of Hank Azarrio. Byron's mom seemed like she wanted to fold in on herself. Her eyes were wide enough to fall out of her narrow face.

"What...what would I say...?" She looked quickly at her glaring husband, then at her own lap. She shrugged her shoulders.

A vein along Marc Teslowski's jaw thumped. I found myself fixating on it. I wondered what it would be like to grab it and pull it right off his face like a magic trick with a ribbon...just pull and pull until he unraveled.

My stomach grumbled. It had been too long since I'd fed my hyper metabolism.

Teslowski stepped up for his wife. "I'll tell you what I would say." He looked from camera to camera until one moved closer. "Listen up."

He leaned forward, red-faced, and faced the camera.

"You're just...you're just a suit, Donner. You're a little, small man. I've seen the pictures. I could snap you in half."

Azarrio stage-chuckled. "Those are some harsh words, Mister Teslowski. No doubt under—"

"I'm not done." He jabbed a fat finger at the camera, at the demigod who, we could all pretty much assume, wasn't watching.

"You put aside that shit you do, Donner, and let's see what happens. You be a man, and you give me back my son, and you answer to me." He stabbed at the camera again. "Then. Then we'll see, won't we?"

Teslowski sat back in his chair. I had to give it to him... even if he was an abusive, puffy asshole, if he had any anxiety about threatening a guy who could pretty much literally do anything he set his mind to, he sure didn't let it show.

Azarrio looked at the audience and shrugged before turning his attention back to Byron's dad. "Mister Teslowski...are you saying you would challenge Doctor Donner to a...to a physical fight?"

Teslowski's lip curled. "What is it with this 'doctor' thing, anyway? Why does everyone refer to this guy like he deserves our respect? What's he done to deserve that?"

A few low voices in the audience seemed to agree.

"I mean, do we give that kind of respect to the Ayatollah? To Qaddafi? To Idi Amin?" For a second I thought Teslowski was going to spit on the stage. He swallowed, sneering.

"He's a punk."

Azarrio didn't let it go. "So, you really do want to fight him."

Teslowski's fingers pressed the vinyl of his chair. "Jesus! Why don't we all want to fight him? Why don't we have all those freaks rounded up and locked away before they do something worse than Philadelphia, or whatever else they've got up their sleeves?"

Outright cheers in the crowd at that. Who would have thought Marc Teslowski would be a voice of inspiration, even if it was for a bunch of idiots?

"Hell," Marc said, "there's gotta be a few hundred of them at that camp of theirs. Once I get my kid back, why don't we just firebomb the place? Let 'em burn."

"Now, Mister Teslowski," Azarrio said, "I know the tabloids, talk radio, blame the flooding in Pennsylvania on a Sovereign with elemental powers, but do you really believe that? People controlling the weather?"

Teslowski looked at Azarrio for a beat, then he looked right at me. He spoke slowly.

"They're...not...*people.*"

I admit it. Even though I'm not a Sovereign and really didn't like being lumped in with them, the fucker got to me. I forgot we were in the studio. I forgot we were on television. I forgot about the cameras.

It was just me and this prick.

I was still more or less in my chair, but my ass was off the seat. I leaned forward, knees bent, balanced on the balls of my feet. My arms were out; my fingers curved. I could cross the stage and be on him with one easy leap.

I pulled my lips back, revealing unusually long canines.

I did something I'd only recently learned how to do on demand.

I growled.

I heard the ripple of gasps and exclamations from the audience as they freaked out. My sensorium—the combined input of my hearing and sense of smell—told me the big guys in black T-shirts were emerging from the wings, ready to step in if they needed to. If they did...well, dealing with me would be a lot harder than handling the usual paternity-case dads and jilted lovers.

Marc Teslowski looked about as ready to go as I was. The fact that the guy was so full of frustration he was willing to physically attack a sixteen-year-old kid on national television pulled me out of my own semi-bestial state.

After all, much as I didn't want to, I could relate.

I flopped back in my chair and shot the audience a nice, friendly, goofy-kid grin; no teeth. Gee whiz, guys, I'm just joshin'!

The security bruisers faded back offstage.

Azarrio's chuckle was a lot less hearty than last time. "That was a pretty convincing display, Nate." His hard eyes were just for me. "You've reminded us: while the reasons may be in dispute, you are not an ordinary teenager. Do you mind if I ask you a question?"

I shrugged.

"Do you feel human, Nathan?"

My mother snapped, "That's a ridiculous question. Do you feel Hispanic?"

Azarrio didn't hesitate. "One hundred percent." He didn't look away from me. "Let me be clear. I'm not judging. I sincerely want to know how you, personally, feel."

The cameras were close. I felt a sweat bloom and cascade down my spine.

"I…I don't know what that means."

I found out later we were in the shot together, and he looked a little bullying, until I said that.

"To be human?"

"Yeah."

I really, really wanted that moment to be over. Thankfully, I picked up a little buzz from the little thing in Azar-rio's ear. He turned, straightened up, and faced a different camera.

"That may be the question we all have to answer, for ourselves, before this story is over," he intoned. "We'll be right back."

We were at commercial.

My mother leaned close to me. "What was that?"

My shirt was sticking to the chair. I leaned forward gingerly. "What?"

"The growling." She lowered her voice. "Provoking Teslowski. This isn't going to help in court. Jesus Christ, Nathan...."

Apparently her voice carried farther than she expected. Marc Teslowski said, "Your snotty son doesn't scare me, woman."

She sat up, stiff. "What did you say to me?"

Teslowski gave me a dismissive nod. "The kid. He's a punk. He's what you raised. Your fault."

Jeri Teslowski, just over her husband's shoulder, looked pitifully apologetic.

My mother was good in a fight, I'll give her that. She didn't miss a beat.

"My son is still at home," she said. "Where's your boy, Marc?"

It was a pretty great shot. Even if it was barely true.

From The Journal Of Nate Charters
Two

I left the television studio feeling okay, all things considered. Since my mother barely spoke to me from when we left the studio lot until we were well down the 405 freeway, I could tell she had a different view.

Just inside Long Beach, she said, "I don't know if that did us any good or made things worse."

I took my third Tiger Milk bar out of the glove compartment. "I thought we did okay." I unwrapped it. "I mean, I never want to do that again, but at least Byron's dad ended up looking like a crazy man, all told."

"Marc Teslowski would have done that regardless," my mother said. "We could have done without your theatrics, though."

"He...pushed me." I tore off a mouthful of the bar and chewed it down. Fuel. "You heard what he said."

She nodded. "That was uncalled for. But...really, Nathan. Growling? When did you start that?"

I smiled and chewed, remembering Lina and me making out a few days before. We still hadn't gone all the way, but we pretty much did everything else. She was playing with me, and she surprised me by using her fingernails. The growl came when I did.

We laughed about it, and I'd practiced it—without the extra...stimuli—a few times since then.

I told my mother the G-rated, abridged version, of course.

"Tried it out a few days ago. It just sort of...came to me."

"You can see why it's better not to mess around like that, I trust."

"I was just giving him what he deserved." I didn't bother mentioning that I was only half-aware of what I was doing at the time. "I thought...I thought it was funny."

My mother sighed quickly. "No. It really wasn't." She focused on changing lanes of a couple of seconds. "Listen to me. They would like nothing more than to show that you, and so, even more so, your father, are somehow less than human. Capable of violence." She glanced at me. "Give them any rope at all, they'll make a noose. You get it?"

Little speeches like that from my mother made me feel cornered. I stared out the window and focused on the last bite of my bar.

"Nathan?"

"Yeah. Sure."

"What is it."

I swallowed. "Nothing."

"Try again."

There was a time when her firm but sympathetic tone would have been enough to get me to spill it all. Since the battle of Kirby Lake, I was far less interested in sharing anything with the woman who had kept so much from me my whole life.

On the other hand, I knew my grudge hurt her. Sometimes I felt like she deserved a little hurt.

"Look, Mom. I'm tired of worrying how to act, trying to figure out how this side or that will take my every move. I'm...I'm not human, I'm not Sovereign; I can't just pick one or the other or something in between to make things all pretty for the lawyers, or the reporters, or whoever. They just need to deal with me."

"You're sixteen years old," she said. "You don't even know who 'me' is yet."

"That's my freakin' point!"

We didn't say anything as a couple of off-ramps slipped by.

"Nathan, sometimes I don't think you understand just how—"

"Oh, come on, Mom! I get it! I know how important it is! I know what's at stake! Jesus Christ! Maybe I'd be better off if I just disappeared! 'Brave men run in my family,' right, Mom?"

I shook my head. The seatbelt felt like a clamp across my chest. The inside of the car was way too small.

"What a load of shit."

"Nathan…"

I remembered bawling like a baby in front of Lina when I read the stupid note my father had given Spencer Croy to deliver to me, a few days after the one and only time I'd seen Andrew Charters in my entire life.

"Do you know where he got that little bit of wisdom, by the way?"

A kid knows their own mother. Add my hypersenses, which make her scent and body language as clear as a road map, and my mother didn't have a chance in hell of masking her emotions from me. I barked a bitter laugh.

"You do," I said. "You did."

She kept her eyes on the road and nodded, frowning.

"Yeah? Tell me."

"Nathan."

"*Paleface*," I said. "A freakin' Bob Hope movie. Right?"

She nodded. "That's right."

"A joke," I said. "The best that crazy fucker could manage was some joke from some movie he probably doesn't even remember seeing."

She stared at the road. "I think he remembers."

I had a pretty much permanent mad-on where my mother was concerned, but just then, I felt like a heel. Her husband was out there somewhere, half-crazy three-quarters of the time and full-crazy the rest, and she'd lived with that for a decade and a half. Sometimes I forgot it had to be a drag for her.

Huntington Beach came and went as we drove down the road.

Finally my mother said, "Are you still getting the dreams?"

"Not really. Lina, though…"

"That's…" Her sigh sounded exhausted. "That's terrible. Tell her I'm sorry."

Sure. Hey, Lina, hon, my mom says sorry about all the leftover stress and stuff from that time you had a gun shoved in your face and watched your boyfriend's dad tear a guy's guts out with his toenails.

"Yeah, I will."

"Is she seeing anyone?"

My face got hot. "What? Besides me?"

My mother chuckled. "No, Nathan. Someone to help with the nightmares. A therapist, or something."

"Oh. Right." I took a deep breath and listened to my

heart slowing down for a second or two. "No...she's been painting. A lot."

We were getting close to our off-ramp.

"Speaking of Lina," I said. "Can you just drop me off at Carson's, and she'll take me home later? I told her I'd come by after the show."

She tensed immediately. "You spend a lot of time at Carson Meunetti's."

"He's a good guy."

"I know. I like him. But..."

"Mom, I'll be home later. It's Friday. There's practice, and a bunch of people will be there. Like every Friday."

She nodded. "I get it. I was just hoping, after this big thing we just did, maybe you and I could...celebrate. Go out to dinner."

I hated my mother in sheepish-guilty mode almost as much as I hated the reasons for her guilt. It was totally the opposite of the mother I'd known up until a year ago. I didn't always like that I'd traded my old mom for the truth.

In fact, I resented the hell out of it. It just made me want to get away from her that much faster.

"I thought there wasn't much to celebrate, remember?"

She laughed, a concession. "Well, we got through it, didn't we?"

I sighed. I just wanted to be out of the car, away from her, and with Lina.

"Can we do it tomorrow?"

She sighed. "Fine. You're not going to be any fun with your mother when you want to be with your friends, anyway. I guess I'll settle for calling Denver Colorado and telling him all about it."

"Thanks." Denver wasn't among my favorite people; he'd helped keep my father's secrets for years. But he and my mother went back a long way. "I bet he'll want a blow-by-blow."

We passed the Abbeque Valley exits and headed south to San Clemente. I kept my face against the passenger-side window the rest of the way.

From The Journal Of Nate Charters
Three

My mother dropped me off in front of Carson's house. I found myself waving automatically as the car drove away, then jerked my hand down, feeling like a stupid kid.

Carson's house was two stories stacked on top of a three-car garage that took up the entire ground level. I glanced up at the balcony, but no one was watching me. I felt even stupider for thinking anyone would give a shit if I waved goodbye to my mother.

I've mentioned that my hearing is better than...well, anyone's, probably, with the exception of my father's. I could hear Car's stereo blasting through the walls and closed windows despite the sound-deadening foam he'd set up on the walls of the living room. Lots of fuzzy guitars, a grinding bass...I didn't recognize it.

I walked to the front door and turned the knob. It was locked, which kind of surprised me. Why bother locking it when Carson and Lina, at least, judging by the cars in the long driveway, were home?

I don't think I'd ever come around when the door was locked. Feeling a little resentful that I had to do it at all, which was another stupid thing given that I didn't actually live there, I knocked.

Like they'd hear me, with the music so loud.

I pounded, then I pounded harder, then I put the strength of my deceptively lean muscles behind the knock. The door rattled in the frame.

Then I remembered the grungy little garden gnome in a planter next to the door. I tipped it over, grabbed the hidden key, and unlocked the door. I replaced the key with a quick glance at the street to make sure no neighbors had seen the deep dark secret hiding place.

I opened the door and flinched. The music was loud. Very, very loud. It hurt. It made my sternum ache. It made me a little nauseous. I couldn't get a deep-enough breath in.

"Hey!"

No good. Fingers in both ears, I made my way to the living room, cringing with every step.

Lina and Carson were seated on the floor in front of the wall unit that held the stereo and TV, their backs to me. Lina had one of Car's graph-lined composition books in her hand.

Carson leaned forward and turned the stereo down by about half until it was just unbearable, not agonizing. He shrugged and said to Lina, "No vocals laid down yet," in that voice people use when they want to be heard above the buzz of a crowded party. "But you get the idea!"

The ends of her hair—only those tips were still the pale blonde from when I'd first met her—bounced on her shoulders as she nodded. "I like it!"

I hovered at the edge of the room. For no reason in particular, I felt like I was intruding on something. Maybe I was.

Lina and Car met when they were both in grade school, and I know things got pretty heavy for them a couple of years ago, when Car's parents died right around the guy's eighteenth birthday.

It was never really talked about, and I never asked, but I was almost positive things got heavy between them, back then. At least for a little while.

Lina and I were a little over a week away from our first

anniversary, and sure, we'd been though some pretty damn heavy shit of our own...but I still felt like an outsider around them sometimes.

"Nate! Hey, TV star!" She put one hand on Car's shoulder to balance herself when she stood up, which didn't thrill me. "C'mere!"

Car stopped the tape at the same moment Lina hugged me. The sudden, blessed drop in the decibel level gave me a moment of swaying vertigo.

Lina shifted her stance and held me tighter. "Easy there, tiger. You all right?"

I squeezed her. She felt really great. "Just the...loud." I caught Car's eye over Lina's shoulder. "Hey, Car."

"Hey, Nate! Nice job today."

"Thanks." Lina and I downgraded our hug to holding hands. "It was...crazy."

Car said, "Did you—" at the same time Lina said, "What did you think of Car's new song?"

Car closed his mouth and grinned, eyes wide. Whatever he was going to ask me about the show was forgotten.

"Oh...well..."

"Oh, don't sweat it, Nate." Car waved a hand at me. "It's not even done."

"It's not that." I matched his smile. Car's enthusiasm about his own music was easy to catch and not at all egotist-ical. "It was...y'know...these ears!"

Car winced. "Ah, yeah, right. Sorry, man. Here..." He twisted around and turned the stereo volume knob way to the left and pressed the play button on the tape deck. "Here, try this."

The sound poured out at a level I could handle. Turns out I thought it was all electric guitar and bass guitar because that's all it was—no drums. The guitars sounded like a swarm of angry bees armed with chainsaws. The bass snapped, crackled, and chugged like a barbed-wire snake around the guitar.

"I'll have Alex play on the actual track, of course," Car said. "I just wanted to lay this down to give him an idea of what I'm shooting for." He stared into space for a couple of seconds, then raised his index finger.

"There. It's kinda Hüsker Dü…Have you listed to *Candy Apple Grey* yet?"

Car had loaned me the record the week before.

"No, not yet."

"That's cool. Here…wait…right here…"

I nodded and stuck my lower lip out in an expression of appreciation I wasn't a hundred percent committed to. There was so much distortion on the guitar—or guitars—I could barely make out any notes. And if anyone could, it would be me, after all.

"Yeah, totally."

Car sat on the floor playing invisible bass strings against his thigh while the demo played on for another minute or more until it ended in a waterfall of feedback.

"You wanna read the lyrics…?" Car slid the composition book across the carpet to my feet. "Oh—shit, what time did you get here, Nate?"

I didn't wear a watch. "I…I'm not sure…"

Lina moved back so she could see the clock on the kitchen stove. "You gotta go."

"Crap." Car stood up in a fluid unfolding motion. "Gotta go pick up Tim. Won't be long." He walked past us to the counter that separated the living room from the kitchen and grabbed keys from an ugly bowl that looked like it might have been a school project. "Nate, you sticking around for practice?"

"You bet."

"Awesome. Be back. You guys have fun."

He was headed out the door.

"I'll tell you about the show later!" I called to his back.

"Later!"

He pulled the door shut, leaving Lina and me alone in the house.

"The show!" Lina bounced. "Screw the song—tell me all about the show!"

I knew she was mostly joking, but I liked the sound of that.

From The Journal Of Nate Charters
Four

Lina's bright eyes cheered me up. I took her hand and we sat on the long couch across from the fireplace in Carson's living room.

"You saw it," I said. "What did you think?"

She rolled her eyes. "Tch! I think Hank Azarrio must be an asshole."

"Yeah. He's like a circus ringmaster." I laughed and shook my head. "Dude can't lose, when you think about it. No matter what happens, he can get some drama out of it."

"Seems like he managed to do that with you and Byron's dad."

"It's pretty easy to push Marc Teslowski's buttons. My mother wasn't happy with how I handled it."

Lina edged closer to me. Her fingers lazily traced random paths on my thigh through my dress pants. "You mean the growl." Her eyes narrowed as she smirked.

"Yeah."

"I bet they play that on the 'best of' episode."

I shrugged. "She wants me to be a good little boy. She's freaked out that if people think I'm some kind of...you know...they'll think even worse of my dad, and that'll work against us in court."

Despite finally getting the spotlight on me and off of Car's new song, rehashing the whole ordeal was a drag.

This was one of the few times Lina and I were alone together in Carson's house. I found myself thinking about when Car's parents had died, about a year before I'd met her, and what might have happened between him and Lina around that time.

What might have happened on this very couch…

I stood up.

"I mean…" I looked down at Lina. Her face was open and attentive. "Well…what do you think?"

She smiled up at me. "I think you should be you. Who else?"

I wasn't sure what that meant. "Right." The idea irritated me, like "being me" was one more role I was supposed to play.

Lina's smile faded. She leaned forward on the couch, her elbows on her knees. "What's up, Nate?"

Instead of looking at Lina, I glanced in the direction of the front door. "I didn't expect the door to be locked." I wanted to sound all casual. It wasn't a very good performance.

"Heh. Funny story about that." My tension must have been contagious; I heard it in her voice. "Funny-strange. Not funny-ha-ha." She considered. "Well, maybe both."

"Yeah?"

"Have you ever met Cordelia? I think she used to go out with that friend of Crystal's…K.C.?"

I shrugged. There were a lot of people in orbit around Car's band, and they were all a few years older than me. They kind of blended together.

"No biggie," Lina said. "I guess a few nights ago, Car was the only one here, and he was playing bass along with the radio, or whatever. There were like, barely any lights on in the house, and, y'know, Car was all into it."

Yeah, yeah.

"So he finishes playing a song, or the radio goes to commercial, I don't know. Thing is, he looked up from his bass and nearly shits his pants because, there in the doorway of his office...just, standing there...is Cordelia."

I couldn't deny that was a little funny. I liked the image of Car freaked out. That made me feel confused and guilty. I liked Car!

I didn't like Car having a history with Lina.

Or maybe I didn't like not knowing exactly what that history was.

Or maybe it was both. The jury was out on whether I really wanted to know the details, or not.

That all went through my head in a crowded split second.

"What'd Car do?"

Lina laughed. "He's all, 'Oh...hey...Cordelia...I didn't see you there.' And she's all, y'know, all sultry and weird, like, 'You don't have to stop. I like watching.'"

That made me laugh out loud.

"No!"

Lina's head bobbed up and down. "Yes! So he's all, 'Well, I was gonna finish up anyway...it's kinda late...' and gets her out of there." She spread her arms in the universally recognized "ta-da" gesture. "And that's why Car keeps the door locked now."

"He...wait." I felt my mood flip, like a physical thing, like something happening just outside of my skin. "He needs to keep the door locked in the middle of the afternoon when he's here with another person because Cordelia might come in and try to jump his bones?"

Lina frowned. "I guess so? We were playing the music

really loud."

"I know."

She squinted at me and turned her head a little to the left. "Nate?" A beat. "You're freaking out." She patted the couch cushion next to her. "Come back and sit with me."

I obeyed. I didn't want to feel how I was feeling. I didn't even understand it.

She took my hand and kissed it. "You didn't have any fun at the thing, did you."

I shook my head. "There were moments. It's always a good time to make Byron's dad look like an idiot. But...yeah, no."

"I'm sorry, baby."

I shrugged. I looked down at our intertwined hands.

She leaned close and whispered against my ear. "Would it help to know you were super sexy on TV?"

She gave the whorl of my ear a light lick that sent a jolt of electricity down my side and into my leg. I was hard before the lightning reached my toes, grouchy mood be damned.

"Sexy...?"

"Yup."

She reached up and guided my chin until we our foreheads touched. "We've got the house to ourselves for a little while," she whispered, "and I'm pretty sure the door is locked, Nathan."

There was the slightest bit of chiding there, but I guess I kind of deserved it.

"Pretty sure..."

I didn't resist when she pushed me back on Carson Meunetti's dead parents' couch.

From The Journal Of Nate Charters
Five

Maybe it was the frustration of the day. Maybe it was the way Lina's hair, longer than I'd ever known it, slid across my bare chest. Maybe it was the edge of annoyance in Lina's first kisses.

Maybe it was the intensity of sensations against the warm animal scent of our skin against the couch; Lina's sweat, her breath, the taste of her saliva; the tangy bite of her on my hand when I slid it out from between her legs.

Maybe it was being bare-assed naked with my girlfriend in Carson Meunetti's living room, knowing the odds were good my girlfriend had been here with him, like this, a couple of years before.

Conscious thought was nearly suppressed by feeling and by lust, except for a driving need to lay my claim, to mark this territory and erase any impression, any trace, any mark left by the guy who'd been here before.

I'd never been so turned on.

We'd talked about it over the last eleven months. Lina would do anything, really anything, with me, so long as I didn't actually put myself into her. I'd always gone along with that, even if I didn't understand it. I was nearly certain she wasn't a virgin. What was it about us that made that off limits?

Her fingernails dug into my shoulder, and her breath was short and hot against my neck. I was pushed up hard against her hip. She pushed, soft and wet, against my moving fingers.

Today was the day. No more limits. No more boundaries. No more excuses. I was hers. I needed her to be mine.

It's easy to tell when your girlfriend is about to come when your sense of smell is discerning enough to read a person's mood and physiology through their sweat and pheromones, when you can sense a heartbeat and blood flow from your fingertips. I brought her over the edge with my hand.

I was utterly engulfed in her scent, her sounds, her taste. I was past thinking; at that moment I was nothing but want.

While she bucked and gasped, I pulled her arms above her head, took both her hands in mine, positioned myself between her legs, and sought her out.

Her body came back to her as her orgasm slid away.

"Nate...c'mon..."

Her tone wasn't encouraging.

I could feel her wet, warm lips against my dick. So close. I bit into the underside of her upper arm; not hard, just enough to hang on, to hold on.

My peripheral vision contracted to narrow focus on pieces of her. Her ear. Her hair. Her breast. Her lips.

She had become discreet instances of stimulation, each adding to my exponential drive to possess the whole.

"Nate...I don't..."

She twisted her hips, denying me. I slid along her inner thigh.

I let go of her arms.

I propped myself above her on an elbow and a knee. Her eyes were cloudy with afterglow and just a degree away from being entirely with me.

The hazy, humid dream of her snapped.

I sat up.

"Sorry." I was shaking. My dick twitched in time with my racing pulse, unaware the rest of me had been reintroduced to my humanity.

"Sorry. Sorry."

Marc Teslowski
One

A shitload of Friday afternoon traffic turned the drive home from the TV studio into a three-hour ordeal Marc was sure they could have avoided if the damn lawyer hadn't wanted to debrief after the show. Shyster was right there for the whole damn thing. Debrief, why, exactly? Just another excuse to rack up some billable time.

Marc listened to KABC for most of the drive until—like it damn near always did, eventually—the discussion on the talk radio station turned to the Sovereigns and Declaration Day and even some talk about Byron. After the taping, Marc was pretty well fed the hell up on that subject. He flipped back and forth between KMET and KLOS the rest of the way and let Van Halen, Led Zeppelin, and Zebra take his mind off things for a while.

Marc opted to pass the El Toro Road exit—it would be a bitch in the middle of rush hour—and got off on Abbeque Valley Parkway. He saw Jeri's face tighten as they passed the high school. He felt the same tension in his jaw and neck.

Byron had ruled that school. Lorded over it. Any sport, you name it, if the school had a team, Byron tried out, and when Byron tried out, he got picked. And when he played, he was the best anyone had ever seen.

Marc had loved imagining the other dads giving their kids shit, pushing them to be as good as Byron fucking Teslowski. He remembered hearing the other schools' coaches digging into their players when no one—no one—could get anywhere near his kid.

Byron Teslowski had been on his way to any athletic

scholarship he wanted, and after that, Marc was certain his son would have had a great collegiate career and a record-breaking pro run.

Football, baseball, basketball—it wouldn't have mattered. He would have done everything Marc himself had worked to accomplish when he'd been his age, except Marc had never had his son's agility, his strength, his speed, or his endurance.

And then, as it turned out, if some people were to be believed, Byron cheated. He wasn't a superstar athlete worthy of the drooling attention of the scouts.

He was a fucking Sovereign.

Or so said the Sovereigns themselves.

That was like trusting the goddamn fox to guard the henhouse, that's what that was. Fuck that.

The lawyers, the Metahuman Affairs people, the turn-coat normals from the Donner Institute for Sovereign Studies, they had their reports to point to: Byron Teslowski was a straight-up Standard Class Sovereign with highly developed adaptive capabilities—in layman's terms, he changed according to what the situation required, which was why he showed off such a wide range of talent when it came to sports.

Of course, the Sovereigns *would* make up shit like that, to justify taking him.

They said his Sovereign ability was what saved him when he was injured in the fight at Charters' place up at Kirby Lake, too. That a normal human would have died from shock and blood loss. Why wasn't it good enough to say the kid was talented? That he was healthy, and strong?

What the hell was wrong with admitting he had damn

good genes that he inherited from his old man, and from Marc's old man, all the way back? Was it so hard to believe?

It was an insult. An affront. It pissed Marc Teslowski off to no end.

They had his boy.

Marc pulled the Dooley into the driveway. As soon as he put on the brake, Jeri got out and went for the mailbox. There wouldn't be anything there except for bills and junk.

Not what she was looking for.

Marc went inside without bothering to wait for his wife. He wanted to get out of his uncomfortable dress clothes, get into jeans and a T-shirt, sit down in his chair, and have a goddamn beer while Jeri threw something together for dinner.

The house was stuffy; close and silent.

Marc tossed his slacks and shirt into a pile next to the bed, pulled on an old and worn pair of jeans, and found a nice loose tank top. So. Much. Better.

On his way to the kitchen, he passed Jeri organizing the mail on the dining room table.

"Nothing," she mumbled.

"Shocker." Acid reflux tightened his chest. He clenched his teeth, sucked his lips tight against his gums, and focused on the fridge.

Wherein, he discovered, there was no beer to be found.

Jesus fuck.

"Jeri."

He could feel her hovering behind him. She was probably waiting to pull the lasagna from the other night out. Microwave leftovers, and no beer.

"Yes, Marc."

"When did you go to the store?"

"I...I haven't, yet."

"Don't you go on Thursday?"

"I—usually, sure, but I needed to find something for the show, and I knew we had enough to get by until Saturday if we needed to, so—"

Staring at the beer-less inside of the fridge wasn't helping with anything. Marc turned around and faced Jeri.

"'Find something for the show.'" His lip curled. "Are you kidding me? So you'd, what, look nice and pretty for the cameras while you sat there and said absolutely not one thing?"

"It wasn't..."

He didn't want to hear it. "All I ask for—all I ever ask, Jeri—is that this goddamn shitty house is kept up and there's food in the fucking pantry. Beer in the fridge!"

His fingers curled into tight hooks. It would serve her right if he finally did just off and belt her one, but she was so damn frail, she'd probably snap in half. Not like his own mother, by God. She could take a punch, and more often than not give as good as she got from Marc's pop.

Marc rolled his eyes. "Who the hell do you think gave a shit if you had a new sweater, Jeri? Seriously"

She looked at the linoleum of the kitchen floor. "It wasn't for them," she whispered.

"That's right, because how would those..." He thought of smart-mouthed Frank in the studio audience. "...lazy assholes know you went out of your way to look nice, for Christ's sake? Who cares?"

She looked up. He was mildly surprised to see her eyes were wet.

"I wanted to look nice for Byron," she said. "In case he was watching."

Marc opened his mouth. He closed it again.

It had not occurred to him that the Sovereigns might let Byron watch *The Azarrio Show*. That Byron might have seen them there. Or would have wanted to.

She studied him.

"Didn't that occur to you?" Her voice was steady but subdued, like she had to stoke up the energy to let a sentence fall out of her mouth. "Don't you think Byron would watch?"

Marc shrugged. "Who knows if they even let him watch TV? They probably have him all...isolated, or shut away. That's what kidnappers *do*. It's part of the damn brainwashing shit."

Jeri kept looking at him. Marc disliked the attitude he was reading from his wife.

"Brainwashing him," she said. "Is that what you think they're doing?"

Marc spoke as if his wife was a retarded person. "Can you think of another reason your own son wouldn't write or call for a year, Jeri?"

Another two breaths, in and out, until Jeri looked away and slipped past him. She opened the refrigerator and pulled out the lasagna.

"Of course not, Marc."

She was not the woman he had married twenty years before. There was little left of the spitfire in the miniskirt he had chased all over the Santa Monica Pier that summer.

Something had happened to her, something that made him almost sick to look at her.

She had caved.

Every now and then, though, he could still pick up the slightest hint of sarcasm, or even anger, in her mumbling whimpers. Every once in a while, she dared to stand up to him.

Not often enough for Marc to respect her for it, though. She was too far gone. Too weak.

"What was that?" Let her try to push him today, of all days. Let her try.

She kept her back to him while she fussed with the plastic wrap on the casserole dish. "Nothing."

He realized he was a little disappointed she had rolled over so quickly. "Right."

He was still pissed off from the stupid show. Still worked up. He wanted to scrap, and Jeri was worthless as a sparring partner.

He also needed a beer.

"I'm gonna go have a few down the street," he said. "I'll eat when I get back."

He retrieved his wallet and keys from his discarded dress slacks. Jeri met him in the living room.

"Can't you just eat dinner? It's been such a long day. What if Byron…"

Marc grunted. "Byron, nothing." He opened the front door. "Tell you what, Jeri. You sit by the phone.

"Me, I'm gonna go get drunk."

From The Journal Of Nate Charters
Six

Lina scooped her black T-shirt off the floor and slipped it over her head. I pulled up my pants.

She gathered her bra, panties, and skirt. I picked up my shirt, but I was suddenly lacking the initiative to put it on. I looked at it, there in my lap.

Lina took her clothes down the hall. I heard the bathroom door shut.

Alone in the living room, half-dressed, I felt self-conscious.

I felt stupid.

I put on my shirt.

I put on my socks and shoes.

There. I was all dressed for *The Azarrio Show* again. Just a little more wrinkled.

Lina came back in the living room. I looked up at her.

Her lip twisted. "So." She crossed her arms over her chest. "What was that?"

"I..." I wanted to shrink into the couch. I felt cornered. "I'm not...I don't know."

"I thought..." She looked like she could be as uncomfortable as I was, except for the residual anger hardening her eyes. "Nate, I've told you how..."

"I know. I know." Where had I gone? Where was I? "I didn't...I felt..."

"You got carried away."

She sounded like a mother scolding a child. Not my mother, exactly, thank fucking god.

"It's not like that." I never liked the sound of my own

voice when I whined. I reined it in. "Look. I know you're... not ready. I...I respect that." She shifted her weight, and her eyes widened in protest. "I do, Lina. I do."

"So?"

I shook my head. "I...lost myself. I couldn't...it's like I couldn't think."

Once I'd said it, it was a lot scarier. I guess she sensed that. She sat down next to me. Not touching, but next to me.

"What do you mean?"

"Like I was more...whatever that part of me that's...like it is."

I thought of my father, his beard tangled with leaves and mud and dried blood, wild-eyed and grinning while he used his filthy toenails to rip the intestines out of a guy named Earl Pratt.

"Like...him."

Lina was emphatic. "You're not him, Nate. Not even."

"I've got his genes."

"But that's not your whole deal," she said. "You know how it works."

"Sure." It took two sets of DNA to make a kid. Birds and the bees and whatever. But half the DNA that made me was...fucked up. *Augmented.* "But sometimes...I don't know. I just get...submerged. I don't know."

Lina studied me. "Submerged."

I nodded. "It's stupid stuff, too. Like, my mother will ask me to do some chore or something, and all of a sudden I just feel so...angry." I frowned and shook my head. "Like I just want to break shit. Tear into something."

Lina nodded slowly. She seemed less angry now. Her

heartbeat had slowed, and her skin was cooler, drier. "So that's how you felt with me."

Her voice was perfectly flat.

"Like you wanted to...break me."

"No!" I wanted to touch her; I reached out my hand and stopped short of her arm. "Not...exactly."

She sat back, which put her a little farther away from me.

"I think I get it," she said.

We sat there. I stared at nothing.

"Lina."

"Yep."

I didn't want to ask. I couldn't not ask.

"Why don't you want to make love with me?"

She let her head fall to rest on the couch back and closed her eyes. "I'm just not...I'm not there yet. I told you before."

"Not there." I pushed through swirling, irritated jealousy. "Not there with me, you mean? Right?"

She opened her eyes and stared at the ceiling.

"Why don't you ask what you want to ask, Nate."

Fine.

"You've done it before. You're not a virgin. Why not with me? What's different about—Lina, c'mon. Look at me."

She turned her head to me.

"Why not me?"

She sighed. "I'm not a virgin. You're right. I've had sex exactly one time. It was...I don't know. It probably shouldn't have happened. It wasn't..." She huffed. "How much of this do you want to know? I mean, really? You should think about it."

I swallowed. "It was Car."

"Yes, it was Car."

It hurt to hear it out loud, but I'd half believed it for so long it didn't hit me like I guess I'd thought it would.

"Okay."

Now she reached for my hand, and I let her take it. "It was right after his folks died. He was a mess. So was I. It just...it was like...comfort. It wasn't a love thing. It wasn't even a lust thing. It was...I don't know. It was what happened."

I'd managed to put this information into some safe zone in my head. I felt a little numb.

"So...but...you and I...it *is* a love thing. And it's a lust thing. Isn't that..." I shrugged and realized I sounded a little silly. I smiled ruefully. "Isn't that all the right stuff?"

She smiled back. We were a notch closer to having a nearly normal conversation, like two people who could and should be able to talk about anything together.

"It should be, yeah," she said. "I wish it was."

Something occurred to me.

"You said you were a mess, too. But it wasn't because of Car's parents."

She glanced to one side and bit her lip. "No."

I waited.

She looked at me and spoke in a rush. "I'm gonna tell you something I should have told you already. I'm sorry I didn't. We've had...other things to deal with this last year. I didn't want to add to it."

"Okay..."

"But, you have to promise me, Nate—you can't freak

out. This is my thing, and I'm talking to Dr. Creighton about it, and I'm working through it, along with the whole cabin thing; I'm figuring it out, but it's something that takes time. Okay?"

"Okay."

"You have to say it, Nate."

After confirmation that she and Carson Meunetti had had sex—that Carson knew her in a way I still, after almost a year, didn't—I didn't think there was much left to freak out over.

I nodded. "I promise not to freak out."

She took a deep breath.

"Okay. Okay." She exhaled hard. "Okay." She looked at me.

"So, right before the day of Car's parents' plane crash, we were all at a party at Preston's. I got...I got a little messed up, and...I came really, really close to being raped."

She closed her eyes, took another breath, and opened them again.

It was her turn to freak out, so I figured it was my turn to be the stable one. I found another slot in my skull for this new information.

"Really close, you said. So...it didn't happen?"

"Not, like, technically. You know."

I understood perfectly.

"Okay. So, this guy. He's, what, off in jail or something? He can't get to you now, right?"

As if he'd have a fucking chance, with me around.

"He got taken care of," Lina said. I could tell that wasn't the whole truth.

"What does that mean…?"

"He never bothered me again. He wouldn't."

"He's…wait, he's not in jail? He got away with it?" The safe zone was dissolving around this new knowledge. "How'd he get away with it?"

"You said you wouldn't freak out!"

"I'm…" I checked myself. "I'm not. Sorry. But, who is he? What happened?"

She shook her head. "No, Nate. Please. This is something I'm working out. I'm trying to handle it. My own way."

I gaped at her. "You won't tell me?"

She threw her hands in the air. "You just got done telling me you're going all Andrew-crazy, and shit! Look what just happened!"

She held her open palm in front of my face and shook her head again. "No. Please." Her hand dropped, found mine, and squeezed. "Let me deal with this my way, Nate. You promised. Please. Be patient about this."

I didn't get it at all. Somewhere out there was some fucker who tried to rape my girlfriend. Somewhere out there was some fuckwad who had messed with Lina's head so badly, we couldn't be what we should be to each other. Some fucker had hurt her—had stolen from us, damn it—and he never paid for it.

"Why didn't you turn him in, Lina?" It was driving me crazy. It didn't make sense.

"Everything happened so quickly," she said. "I mean— literally. The time between that and Car finding out about his parents…it was hours. What happened to me, what happened to him…it doesn't compare."

"Sure it does!"

"No." She shook her head firmly. "It doesn't. Something really bad almost happened to me…and that was bad enough. But something horrible did happen to Car, Nate. There's no comparison."

"I don't know."

"You couldn't."

I wanted to argue that. I wanted to mention my father was a half-crazy homeless animal man and my mother had kept it a secret the first fifteen years of my life, and, hey, that's got to count for something.

I bit my tongue.

"Who else knows?"

"Please don't ask me, Nate. You do, now. I hope that makes our…stuff…easier to understand. I just…I want to keep it mostly my thing. For now. Okay?"

"Is that what Dr. Creighton wants you to do? For your therapy?"

"He thinks it's important."

She was lying.

"Okay." I sighed. I pulled her hand to my lips and kissed her knuckles gently. "I'm glad you told me. It's…hard to think about. But I'll leave it alone."

I was lying, too.

From The Journal Of Nate Charters
Seven

If Carson's band didn't have a gig on Friday nights, they practiced in his big converted three-car garage. I usually hung out.

Car and his friends were all, like, twenty, twenty-one, twenty-two or something—all older than me by a few years—but Car was friends with Lina, and I was with Lina, so everybody pretty much took me in.

Lina and Car.

I didn't really understand how I felt about that. It hurt, a little. It was...weird.

Thing was, Carson Meunetti had never been anything but awesome to me from the moment we met, when he shook my hand and looked me in my crazy eyes and never flinched, never acted like I was anything more unusual than Lina's (at the time) new boyfriend.

When things got crazy and we hatched our stupid plan to get Byron Teslowski away from maybe being experimented on by Prentice-Cambrian's flunky scientist Lester Brenhurst, Carson covered for us at no small risk to himself.

The guy was like an older brother to me.

And I had to admit it: no matter how much I looked for it, he never treated Lina like anything more than his best friend. Now that I knew what I knew, somehow, it was obvious to me that I'd never had a thing to worry about.

So, sure, it was a little weird when Car came back with Tim, and the rest of Jesus Horse showed up with their girlfriends and everybody else. But after everybody settled in with their pizza and beer (I got my own pizza, but a while back everyone had come to agree that no one let me drink anything stronger than soda), things almost felt normal.

Lina stuck close by me. I felt a little guilt when she'd hold my hand or touch me; I think I wanted her to be angrier with me over what had happened that afternoon. Maybe she wanted things to feel normal, too.

I tried my best to go along. We went down to the converted three-car garage when practice started, and I hung out there with her as long as I could take the volume. I tried to convince myself life would keep moving forward and we'd work through this stuff.

Except for the fact of some dude out there in the world who had never been punished for almost raping my girlfriend.

The thought of it twisted through my brain like a worm through dirt.

I tried to be cool. I sat there with Lina, earplugs jammed in my ears to protect my inhumanly sensitive hearing, and watched Car, Crystal, Alex, and Tim run through their set.

With every tune, horror movies played in my head. Lina, helpless, while some faceless fucker hovered over her...or Lina, struggling but not strong enough to twist free, the weight of her would-be rapist pressing down...

If I sat through another song, I felt like I would rip out of my own skin. I had to get out.

Even with my ears plugged, the vibrations of the bass guitar and drums always get to be a little much for me, physically. Lina was used to my sensitivity, so when I got up to go back up to the house she didn't seem to realize I was messed up. She kissed me on the cheek, squeezed my hand, and mouthed "I love you."

I silently said it back to her and pushed down the urge to cry as I passed through the side door of the garage and around to the front door of the house. What a day, and it wasn't over yet.

In the house, Katrina Lombaugh and Tammy Akui were sitting at the dining room table drinking Corona beer and playing some card game.

"Hey, little Nate," drawled Katrina. She raised her beer bottle. "They taking a break?"

"Just me." I dug the earplugs out of my ears. I could still feel the vibrations of the music through the carpeted floor, but the Cocteau Twins record playing at a reasonable volume in the living room was still a nice break. Elizabeth Fraser's otherworldly caterwauling was almost soothing.

"Want in?" She indicated an empty chair at the table with a nod of her head.

I shrugged. "I'm just gonna hang out. I'll watch you guys play."

Tammy smiled, and her eyebrows went up. Katrina caught the expression and smiled slowly. "Big fun, you betcha."

I laughed, and sure enough, rather than actually watch them play Go Fish or whatever, I dug around in the bookcase between the dining room and the living room.

"How'd your TV thing go, little Nate?" Katrina shuffled the cards.

"It was awesome." I groaned with enough exaggeration to convey the opposite.

Tammy said, "That host looks like a child molester." Her voice was low, her short laugh even lower.

"He smells like shit," I said.

"Figures." Katrina, no different from everybody else in that crowd and, hell, might as well face it, everybody else in the country by now, knew the score with my enhanced senses. "Must have been a nice treat for you."

"Not," I said.

"The world is asshole-heavy," Tammy said. She nodded to Katrina. "Gimme three."

The world is asshole-heavy. Fuck, yeah.

I put down issue of *RE:Search* I'd been thumbing through.

"Hey, you guys."

"Yeppers, little Nate?" Katrina frowned at her cards. "Dealer takes two."

"Um…you two remember a party at Preston's, a couple of years ago? Were you guys there?"

I'm a body-language speed-reader; it's a side-effect of my super-sensitive sensorium. Katrina, she was a smart one; I could see her try to control her reaction. Tammy, on the other hand, didn't seem to care.

"Whoo! That was a pretty big night!" She laughed.

Katrina glowered at her. "You were still with Ian, right, honey?"

Tammy frowned. "Yes, Katrina. Thanks for mentioning. And you were with that alcoholic guitar player…what was his name, again, honey?"

Katrina's nostrils flared. "His name is Ernie."

The two of them exchanged a steady look that I guess signified some kind of truce: no territory gained by either side. Not that I had any clue what had them suddenly so bitchy with each other. There was so much history in this crowd; sometimes I felt like I'd never know everybody's whole story.

Tonight, though, I was only interested in one little part.

"So, um…yeah…"

Katrina gave me a big-sister smile. "We aren't gonna tell you about it, little Nate."

I laughed. "You don't even know what I'm talking about!"

"Sure we do," Katrina said. "But you're not getting anywhere with us."

Tammy snorted. "Oh, c'mon. Who cares? It was two years ago. Everybody was stupid."

Katrina pointed at her with a long, elegant finger. "Tammy!"

"What? It's not like Crystal didn't give Eric way worse than he tried to do to Lina. That asshole could barely walk when she was done with him!"

Eric.

I had a first name.

Eric. Eric *what*?

Katrina tossed her cards across the table, not quite at Tammy. "You are such a fucking bitch."

"It's cool, Katrina," I said. "I know what happened. Lina told me."

Katrina looked dubious. "She did?"

"Yeah. Just not the guy's name." I looked at Tammy. "What's his last name, anyway? This Eric guy?"

Katrina's second "Tammy…" was thick with warning.

Tammy smiled coldly at Katrina, gave her the finger,

and turned to look at me. "His name's Eric Finn, little Nate." Katrina's nickname for me sounded wrong coming from Tammy. I couldn't tell if she was making fun of me or digging at Katrina for whatever reason.

I didn't care.

I had a name.

Katrina stood up. She was tall and long, over six feet in her cowboy boots and the silly thrift-store top hat she liked to wear.

"Tammy," she said with acid sweetness, "will you kindly have a word with me outside for a moment? Cunt?" Tammy's face darkened.

"Don't bother, Kat." She got up, scooped her purse off the floor, and went for the front door. "You are way too hung up, woman. It was two years ago. Everybody's moved on."

"That's not up to you!"

"Oh, for fuck's sake," Tammy said at the door. "Get over it!" She left.

Katrina seethed a moment, then looked at me. "Believe it or not, that had nothing to do with you."

I nodded.

"Sit down."

I took Tammy's place at the table. The name of Eric Finn swirled in my head.

"Nate."

"Katrina."

"You shouldn't have asked."

She didn't seem mad, just concerned. I was pretty sure Katrina was one of the more fucked-up members of Car's little tribe, but right then and there, she seemed pretty damn cool to me.

"I...I just had to know."

"You shouldn't." I felt guilty for pushing things, a little, but damn it, I couldn't handle how the whole thing made me feel so helpless. There was too much of that in my life.

I guess Katrina read that on my face. Or maybe she just thought I was an idiot. She sighed, shook her head, and reached into her coat pocket for her cigarettes.

"Tell you this much, little Nate," she said. "That was one fucked-up party."

"Guess so."

Lina drove me home after practice wound down. She pulled into my driveway and turned down the radio.

"You've been pretty quiet," she said. "Tired?"

I was way tired, but I knew she didn't think that was it.

"Pretty big day," I said. My smile felt weak.

She squinted at me. "You okay about everything?"

I flashed on my sex-crazed episode. I felt a rush of guilt about pushing to get the name of Eric Finn from Katrina and Tammy. "Are...you?" The reversal was automatic evasion, standard equipment in any teenager's tool box.

"I'm worried about you," she said. "This temper thing of yours."

I looked out the windshield at the headlights on my garage door. On the radio, low, the Clash's "Red Angel Dragnet" played on KNAC. "Yeah. Well. Hopefully it's not a thing."

"Yeah."

She waited. I knew she was waiting for more.

I closed my eyes, opened them, and said, "Tammy told me who he is."

"What?" Her voice was loud and sharp in the confines of the car.

"She told me. His name's Eric Finn."

Her anger felt like buffeting waves to me. "Why did you ask her? Fuck, Nate, you fucking promised!"

I remembered Katrina, so pissed off that Tammy had spilled the beans. What was it about that night? What was with all the secrecy?

"I just wanted a name." I realized I was angry with Lina, and for a moment the realization threw me, but then it made sense.

"You promised!"

She was my woman. I'd risked my life for her.

"I think I have a right to know," I said.

"Isn't that nice for you." She looked straight ahead. "Now you know. You have your name."

"Yep."

"Better take your precious name and get out," she said. "I want to go home."

I didn't like parting angry. It scared me.

"Lina…"

She looked at me. "Don't do anything, Nate. You promised."

Whatever anger I felt was wiped out by the mix of disappointment and pleading I saw on her face. I thought I was right to find out. I did. But I hated the way she looked at me.

"Okay," I said.

"Good night." She turned away. Her hand floated over

the gear shift, ready to put the car in reverse.

"I...I'll call you tomorrow?"

"I want to go," she said again.

I got out of the car. She put it in gear and started moving before I'd even finished shutting the door. At the corner, I saw her stop to reach over, open it, and shut it securely before she took off.

The exhaust filled my sinuses, blocking out the scents of the night and making my head a little light.

Out of nowhere—maybe because things on the ground were not so hot—I remembered that, this very night, Halley's Comet was as close to the Earth as it was going to get this time around. That would be something.

I looked up at the sky.

It was covered with clouds.

Marc Teslowski
Two

Marc hated what this place had become.

For twenty years, the bar had carried the name of its owner: Grayson. Not "Grayson's." When the original sign arrived for inspection, Red Grayson hadn't noticed the apostrophe and the "s" were missing on the sign until two days after the thing was hung. When some people laughed about it, Red just laughed along with 'em.

When it came time to replace that sign, Red made sure that apostrophe "s" stayed off. Twice.

Throat cancer took Red about a year and a half ago, and his family sold the place pretty quickly.

To a woman.

Nothing wrong with that in principle, Marc knew. But this was Grayson. It was Marc's place. Hell, it was the place for a lot of blue-collar types like Marc who wanted to relax and drink where they didn't have to be too concerned with who they might offend.

Worse, the clientele took a turn for the younger when the woman—Kelsie or Karly or some other horrible, cutesy, sorority-princess name—took over.

Still, Marc had nowhere else to go. He could sit at the bar and drink the same beer Red used to serve and watch sports on the TV hanging in the corner and willfully ignore the shrill, over-loud voices of the kids and their dart games and pinball. He could be alone in this crowd.

At least there wasn't any live music this Friday night. Even though the jukebox was loud enough to raise Christ, he'd gotten real good at blocking out most of the new-wave shit the punks paid to hear, and every now and then someone would drop a quarter for REO Speedwagon or Loverboy or Pat Benetar or something Marc could appreciate.

Bottom line, even with the kids and the yuppies and the goddamn woman behind the bar when it should be Red Grayson and the name should also be Grayson…

It still beat the shit out of sitting at home.

A man's home was his castle. Yeah, it was corny, but it was true, too. When Marc was growing up, his pop ruled over his castle, that was for damn sure. Marc had done his best to follow suit, keeping on Byron's ass and making sure Jeri kept the house up, and if either of them fell short, well, Marc didn't let that shit slide.

If he did…well, Marc could almost hear the old man's voice, riding him. It sure as hell wasn't too difficult to call up any of the times he'd taken the belt to Marc's ass.

Now, though…with Byron gone, there wasn't much of a house for Marc to be master of.

He reflected, for the millionth time, that he was running out of things he *could* control. They'd been pulling responsibilities from him at the distribution center where he worked, little by little, citing "all you're going through," but Marc didn't need their fake kindness. He knew his fight with the Sovereigns was a distraction.

His so-called friends sure thought so. He didn't even bother calling Vic or Sam or anybody. Over the last eleven months, they'd all gradually gotten too busy to come down to Grayson and have a beer with ol' Marc.

He knew what that was.

On this barstool, he could at least pretend things were

still the way they were supposed to be. In fact, if he stopped coming here, that would be like giving in to the whole fucking mess the last year had been.

On the TV, a promo for the eleven o'clock news played. Marc couldn't hear what the anchorman was saying.

Then Marc saw his own face, livid, blotched and red, followed a split second later by fucking Nathan Charters *growling* at him.

Apparently they would be running something about *The Azarrio Show* on the news that night. Like that was really news.

"Hey! That was you!"

Marc had not registered the presence of the kid on the next barstool. He looked at him now: clean cut, smooth-faced, wearing a light blue suit coat over a pale pink dress shirt. The guy's tie was loose around his neck.

Fucking yuppie.

The game was back on the TV. Marc focused on it.

The kid yelled cheerfully in Marc's ear. "You're that Tekonski guy!"

No escape. Not even here. Not anymore.

"The name," Marc growled, his eyes on the television, "is Teslowski."

"Yeah! Teslowski! Dude!" Marc peripherally sensed the kid turning on his stool. "Shane! C'mere!"

Another off-duty day trader fresh out of business school crowded up on the far side of the first guy, who slapped the bar very close to Marc's hand.

"Check it out! You know who this is?"

Marc said, "I'm trying to watch the game. You mind?"

Shane gawked at him. "Whoa! You're that Sovereign kid's dad! Check it out!"

Marc turned to face them both. He stood up.

"My boy is not a Sovereign."

The yuppies grinned at each other. The first one nodded up at Marc, all casual, baby-practice intimidation.

"Sure, man. Sure."

They laughed at him.

They.

Laughed at him.

In *his place*.

It didn't take a thought. It didn't take a second. Marc slapped his open palm against the back of the seated kid's neck and shoved it firmly against the bar. Condensation splashed.

"The fuck?" Shane yelped. The first yuppie flailed. Marc applied pressure.

"My kid," he said, louder, "is not a fucking Sovereign, you little shit!"

The new owner, Kristy or Karly or what the fuck ever, sauntered over behind the bar.

"Marc," she said. For a tiny moment, he didn't understand how in the hell she would know his name. Then he realized how stupid that was. He was on the damn news, all the time. Who didn't know his name?

"My kid," he said to her, "is not a Sovereign."

"I don't give a shit, Marc," she said. "You gotta let this man go, and get out of my place."

One of her workers, a big dyke, flanked her. She held a serving tray like it was a discus. Marc could see she'd love him to give her an excuse to do something.

The little shit under his hand pushed against the bar with both hands. Marc increased his pressure. He might not be in the best shape of his life, but he was still stronger than this white-collar maggot. "C'mon, man!"

The crowd behind Marc—no doubt all buddies of the sniveling little fuck—started shouting shit at him.

The dyke looked at her boss. "Say the word, Christine."

She held up her hand, restraining her employee. "Make it easy, Marc," she said.

"Fuckin' come outside with us, old man," Shane said to him.

"Nope," Christine said. "You will not." She said to Marc, "C'mon. Just today."

Marc felt the kid pushing hard against him. When Marc let go, all that force sent the kid backwards off the stool and onto his ass.

"Fuck you," Marc said to the kid. "Fuck you," he said to Shane. He looked at the women behind the bar. "Fuck you, too."

He muscled his way through the crowd and burst out the door. The night air was jarringly cold compared to the crowded heat inside. Marc was chilled by his own sweat.

He heard them laughing inside.

He thought of the guy in the audience during *The Azario Show*. That fuck had been laughing at him, too. He wasn't obvious about it, but it was clear enough.

They thought he was a joke.

The world thought he was a joke. An item of interest on the eleven o'clock news. An old man being disrespected by a little fucking monster and sitting there and taking it.

Taking it.

The Sovereign—starting with that smug fuck, William Donner—had spent the last year laughing at him.

No wonder his friends wouldn't talk to him. And Jesus, if his pop was still alive, grown man or not, Marc would have deserved the belt. He'd bend right over. Fuck it. No more.

No more.

From The Journal Of Nate Charters
Eight

Lina didn't take any of my five calls on Saturday. On the fifth, her dad told me to "Relax, Nate. Give it a day or two for her to get done being mad at you for whatever you're in the doghouse for." He paused, then said in the same bemused tone, "You didn't do anything too stupid, did you…?"

Debatable.

"No sir. Thanks."

My mother took advantage of my apparently open schedule to hold me to our "celebratory" dinner. It wasn't much fun for either of us. I was too distracted by the Lina stuff, and I think whatever rush my mother had felt from the television show had faded. We didn't order dessert. At least she let me drive the car to the restaurant.

We got home in one piece, and I retreated to my bedroom. It felt sort of poetically appropriate to put on the new Hüsker Dü record Car had loaned me, given how tangled up we all were. I put on my headphones, turned out the lights, lay on my bed, and let it spin, hoping I could turn my brain off for forty-five minutes.

That didn't work so well. Pretty much every song on the damn record might as well have been written for my life. I put myself through it anyway, even getting up to flip the record over after "Too Far Down."

Maybe I felt like I deserved it. By the time the mournful piano of "No Promise Have I Made" came around, I had tears on my face.

One more song, and the record was done, and so was I. I pulled the headphones off my head and spaced out, staring at the maps on the wall over my desk for a few minutes.

I'd had a thing for maps as soon as I'd been old enough to understand what they were. The idea that I could look at a piece of paper, a drawing, and see places far away from what I knew, far away from what I had to deal with day in and day out, was a powerful distraction.

It didn't do much for me that night. Maps represented all the people in all those places, too. In one of those places, somewhere in one of those little dots, was Eric Finn. Somewhere else, probably not far away, was Lina Porter. And too far away from her…was me.

Eventually, I fell asleep on top of my bedspread.

My head wasn't in any better place Sunday morning. I tried to take Graham Porter's advice and not bother his daughter. The whole thing was driving me buggy, though. I had to talk to somebody about it.

So I called a conference with Mel and Jason, my closest and oldest friends. As usual, we convened in Mel's bedroom, where they were already waiting for me when I arrived.

Mel's bedroom had all the same stuff on the walls—framed Disneyland prints, album jackets, and a giant foam-core Duran Duran display he'd managed to finagle from Pinnacle Records—but I felt a little out of place there. I realized it had been a month, at least, since the three of us had hung out.

"Nathan!" Mel and I clasped hands. I noticed he'd shaved the wispy chin-hairs he'd been sporting, but seemed to be cultivating something on his upper lip. He smiled but seemed a little on edge to me. "We haven't seen you in a while, good sir." He glanced at my hair. "What's with the leopard spots?"

I ran my hand over the dye job on my short hair. "I dunno. Just something to do."

Jason and I shook. "It's boss, dude." I was relieved to see his own snaggle-toothed grin was as cheerfully unburdened as always. "You been pretty busy hanging out with the big kids, I guess, huh?" He punched me in the shoulder, a tap.

I laughed. "I know, I know. It's been weird since I got on independent study. Makes it harder to see you guys."

Mel nodded. "It's a long walk between our houses, that's for sure."

We lived two blocks apart.

"Uh...yeah." I didn't need to be hassled, not now. Not today. I needed their help.

Jason shrugged and ran his thumb and index finger across his own bushy blonde mustache. "Hey, everybody's busy. Y'know, doing homework, ditching class...being on TV shows..."

"Ugh." I grinned. "Did you watch that horrible thing? I'm trying to forget it even happened."

"Dude. I watched it, then it was on the news that night, too."

"National news, that is." Mel gave me a pointed look.

"What?" This wasn't good. "Why?" My profile was high enough as it was.

Mel sat down cross-legged on the floor in front of the four milk crates holding his record collection. "Who knows? Slow news day?" He looked up at me. "Whose idea was that fiasco, anyway?" This time, his smile carried some genuine sympathy.

"The lawyers," I said. "My mother. The Sovereigns, I guess. I don't think it did any of us any good—me or Byron's folks."

"Is that why you called us?" Jason asked.

I sighed and sat down on the edge of Mel's bed. "No."

"Hold on." Mel put the Golden Palominos on his record player to cover our conversation and keep his little sister from her occasional eavesdropping from the other side of the closed bedroom door. He held up an index finger until the dude from R.E.M. started singing. "Okay, boy. Go."

I mustered a small smile to acknowledge his pun on the first song. I sighed again and looked at my two best friends while Mel bounced down his bed.

"I...found something out about Lina."

Jason's jaw dropped. "No fuckin' way. She's cheating on you!"

I frowned. "Way to go right to the worst possible thing, ever, Jase."

"Well, she's always hanging out with that Sting wannabe...I dunno..."

Carson. Jesus.

"It's not that," I cut him off. "It's something that happened a while ago. Before we knew her."

"What?" Mel's dark eyes were steady on me.

"Okay." Another deep breath for me. "Okay, this is pretty shitty, and it's...okay, look. She was almost raped."

"Dude!" Jason barked.

"Almost...?" Mel would have looked calm to Jason, but I could smell his skin pop with a burst of adrenaline and testosterone.

"Yeah. I guess this guy came really close—she was all wasted or whatever—but Crystal Dubois pulled him off of her."

"Fuck."

"Fuck yeah, fuck," Jason echoed.

Mel scratched at his chin like he expected to find his old scraggly beard there. "So…what happened?"

"Nothing." I chewed on the insides of my cheeks and exhaled through my nose. "That's the problem. That's why I needed to see you guys. Get your opinion."

Mel shook his head. "What do you mean, 'nothing'?"

"I mean, nothing. The guy who did it didn't get in any trouble," I said. "He's still out there. He got away with it."

"Lina didn't, like, press charges?" Jason looked indignant.

"Nope."

"Why the fuck not?"

I closed my eyes and struggled with what to tell these guys, how much to share. I shook my head, shrugged.

"There's…stuff. It happened pretty much right when Car's parents were killed. The plane crash. That kinda overshadowed everything else."

Mel's lips puckered, and he blew air. He never did learn to whistle. "Wow."

"Yeah." Jason stared into space for a second before looking at me. "So—who is this asshole?"

"Guy's name is Eric Finn." I looked at them both in turn. "Ring any bells?"

"No," said Mel.

Jason shook his head. "So, you gonna turn him in, or

what?"

"Heh. Yeah. No."

"Why the fuck not?"

"That, right there, is why I needed to talk to you guys," I said. "Lina made me promise not to do anything about it."

Jason barked again. "What?"

"It's part of..." I realized these two didn't know Lina was in therapy after the shit I'd dragged her through at the cabin last year. "It's...personal. Stuff she's trying to work through."

"Well," Mel said, "okay, then." He looked at me and crossed his arms across his chest.

"It's not right," I said. "Fucker shouldn't get away with it."

"Fuckin' A," Jason said.

"But," Mel said, "Lina wants you to let it go. Right?"

"Yeah." I looked at my hands. My fingers were curled and stiff. "But...it's not fair. And it's kinda driving me crazy."

"But," Mel repeated, "Lina wants you to let it go, Nathan. Life sucks. What can you do?"

"Fuck that," Jason said. He looked at me. "Hey. What would you do, if you could?"

His question broke down a door to a little room in my head I'd been keeping locked down. I stood up and paced a square of carpet. The words came spitting out.

"Fuck with him. Scare the shit out of him. Make him know it wasn't over. Make him know he wasn't dealing with a teenaged girl. That he had...he had me watching him."

The frustrated anger built in me, moving fine-grained sandpaper over the surface of my brain and down the nerve endings in my skin. I imagined Eric Finn's face—a face I had never seen, a face that was a vague amalgam of fear and cow-ardice—in tears in front of me while he cowered on the ground. "Make him sorry." I blinked and looked at Jason. "That's what I'd do."

Jason nodded. "Sounds like a good start."

"Sounds nothing at all like letting it *go*," Mel said. "Fuck's sake, Nathan. Lina'd kill you. Shit, your mother would kill you. And the cops. And what about the legal shit?"

Jason gave Mel a look. "Screw that." He looked at me. "M.Y.O.J., right, dude? Make that part of the deal."

"What deal?"

"When you face him. Make that part of the deal: that if he talks about it to anyone—anyone—you'll, I don't know, fuck him up."

Mel threw his arms into the air. "Blackmail? Seriously, what is *wrong* with you two?" He stepped in front of me and stopped my pacing. "Nate. This is a bad idea. You know it."

Of the two of them, Mel had been my friend the longest, ever since he first moved into the neighborhood in the summer of sixth grade and struck up a conversation at the bus stop. He had always been the steady one, the comparat-ively calm one. I think he recognized that his role was to provide a foil to Jason's flailing bravado, and he embraced that. He was sure playing it to the hilt right now.

"Mel," I said, "I can do something about this. I can make a difference. I can make that fucker feel something about what he did to Lina.

"Maybe," this thought had not occurred to me until just then, "even keep him from trying to rape someone else."

"Yep," Jason chimed.

"I can *do* something, Mel. For once."

Mel frowned. His lips twisted. "For once?"

His body language broadcast "gotcha," like he'd made some big psychological victory, like I'd see reason and let it go, let the world keep spinning, let Eric Finn keep going through life as a guy who thought he could get away with nearly raping my girlfriend.

Fuck that.

"Yes, Mel. For once." I felt my upper lip tremble. For a lot of people, I know that's a signal they're about to cry. On me, it means I want to bare my teeth. It means I want to leap.

I forced myself to look away from my best friend. My eyes found Jason.

"Can't let it stand, man," he said.

I took a breath and exhaled explosively. Right then, for a moment, that's when I felt like crying. I didn't.

"Yeah." I looked at Mel. I wanted to see understanding in his face. "I don't think I can."

All I got was disappointment.

"Guess you'll tell me all about it when it's over."

He turned away and made a fuss over picking another record to play.

Marc Teslowski
Three

Marc stowed his carry-on bag and sat down in his window seat. The curving wall of the airliner cabin was cool where he leaned against it, raising gooseflesh on his bare arm. The sensation made Marc's lips split in a steely grin.

He was going to Missoula.

When he got there, he'd pound on the doors of the Donner Institute for Sovereign Studies until they let him in and let him see his son.

Nobody liked it. Baldwin threatened to no longer represent Marc and Jeri, which was an empty threat, since far as Marc could see, the lawyer had so far done for them exactly jack shit.

Jeri was as close to pissed off as he'd seen in years. He would have thought she would have gone along with whatever Marc wanted, especially if that meant even a tiny chance it might get Byron to come home. Faced with the possibility, it was almost like she didn't want Byron to be back under Marc's roof.

Maybe she didn't. She'd never approved of Marc's parenting philosophy; he knew that. Tough. He was the father. He was the husband. His authority had to be final, and besides, if she'd had her way, Byron would never have been challenged, never have been pushed to accomplish everything he'd done.

Her unspoken, suspected betrayal only served to strengthen Marc's resolve. He would go to Missoula, and he would come back with his son if he had to drag Byron out by his ear and punch William Donner in the throat on the way out.

Yeah.

Marc straightened in his seat and watched people file onto the airliner. A few people back was the second strangest-looking guy Marc had ever laid eyes on. He was probably six and a half feet tall, but gawky and skinny as all hell. He had tiny little ears, like they'd stopped growing when he was a kid or something, underneath a sloppy, spiky shock of feathery black hair.

The guy's nose was enormous, narrow and hooked at the end like a beak. His lips were thin and pale. His eyes were black and wide, and he kept them pointed at the ground as much as possible.

The first-most strangest-looking guy Marc had ever seen was Nathan Charters.

Marc's eyes narrowed and his nostrils flared.

Right.

The Sovereign freak sat down next to him.

Marc didn't bother to hide his revulsion. He recoiled and shoved himself as close as he could to the inner wall of the cabin. He stared out the little window.

Mother *fuck*. It was like the whole world was trying to get his goat. Put a fucking Sovereign on the same plane. Put him in the seat next to Marc.

It couldn't get any worse.

"Oh my god." The guy's voice was a grating, piping screech. "You're Marc Teslowski."

All right, then. It could get worse.

Marc kept his eyes on the tarmac below and said nothing.

"You are. You're Marc Teslowski."

This could go on for hours. Marc had to put an end to it.

"I'm not interested in talking to you," he growled.

The gawky freak squawked a laugh. "Well, we're traveling companions, Marc Teslowski." Marc felt him shifting in the next seat. "Might as well be companionable, right?"

Marc kept his tongue. How many hours was this flight?

"My name's Eddie. Eddie Schwippe." Some of his vowels came out choked, like his tongue was hitting the roof of his mouth at the wrong time as he talked. Maybe his fucking tongue was deformed thanks to whatever kind of freak he was.

"And you are the infamous father who wants the Sovereigns to give back one of their own." His chirping wasn't so strange Marc couldn't hear the subtle teasing in his tone. "Well. One of our own, I guess I should say."

The plane started to move into position on the runway. Marc watched the pavement flow past, the swift flash of lines and letters coming and going in the small square of the world he could see.

Eddie Schwippe clucked. "I bet you're not too happy right now, eh, Marc? Mister Teslowski? Right?"

Marc gave up and turned to face him. Eddie blinked and smiled. His eyes, Marc realized, were entirely black, all pupil. It was disturbing.

"I told you. I'm not interested in talking. All right?"

Schwippe shrugged, and knobby shoulders rolled under his baggy dress shirt. "Got it! 'Course, that doesn't mean I won't be talking to you. It's too long a flight to just sit here and space out, right? Besides, I forgot my book."

Schwippe held out his right hand. The fingers were long, the knuckles like walnuts. His fingernails were so black and glossy you'd think they were painted, but Marc guessed they probably weren't.

"So as I was saying," Schwippe said, just slightly more seriously, "my name's Eddie. Pleased to meet you."

Marc turned away from him and locked his focus on the back of the seat directly ahead. He still couldn't help peripherally seeing Schwippe pull his hand back, slowly.

"Really?" Schwippe clicked his tongue. "And to think I went to the trouble of filing my nails. They weren't always like that, you know. I mean, I was always a little...awkward-looking, if you want to put it kindly...but after Declaration Day..."

His sigh carried the hint of a whistle.

"I just...blossomed. I'm going to see if the Institute can help me figure it all out."

The insistent, winking enthusiasm returned to his voice. "Why are you going to Missoula, Marc, Mister Teslowski, I wonder? Hmm?"

Marc said nothing. Schwippe left him alone while the stewardess ran through the pre-flight safety demonstration and the airliner took off. Maybe the freak finally took the hint.

Marc watched the plane turn over the Pacific Ocean before angling east and north while the earth dropped farther and farther away.

He was going. He would be there. Today.

He was doing something, something real. Nobody liked

it, and it was putting him into some serious debt, and it would eat every hour of vacation and sick time he had left, but he couldn't let any of that matter. He was taking action. Taking responsibility.

Finally.

"I love flying, too," Schwippe quipped.

Marc hadn't realized he'd been smiling. He tamped it out.

"So, seriously," Schwippe went on. Marc realized his break from the freak's fun-time poking was over. "I'm sincerely curious. Why are you going to Missoula, Mister Teslowski?"

Why not? Nothing and no one could stop him now. He might as well tell the Sovereign beanpole. Call it practice when he had to talk to a whole freaking compound of them.

"I bet you can guess." He glanced at Schwippe.

Schwippe's alien black eyes popped. He jumped in his seat a little, a show of being startled. "Well, I'll be! I get an audience, after all?"

Marc scowled at him. "You're a sarcastic little shit, aren't you."

Schwippe looked down at his long torso and at his legs, which were bent sharply to fit in the space between seats. "Little, I'm not. The rest...well, a guy's got to find a way to get by."

Marc snorted at this. "By being an asshole."

Without an ounce of venom, Schwippe said, "Hey, look how well it's worked for you, right?"

Marc turned in his seat to face him. "What the hell do you know about me?"

"Seriously?" Schwippe looked all the long way down his nose at Marc. His eyes narrowed and he smiled wide. "And I quote: 'Why don't we have all those freaks rounded up and locked away?'"

For the millionth time, Marc wished he'd never agreed to do that goddamn TV show, and not because of what he'd said. "Good for you. You watch TV."

Schwippe's Uncle Remus impression suffered from his croaking, high-pitched delivery. "Just like a reg'lar ol' human bean! 'Magine dat, Misser Marc, sir!"

Marc got the message. He thought it was bullshit. "Except you're not. Your boss made sure we all know that."

Schwippe blinked. He sat back and tilted his head back on the seat. "Wow." He shook his head. "I don't get how you do that."

"What."

"How you can turn it off and on like that. Be so select-ive."

"What," Marc repeated, harsher.

"Your bigotry." Schwippe's voice was casual, but most of the humor was replaced by a bewildered tone that was some-how just as insulting to Marc. "You know you don't make any sense, right? Does it just not matter to you?"

Marc pushed the words out with as much disgust as he could muster. "You don't get to tell me what to do or how to think, freak."

Schwippe's head tilted. "Wha'?"

Marc leaned forward. "That's your whole thing, right? Set the terms, show up and tell the rest of the whole damn world how we're supposed to treat you, how we're supposed to act." He forced himself to keep his voice low, conscious of the tight quarters and the dozens of people in the seats around them. "To hell with you, Sovereign."

"Hold the phone, there, buddy." Schwippe seemed to roll his eyes, but it was hard to tell where those glossy black balls were pointed. "I'm just a skinny dude from West LA with a next-to-worthless metahuman bag of tricks and a cheap tailor. I can't make you do anything, Marc, and you're even more delusional than I thought if you think I can."

"Delusional!"

Schwippe took a breath, glanced around and seemed to find the same restraint Marc had a moment before, and huffed through his narrow nostrils. "Listen, man: your son is a Sovereign."

Marc leaned quickly back against the window. "Bull-shit."

Schwippe's laugh held disbelief. "How can you say that?"

"Just because they took him doesn't mean he's one of you. There's no proof of that. Just their word."

Schwippe's shiny black eyes fixed on Marc. He tilted his head to the left and tapped a long, knobby finger against his lip.

"I'll give you that one," he said. "Technically. But...why would they lie?"

"To give them a reason to hold my son captive for the last eleven months." Marc relaxed slightly. "Of course."

"But..." Schwippe kept looking at him. "But...why? Why your kid? What for?"

Marc had no idea. There had to be a reason, though. Something to do with the business between the Charters family and Tyndale Labs, maybe. That whole ugly mess last year. There had to be a reason.

"I don't know," he muttered. "I'm sure you'll be able to ask them."

Schwippe laughed. "Oh, sure, what, during the weekly Sovereign poker game?"

Marc didn't laugh. He imagined strategy sessions—had the vague idea of a war room, like in that movie with the Pink Panther guy and Slim Pickens. The image gave him a bad feeling.

Schwippe said, "What if your kid…Byron, right? What if he just…wants to be there?"

"He wouldn't." Marc's voice was flat. "There's nothing there for him. He's a prisoner—don't you get that?" He kept his jaw tight to avoid yelling. "Your…you freaks…are holding my kid a prisoner. That's the kind of p—" He stopped himself. "The kind of trash you're running to. Get it?"

"Boy," Schwippe said with a small smile, "you have no idea of the kind of trash I'm running *from*. Seriously."

Marc fell back against his seat. Fucking freak.

Schwippe didn't say anything for a few blessed minutes. Marc ground his teeth and tried to get his ears to pop. He wondered how much farther it was. How much longer he'd have to endure Eddie Schwippe's company.

"But…" Schwippe said.

"Fuck. Give me a break, would you?"

"But…seriously, even if he's not a Sovereign—what will you do if he says he wants to stay there? What if he's not a prisoner, after all? What if it's something else?"

"Like what?"

"I don't know! Sake of argument."

Marc shook his head. "He's a minor. He's my kid. He does what I say. If—and I mean it's a big fucking if—he's just sitting up there...laughing at me and his mother..." Marc couldn't deny the thought had crossed his mind. The kid might think he had plenty of reasons to get back at his dad. Marc would have thought the same at his age.

He shook his head again.

"No difference. He comes home with me. He doesn't get to do what he wants until he hits eighteen years old and gets a job."

Schwippe's eyes went wide. He stared at Marc and covered his mouth with a spidery hand. His Adam's apple bobbed as he did his best to stifle a laugh.

"Oh, right," he finally said. "Eighteen. Totally." A single laugh burst out. "That's when us big kids get to do whatever we want. You bet."

Schwippe calmed down. He shifted in his seat, stretching his left leg into the aisle before slowly, apparently painfully, bending the hinged stick back in place.

"Hit eighteen, the world's your oyster!"

He whistled another sigh, gave Marc one more crooked-head, glassy-eyed glance, and didn't say another word the rest of the trip.

Marc had no idea why that bothered him more than anything Schwippe had said or done so far.

Marc Teslowski
Four

Marc didn't have any baggage other than the carry-on duffel bag hanging from his shoulder, but he couldn't help stopping near baggage claim to gape at the display of a stuffed mountain lion chomping on the neck of a billy goat.

The exhibit made him grin until his cheeks hurt. He was not in Orange County any more. He was in Missoula, Montana, unlikely as it seemed the closest city to the Donner Institute for Sovereign Studies.

Tomorrow morning, he would be at the gates. By tomorrow night, he would be back on a plane for home, and instead of a chatty, sarcastic Sovereign freak in the next seat, it would be Byron, his son.

Marc tore his eyes off the garish taxidermy display and turned toward the car-rental stations. On his way, he caught sight of Eddie Schwippe, the sarcastic Sovereign freak himself.

Hard to miss. The Sovereign towered over everyone else, even if there were teenaged girls in the terminal who probably outweighed him.

Schwippe was talking with three redneck-lumberjack types. Other Sovereign come to meet him, right out in the open? Marc's lip curled, but as he watched, he realized his initial assumption wasn't quite right.

He was too far away to really make out what was being said, but it was clear the three guys around Schwippe weren't very friendly, despite their smiling faces. Marc had used that same sneer himself to throw people off balance. It was almost a reflex.

They crowded around him, gradually herding him toward the door. Schwippe seemed resistant to the idea, but he was going, all the same.

One of the rednecks put a hand around Schwippe's pipe-cleaner bicep. Marc could see a splash of red and blue on the back of the redneck's hand. Jesus, a tattoo there would hurt like hell.

The whole thing seemed weird. But Schwippe was a Sovereign, so Marc figured he could take care of himself. In fact, the idea Schwippe might cut loose made him a little nervous. What if the freak caused an earthquake, or started shooting lightning bolts out of those black-marble eyes?

Marc didn't want to be around for that. He started for the car-rental counter and hoped it wouldn't take long to put some real distance between him and Schwippe.

Last he saw of Eddie Schwippe were those wide alien black eyes aimed in his direction as the freak left with his pushy friends. Marc wasn't sure if the Sovereign was looking at him or not.

Andrew Charters
One

Reality, as perceived by Andrew Charters, was more than the discriminate input of five senses. For Andrew, the universe was a torrent of metasensory, aggregate sensation that pelted him, from all sides, at all times.

The dry soil delivered granular data through the soles of his filthy, calloused bare feet. He knew, in quantifiable terms he could not elucidate, how long ago the dew had burned off that day. He knew, from his impression of the relative warmth of the earth, how soon the ants would wake up from their winter torpor. If anything down to the mass of a rabbit moved anywhere within a fifty-foot radius of his crouched position on the ridge, he would feel the vibration like a super-human version of the proverbial Indian with his ear on rail-road tracks predicting the arrival of a train.

The slightest breeze carried libraries of information to Andrew's olfactory bulbs. Turning a slow circle, he could pin-point the locations of edible plants, animals alive and dead, and their droppings with an accuracy that depended on intensity and distance but far surpassed the inherent sensitiv-ity of any other living thing on the planet.

Andrew's hearing was equally discerning. If the rabbit fifty feet away happened to scratch itself, Andrew would, if he concentrated, be able to count the strokes of its leg.

His eyes soaked up photons with such vociferous appet-ite, he could successfully navigate a china shop crowded with playing-card houses, with the shades down, on a moonless night, if called upon to do so. In full daylight, his visual acuity was, like his sense of smell, without parallel among life on earth.

His sense of taste, tied closely to his sense of smell, was delicate enough that he could distinguish ingredients very nearly by their constituent long-chain molecules.

Working together, Andrew's sensorium plowed unending information into a brain that had failed to successfully adapt to the augmented, collective assault of sight, hearing, scent, smell, and touch.

The overload had driven him crazy long ago.

It was so much worse where people were, with their cars and televisions and phone calls and music and perfumes and talking and sweat and pheromones and smelly emotion. So Andrew preferred to spend as much time as possible in the wilderness, where the sensorium was not necessarily less intense, but the individual data, at least, were smaller and more...natural.

Surrounded by dirt and trees and lizards and bugs and birds and furry things, he didn't have to put himself through the painful effort of making room for thoughts, for words. He could just...be.

The problem with this was, despite the extreme modifications and augmentations Project: Rancher had inflicted on his physiology, Andrew Charters had begun life as a human being and he was still a human being in several ways that mattered very much. Self-imposed solitude was all well and good until loneliness grew and ached and gnawed through him like a twisting feedback loop.

That kept him from retreating too far into the wild

places, literally and psychologically. He lived on the periphery, wandering all over the western United States, but most often staying no more than a day's loping walk from Kirby Lake in the San Bernardino mountains.

He'd been skulking around the mountain town last year, toying with the idea of breaking into his mother's vacation cabin and enduring the deliciously melancholy impressions of history to be found there, when his uneasy balance of exile and need was thrown all to hell by the appearance of his son.

He knew it was the boy before he'd actually seen him. The scent was too much like his own—but cleaner, newer, and yes, inhuman...but not *so* inhuman.

The kid didn't seem to have as much trouble with his gifts as his father. Andrew stayed upwind, and when he'd caught sight of Nathan's face in the pale light of the cabin porch light, he understood. The scientist he had once been extrapolated on what he saw:

Andrew's own augmentation was forever in conflict with his human origins. The changes had been forced upon his genetic structure by the Augmentation Regimen.

Conversely, those chimeric genes went into what made Nathan Charters from the moment of conception. Nate's face showed that: unusually large eyes set in appropriately large sockets, with the bone structure to support it. A barrel chest to accommodate vigorously pumping lungs and heart, which were required to drive a metabolism designed to fuel the extra dense muscles of the boy's body...and the extra neural connections in the boy's brain handling the input of his senses.

Trembling with fascination and yearning and regret, Andrew had watched his odd, tentatively graceful teenaged son that night and realized, correctly, that the boy would not equal the father's remarkable abilities, being entirely half-human.

Nathan would be at least half again better at living with the abilities he had, though. With luck, the kid would never be more than a little crazy.

Andrew found it hard to stay away after that April day nearly a year ago. It was a good thing, too—Nathan wasn't crazy enough to deal with the augmented thugs Lester Brenhurst had sicced on him. Andrew was, though.

He grinned, his snarled beard pulling back to reveal strong yellow teeth, and remembered how it felt to have the hot guts of one of Lester's agents slap against him. That was a good day.

But Andrew knew it was not so good for his son, or for Nathan's mother. The complications presented by his very existence helped Andrew decide the best thing he could do was disappear again.

Over the last eleven months, though, it had become difficult for Andrew to deny that running mostly only made things easier for him.

Andrew saw newspapers in people's trash. He watched television, when he could bear it, through people's windows. He knew Nate and Lucille were going through a rough time.

Andrew Charters
Two

A delicious scent, tangy and warm, pulled him out of his reverie. Unconsciously, his whole body tensed. Crouched on the ridge, he balanced on the balls of his feet and the fingertips of his left hand. He right hand automatically curled into claws tipped with half inch long, filthy fingernails.

Just down the ridge, maybe forty feet away, a field mouse made its way through the chaparral in halting, jerking bursts. Andrew couldn't see it—yet—but between a headwind and the remarkable sensitivity of his ears, he could plot its position from point to point as it moved.

It would make a fine little snack.

Andrew let himself be whittled down to the input of his sensorium. It was easier to hunt—easier to live—when he subsumed thought and memory and feeling and let his body be guided by hunger and sport.

He inched down the ridge. The breeze was still in his favor. He visualized the vector of the field mouse as if lines were traced on the ground ahead of him.

A flutter, above.

Andrew unlocked his eyes from the triangulated location of his prey and glanced up. A hawk circled.

Andrew bit back the urge to growl behind his spreading smile. Did the hawk think it could dive and reach the mouse before Andrew would?

For that matter, did the hawk suspect that if it tried, it would be in danger itself?

Thought pushed for bandwidth in Andrew's mind as choices presented themselves and, consequently, delayed him.

The bird would be more meat...but feathers were more of a hassle than fur.

The field mouse had frozen.

The hawk circled. Andrew knew he was being watched, that the bird was running its own kind of instinct-driven assessment.

That was the thing, though, wasn't it? Andrew didn't have to run on instinct. His choices were colored by, and benefited from, something else.

It wasn't that his choices weren't simply black and white, on-off, instinct-driven impulses. He had more than instinct ticking away inside his skull. That was what made things so...hard.

The revelation literally knocked him on his ass.

The hawk dropped like a spear, cried out, and snatched the field mouse in its talons. Flapping powerfully, it ascended again and made for a nearby treetop, where it could enjoy its morsel well away from the foul-smelling predator.

Andrew sat in the dirt and laughed, a hoarse croaking from his underused vocal chords.

"You can have it, birdie," he chortled.

He watched the bird tear into the field mouse with quick strokes of its beak. It seemed to be enjoying itself...but really, it was just a machine.

"Not me," Andrew husked to himself. "Don't have to be."

He could decide to be something other than what he was made to be, if he wanted to be. If there was *reason* to be.

Hazy memories coalesced in his mind. A fight—no, an argument—between him and Lester, a long, long time ago.

Someplace bright, but there was a dark place there, too. With frightened people inside.

Andrew made a choice, back then. An important choice. A life-and-death choice. He couldn't pin down exactly what it was, but he was sure he'd made a decision Lester hadn't liked. He made a choice that kept the frightened people safe.

It had scared him. He remembered that feeling. But he did it. He did it.

Somewhere out there, fifty miles or so to the south and west as that hawk might fly, was his boy. Andrew knew something about the forces allied against his son, against his...wife.

"Damn," he whispered. He gripped the earth with toes and fingers to combat the physical urge to flee, to head for the hills in every sense of the word.

He could make a choice. He had *good* reasons.

The hawk preened, watching him.

Andrew let go of the ground and stood up, straight. Like a man.

"Gonna need help..." He grinned as his eyes watered from giddy exhilaration. "Gotta go see Denver..."

Marc Teslowski
Five

Marc wasn't a huge fan of the Hyundai Excel they'd given him at the rental office, but it was good enough to get him up the three thousand feet into the mountains east of Missoula. It would be good enough to bring Byron back. The kid probably wouldn't even notice the junky car. He'd be too excited to care.

Marc stamped down the possibility that Byron might just as likely be too angry to care. That was Jeri talking. That was not reality.

He was distracted from that line of thinking by the traffic on I-90 and MT 200. There were a lot of out-of-state plates. Finally, he realized with a mix of irritation and nerves that at least some of these cars probably held Sovereign on their way to…how would they think of it? Sanctuary? Asylum? They were like those Arabs on their way to that city, whatever it was, and it looked like some had come a long way.

It was three days until the first anniversary of Declaration Day, when the king of the freaks, William Karl Donner, had appeared in Washington, D.C., did his flashy David Copperfield magic tricks, and announced to the world that people like him (who even knew that there were people like him until then?) would henceforth be considered Sovereign, separate and apart from the laws of the nations of the world.

Not a week later, Reagan—*Reagan*, of all the guys—rolled over and basically went along with the idea. They called it the Sovereign Compromise. The Sovereign would be left alone, allowed to build their hideaway on land Donner owned out here, and in return, the government and the Sovereigns would share any information they got on what the Sovereigns actually were.

The thing that pissed off Marc, and a whole lot of other people, too, was that the Compromise allowed the Sovereigns to police themselves. If a Sovereign broke a human law, a law of the United States, they wouldn't be tried in a human court, spend time in human prison, or fry in an electric chair built for humans.

Nope. The Sovereigns answered to their own law, which, from what Marc had seen in the last year, pretty much amounted to whatever William Karl Donner said it was that day.

Which was why the Teslowskis hadn't been able to get to their son. All it took was for those freaks to declare that Byron was a Sovereign, too, and that was supposed to be that.

Well, today, Sovereign law would meet Marc's own law: the right of a father's jurisdiction over his own flesh and blood.

A final right turn off Garnet Range Road, and Marc found himself, along with most of the other cars he'd been following, driving beneath a green metal sign that told him he had arrived at the Donner Institute for Sovereign Studies Visitors Center.

Marc could barely believe the smaller sign on right shoulder:

YOU ARE NOW LEAVING UNITED STATES
METAHUMAN SOVEREIGN TERRITORY
BEYOND THIS POINT
(EO 12512 APRIL 26 1985)

Un fucking believable.

Marc didn't feel like he was leaving his country. He drove onto a large, well-paved parking lot that wouldn't look out of place outside a K-Mart or GEMCO, except there weren't any of those metal things holding shopping carts, just row after angled row of painted stripes on black tarmac.

"Jesus..."

The parking lot was about half full. Marc didn't bother being choosy. He glided into the first spot that presented itself.

Marc strode for the only building, a low, modern/rustic-looking structure on the south edge of the lot. He tried to keep his eyes on his destination, but the temptation to scan his fellow travelers was too great.

Individual and small groups of two or three got out of their cars, stretched, and checked their backpacks or fanny packs or maps or cameras just like tourists anywhere. Some people turned in slow circles, taking in the pine- and fir-tree-lined slopes all around.

Marc saw a woman get out of her car, fall to her hands and knees, and kiss the asphalt. A man and a woman from a nearby car approached the woman, and the women embraced. They went toward the Visitors Center as a group, speaking in low voices punctuated by bright, exhausted laughter.

Everyone looked entirely, completely human.

That was weird. Where were the freaks?

Were these people just...people? Tourists here to gawk?

Marc steeled himself for what he'd find inside the Visitors Center. It was sure to be staffed by monsters.

Marc went through automatic sliding glass doors and

found himself in an open space that could have been designed by the same architect who had built the Missoula airport. Huge, polished wooden beams overhead. A shining floor that looked like, but couldn't possibly have been, a single huge slab of marble. Tasteful kiosks of wood and brassy metal displaying television touchscreens.

Employees, distinguishable by their teal vests, approached some people with open smiles. Two employees met the pavement-kissing woman and her new friends.

No one bothered Marc.

He noticed guards, armed with nightsticks and sidearms, their uniforms traditional but unlike any with which he was familiar, were stationed every dozen yards or so throughout the space. They nodded and smiled at anyone who came near.

Over a centrally located circular booth bearing the word "Information" in carved wooden beys-relief, a long banner hung that read, "Freedom To Be Better ~ The Sovereign Era: Year One."

Marc made for it. A young woman—an apparently utterly normal, human, young woman—smiled from behind the counter as he approached.

"Good morning, sir. Welcome to the Donner Institute for Sovereign Studies."

He was disappointed, and slightly disgusted, that regular people would sink to working for the freaks like it was just another job. Couldn't this chick be a waitress or something? Was the economy that bad?

Marc took a deep breath, sucking in his gut and sticking out his chest. He put his palms flat on the counter and leaned in.

"I'm here to see my son," he said.

God, it felt good to say that, here.

Her smile faltered slightly, mostly in her blue eyes, where confusion took over. "And does he work here...?"

Her reaction was a little confusing for Marc, too. "You mean you don't know who I am?"

"I'm sorry, sir...I sure don't."

A staff member to her right handed a tourist a pamphlet and turned toward them. Marc saw right away that this guy, at least, knew who he was. The guy's eyes widened. He quickly came up next to the young woman with a couple of long steps.

"How can we help you?" He smiled, too, but Marc knew how to pound through that dodgy shield.

He bared his teeth in his own kind of grin. "My name is Marc Teslowski." He raised his voice on every word. "And I demand to see my son."

The man was sweating over the same firm but polite mask Marc had seen on the salespeople at Wards when he tried to return some underwear not two weeks before. "I'm very sorry, Mister Teslowski, but we can't help you with that."

"You don't have to help me. Just point me down the road to Donner's hidey-hole." He kept his feral grin in place. His eyes danced with intimidation. "You just tell 'em I'm coming so they can open the gate or whatever they need to do."

"Sir...I'm sorry."

Marc shrugged. "Okay, well, how about this. I'll wait here—heck, I'll even wait in your office, or whatever, so people don't stare—and you call up and have them bring my boy down here. You're right. I don't need to go to the Institute." He laughed. "I'd just as soon not get any closer than I am right now, know what I mean?"

The guy looked down a moment, eyes widening, steeling himself. That's right, Marc thought. Your day just got interesting, you traitorous little shit.

The guy focused on Marc again. "Sir, again, I'm sorry, but we can't do that. As you know, your son, as a Sovereign —"

"My son is no such thing!" Marc bellowed. He slammed his fist on the counter.

The girl who had initially greeted him flinched and took two steps back. The guy threw an imploring look over Marc's left shoulder.

And just like that, Marc was flanked by two of the guards. They weren't smiling now.

"Sir. We'd like you to leave now," said the one on his right.

Marc whirled on him. "Are you a person? Or one of them?"

The guard's jaw moved. His nostrils flared. Marc sized him up. He had about two inches on the guy, but the guard's right hand was at the holster on his hip.

"We would like you to leave, sir. You won't be asked again."

Marc smirked. "Hah! You haven't asked me in the first place!" He looked for a sign, any small thing, that would clue him in as to the guard's pedigree. "You didn't answer my question—are you one of them? Or are you a stinkin' traitor?"

The guard on his left gripped Marc's shoulder. He had a pretty good grip. Marc twisted out of it. Something in the middle of his upper back pinched like it always did when he pivoted too fast—a reminder of his so-called glory days on the high school gridiron.

"Don't you fucking touch me, traitor."

The guard didn't say anything. He just nodded once, and Marc felt the hard, prodding tip of the other guy's nightstick on his back, twisting into the exact location of his pulled muscle.

Marc flinched automatically, arching his back. The nightstick jabbed, and Marc stumbled forward.

The guard on his left got a better grip the second time. He used both hands.

In that fashion—prodding and dragging him as he howled a string of invectives—Marc was ejected from the Visitors Center of the Donner Institute for Sovereign Studies.

Once outside, a third guard met them and handcuffed Marc before extracting his car keys from his front pocket with the smooth skill of a street thief.

"You fuckers! Fuck you! Fuck you!"

A sedan pulled up to the curb in front of them. Marc didn't have time to get a good look at the golden seal on the passenger-side front door before one of his captors opened the back door and shoved him in, one hand on his shoulder and one on the back of his head, cop-style.

The car had a thick metal mesh dividing the rear seat from the front, just like a police car. The driver didn't turn around or say a word. He navigated out of the parking lot, which was getting crowded with cars and people, and drove back down Garnet Range Road.

He parked in a turn-out about fifty yards from the Institute road, got out, opened the back passenger door, and dragged Marc out.

"Do nothing," the guard said before he unlocked Marc's handcuffs and scraped them off.

"Your car will be delivered in a few minutes," the guard said. "When it is, get in and drive away, Mister Teslowski. Go home." The guard's voice lowered. "This was the nice one. Next time, it won't be us. It'll be," he glanced back in the general direction of the Institute, "SCET. You don't want that. Be smart."

The guard waited, but Marc was too furious to speak. The guard shrugged, got back in his car, and left.

It was a half-hour—thirty minutes of standing in the dirt watching lots of cars head for the Institute and very few pass him headed the other way—before three guards rode up in his rental car.

He spat on their boots before he drove back down the mountain.

Byron Teslowski
One

Byron Teslowski, a little cold in his athletic shorts and Abbeque Valley High sweatshirt, stood in the meadow between the Institute and Donner's weird old house and waited for Spencer Croy to shoot him in the leg.

Again.

Byron couldn't get it out of his head that his dad had shown up at the Visitors Center just a couple of hours before, been not even a mile away, and that he was still probably down in Missoula.

It made it hard to focus on the task at hand, and that could be a problem.

Mister Croy called to Byron from fifty paces away, where he stood with his right arm extended and a pistol in his hand. "You're distracted."

Byron glanced at Dr. Mazmanian, who was crouched a few yards to Byron's left. Mazmanian shrugged with sympathy.

"Sorry, Mister Croy." Byron swallowed and shook himself out like a boxer preparing to enter the ring. "I'll get it together. Just gimme a sec—"

The impact grabbed him on his right upper thigh and spun him around. The crack of the gunshot reached Byron just as he lost his balance and hit the tall grass on his left side.

His entire leg was numb save for the burning throb where the bullet hit him. He looked down at the massive, purple bruise he could almost see spreading as he watched.

He told himself he wouldn't throw up.

He managed to tilt his head toward the dewy grass

before he did.

Doc Mazmanian got to his side quickly and gave the leg a glance before looking at Byron.

"What day is it, Byron?" Mazmanian smiled.

"Ow. Tuesday." Byron wiped his mouth, and then wiped his hand on a dry patch of meadow grass. "Fuck. Ow."

Croy holstered his pistol and strode to stand over Byron. "How is he?"

Mazmanian balanced his hands on his knees and stood up. "Much better than last week. Didn't even break the skin."

"Good."

Careful to avoid the stinky mess in the grass, Byron gingerly shifted onto his back, propped on his elbows. The pressure of the ground on his ass made his right leg hurt even more. He winced and squinted up at Croy.

"You didn't give me a chance to get ready!"

"Closer to reality," Croy said. "There will be distractions in the field. Your state of mind this morning served its purpose."

Byron shifted back to his left side and carefully stood up. Neither of the adults moved to help him.

He had to keep as much weight on his left leg as he could. His right leg was beginning to come to life with fiery pins and needles.

"Served its—?" Byron gaped at Mazmanian. "That's, like, totally why you told me about my dad before we came out here."

Mazmanian, still grinning, nodded.

"Jesus!" Byron looked at both of them. "Was my dad even here? Or was it all just part of the test?"

"Oh, your dad was here, all right." Doc Mazmanian's smile leveled off. "He made a big scene. They had to eject him from the Visitors Center under guard."

Byron took a second to picture that. He decided he needed some flavoring. "Did they mess him up?"

Mazmanian raised an eyebrow; Byron knew the doc well enough to recognize that as a minor rebuke. "They only hurt his pride, Byron. Just his pride."

Byron's leg was on fire from the pins and needles, but he had to resist stomping his foot because of what the impact would do to the bruise. All the same, he smiled, just a little.

"That'll work."

Mazmanian furrowed his brow and shook his head. "Great attitude, Byron."

Croy turned for the Institute grounds. "Time for your follow-up work." He didn't wait for them.

Mazmanian kept Byron's limping pace but made no move to help him. Byron didn't take it personally—it was all part of the exercise. They needed to see how fast his adaptive abilities would work; any outside assistance would mess up the, whatever they called it, the data.

Croy went directly to the research center; if Byron wasn't bleeding or in shock, there was no reason to bother with the infirmary. Byron, eyes down, struggled with the stairs leading to the entrance. His leg really, really hurt.

"You can do it, soldier boy."

That throaty female voice sure wasn't Mazmanian.

Byron lifted his head and saw a girl about his age, sixteen or seventeen, leaning with deliberate cool against the rail on the far side of the wide steps.

She was skinny. Her holey, strategically bleached blue jeans hung off narrow hips. She had freckles all over her bare arms and, Byron noticed, across the belly beneath her gray half T-shirt. Her freckled face was topped by a shock of spiky red hair. If her wardrobe made her cold, she did a good job of hiding it.

Her smile was mostly mocking. She brushed lightly at her chin. "You got a little bit, right there."

Byron automatically scraped at his chin, mortified that he might have puke caked on his face.

There was nothing.

She laughed. "Sorry, dude. Couldn't resist." She pushed off of the rail, briskly descended the stairs, and strutted toward the residence center while Byron watched.

"C'mon, Byron," Mazmanian prompted. "Let's get you wired up and cleaned up. You'll be properly introduced before long, I'm sure."

Byron scowled and painfully ascended the remaining stairs. "Can't wait," he growled.

From The Journal Of Nate Charters
Nine

Every Monday, I had to get my weekly independent study assignments from school, which meant getting a ride from my mother, who always took that day off or worked from home. I didn't have much time for myself.

I'd been following the advice of Lina's dad and hadn't called her. She didn't call me, either.

Tuesday, my mother left for her office and I had the house, and more importantly, the telephone, to myself. I went for the White Pages as soon as my mother's car was out of sight.

There were four listings with the last name of Finn. Finn, Vincent; Finn, F.; Finn, Albert; Finn, Michael.

No one answered at the first number, even though I let it ring ten times. The second number clicked over to an answering machine on the third ring.

"Hey, there, hi! The Finns aren't in! Get it? Ha, ha... well, you know what to do. At the beep, leave a message for Frank, Ricki, Bill, or Dawn!"

Beep.

No Eric.

I called the third number. On the fifth ring, a kid's voice said, "What? I mean, Finn's residence."

I closed my eyes and crossed my fingers.

"Is Eric there?"

"Who wants to know?"

"A…a friend of his. From school."

"Eric don't go to school, dummy."

I raised my fist and mouthed a silent, "yes!"

All excited, I found myself taking on the kid's attitude. "Duh," I said. "We used to go to school. Together."

"What," the kid giggled, "like a couple of fags?"

"Ha, ha. Good one. So is Eric there, or not?"

"He's at work, of course."

"Oh, yeah, right. Hey, where does he work again?"

"You don't know?"

"It's…been a while. Hey, why aren't you in school?"

"The car place," the kid said. "What's it called…oh yeah." The kid made like he thought he sounded like a radio announcer. "Sunrise Import Shop!" His voice went back to its high, piping normal. "I'm home sick!"

Sunrise Import Shop.

I hung up on the kid, grabbed the Yellow Pages, flipped to the right page, and there it was. Even had a quarter-page ad.

I wanted to go right then, but it was all the way across town. I'd need to fuel up before I got on my bike.

As I put second breakfast together, I started playing fantasies of my meeting with Lina's would-be rapist through my head. None of them ended well for Eric Finn. Some of them involved tears, and not mine.

It wasn't a short bike ride to Sunrise Import Shop. The place was in an industrial park on the far side of El Toro, which meant going all the way down by the freeway.

At least the weather was decent. A little chilly, but that gave me an excuse to wear my hooded sweatshirt. I could be incognito until the right moment.

I wasn't sure when that right moment would be, or how

it would unfold, but I had ideas that there would be some public humiliation.

It was around one in the afternoon when I coasted into the parking lot. Sunrise Import Shop was what looked like one of those places that customizes cars, puts spoilers and headers and superchargers or whatever on them. It sat kind of in the middle of a row with a wrought iron fence place, a transmission place, and so on.

From the parking lot, the shop might as well have been an office. I pedaled around to the back, where I saw the rear of the building was, in contrast, almost entirely open to the elements: a nearly unbroken row of roll-up garage doors.

In Sunrise Import Shop, five guys were tinkering around four import-looking cars—like Nissans, Datsuns, Toyotas and what-not—in various stages of disassembly or whatever.

I rode back and forth along the alley behind the building, my hood tight around my head. A cold feeling swept through me. I felt like I'd just figured out the dream where I'm at school with no pants on wasn't a dream.

I stopped a dozen yards down from the three garage doors that made up the back of Sunrise Import Shop and balanced my bike on one straight leg.

It occurred to me that I had no idea what Eric Finn looked like.

I was fucked.

Fucked.

A guy in coveralls walked out of Sunrise and into the alley. He wiped his hands on a dull red rag and put his hand above his eyes, shading them from the sun behind me.

"Hey, kid," he called.

Great.

I stood there on my bike.

"Yeah?"

"C'mere, kid."

I realized there was a one in five chance that this was Eric Finn himself.

Yeah. Game time.

I pedaled casually toward him. It didn't take long for my excellent eyes to pick out "Len" stitched on his breast. Okay. Not Eric Finn.

I stopped so that Len had to turn his back on the shop interior to face me. Meanwhile, I had a pretty good view of the people inside.

"Yeah?" I tried not to sound too much like your typical sullen teenager. I hoped my hood provided enough camouflage; I didn't want to be recognized right off the bat.

Len smiled; he thought I was suspicious, that I was like most kids, and assumed I was in some kind of trouble, or at least about to be wrongly accused of something. "Nothin'—I just saw you going by a few times. Did you wanna check out the shop?"

Over Len's shoulder, I *was* checking out the shop. Most of the guys inside hadn't looked up from the cars.

One did. He appeared when he dropped the hood on the car he was working on.

He had jet-black hair that looked like it would make a pretty tall pompadour if he took the time. His eyes were brown. He had high cheekbones on a face that looked narrower that it probably was thanks to the pointy black Vandyke on his chin.

He pretty much looked like a music-video handsome version of a carnival devil.

"Oh, no," I told Len. "I'm just, y'know, riding my bike."

Len laughed. "Sure. Sure." He wiped his hands on the rag again. "Well, look, if you feel like taking a break to check things out, that's cool. We're all cool; it's no big deal."

Lazy pompadour male-model guy was watching us with intelligent, curious eyes. He moved around the car and started walking toward us.

"It's cool... no, I'm...I'm good."

The stitching on rockabilly Satan spelled ERIC in embroidered cursive.

I started sweating. My gut felt empty and rebellious.

I stood on my pedals and started pumping until I was out of the parking lot and all the way down at the intersection.

I screamed at the passing cars.

"Fuck!"

I felt like my body was being held inside my skin and every point where they met was barbed wire and Teflon. I wanted to explode. I wanted to break something. I wanted blood.

I wanted to cry. Suddenly, I was so frustrated.

The light had changed. Cars were stopped in the lanes next to me. People were looking.

"Fuck you!"

I had to get away. I hauled ass until I got to Bridge Park, off Los Gatos Parkway. I got off my bike, let it fall, and dropped myself onto the damp grass.

I would not cry.

I sat there, the smell of the grass and mulch and exhaust from the cars on the street tickling my sinuses and itching at the back of my throat, and tried to take stock. I tried to figure out why I'd gone rabbit.

The only reason it took as long as it did was because I didn't like the answer.

I'm stronger than anyone my age and most anyone older, for that matter. I'm faster, too. I can jump almost fifteen feet, and almost seven feet straight up, standing. I can see in the motherfucking dark, hear things you can't hear, and smell people before they come into the goddamn room.

I've fought honest-to-fuck monsters, human and other-wise. I'm not a coward. I'm not.

That stuff doesn't matter all that much when you can't pass for a normal in a crowd. When you spent pretty much the first decade of school being picked on, singled out, ostra-cized, you name it.

To see Lina's fucking wanna-be rapist is all handsome and sharp, like he stepped out of a Stray Cats video or the set of fucking *Grease* or something…and to know that this is the guy that Lina never even bothered to turn in…and to know that…

I stopped myself. I squelched the tirade in my own head. I had succeeded in shaming myself.

You can't unthink a thought, though.

"Fuck."

I got back on my bike and headed home, knowing that baby rock-star Carson Meunetti and Eric male-model motherfucking Finn had known Lina in all the ways I had, and some ways I never had—the way things were going, maybe never would, now.

It made me feel like I was ten years old again, wondering how I was going to explain that my homework was in my backpack, and my backpack was hanging from the top of the elementary-school playground backstop, where Byron Teslowski and his wingmen had thrown it.

Where I had let them throw it, even though I could stop them if I only had the guts. If I wasn't paralyzed from the desire to just be normal.

I didn't feel strong, or special, or brave.

No. I felt small. Different. Stupid.

Byron Teslowski
Two

Getting shot made Byron hungry, even though it also usually made him barf. He'd have to work on that.

Doc Mazmanian would tell him adapting and healing after being shot gave him the appetite. Made sense. Byron remembered when he and Nate got in their fight that one time. Terry and everybody had been freaked out by all the blood, but all Byron could think about was tearing into the spaghetti leftovers he knew were in the fridge at home.

He guessed that he would have been starving after the fight at Kirby Lake if he hadn't been unconscious.

He kinda missed his mother's spaghetti.

The residence building's ground floor was dominated by the commons area, which had a cafeteria. It made Byron think of what a food court would look like in a mall designed for billionaires.

It was the middle of the afternoon, after lunch and well before dinner, but the cafeteria counter was always open. Byron cut under the metal line dividers, grabbed a tray and a place setting, and smiled at Sal, who waited behind the counter.

"What's up, Sal?"

The cafeteria worker looked past Byron, indicating the line dividers with his glance. "How's the leg, Byron?"

Everybody knew when Byron was having a test; Mister Croy didn't want anyone to be alarmed when they heard the gunshot.

"A little stiff, but it's cool."

Sal shook his head. He smiled under his mustache. "You

get shot in the leg and two hours later you're limber like a piece of rubber! Me, I couldn't bend my knees like that if my life depended on it."

Byron liked chatting with Sal. It almost made him feel like they were anywhere in the world, and that more than one of them was a totally normal...human. "Aw, I bet you could."

"Let's not find out. So...pasta today, kiddo?"

"Yes, sir."

Sal piled a plate high with angel-hair pasta, poured on the marinara, and snowed Parmesan cheese all over that. Byron thanked him and sat down at one of the smaller tables.

He had just rolled a mouthful around his fork and shoved it in his face when the girl from the stairs sat down across from him.

"Hey, soldier boy."

Her eyes were greenish-gray and large on her small, angular face. She smirked at him.

Byron wiped his mouth and tried to chew faster.

"Take your time, dude. Don't choke."

Byron finally swallowed. "You're new."

"Am I? I mean, I've been around...lemme see...sixteen years and..." She counted off on her thin fingers. "Four months. Newer than some, I guess. Not as new as others."

Was this chick crazy, or just being lame?

"I mean...you're new here. Obviously. Jeez."

"'Obviously. Jeez.'" She laughed. "Relax, man. I'm just having fun."

That made one of them. "Good for you."

"You're Byron. The famous kid with the jackoff dad."

"Hey, you can read a newspaper."

"Faster than you, I bet." She smiled, showing a mouthful of big teeth. "I'm Haze." She stuck out her hand.

It would be rude not to shake her hand. Byron took it.

Her hand was very, very warm. Like picking up a rock on the beach on a hot day. Byron didn't flinch, and the skin on his palm quickly adjusted to it.

"Nice to meet you."

Her light eyebrows bounced once. "You're curious... aren't you?"

Byron shrugged. "Sure."

She poked the garlic toast on the edge of his plate. "You gonna eat that?" She pushed her finger in and kept it there.

Byron thought that was kinda rude. "Not now, I guess!"

"Heh." Haze pulled her finger away to reveal a dark, charred circle on the bread. A thin tendril of smoke twisted up from it. It smelled like a fresh oven.

"Huh!" Byron picked up the toast, held it to his nose, and sniffed. He loved the smell of fresh toast. It was a thing. "You're a...what's it called, a pyro...pyrotech..."

"You're thinking 'pyrokinetic.'" She sat back a little. "That's what the mad scientists say, anyway."

"That's pretty cool..."

She shrugged. "I guess."

"So is Haze your...y'know, your real name?"

She rolled her eyes. "You mean, is it, like, my call sign, or, whatever, my 'Sovereign' name, or is it the name on my birth certificate?"

Byron knew he had offended her, but he was damned if he knew how. "Well, yeah. I just thought, you know, a girl who starts fires, smoke, haze, all that..."

"I'm not one of your SCET goose-steppers, dude. Yes, it's my real name. Haze, short for Hazel, which you are never to call me, not ever…get it? Hazel's a maid on TV, not your new best friend."

His new best friend?

"Okay, sure. Cool. Whatever."

"All right." She had a cruel twinkle in her eye. "You gonna call yourself something stupid when you're a full-on Sovereign enforcer? Got your call sign all picked out?"

Byron felt himself redden. "It's not like that. And they're not goose-steppers, either."

"So you don't have a name yet."

"You don't get to pick your own nickname. That would be…lame."

"Oh, *that* would be lame." Her grin was three parts irritating and one part…something Byron couldn't name. "I see. Okay."

"What do you have against the SCET?"

She looked to the left and stretched her arms above her head. Byron couldn't help watching the bottom of her half-shirt move up her torso. She had so many freckles…

He brought his eyes up as her arms came down. "Same problem I have with all cops." He was sure she hadn't noticed his looking, but there was something in her eyes that unnerved him.

"Um…" What was he supposed to do? He was a guy! "Is that why you're here? Trouble with the cops? Did you…set something on fire?"

She shook her head. "Huh-uh, soldier boy. Not on the first date."

The drill team and cheerleader girls back home were not like this. Byron wasn't used to feeling so off-balance with a girl. Why didn't his adaptive power work for *this*?

"First date?"

She winked. "Close enough. We're the only teenagers here…and least for now, far as I know. There's that glowing girl, but she's just a kid. We're supposed to be buddies; it's right there in the script."

"What…script?"

"Figure of speech, Byron." She made googly eyes at him. "Like, a joke…?"

He shook his head and tried to get back to eating his spaghetti while it was still warm. "You are one weird chick." He took a bite. It was too late. The pasta was rubbery and the sauce was cold.

"I get that a lot." She must have seen the look on his face as he ate the cold spaghetti. "Here, let me."

She put her hands around the sides of his plate. A wave of heat, like opening an oven door, rolled across him.

Haze let go of the plate and stood up. "I'm outta here. See you around, solider boy."

She stretched again, all ribs and freckles and sharp elbows. Byron could not help noticing that she wasn't wearing a bra under the cut-off T-shirt.

She pointed casually at his food. "Oh…is that hot enough?"

"Uh…totally. I'm sure."

Nope. Not like the Abbeque Valley girls at all.

From The Journal Of Nate Charters
Ten

Thankfully, I didn't have a lot of time to wallow in my insecurities. A car horn I didn't recognize blared from out in front of the house (need I mention what a shitty sound that is when you have ears as sensitive as mine?), and I went to the window to investigate.

Jason's dad's big Bonneville was in my driveway. With Jason behind the wheel. Curious, I stepped outside. Jason leaned out of the driver's side window.

"Come on!" His eyes were full of mischief.

"Two secs!" I went back into the house, grabbed my sweatshirt and backpack, went back out, locked up, and slipped into the passenger seat.

Jason nodded to me. "What's up!"

I looked around. "Since when does your dad let you drive around in the family car?"

"Since never!" He shifted into reverse and backed into the street like he'd been driving for years instead of months. I was a little envious. With my senses and reflexes, I was sure I'd be totally fine driving on my own, but my mother was sticking to the letter of the law. I wasn't allowed to use the car unless she was in it.

"Since…huh?"

He grinned maniacally. "I stole it!" He maneuvered away from the house and turned at the corner, headed out of the neighborhood and down to Los Gatos Parkway. "Technically."

"You stole your own family's car." This was totally Jason. I was feeling better already.

"Technically." He laughed lightly. "My folks had to leave town—my aunt is having a kid, and the guy who knocked her up isn't around, so they're helping her out for a few days. I'm supposed to watch Reggie."

Reggie was Regina, Jason's twelve-year-old sister. "I bet she's stoked about that."

"She's got a new boyfriend." Jason shrugged. "They're playing Intellivision."

"Sure they are."

Jason wrinkled his nose and bunched his shoulders. "Gross, man. It's my sister."

"Yeah. And when did you lose your virginity, again?"

"I was fourteen." He smiled and sang, "Frances Gallagher..."

I didn't know who she was. No one did. Jason claimed she went to Dana Cove High. Now and then, Mel and I teased him, telling him she might as well be "from Canada." But I could tell: Jason wasn't lying.

I didn't really hold it against him, but the fact that he'd lost it so long ago and I still hadn't done it with my steady girlfriend of nearly a year brought me down.

Jason drove a few blocks until he must have noticed my silence. "Something up?"

I sighed. "I—yeah."

"Is it the thing with Lina? Have you talked to her yet?"

"Yes. And no." I turned my head to look out the passenger window, then turned back to face front. "I saw the guy. Eric Finn."

"No fuckin' way. What'd he—no, hold on. I want to hear this with no distractions. Hold on."

"He's—"

Jason took a hand off the wheel to wave it at me. "Wait! Wait-wait-wait!"

I waited. He turned left at the next light and headed back the way we had come, but instead of making a left toward my house, he went right, up to Romita Park. He parked at the curb, turned off the ignition, and pulled the parking brake.

"Okay." He shifted on the bench seat to face me. "Hit me. Hit me."

I told him about Sunrise Import Shop, about how Eric Finn was all...adult, and stuff. I didn't tell him about my little meltdown in the park.

"Dude sounds like a putz," Jason said helpfully.

I huffed. "What was she doing with him, when she was, like, fifteen years old? He must have been almost eighteen! What if he was eighteen?"

Jason nodded sagely. "Statutory rape, that's what."

A rush of unfocused anger flowed in me. "Except, not, right? If he never went through with it."

"Right." Jason scratched his temple. "You ever talk to that one chick? The one you said pulled this asshole off of Lina?"

"Crystal? No. I didn't get the chance at their last practice."

"Oh. Huh."

"What?"

"Well...dude, I don't want to be a dick, but...maybe that's not how it went down, right? Maybe the guy...sorry, but maybe the guy really did it, and Lina doesn't want anyone

125

to know. Especially, like, you." He made clawing motions with his hands. "Considering."

"Considering…what?" My guts shook. "Considering I'd kick his ass?"

Jason sat back and looked out the windshield. "Fuckin' A. I would."

Was he judging me?

"You think I should…go after him. Like, really. Go after him."

"Dude." Jason turned back to me. "You are…you, man. Who gives a shit if this fucker's all whatever you think he is? You're a fuckin' Sovereign—"

"I am not a Sovereign." My voice was a little louder than it needed to be. Jason knew better than to put that on me.

He pushed. "You might as well be, dude. You know those guys would back whatever you wanted to do. You're untouchable."

I laughed. He was crazy if he thought that. "Seriously? You haven't been watching the freak show I've been living since last year? Dude…seriously?"

He shook his head. "Huh-uh." He held up his middle finger and flipped off the world outside the window. "They're going through the motions with that bullshit, man, you ask me."

Jason had absolutely no idea what he was talking about. But there was some kind of sense, sort of, around what he was saying.

I said, "I'm so fucking sick of it."

Jason looked at me for a second. "You should be, dude."

We sat in the car a few minutes.

"I mean…if she was with that guy…what's she doing with me?"

Jason shook his head. "Nope. Don't even."

"Makes me wonder."

"My ass. She digs you." He smiled. "Fuck knows why, seein' as how she met me the very same time as you…but Lina's lousy taste aside, the situation's the same. It's MYOJ time, dude."

Was it?

Could I?

"You think so?"

"No doubt."

"What about Lina?"

"What about her?" Jason scoffed. "That fucker did her wrong, and it's obviously totally fucked her up. You're the guy who's supposed to do right…right? MYOJ. Totally MYOJ."

Eric Finn's Stray Cats knock-off male-model Sha Na Na reject face floated in my mind. I wondered what he'd look like scared out of his mind.

"I…I fought monsters." I looked at Jason. "I mean, they were like monsters."

"And here you are. And where are those monster guys?"

"You know."

"Tell me."

"They're dead." They died horribly, in fact. "But I didn't —"

"They're dead. And here you are," Jason said again. "You're a fucking badass, dude." He shook his head and laughed. "I never got why *you* don't just get that."

It was hard to.

I considered. "I wouldn't even really have to do anything, right? I mean, I could just freak him out. Scare him. Make him know…someone knows."

"Someone who could fuck him up," Jason said, "any time you wanted."

I shifted on the seat. "I was just thinking, someone who could turn him in, any time."

"Either way. It's MYOJ time."

I thought about it.

Eric Finn was just a guy.

Eric Finn was just a fucking bully.

Eric Finn…was just human.

I took a deep breath.

"You think it is?"

"Totally." He nodded. "You do, too. Say it. MYOJ time. C'mon."

I looked out the window at the movie in my head of Eric Finn blubbering at my feet.

"Okay."

"Say it."

I took another deep breath.

"It's make-your-own-justice time."

Marc Teslowski
Six

The restaurant next to the hotel had a dim wood-paneled lounge that was nearly empty. It did not have a television or a jukebox. That suited Marc fine.

Two hours ago, he had found the corner farthest from the entryway to the restaurant and set himself up in a booth. He gave his credit card and instructions to the waitress: set him up with a steak, french fries, and a new beer and fries every time either one was depleted.

So equipped, Marc proceeded to kill his hunger and sobriety. He heard activity in the main restaurant rise and fall through the dinner hour, but the lounge never attracted more than a few old men, who sat at the bar, and a few tourist couples, who came and went.

They all seemed human, not that that made any difference anymore. What was happening to the world?

It was three days until Declaration Day. A little over two weeks later would be the anniversary of Byron going to the Donner Institute.

"Not 'going,' damn it," Marc muttered into his beer. "Taken. Taken."

He wanted to punch himself in the face. Was he starting to believe what everyone else wanted him to think? That Byron wasn't the victim of a Sovereign kidnapping and propaganda campaign...that he just...left?

"Taken," he said again, probably louder this time, as an old-timer at the bar looked curiously over his shoulder at Marc.

Marc ignored him, putting his attention solidly on the

ruins of his dinner. He picked at his fries. Where was the waitress? The damn things were soggy and cold.

He sensed someone near the table. He looked up.

It wasn't the waitress. It was a couple of guys, one older, one younger.

Great. Someone had recognized him.

The older guy took off his white cowboy hat and extended his right hand. "Mister Teslowski, my name is Ray Greene. This is my boy, Arby. We'd very much like to buy you a drink, sir."

Marc straightened, bracing himself with one hand on the booth bench. "No, thanks." He put a horrible french fry into his mouth and chewed, looked away from the pair and at nothing.

"I don't mean to disturb you," Marc heard Ray say. "We're...well, Mister Teslowski, I guess you could say the boy and I are fans. Wanted to say thanks."

Marc put his focus back on them with a tinge of difficulty.

"Thanks?"

"Yes, sir." Ray gestured at the empty bench across the table from Marc. "You mind?"

Marc squinted at them. "Whatever."

Ray slid in, resting his cowboy hat on the booth next to him. Arby sat on the edge. Under the table, Marc shifted his legs to avoid those of his guests.

"Appreciate it," Ray said. He looked at Arby. "Go fetch us some beers, kiddo." He turned to Marc. "What're you drinking? Miller?" Marc nodded, and Arby went for the bar.

Marc looked at the man across the booth. Ray Greene

looked to be a little older than Marc, maybe in his early fifties. His face was deeply tanned and on its way to weathered. His swept-back hair was mostly pepper, headed for salt. He wore a red and black flannel shirt with a bolo tie with a turquoise and steel steer's head at the collar.

"How'd you know I was here?"

Ray looked apologetic. "Local news mentioned what happened."

Marc grimaced.

"Don't misunderstand," Ray said quickly. "We don't care what the news says. I got a boy." He looked over to where Arby was carefully counting money to pay for the three drinks and inclined his head tolerantly. "I know I'd do just about whatever needs doing to keep him safe. So we…I have a great respect for what you did today."

Marc snorted. "Well, Ray, it didn't do a hell of a lot, did it?"

Ray shrugged. "Got my attention. Probably some other folks', too."

Arby returned with the three steins of beer just barely held in his two hands. Ray took one and put it down in front of Marc. Arby set the other two down and slid back into the booth.

"Damn near spilled Mister Teslowski's drink," Ray said to his son. "That wouldn't have done nobody any good, boy. We'd be done before we started, you might say. Have a care."

"Yessir." Arby kept his eyes low and deferential. Marc thought that said something about Ray's skills as a father, something Marc approved of.

"Thanks," he said to both of them. He lifted his stein.

"Hold on." Ray held up his own glass. Arby did the same. Ray lifted his a little higher. "To...*Homo sapiens*. And brave deeds." He nodded to Marc.

Sounded a little formal and weird, but, hell, Marc wasn't paying for the drinks anymore and was all out of give-a-damn. He clinked his stein against the other two and drank.

Ray smacked his lips. "That's been my go-to toast these days. It's never been more appropriate than right here and now, though."

Marc wasn't an idiot. He knew this guy was flattering him. He'd seen a lot of this when the college recruiters courted him his senior year of high school. But after the day he'd had, he didn't care what kind of bullshit the guy was shoveling. Right now, it smelled just fine.

So he played his part.

"I don't know about brave deeds. I was just...fed up. You know?"

"You bet I do," Ray said. "The way I see it: that's how most things are. We get tired of it; everything else is all played out...what's left? Sometimes...you just have to take it into your own hands."

"That's...yeah. That's right."

"I get it." Ray sipped at his beer. He put a finger on the low stack of extra napkins next to Marc's plate. "You mind?"

Marc dipped his head. Ray took a napkin and dabbed at his mouth.

"I get it," he said again. "And here's what else: it doesn't even matter if you succeed."

Marc remembered his humiliation at the hands of the Visitors Center guards. "I don't know about that."

Ray lowered his eyes, pursed his lips, and shook his head. "No, sir. It doesn't matter. Because even in failure, we can inspire others to greatness. To...risk, even."

Marc laughed. "What're you, a preacher?"

Ray's eyebrows arched. He smiled and looked at Arby, whose lips curled slightly. Ray looked back at Marc.

"Oh, hell... no," he laughed, "no, I'm no preacher. I do a little writing, a little organizing. I help bring...I guess you could say I help bring like-minded folks together."

"They pay you for that?" Marc smelled a pitch coming. What the hell. He didn't have anything else going on. They could keep plying him with compliments and beer. He'd return the favor by humoring them until he closed the place closed down. Might as well.

Ray laughed again. "Well. Sometimes. I have a little put away." His face leveled out. "My wife passed a couple of years ago, so there's the insurance."

"Sorry."

"Obliged," Ray said. "Anyway, I don't do it for the money. Some things are more important."

Marc tipped a mouthful of beer down his throat. "Gotta have money to do the important stuff, though, right?" He thought of the lawyers and all the money he'd wasted on important things.

Ray grinned. "Sometimes it's enough to surround yourself with the right people. Hell, sometimes that's better than a boatload of money."

Marc waited.

Ray's grin widened a little in acknowledgment. "Yeah, okay. You're waiting for the pitch. You're not an idiot."

"You're buying, Ray, so I can be polite."

Ray laughed and slapped the edge of the table. "So I am. So I am. And I appreciate it." He leaned forward a little. "Look, Marc—you all right with my calling you Marc?"

Marc sat back and waved his hand at the drinks Ray had bought. "Sure."

Ray laughed again. "Right. Look, Marc, I wish I'd known you were coming to Missoula. I have resources. We could have helped you some."

This wasn't what he'd expected. "How?"

"Well, for one thing, had I known, you never would have paid for no rental car. You sure as hell wouldn't be staying in no hotel. I wouldn't have it."

Marc shrugged. "How would that have made anything turn out different today?"

"It's all about appearances, Marc. All about it. That's the thing. I told you—and I mean it—that we respect what you tried to do today. But, I've got to be honest with you, there's no way it would have turned out any different so long as it's just you headed up there and just, well, just telling those Sovereigns you want in." He smiled sympathetically. "One doesn't just walk into the Donner Institute."

Marc figured he better drink up. This was getting old.

"You think you coulda got me in?"

Ray shrugged. "I think we could have worked up a little attention beforehand. Talked to KPAX and KGVO ahead of time—we have some sympathetic folks over there—so if there was going to be any news coverage, we could have a little influence in that regard. You follow?"

Marc shook his head. "You want me to hire you as a...

what, a publicist or something?"

Ray laughed again. Even Arby chuckled, looking at the table.

"Oh, hell, Marc. That's not it. I'm telling you: we want to help you."

"Sorry, Ray," Marc didn't feel at all sorry. "I've had a lot of people say they wanna help. Usually ends up with a hand on my wallet."

"I told you. I don't need any money." Ray seemed a little frustrated. That was fine with Marc. "Look. I've got 'pert near seventy acres. A nice house. A little business—but here's the thing, Marc: it's not just a business. It's a mission. And it's your mission, too."

"All I give a shit about is getting my kid back where he belongs."

"Sure. Sure. But I know it doesn't stop there for you. I know it. This whole thing—doesn't it offend you?"

"What whole thing?"

"The Sovereigns, Marc." Ray sighed. "The damn Sovereigns. What else?"

"Fuck 'em."

Ray shook his head slowly. "It's not as simple as that, though, is it? They've set themselves up just a few miles from my land in their...compound." He sneered. "Do you know their Institute, that it's on the site of the old Garnet Ghost Town? Damn, I used to go there all the time as a kid, thinking about how things used to be, all the miners and saloons and gunfighters and whatnot.

"Now...now it's ground zero for those...I don't know what they are."

Arby spoke up. "Ain't nobody does."

Ray nudged his son's shoulder. "Nobody does. Damn right. And yet."

"What?" Marc said.

"Hell. A year ago, where were they? Before Donner? Where'd they all come from?"

Marc thought about it. "Don't they say they were always around? That the government knew…?"

"Who says that? The Sovereigns?" Ray snorted. "I'm not prepared to take them at their word, are you?"

Marc shook his head.

"No one knows who they are, what they are, for the love of Pete…or where they came from. And here we are as a country, in bed with them."

"All right, fine." Marc said. "It's shitty. Sure."

"And they've set up their base of operations in my back yard, which, if you'll give pardon, pisses me off, Marc."

"Sure."

"And," Ray said. "They've got your son."

"Yes they do."

Ray nodded slowly. "You're someone I've wanted to meet for some time, Marc. I was thinking of writing you, but I figured, hell, this guy probably gets bombarded by all kinds of crap. He won't pay any attention to me or mine."

Marc smiled. "You were right."

Ray raised his stein casually. "Thought so. So when I heard you were here…I had to meet you and introduce myself. Because I think we can help each other, Marc."

Marc scowled, less irritated by Ray and Arby and more simply frustrated. "I don't see how, Ray. Sorry."

Ray looked at Marc. He studied his beer. He looked over at the old men at the bar.

"I know." He looked back at Marc. "Look. Let me extend this to you. Call it a thank-you for being enough of a man to do what you did today, which, even though I get that you don't see it like this right now, I take as no less than your taking a stand for normal human beings."

He smiled a little. Marc thought maybe Ray had heard his own voice and thought it sounded a little ranty.

"Let us put you up tonight, out at the ranch. Sleep in a proper bed. We've got a couple of sweet little guest rooms, all homey, set up just like my wife left 'em, only we've, you know, kept them clean and all.

"Have a proper breakfast with us. We can talk some more. I'll show you around. And if you want, I'll drive you back down to the airport myself, when the time comes."

Marc looked at Ray's open face.

"What the hell," he said, finishing his beer. "Figure I can't say no to the help."

Ray beamed. "I consider it a privilege, Marc. A real treat." He nudged Arby.

"Go settle up Mister Teslowski's bill, kiddo."

Automatically, Marc started to protest. Ray cut him off.

"I won't hear it. From here on out, we're taking care of you."

Arby slid off the booth and ambled over to where the waitress hovered near the bar. Marc and Ray pulled themselves out and shook hands.

Byron Teslowski
Three

The first coherent thought in Byron's head when he was jarred out of a very sound sleep by a grating, repetitive, achingly loud claxon was "fire drill."

He pulled on his jeans and put on shoes, skipping socks to save time in case this was the real thing. How would his adaptive powers handle extreme heat or, worse, actual fire?

Blearily, he decided that was something he wasn't going to suggest to Doc Mazmanian, at least not where Croy might hear. It was stressful enough learning how to be bulletproof.

He had been sleeping in a T-shirt. He threw his old varsity jacket over that. It was two-thirty in the morning; it would be cold outside.

Byron's small apartment—as an individual, he was assigned a studio—was on the third floor. After checking the door with the palm of his hand and not feeling any heat, he opened it and went into the corridor. A few residents were doing the same.

Bethlehem Franklin, a nice older lady who could some-times tell the future, smiled at him as he joined the queue down the stairs.

"Fire drill?"

She nodded. "Must be."

He grinned at her. "Are you...sure?"

She tapped him on the arm with a small, veiny hand. "Be polite. I didn't have one of my spells, so no, I'm not sure. But what are the odds?"

"Guess so."

They descended to the ground floor and went out onto

the commons. The grounds of the Institute looked strange at this late hour, like the world wasn't accustomed to having so many people around at once.

Residents, most dressed in sleep clothes or haphazard combinations of jackets and sweatpants, milled in small groups and waited for word. It was just like high school, Byron thought, except that most of the people hanging out were adults and a few of them smoked cigarettes.

Byron tried to remember the last time he'd been in an actual fire drill. Probably 1984. He didn't think Abbeque Valley High had done one after the Christmas break.

Standing a few feet away from an old lady who had seen the death of her daughter miles away and seconds before it happened, and a few more feet from a woman who could go unnoticed in a crowd unless she wanted you to notice her, and so many other Sovereigns and the regular humans who worked alongside them, Byron felt heavy. High school seemed like forever ago.

The loudspeakers set on poles around the Institute grounds crackled.

"Evening, everyone." Byron couldn't place the voice, especially through the crackle of the speaker. "Sorry for waking you, but safety first. Everything's fine now. You can go back to your homes."

Byron thought it was weird the Institute called their little apartments "homes." He didn't feel like he was home.

That didn't mean he *wanted* to go home, though. He just didn't know how long it would be before he stopped feeling like he was getting away with something.

He sighed. His breath flowed like white smoke.

The other weird thing: they didn't call this a drill. Somewhere in the living center, something caught on fire.

"Huh," he said to himself.

Ms. Franklin, who was walking back to the building, turned and looked at Byron over her shoulder. "You coming, kiddo?"

Byron was wide awake. It wasn't too horribly cold outside—or at least it didn't seem that way to him. He lifted a hand in acknowledgment. "Nah. I'm, like, too up now. I think I'll take a walk."

She nodded. "Good night, Byron."

"Night."

He was pretty sure she was the oldest person there, except for maybe Dr. Donner's uncle Walt. Byron liked that she was around. She was kind of like a grandmother to him— to the whole Institute, he guessed.

Byron wandered along the footpath. He thought of his own grandmother. Gram Ursie wasn't much like Ms. Franklin. Not black, for one thing. Or as nice.

You didn't get to choose your relatives.

Or your father.

Byron cut across a patch of lawn and over a low dividing wall separating the meadow from the grounds of the Institute. Away from the buildings, the night was cool and damp, and the meadow quiet and still. Frost reflected the light of the waxing moon.

It was...pretty, Byron decided. Much nicer than the last time he'd been out here, getting shot in the name of progress, or whatever.

He walked slowly. The ground crunched under his

shoes. The grass made the cuffs of his jeans dark with moisture. Except for a low hum from the Institute behind him, there was almost no sound.

Byron couldn't get away from thinking about it.

His father was in Missoula. Tonight. Right now, probably sleeping in some little hotel room. Maybe drunk.

He considered that and chuckled to himself. After having his ass handed to him by the Sovereign? Definitely drunk.

The idea of it didn't make him as happy as he thought it should. He was more irritated than anything.

Everything had been fine. The lawyers were keeping his dad off Byron's back, running in circles, as much as Byron understood what they told him, while Byron got to have a… well, an interesting time among the Sovereign.

He still didn't think of himself as really being one of them. Sure, he had the adaptive power, and he was classified as a straight-up Standard on the ability class rankings, all official.

But shit, he was just some dude, right? Powers or not, he was just a high-school jock who might get lucky and be a college jock and maybe even go pro. He didn't feel too much like he was part of anything bigger than that.

He turned and looked back at the buildings of the Institute. They were sharp and bright against the black night of the mountains around them.

He *was* part of something. No way to ignore that. He was about to become the third field member of the new primary Sovereign Conduct Enforcement Team, the group Spencer Croy referred to as "alpha."

Someday soon, Byron would be somewhere out in the

world, keeping folks safe from Sovereign crazies…or, if need be, keeping Sovereigns safe from regular-people crazies.

It was super-important. The majors.

He hoped his father would just go home. Not wreck everything out.

Byron turned and walked a little farther into the meadow. He stopped and squinted at a ripple in the air ahead.

It was steam, coming up off the ground. Weird.

Caution was drilled into their heads, even out here, where someone would have to have a death wish to cause any trouble for the Sovereigns.

"Somebody there?"

A thin shape, all narrow, with long arms and legs, rose up from the ground.

"Hey, soldier boy."

It was Haze. She held her arms in front of her, linked her fingers, and stretched. Wisps of steam curled from her shoulders and from her hair, which was even more fucked up than when he'd first met her.

"What are you doing out here?"

She shrugged and looked around. "Just hanging out." She bobbed her head in greeting. "You?"

He walked over to her. She wore a gray hooded sweatshirt that seemed too big for her, and men's boxer shorts. On her feet were pink fuzzy bunny slippers.

Her slippers looked dry. In fact, her hair was dry, too, even though Byron could feel the moist night air beading on his own head.

"There was a fire drill," he said. "I couldn't sleep."

She smelled like sage.

"Oh, yeah. I guess that's what that alarm was, right?"

She also smelled like smoke.

He frowned. "You know anything about that, by chance?"

She raised her eyebrows and stepped back. "You getting all SCET on me, Byron? Come out here to check up on the firebug?"

He flinched. "What? No—I was just taking a walk." Why did she make him feel so defensive? "I didn't know you were out here hiding out."

"Who's hiding? I'm right here, right?" Her eyes twinkled.

Byron crossed his arms on his chest. "Oh, yeah, totally. Right here. In the freakin' meadow in the middle of the night. Nothing weird about that."

"Not as far as you'd know," she said. "I might come out here every night. You don't, though."

"How do you know?"

"Because I do," she said.

"Oh."

She laughed. "No, I don't. I'm fucking with you, Byron."

He uncrossed his arms and flung them out at his sides. "Whatever! Fuck!"

She toned it down to a smile. "Chill, soldier boy." She indicated the Institute behind him with a tilt of her head. "Everything okay back there?"

Byron relaxed. "They say so, yeah."

She looked at him. "Okay. Good."

"Yeah." He didn't want to be a dick, but… "So…what

happened?"

Haze put on big innocent eyes. "With what?"

He laughed, not quite in spite of himself. "Tonight. The fire."

She looked at her bunny slippers. "Not much of a fire, really. Just a little smoldering."

"In your room?"

"Yeah." She kicked at invisible rocks. "Had a... dream. Woke up and my blanket was a little bit on fire."

"A little bit on fire?" he laughed.

"Yeah." She shook her head. "You know the worst thing about a room fire in that place? Don't have a room fire, by the way."

"I totally won't," Byron said. "What's the worst thing?"

"It's not the fire." She snorted. "Fires, I can handle. Watch me, sometime. No. It's the fucking sprinklers."

Byron imagined it.

"Oh. Right."

"Yeah. I managed to get this thing on me, and my slippers, and get out of there only, y'know, a hundred and ten percent drenched. Came out here to dry off in peace."

Byron's voice was casual. "Sure. Dry off."

She looked at him.

"They're gonna know it was you," he said.

"No shit, Sherlock. Far as I know, I'm the only firebug in residence." She looked up and to her left, thinking. "Maybe the only one, period, if the Stiff is right."

"Well, why bother hiding out?" Byron shook his head. "Wait...who's the Stiff?"

"Your big boss, obviously. Donner."

Byron laughed. "Oh, shit. That…that is fucking hilarious, dude."

She smiled. "I'd say don't tell him I called him that, but we both know he probably already knows."

That was a creepy thought. "You think so?"

"I just figure that's the case. Saves me from being freaked out about it later." She shrugged. "Anyway. I'm not hiding out." She looked away from him, at nothing.

Byron knew he was not the sharpest tool in the shed, but he thought he read this one right. Whatever the real reason for the fire, assuming it wasn't some bad dream, she wasn't happy about it happening.

"So," he said after a bit. "Can I…help out? With the fire stuff? If you need it…?"

She blinked at him. Held his gaze for one fraction of a second long enough for Byron to feel a little funny, right below his ribcage.

"You have a blow dryer?"

"Huh?"

"A blow dryer." She enunciated with exaggeration. "Do-you-have-one. Or any extra towels. Clean ones. Dry ones?"

Byron remembered. Her room got the ceiling sprinklers treatment.

"Yeah," he said. "I do. Blow dryer and towels. But… couldn't you just do what you did out here? Make everything dry?"

She walked back toward the Institute. "It's tricky. Sometimes I have a little trouble staying on the toasty side, and not on the toasted side." He stepped to catch up with her, and she looked up at him. "So you'll help me fix up my room, soldier boy?"

Byron was shocked to discover a serious case of pregame jitters washing through him at the thought of being in Haze's room, alone, with her.

She smiled, just a little teasing. Did she have his number?

Byron pulled it together. He put a little extra-casual swagger in his stride.

"No sweat," he said, "but fuckin' stop calling me that, all right?"

Her laughter bounced off the concrete and glass of the Institute and all over the night.

Marc Teslowski
Seven

Marc lay in bed for some time after the smell of coffee and bacon and the low noises of a household coming to life beyond the closed door of the guest room woke him. The bed was so much more comfortable than the old queen he shared with Jeri.

A light knock on the door preceded a man's voice that was not Ray Greene's. "Breakfast is nearly ready, Mister Teslowski."

Marc cleared his throat. "Thanks." He sighed. This sure as shit beat sleeping in the hotel room, but he wasn't so sure he was up to spending the morning with a bunch of strangers. Ray was friendly enough, but something about the whole thing felt just a little...off.

He slipped out from under a thick quilt and stood up next to the bed. The thick carpet felt fancy and expensive on his bare feet.

Marc scratched his balls, farted, blinked, and looked around, which was something he'd been a little too toasted to do last night. It was all he could do to strip down and fall into that fucking amazing bed.

Probably "quaint" was the word for the room. Like one of those home-decorating magazines at the doctor's office. There were doilies on the nightstand, and the lampshade had ruffles. Embroidery—a big-eyed cat, some Bible verse, that kind of thing—hung in frames on the walls. The dresser across from the foot of the bed was a monster of distressed wood, rustic and cozy.

Marc figured this was how it was at one of those bed-

and-breakfast places Jeri used to get on him about going to. Nice, if you were into that. Marc wasn't.

That bed, though…that would almost be worth shelling out for a place like this for a weekend, even though he really couldn't stand the idea of being stuck with Jeri that long. If the kid was there, maybe.

Marc felt a sharp pinch at the base of his neck as his shoulders tensed. The kid was *not* there.

The comforts of the bed were fading fast. Grimacing, Marc went into the room's small bathroom. He took a piss, rinsed his mouth out with a handful of water from the tap, used his damp hands to tame his bed-head hair, and looked at himself in the mirror above the sink.

Damn thing had little cherubs carved in the upper corners of the frame.

Marc's eyes were bloodshot, and his bags were dark and puffy. His tongue was coated and swollen. Whatever. He just woke up, and he'd tied one on the night before. Plus, he was a guest, right? No one would give a shit how he looked.

He found his clothes piled on a chair that looked stolen from the Walton family. He dressed. He would shower and put on fresh clothes after breakfast.

Marc left the room and followed sounds of activity down the hall and into the kitchen. Five people moved around each other, filling their plates.

Ray Greene hovered near the stove. He wore a white apron over a red, checkered, flannel shirt. He waved at Marc with a spatula.

"Marc! Good morning. How'd you sleep?"

"Great, thanks."

Ray chuckled. "Everybody loves that bed." The thin guy standing next to him nodded when Ray glanced at him. Ray said to Marc, "I'll let everybody introduce themselves once we're all seated. G'won—grab yourself a plate and get some grub."

Marc watched as Ray shoveled a slab of ham, some home-fried potatoes, and scrambled eggs streaked with grease onto his plate. Ray instructed him to take the spot to the right of the head of the long table in the adjacent dining room, and Marc did so.

The skinny guy from the kitchen was on Marc's left. They shook hands. "Abe," he said. "It's a privilege, Mister Teslowski."

"It's just Marc."

Abe laughed at that, his Adam's apple bobbing when his chin tipped back.

"Well, imagine that."

Marc didn't understand. Fortunately, Ray took his place at the head of the table then, and everyone's attention shifted to him.

"Marc, we're gonna have a little prayer," he said. "Hope you don't mind." He chuckled and looked around at the others. "'Course, we'd do it anyway, but I'm just being polite."

Marc shrugged. "I don't mind."

"Figured you wouldn't." Ray's voice was strong with approval.

When he saw everyone else bow their heads and close their eyes, Marc did the same.

"Heavenly Father," Ray intoned, "we thank you for bringing us together in this house of Patsy and mine's, where we gather to celebrate you and the purity of your Creation. We thank you for bringing Marc into our midst, and we pray for your wisdom to guide us on our path in these days of trial. Bless this food you have graced us with, Lord, bless us all, and God bless the human race. Amen."

Marc's mumbled "Amen" was less strident than what he heard echo around the table, but nobody seemed to notice.

Marc thought he should say something nice to Ray. "Thanks for your, uh, hospitality."

Ray's head dipped slightly. "It's our pleasure, Marc. Think nothing of it."

A heavyset man eating near the far end of the table, maybe close to Ray's age but no older, took a roll from under a towel over a basket and buttered it. "Mister Teslowki," he said, "that was some awesome work you did up there at the devil's nest. You got reason to be proud, sir."

All the kowtowing made Marc uncomfortable. He could feel himself blushing. "I don't know." He scowled. "Didn't make any difference."

Another man, younger, with lean, muscled arms and a dyed black mullet sprouting from his head, made haste to chew the food in his mouth before he said, "No, sir, Mister Teslowski, no, sir. Made a difference to us, and a lot of other folks, too." He looked down at his food, momentarily bashful. "Sir."

Marc laughed nervously. "Listen, you guys can call me Marc. I kinda wish you would."

Ray laughed. "Mister Teslowski's your father, right, Marc?"

"Uh, yeah. Something like that."

Ray looked around. "You heard the man. No more puttin' on airs for Marc. Make him feel to home."

The thin man next to him spoke up again. "Hey Marc. You're goin' back up there, right? You're not done up there?"

Marc frowned again, chewing slowly.

Ray spoke up.

"You bet we are." He looked at Marc. "If you'll allow me, Marc—I hope you'll let me go back into the devil's nest with you. They know me up there," some laughter around the table, "and I bet things might turn out a little different next time."

Marc felt a jab of suspicion, that something strange was going on with Ray and his friends. "What do you mean?"

"They know me. They know my work." He passed his gaze around the table. "Our work, for humanity. God's work." He jabbed a forkful of egg into his mouth and talked around it. "Look here—when we're done with breakfast, and I'm not rushing you; you eat all you want—I hope you'll let me take you on a little tour. Show you around. Explain our mission here.

"I think," Ray swallowed and smiled slowly. "I think you'll find you have a lot of friends in the world, Marc. And some pretty damn good friends in Montana."

"My flight..."

"Hell with that. You let me take care of it."

Marc said automatically, "Oh, I can't let you—"

"Marc. Marc." Ray looked at him. "I'm not kidding you. I have more money that I'm ever gonna be able to spend, even with these freeloaders leeching off me." Laughter around the table and a twinkle in Ray's eye. "There ain't no

153

shame in it, accepting some help now and then. And you'd be helping me."

"I don't see how, Ray."

"You give me the afternoon, so I can show you. All right?"

Marc could feel hopeful eyes on him from all around the table. This place wasn't right, but it wasn't any more wrong than the rest of the world.

He picked up his coffee mug and raised it to Ray.

"All right, then."

Byron Teslowski
Four

Byron's appointment with Doc Mazmanian was scheduled for nine o'clock Wednesday morning. Mazmanian didn't look up from the papers on his desk when Byron came into the small but warm office at nine-eighteen.

"Watch stop, Byron?"

Byron's whole morning had been a rush to chase the clock. He hadn't stumbled back to his own apartment and into bed until four-thirty last night. His Sovereign ability apparently adapted his ears to totally ignore the alarm clock when it went off at seven. Ha, ha.

"Fire alarm." It wasn't a lie. The fire alarm led to meeting Haze in the meadow, and hanging out in her apartment and trying to wring out and dry her clothes, which had kept Byron up and made him late.

Mazmanian looked up. "Hm." He smiled. "How's Haze?"

Byron's heart jumped. Busted. "What…?"

"Don't worry about it. I'm sure you were a perfect gentleman."

Thing was, he had been. It bugged him that Doc Mazmanian might not think so. "We just hung out," he said quickly. "Her room got messed up."

Mazmanian dismissed the topic with a wave of his hand. "I'm just messing around." He stood up and held out his hand.

Byron didn't get why they were doing it, but he shook Doc Mazmanian's hand.

"Congratulations," Mazmanian said. "You're officially

bulletproof."

Byron couldn't help his smile. "That's...that's a trip."

"Well. Don't let it go to your head." Mazmanian looked at him. "In fact, if it comes to that—and to be honest with you, I hope it doesn't, and to be more honest with you, it probably will—just...keep your head down. You could still get a pretty serious head injury from the impact. And I can't guarantee your eyes are as tough as your skin."

It didn't sound all that real, but Byron took it seriously. "Got it." He had an idea. "Maybe I should wear a helmet?"

"I'm sure you will." Mazmanian squeezed the end of his nose and studied Byron. "You sure this is what you want to do?"

Byron nodded. "Yes sir. I want to be part of the team."

"But you know it's not required, right? This place—you can just be here, you know."

Byron squinted. "Sure, but...that doesn't seem, like, right, I guess? You told me Sovereigns in my ability class were pretty rare, right?"

"There are a hundred and fifty Standards in the world if we're lucky...and we'll probably never meet most of them," Mazmanian said.

"Yeah. So if I'm lucky enough to be that, it'd be...kinda lame, I guess...to bench myself." He nodded firmly. "I'm totally in."

Mazmanian came around the desk and slapped Byron on the shoulder. "Okay, 'dude.'" That brought Byron's smile back. "Get on over to the barracks, then. Spencer's expecting you."

"Will do. Thanks, doc."

Mazmanian went back to his desk chair and waved Byron off. "Keep your head down!"

Byron left the research building and took advantage of one of the Institute golf carts to zip over to the barracks, nestled way off in the corner of the grounds farthest from the Visitors Center and, just maybe, prying eyes.

He'd heard there were plans in the works for something fancier, but for now the building everyone called "the barracks" was a corrugated-steel half-cylinder pre-fab structure on a broad concrete slab. Byron parked the golf cart in a painted slot and walked over to the wide, open doors that made him think of an like an airplane hangar. Spencer Croy waited just inside.

"Sorry I'm late," Byron said as he approached.

Croy, as usual, skipped stuff that was not essential. "Follow me."

He led Byron through the twenty-foot-high doors and into the interior. Byron forced himself to at least appear relaxed and confident. Game face. Game face.

He almost lost it when he saw the giant.

Byron was peripherally aware that there were other people there, but he couldn't take his focus off the fifteen-foot-tall, leanly muscled guy, maybe about twenty-five, dressed in black sweat pants and a white tank top and sitting on the edge of a huge bed that was dressed with sharp military corners. The giant's voice wasn't as loud as Byron expected.

"Colonel! Take a look. I'm getting pretty good at regulation corners, eh?" The giant smiled at Byron. "I don't have to do it, of course, but hey, I like a challenge." He waggled his fingers. "These babies aren't so good with the precision stuff. Big surprise. No origami for me. Not anymore!"

He looked at his own hand for a beat, then used it to present an exaggerated wave to Byron. "I'm Ed Kelso. You're Byron?"

Byron's voice, when it came out of his throat, sounded undeniably small in the wake of the giant's speech. "Byron Teslowski."

"Howdy." Kelso looked to his left. "Say hi, Jon."

A thin, small man with a neat blond flattop came forward and extended his hand for Byron. "I'm Jon Schulmann. It's good to meet you." He looked to be around the same age as Ed Kelso

Byron shook his hand. "I'm Byron." He tilted his head slightly. "Hey...do you have an accent?"

Schulmann let out a short laugh. "My dad's fault. He's from Austria. I'm born and raised U. S of A., though. New Jersey."

Byron grinned and nodded. "My grandparents are from Poland. I kinda thought I heard something."

"The Old World...and the Garden State. Can't seem to shake it."

Kelso boomed, "Give it a couple of days, Byron, but make sure you ask Jon to say," he switched to a horrible Sylvester Stallone impersonation, "'Yo, Adrian,'" and then an awful exaggerated German accent, "'I know nuh-ting!'"

Schulmann looked up at Kelso and shook his head. "You're an idiot, Beau Bridges. Rocky's from Philly. And I'm not German. I'm Austrian."

Byron looked at Spencer Croy. "I'm lost. Beau Bridges?"

Croy looked as though he wished everyone would get on with it. "Mister Schulmann references a movie called *Village of the Giants*."

"Oh."

Schulmann looked like he was trying hard to stifle a laugh. Byron looked away before he caught the bug.

This was crazy. These guys were the core of the Sovereign Conduct Enforcement Team Alpha? It was like an episode of *M*A*S*H* or something.

"Phht." Kelso blew air through his lips. "You'd never catch me in a toga made out of curtains. Not since Doctor Donner got me my very own tailor, at least."

Someone cleared their throat behind Byron. He turned to see a guy in his thirties, with tight dark curls on his head and dressed in a sharp black suit, stride into the "hangar."

"Byron," Spencer Croy said, "this is Special Liaison Derek Fontino, from the Department of Defense."

Fontino had sharp features and equally cutting, swift movements. He shook Byron's hand firmly and quickly. "How are you, Byron?"

Fontino kept hard eye contact after they broke their handshake, and that, along with the question, put Byron off a little bit.

"Good, thank you." He figured it out. This guy reminded him of a younger version of the creepy doctor, Lester Brenhurst, who had set everything off last year and nearly gotten Byron killed.

"We'll have to talk later," Fontino said to him. "Your affiliation with the SCET will have some repercussions, all things considered."

The guy made Byron feel like he was in trouble for breathing. Maybe his gut reaction wasn't uncalled for, after all.

"Repercussions?"

Fontino frowned slightly at him, but his eyes stayed bright and on-target. "Of course. Later, as I said." He turned to Croy. "Colonel Croy, you have paperwork on Teslowski for me, yes?"

Byron had spent a lot of time around Spencer Croy in the last year. He knew how to read the tiny changes on the colonel's face that represented all the emotion he typically revealed, and right now, the slight deepening of his faint crow's-feet told Byron that Spencer Croy didn't like the guy, either. Everyone knew Croy didn't like being addressed by his former military rank.

"You know that's an unnecessary question."

Fontino looked quickly at Kelso, Schulmann, and Byron: a kind of strafing farewell. "Of course. My apologies." He strode out of the barracks.

Schulmann snorted. "That guy…"

Kelso shook his head. "Asshole to the max."

"Who is he, again?" Fontino had come and gone so quickly, Byron almost thought maybe the guys on the SCET were hazing him.

Spencer Croy said, "Mister Fontino is our liaison with the DOD. His presence here is part of EO 12512."

Byron looked to Schulmann for help.

"The Sovereign Compromise, to most folks."

"Oh…okay." Byron wasn't thrilled with that. "He acts like he's in charge."

"He is not," Croy said. He turned for the barracks doorway. "Join me outside."

Schulmann walked out past Byron. He wondered what the thin man's abilities were. No one had told him what to expect from his teammates, and Byron had been so caught up with the never-ending tests and exercises of the last nine months or so that, while he'd been curious, he never asked.

With an aching creak of bed springs, Ed Kelso stood up. Byron couldn't help staring.

Kelso wasn't simply a regular person maxi-sized. His body was built to support a two-legged creature of his scale.

Byron saw that Kelso's bare feet were about twice as wide, relatively, as his own. The edges, and, Byron assumed, the soles, were covered in hard, rough skin: calluses on top of calluses.

Kelso's legs were enormous. His thighs were easily as wide as Byron's torso, and Byron was a healthy, strong kid. The giant's barrel chest moved like a bellows below massive, wide shoulders. Byron had the impression that Kelso's arms were a little longer than normal. He'd already seen that his hands were unusually broad, with long, thick fingers.

Kelso's head and face, other than being proportionate for his height, were perfectly normal. If all you had to go on was a mug shot, you'd never know he was almost three times the height of a tall man.

When Kelso bent his corded neck to look at him, Byron's pulse quickened, and a chill ran down his back. His instincts told him to get ready to run from this ridiculously large thing. Byron swallowed and hoped he didn't look as scared as his nervous system demanded.

Kelso smiled slightly. "I am a sight to behold, ain't I?"

"Look, sorry…it's totally uncool of me…"

"Don't sweat it, Byron, seriously. Even among Sovereigns, I know I'm…" He flexed his arms and kissed both biceps, then held his left hand out and, with great critical attention, inspected his fingernails. "…exceptional. But not, y'know, officially *Exceptional*." He grinned broadly, which was saying something.

Byron laughed, suddenly entirely at ease. The dude was hilarious.

"C'mon," Kelso said. "Croy's probably counting the seconds."

Byron trotted to keep up with Kelso's stride as they went out into the late-morning sunlight. Croy and Schulmann were seated at a fiberglass picnic table pretty much exactly like the ones they had in the lunch room back at Romita Elementary, which tripped Byron out.

Byron sat down next to Schulmann. Kelso lowered himself to sit cross-legged on the asphalt. When his ass hit the ground, the picnic table bounced.

Spencer Croy said, "Mister Teslowski has expressed an interest in the SCET. His abilities have been tested and, in some areas, honed, and I have decided he should begin training with the two of you effective Monday the twenty-first."

"Welcome up," Kelso said.

Schulmann nodded. "Byron, what exactly is the nature of your Sovereign ability?"

"I, uh…adapt. Like, physically. Really fast."

Croy said, "The official designation for his ability is 'rapid reactive metamorphic adaptation.' Doctor Mazmanian and his team rank Mister Teslowski's ability class as Standard."

Kelso grunted, "Huh!"

Schulmann looked fascinated. "What...what does that mean, exactly?"

"Well..." Byron had never liked drawing attention to his talents. Last year around this time, he didn't even know he was all that different, just really, really good at sports.

All the sports.

He grinned sheepishly and tried again. "Well...after Mister Croy shot me enough times, I'm, like, bulletproof and stuff."

"Get out," Kelso said.

Encouraged, Byron added, "And...y'know, I heal really fast. And I'm pretty strong, pretty fast. I was CIF All-Star my sophomore year." He laughed a little. "I didn't know it was 'cause of all, y'know, this stuff."

"Remarkable." Schulmann looked at Croy. "Do you think he'd adapt to my emissions?"

Byron was convinced they were messing with him *that* time, but Croy shook his head, once, firmly.

"That will not be part of the exercises."

Schulmann looked at his hands, folded on the table. Byron thought he seemed bummed out all of a sudden.

"That's probably a good idea, all things considered," Schulmann mumbled.

Byron said, "I don't get it. What—sorry, I never found out—what's your ability?"

Kelso spoke up. "Jon's a microwave oven. He makes perfect popcorn."

163

Schulmann raised the middle finger of his right hand and directed it in Kelso's general direction. To Byron, he said, "Best way to put it would be that I'm a living particle accelerator."

Byron had heard the term, somewhere, but it didn't mean a thing to him.

"Huh?"

Schulmann's lips twitched up at the corners. "Like radiation, you know? I...hm. How to put this simply..." He suddenly looked appalled. "Sorry! No offense!"

Byron laughed. "Dude, none taken. Simple is good."

Schulmann caught a go-ahead nod from Croy before proceeding. "Okay, great." He laughed. "So it's like this: X-rays, radio waves, even light and, like the lummox said—"

"Hey!" Kelso chuckled.

"—microwaves, too...they're all pretty much the same thing, just at different levels of energy. I can take atoms and...get whatever energy I need out of them."

"Whoa," said Byron. "I mean, I don't, y'know, totally get all that, but...you said radiation. Like an A-bomb?"

Schulmann coughed into his hand. "Well, uh...not so— not so big. And not...exactly."

Spencer Croy said, "In terms of Mister Schulmann's field effectiveness, he is essentially a ranged energy weapon."

Byron looked at Jon Schulmann and Ed Kelso. "Holy fuck. You guys are...you guys are fucking awesome. I don't even get what you'd need someone like me for."

Croy said, "Your role will be defined through training and, eventually, field experience."

Byron looked at Croy. "You guys always know more

than you tell me. Can I get, like, a hint?"

A muscle twitched on Croy's cheek. A smile?

"Mister Kelso has strength, and mass."

"I'm the hammer," Kelso said.

"Mister Schulmann's energy manipulation abilities offer a range of tactical advantages."

"I'm the needle," Schulmann said. "Or the flamethrower."

"You," Croy looked at Byron, "are very fast and suitably strong and, with training, could prove to be functionally invulnerable. Also, you are not readily distinguishable from baseline humans."

"Wait..." Byron looked at Schulmann. "You look normal."

"Sure," said Schulmann, "but if I want to use my abilities without burning myself, or, I don't know, giving myself cancer in twenty years, I have to wear my containment suit. You'll see; it's pretty conspicuous."

"Oh."

Croy continued. "The expectation is that you will serve in a variety of roles, depending on the nature of the operation."

"Oh, okay." Byron smiled and looked at the three of them. "Good thing I'm, like, adaptable. Right?"

Kelso's laughter was loud, but when he slapped his knee, Byron flinched, hard.

"Great." Schulmann shook his head and smiled. "Another one."

"Laugh or cry, Jiffy Pop," Kelso said. "Laugh or cry."

There was a beat of silence between the two men as the

mood around the table dropped to the ground. Byron was about to ask about it, but Mister Croy spoke first.

"We need to talk about Friday."

"Ah," said Schulmann. "Right."

"Big day." Kelso ground his left fist into his right palm.

Croy said, "We assume the number of demonstrators at the Visitors Center will peak then. We also have intelligence suggesting our enemies will instigate a coordinated act of terror to take advantage of this."

Byron felt like he was a guest at this meeting, but he was dying to ask a question. It must have been obvious. Croy looked at him. "Yes?"

"Our...enemies?"

Kelso said, "You would know, Byron."

Byron looked at him. "Seriously? You think the company that wanted to experiment on me would do something? But...I figured, what with all the court stuff, and the news being, like, all over it..."

"Not Tyndale Labs," Croy said. "Their masters."

"Oh." Byron remembered the parent company of Tyndale Labs, and the one that creep Lester Brenhurst really worked for, was called PrenticeCambrian. It was a trip to think the same corporation that owned a bunch of laundry-soap and snack-cake brands could be behind some organized effort against the Sovereigns.

Byron didn't know a whole lot about it, and no one had seen fit to really fill him in since he'd arrived at the Institute.

Jon Schulmann said, "They're probably a puppet group as well, if I had to guess." His upper lip curled. "But hell, they don't even really need to encourage anyone. Plenty of home-grown hate out there."

Kelso's snort was loud. "Fuck 'em."

Croy continued. "The two of you will supplement our regular security force. It is Doctor Donner's hope that the presence of the SCET in an official capacity will be enough to keep the peace between demonstrators and discourage any blatant instigators."

"Um..." Byron saw Croy's subtle nod and went on. "You said 'between demonstrators'?"

Kelso answered for Croy again. "Heck, kid—we didn't hire *all* the pro-Sovereign people in the country." He laughed. "Got all the ones in Montana, though, I'm pretty sure..."

Schulmann said, "When you say official capacity, you mean...?"

"Full-dress," Croy said, "and your field-rated containment suit."

Byron said, "Will, uh...what about me?"

"Doctor Donner would like you to remain on the grounds," Croy said. "We'll formally announce your induction into the SCET at a proper press conference the following week."

"Benched!" Kelso shrugged and grinned. "Sorry, kid."

Byron wasn't used to being off the court when the ball went up. On the other hand, the idea of facing off with a bunch of anti-Sovereign nut jobs made his stomach a little queasy.

"I'm cool," he said.

Croy was watching him. "You may be needed, and you may not. You'll get a uniform tomorrow. Wear it on Friday."

Byron still remembered how it felt when Lester Brenhurst's augmented assassin nearly disemboweled him. The memory of his own blood, sticky and hot between his body and driveway gravel, made him shiver. He blinked. This wasn't a game. Not even. "Yes, sir."

"Mister Croy," Jon Schulmann said, "how reliable is the intelligence insofar as the chance of violence on Declaration Day goes? Has Mrs. Franklin seen anything?"

The name distracted Byron from difficult memories. "Beth...?" Schulmann nodded at him and turned back to Croy.

"No," Croy said. "We have no precognitive intelligence. Just chatter picked up from the local militia."

"Ah," sighed Kelso. "The speciesists."

Byron had never heard the term. "Who?"

Schulmann said, "There's a militia group headquartered on a ranch not far from the Institute. They used to be white supremacists...you know, neo-Nazi, racist stuff."

Kelso said, "Until we started coming out of the woodwork and gave those fucktards something real to worry about."

Byron didn't get it. "Why be worried about us, though?" He looked at Croy. "I mean, seriously. There's, what, like a few thousand Sovereigns in the world, right?"

"Less than six thousand," Croy said.

"Okay, but most of us can't even really do anything, right? And even if they were all, like...I don't know..."

"Living weapons?" put in Schulmann.

"Yeah. Even if, we're still, like, outnumbered a gazillion to one. Why be scared of us?"

Kelso managed to look dreamy and sinister at once. "I don't know about you, Byron, but as soon as I can find a nice big girl, this guy here's gonna make as many little Sovereign babies as he can. Gotta balance things out for the team, right?" His eyes narrowed. "Let's see how mean they feel when there's sixty thousand of us. Or six million."

Schulmann grunted. "That's why." From Jon's tone, Byron got that he liked the idea.

Kelso said, "Don't get me wrong—I'm not saying we should take things over or anything. But if the norms think we're gonna just hide here in this...gimme a word, Jon."

"Ghetto?"

Kelso pointed an index finger at the other man. "Bingo. That's bullshit. This is our world." He looked a little sheepish, but Byron thought it wasn't entirely genuine. "Our world, *too*, I mean."

Mister Croy said, "We are dangerously outnumbered, and for now, our distribution makes us vulnerable. Some think that makes us dangerous."

Jon Schulmann seemed focused on something far away. "Watch what happens if they make us prove them right."

"Damn straight," Kelso said.

They looked at Byron.

"Yeah!"

He kinda wanted to throw up.

Andrew Charters
Three

Denver Colorado sat in his wheelchair on his back yard deck, reading *The Kirby Grizzly*, drinking coffee, and occasionally picking at a brand-name coffeecake from its long white box.

Denver's backyard blended gradually with the light woods growing around most every house on this side of Kirby Lake. There was plenty of shadowy cover there in the trees, especially for one so preternaturally adept at stealth as Andrew Charters.

Crouched on his haunches, perfectly still, Andrew watched Denver for some time. Once in a while, the light breeze would send Denver's scent, along with the bite of the coffee and the doughy, soft impression of the dessert, across the sixty feet to Andrew's nostrils.

Each time, Andrew smiled. Denver was his oldest and only friend. His scent was calming, encouraging…and stirred in Andrew a bit of rueful regret. For the last decade and a half or so, their friendship had been unfairly one-sided. That wasn't going to change today.

For the umpteenth time, Andrew's hyper-alert nature drew his gaze to the wooden slat fence running up the left side of Denver's yard. That hadn't been there a year ago. Most of the backyards along Denver's street just blended into one another even as they blended into the woods.

The fence disturbed Andrew. It was something different, it was new, and it smelled like chemicals, sealer, and paint. He didn't care for unexpected changes, especially to a place so familiar to him. Who would have put it there? Why was it there now?

Andrew chuffed, a hard sigh through his flared nostrils. He was in for a whole lot of changes. The damn fence was a...

A...

The answer was in his head, tucked away and making itself scarce, what with all the fierce animal stuff crowding higher concepts out of the way. His brain dedicated a lot of itself to processing the world. Switching gears to remember something esoteric, something symbolic—it required an effort part of Andrew deeply resented.

A symbol.

That was it, right there.

Andrew grinned widely. The timid parts of his brain—the scientist, the intellectual—sneaked one in.

The damn fence was a symbol. A symbol.

There might as well be a fence between the woods where Andrew hid and where Denver—poor, unsuspecting Denver—sat reading the paper. Between Andrew staying out in the cold, literally and figuratively, and stepping back into the world in which he had been born as a human being.

Andrew stood up, cleared his throat, hawked a thick ball of phlegm, and stepped out of the cool shadows of the trees and onto Denver's roughly manicured lawn.

"Hello, Denver," he croaked.

The newspaper in Denver's hand quivered for a split second, but if Andrew's appearance surprised him, he did a great job of concealing it.

"Well, now," Denver said. "Look what dragged itself in. Where've you been keeping yourself?"

Andrew couldn't fight feeling dangerously exposed on

the lawn. He loped to the covered deck. "In the woods. Breathing. Hunting. Staying away."

Denver nodded. "Uh-huh. I was a little surprised when you didn't show up this past winter. Kept the blankets out for you. Even made a run down to the DAV and picked you up an old coat."

Denver got him a coat? Andrew licked his lips and focused down. "Thought I should stay away. After…"

"Ah. Yeah." Denver frowned. "You sure did a number on that poor asshole, Andy. Made things pretty bad for the boy, too. For Lucy."

"Deserved what he…" Andrew blinked, flashing on the feeling of the PrenticeCambrian mercenary's flesh parting for him, the hot splash of blood, the slippery slap of entrails against his feet.

Denver said, "Come on back, Andy."

Andrew blinked again. "Deserved what he got," he said firmly.

Denver tilted his head. "You'd know."

Andrew nodded slowly. "Why I'm here."

Denver set down his newspaper. "What's why you're here?" He broke off a piece of coffeecake.

"The boy…Lucille." Andrew swallowed past his tight throat. He coughed. "Want to help."

Denver's handful of cake stopped halfway to his bearded mouth. "You want to *help*?"

Back in the woods, a squirrel scrambled down the trunk of a tree and rummaged in the mulch of pine needles and dirt below. Andrew struggled against the urge to turn around and pinpoint the little prey with his sensorium.

He took a deep breath and nodded. "Yeah. Thought I... thought I could. Should."

"So..." Denver regarded him. "Huh. Well, I guess that could change things. Probably for the better, too. Good for you, Andrew." He squinted at him. "Good for you."

Andrew licked his teeth behind closed lips. As always, his augmented canines snagged on his tongue: a rough, alien feeling, even after all these years. Maybe it was a good sign, that he'd never gotten used to that.

"Thing is..."

He found it difficult to push any more words out of his mouth. Another fence.

Denver put the uneaten morsel of coffeecake back in the box. "'Thing is' what, Andrew?"

"Gonna need your help."

Denver nodded. "Figured as much. I can give you a ride down the hill, if you want. No problem."

Andrew shook his head. "Not going that way. Not first."

Denver sat back in his chair and scratched at his beard. "What do you mean? What's the plan?"

Squirrel smell. Coffee smell. Newsprint smell. New-fence smell. Andrew closed his eyes and gritted his teeth. When he opened them, Denver continued calmly watching him, waiting. He knew how it was. Andrew was grateful for that.

He pulled the words out of his head and out his mouth.

"You know how I...how I am. Need to...need help to be more..." He shook his head. "No. Not as *here*. Less...less... wild."

Denver nodded slowly. "That's been a challenge for you.

I know. But..." He grimaced. "Look, is it...possible? Or did the augmentation regimen, well, go too deep?"

Andrew sighed heavily. "Gotta be possible. Right? Just need...the right help."

Denver was quick. "You're finally gonna take them up on their offer. The Sovereigns."

Andrew nodded. "Gotta go to Montana." He tapped his gray, tangled dreadlocks. "They got rid of the killer bugs Lester put in me that time. What else?"

Denver let out a sigh of his own. He turned his head, drew his upper lip back and sucked on his beard: habitual action Andrew had seen Denver do since he first grew facial hair in the late Sixties. He didn't need the visual cue to tell his friend was conflicted; his scent made that clear.

"You really think this is the best time to pay them a call? You know what Friday is, right?"

Andrew had no idea. He shrugged.

"It's the first anniversary. Declaration Day."

"So?"

"So while you've been hiding out in the scrub, things have been happening in the real world. This last year, with Sovereigns coming out of the woodwork all over the place, William Donner in the news pretty much every damn day, this armed force they're putting together...not to mention the whole legal mess your boy's involved in..." Denver stared at Andrew. "Things are pretty tense out there, buddy."

Andrew thought hard.

"Gotta be now," he said.

"I really, strongly recommend hanging out for a couple of weeks," Denver said. "You can..." He surprised Andrew by

175

exuding reluctance. "You can stay here."

Denver drew himself up in his chair.

"But that's all I can do for you, buddy. Down the hill to Abbeque Valley is one thing. Crossing state lines, all the way to Montana, and while this shit's going down?" He shook his head gently. "I can't do it, Andy. Sorry."

Denver was saying no?

Andrew felt a rush of surprise and frustration that threatened to sour into anger, but the sound of a car pulling into the driveway threw him solidly into flight mode. He leapt backwards off the porch and landed in a crouch in the yard.

"Car!"

Denver raised a calming hand. "Easy, man. That's Sandy." He looked over his shoulder and back at Andrew. "She's a friend."

"Can't be seen." Andrew skulked toward the tree line. "Can't be seen. Bad idea. Not good for you."

"Aw, hell." Denver rolled his chair down the deck ramp and onto the grass. "Just settle down. She knows about you. And she's been bugging me to introduce you." Almost under his breath, which was of course equally clear as anything to Andrew, Denver added, "Like I could just call you up and have you over for goddamn cocktails…"

Andrew heard doors opening and closing. A woman was in Denver's house. She was coming toward them.

Stranger!

"Not good…"

"Just…" Denver kept his hand out, palm out. "Just… stay!"

The back screen door opened, and she was there. A woman, in late middle age, about five-foot-six inches tall, with shoulder-length, wavy, graying brown hair on her round head. She froze when she saw Andrew, one hand still on the frame of the door.

Andrew knew he was growling. He couldn't help it.

"Jesus, Andy," muttered Denver, one hand hiding his face.

The woman closed the door behind her and took a step onto the deck.

"You must be Andrew," she said. "My name is Sandy. I'm a good friend of Denver's."

Andrew caught her scent, which included a hint of men's deodorant (the kind they all thought was unscented) and absolutely no fear. On the contrary. She oozed curiosity.

Andrew swallowed his growl. Still on all fours, he shifted until he faced her.

Denver sounded resigned. "Say hi to my girlfriend, Andy."

Andrew cleared his throat. "Hi."

"Hi." She smiled without showing her teeth, which Andrew appreciated, whether it was conscious choice on her part or not. People made him nervous when they showed their teeth.

Andrew stood up.

Sandy walked right up to him and stuck out her hand.

Andrew looked at it. What was that for...?

"Put 'er there," Sandy looked him in the eye, but just for a moment. Not long enough to be threatening. Another nice touch.

He looked at his own hand. It was black with grime. "Sorry…"

She took it in her own, which made him jump, just a little. She gave his hand a firm pump and let go.

"Nice to meet you, Andrew," she said. "What brings you around? Have you had lunch?"

Denver had a small smile on his face that didn't quite reach the reservations in his eyes. "Sandy—and no offense, Andy, but you know this—he's not so good with being indoors."

"No," Andrew said to Sandy. "I can come inside." He looked at Denver. "Gonna have to start. Have to."

Denver gave him a long look. "Well."

"Well." Sandy nodded once. "Three for lunch." She smiled at Andrew. "You and I can get better acquainted."

With that, she turned and went back up to the porch and opened the screen door. She looked at Denver.

"Make sure he rinses his feet off, first, hon, okay?"

Marc Teslowski
Eight

After breakfast and a shower, Marc found Ray in his office, behind a desk crowded with file folders stacked around an electric typewriter. He wore narrow reading glasses on the end of his nose.

"Hey, there." Ray closed the folder he'd been reading and stood up. "Sorry this place is such a mess. A clean desk is the sign of a sick mind, right?" He laughed and put his hands on the small of his back to stretch. "I told you I run a little newsletter, right?"

"I think so."

"This is where I put it all together. *The Good Human*, it's called." He pointed to a yellowed magazine cover, framed behind glass, hanging on the wall behind his desk. The cover depicted a figure in a white robe and hood ringing the Liberty Bell while the ghost of George Washington looked on. "Kind of a tribute."

Marc stared at the old magazine. "Is that..." He laughed automatically. "Is that a Klu Klux Klan guy?"

Ray stepped around the desk. "A patriot. Yes, sir." His eyes were bright and intense. "You feel like taking a little stroll?"

Marc had never seen anything like that in his life. He pulled his gaze away from the wall. "Sure."

"Great!" Ray strode out of the office and down the hall. "I love that morning air!"

They talked while they walked across the grounds. "Sixty-six acres," Ray declared. "It's like living on a chunk of the

Garden of Eden, dropped right in the middle of the United States of America. The house is…well, it's way more than Patsy and I every really needed, but as you can see, these days there's lots of company around."

"Your family?"

"Heh. Not by blood." He laughed. "Except in the sense that we're all family by blood—by our genes, you know what I mean?"

Marc shrugged. "I'm not up on that stuff."

"No? I figured you would have to be, given what they've put you through in the last year."

"I leave it to the lawyers," Marc grumbled.

"Lawyers." Ray hawked and spat. "'Nuff said."

Marc smiled. "Shit, yeah."

"Anyway. Belial, Abe, Carrie, all them…they're not related to me, but we share a common cause, and we—like you and me, and all but six thousand or so folks on the planet —share common blood. So that makes 'em family to me."

Marc thought about the weird racist magazine on Ray's office wall. He was quiet as they came to the barbed-wire-fenced perimeter of the grounds.

Pine forest carpeted the slopes beyond. He felt a long way away from everything, and even though Byron was probably less than five miles away as the crow flew, he felt like they might as well be on different planets.

"Great view," he said, to fill the air.

"Let's be straight with each other, Marc," Ray said. "You're a little uncomfortable. Am I right?"

Marc kept his focus on the panorama. "I don't think of myself as a racist. No offense."

Ray's laughter echoed off the distant hillsides. "A racist? Oh, hell's bells, Marc. I'm no racist. No, sir."

Marc looked at him. "You've got a cartoon of the Klu Klux Klan on your wall. You've got all these people living in your house, talking about all that stuff. I thought…"

"Hell, look here." Ray's laughter subsided, but his tone was still light. "I'll give you this much: I used to be what some folks would call a racist. But that was way before, Marc. Before."

"You mean before Four Eighteen Eighty-Five."

"Pretty much. I'd heard a little bit, before then, even. I'm lucky in the sense that I know a lot of people all over this country of ours. Some of those people are senators. They knew it was coming."

Marc found the thought offensive. "We knew? About Donner?"

"I reckon so," Ray said. "Doesn't Donner make the same claim, after all?"

Marc scowled. "I don't listen to anything that asshole says."

Ray nodded. "You're angry. I get it." He started walking, and Marc kept pace. "Me, I *have* to listen. I have to know what's going on, best as I can, so I can report it to my readers and keep the rogues' gallery around here in the loop. And seriously, Marc, you'd do well to pay attention, too."

He grunted. "Makes me sick to give them any more thought than I have to."

"But they have your son," Ray said gently. "And the lies they tell…"

"It'll come out." Marc squinted at Ray. "So what's with

the Klansman picture, if you don't believe that stuff anymore?"

"That's the cover of *The Good Citizen*, from the twenties," Ray said. "I keep that—and I named my newsletter after it—because the publisher was a woman of principle and strength. You know she was the first female bishop in the United States? A real trailblazer, full of the strength of her convictions." He took a breath and looked at Marc. "Not too different from my Patsy, God rest her soul. Hell of a woman. Hell of a woman."

"I bet she was," Marc said. "Your wife, I mean."

Ray nodded, his eyes far away for a moment. He looked down at his feet as they walked and said, "When Donner came on the scene and all the abominations crawled out of the shadows where they'd been hiding, I guess you could say I came out of the shadows myself. Figured out pretty damn quick that having different-colored skin or slanty eyes or kinky hair, what have you…those things didn't make a damn bit of difference compared to how different Donner's tribe is from us."

Ray grimaced. "I woke up fast. The way I figure it, the Sovereigns are the biggest threat to the purity of the human race since the time of the Nephilim."

"Purity? You're worried about the Sovereigns having kids with regular humans?" Marc had no idea what the Nephilim was, but he figured there wasn't much point mentioning that.

"Shit, I'm worried about the Sovereigns having kids with each other. How much time we got before a new generation of abominations are born?" Ray shook his head. "Fact is, it's probably already happened. Scares the crap out of me."

"I never thought about that."

"I think about it all the time," Ray said. He stopped and turned toward Marc. "Look at it this way, Marc. You see any Neanderthals walking around?"

"Nope."

"Damn right. We're tough, and we're mean, and we are God's blessed chosen. The Sovereigns're going to find out. Mess with us, you get war. And we have God on our side."

Marc wasn't religious, but he didn't comment on that. He was a guest, after all.

"I just want my kid back," he said.

"You'll get him," Ray said. "I'll help however I can."

They walked along the paved driveway that linked various outbuildings with the main house. Ahead of them to the right was what looked to Marc like an old barn. The big doors were closed. A whole lot of big noisy crows perched along the peaked roof in a thick black line.

A tall, young guy, bare-chested but wearing blue jeans and work boots, hoed stray weeds from the cleared dirt in front of the barn. A Walkman cassette player was clipped to his belt. He was intent on his work and lost in whatever was playing in his earphones.

Marc noticed the kid had the Stars and Stripes tattooed on the back of his hand. Where'd he seen that before?

Ray stopped and called out. "Drake! Hey, Drake!"

The kid straightened up from his work and pulled his earphones out. "Morning, Mister Greene."

"Drake." Ray was smiling, but Marc recognized his tone. He'd used the same tone on Byron more than once. "You know better, boy. Wear some gloves when you're doing yard work, all right?"

Marc saw the kid's face fall. "Yes, sir. I'm sorry sir." He covered the splash of blue and red with his other hand. "I'll go get 'em." He glanced over his shoulder at the barn. "Gotta go inside…"

"All right, then." Ray raised his own hand in a casual wave. "See you for dinner. I'm going on a drive with my friend here; we probably won't be around for lunch."

"Yes, sir."

Marc remembered.

This kid with the flag tattoo was one of the rednecks he'd seen hassling the Sovereign from the airplane. Schmidt, or whatever the freak's name was.

What the hell was he supposed to make of that? Who the fuck were these people, anyway?

Ray was shaking his head. "I tell you what, if that well-meaning dumbass was my blood kid, he'd know to wear his gloves. But one boy's been enough of a challenge to raise." He laughed. "Hell, you know what I'm talking about."

"Yes, I do," Marc said slowly.

"Come on," Ray said. "You up for round two at the devil's nest? I'm driving!"

Andrew Charters
Four

Andrew had never been in Denver Colorado's house. Not in all these years.

He stood just inside the threshold of the back door. Denver, who had wheeled himself in first, and Sandy watched him from a little farther in, at the edge of the kitchen.

It was difficult to figure out if Denver carried the scent of the house on him or if the house represented a kind of superset of Denver's scent. Andrew shook his head and let out a shaky breath. The distinction was unimportant. Except for a little hint of new-fence smell that must have blown in, the place was so...Denver...Andrew felt like he was immersed in the essence of his friend.

It was a lot to take in. Andrew turned back to face the screen door. The yard was there, just past the deck, and the woods were there, just beyond the yard. He could be back in the cool shadows in three leaps. He could be miles away from any houses in hours.

Behind him, in the kitchen, Denver said softly, "How's it going, there, Andy?"

Andrew saw that his hand was moving, apparently on its own, to grasp the screen-door latch. He grabbed his wrist with his other hand, breathed in and out through his mouth, and turned his back on escape.

"Nice...place," Andrew said. He laughed once, a harsh bark. "You. Lots of you."

Sandy slapped Denver lightly on the shoulder. "See that? That's why I'm always after you to straighten up around here a little." She smiled.

"Yes, dear." Denver grinned at her. Andrew had a sense that Denver and Sandy were doing something funny, but he didn't quite understand. It was hard to remember how people acted together.

He had been a person, once. He would have to learn how to be one again.

He laughed again, to see how it felt. Denver and Sandy flinched at the sound. Andrew felt a degree of mortification. Even to his own ears, his laughter sounded like there was something dead slapping in his throat.

Denver said, "Anyway...you want to come into the kitchen? You ready?" He maneuvered his chair farther into the house. Sandy stepped aside, leaving a clear path for Andrew to walk to the table just past the kitchen.

"Yeah," Andrew said. He slinked forward, sniffing and listening.

Wet putridity in the metal bowl—the sink, it was called a sink. He knew this. He knew most of it. He wasn't an amnesiac. It had only been a decade and a half since the augmentation regimen made him into this; that didn't have to represent his whole life. He had a long way to go, a long time to be better than he was.

"There's old food in there." He pointed at the sink.

"Ah." Denver nodded. "I might not have run the disposal last night."

"Or the night before," Sandy said.

"Easy, you," Denver said to her.

Andrew watched them. The way they leaned toward each other, the flood of pheromones flowing from their bodies to their mouths and noses...

It made him feel something.

It felt *nice*.

Denver frowned at him, but the corners of his lips were up, too. "What are you looking at, mister?"

"Heh."

These two, just by being there, helped Andrew pull his old self up from the thorny tiger trap of his more animal nature. They were so human. That was a really good thing.

"Denver."

Andrew wasn't really addressing his friend. Just declaring his existence. Denver nodded. "Andrew."

Andrew's lips felt stiff as they stretched into a grin. "Heh. So...I should sit down, right?" He pointed to the chairs around the table past the kitchen. "On one of those?"

Denver smiled. "Yep."

Andrew did so, though it took a little effort to ignore the whirring noise of the refrigerator when he passed it. It was damn unnatural, but that, he reminded himself, was part of normal. Deal with it.

"Well, look at you," Denver said. "Sitting at my dinner table. How about that."

Andrew nodded, then looked at his legs. "It's strange. Sitting. Feels weird."

"You get used to it." Denver spread his arms and looked down at himself, in his wheelchair. His eyes twinkled and the hint of a smile teased behind his beard.

Sandy slapped him again. Strange. But...funny. That's what it was. Funny. But not funny in the way Andrew was used to. There was violence, of a sort, but no animals or people were in pain.

Denver pulled his chair up to the table, and Sandy started making a few sandwiches.

"You like Braunschweiger, Andrew?" Sandy asked.

"Not sure," Andrew said. He looked at Denver.

"You used to."

"Oh. Okay, yeah."

"Good," said Sandy. Just be a minute. You hungry, Denver, or did you fill up on that sweet stuff?"

"I'm good for now," he said.

"So Andrew," Sandy said, "I've heard a lot about you, of course. I'm glad you came by."

"Had to," said Andrew. "Important." He looked at Denver, who frowned.

Sandy glanced over at them from the kitchen. "Important?"

Denver said, "Andy's decided to finally get some help with his...condition."

She studied Andrew. It made him feel the slightest bit uncomfortable. He wasn't used to being the prey.

"I see," she said. "But...how?"

Andrew struggled against an automatic threat response. He tightened his lips against his teeth to keep the grimace off his face. While he fought with this, Denver answered for him.

"The Sovereigns. They offered, years ago, I gather, but Andrew was a little crazier back then." He looked at Andrew. "No offense."

Andrew swallowed, finally defeating his instincts, and shrugged. "It's...how it was."

"What's different now, Andrew?" Sandy was more focused on preparing the food than she was on him now, which made things easier.

"Need to help Nathan," he said. "That's my son. Nathan."

Denver said, "That's something I don't get, Andrew. Why now? It's been almost a year since you saw him, right? What's happened that you're all worked up about this now?"

Andrew's nostrils flared. "Not just now. Been all year." He sighed. "Took a long time. Still had to...be, right?"

Sandy put a plate with a Braunschweiger sandwich on wheat bread and a side of potato chips on the table in front of Andrew. She sat down next to him with a similar dish for herself.

Andrew watched her wrinkle her nose, cough, and pinch her nostrils quickly. She looked at Denver, who looked apologetic for some reason Andrew didn't understand.

Sandy dabbed her mouth with a napkin. "Go ahead, Andrew." To Denver, she said, "So polite!"

Andrew shoved most of the sandwich in his mouth and chewed.

Denver chuckled. "A real gentleman."

Andrew preferred live prey, and while this was a step below that, it was several steps above human dumpster trash, which he'd had to resort to more than a few times over the years. He swallowed and wiped his beard with the back of his hand.

"Thanks. Good."

"You're very welcome," Sandy said. "Okay, so...how will the Sovereigns be able to help? Will they—can they undo what was done?"

Andrew shrugged. "Don't know."

Denver said, "I think the idea is to be a little more Dr. Jekyll and a little less Mr. Hyde."

Andrew grunted around the second mouthful of sandwich.

"I see. And then...you want to talk to your boy, is that right, Andrew?"

"Yeah! He's in a spot...kinda 'cause of me. I think. Not right."

Sandy said to Denver, "Do you think he could make a difference?"

Denver pursed his lips and tilted his head, thinking. "It might. Not sure how it'll turn out for Andy, though. Somebody's going to jail for the deaths of those PrenticeCambrian guys."

To Andrew, he said, "They might decide you're it. What then?"

Andrew shook his tangled gray mane. "Self-defense. Self-defense."

Denver looked doubtful. "Yeah, well. It's not about what happened. It's about getting a jury to believe it happened the way your side says it did."

Andrew didn't care about the particulars. "Need to go to the Sovereigns. Get help. Get to Nate. Work it out." He looked at Denver. "Need you to take me, Denver. Right away."

Denver scowled. "Now, I told you before, Andy, that's just not a good idea. Especially this week. And I can't take you, man. You gotta find your own way this time."

"Come again?" Sandy looked at Denver. "Let's start with why it's a bad idea that Andrew get some help for himself so he can help his son."

"Well, let's see." Denver started ticking off on his fingers. "I'm depositioned in Lucy and Nate's case, and in the Teslowskis' case. Andrew here is a Federal fugitive considered armed and dangerous. The whole damn world has its eyes on the Donner Institute, what with the Sovereigns planning on making a big deal out of the anniversary this Friday. They've got their hands full with the press, and the crazies...and the crazies in the press.

"And, for Christ's sake, I'm a middle-aged man in a wheelchair whose face has been on television more than a few times thanks to the thing last year. I'm not the guy to be driving Andy across state lines and into the goddamn lion's den." He shook his head. "No way."

Andrew pouted. "Gonna take months if I have to hoof it. Can't wait."

"Why not just call 'em? Have 'em come and get you. What'd you need me for, anyway?"

Andrew recoiled in his seat. Potato-chip fragments fell from his lips. "Don't like 'em. Don't trust 'em."

Denver waved his hand at him. "Aw! They offered to help, Andrew, didn't they? And you need them."

Sandy said, "Denver. He needs you."

Denver gaped at her. "It's not a good idea, Sandy."

"I think it is." She propped her elbows on the table top and leaned toward Denver. "This is a good idea for so many reasons, Denver—not the least of which is that your friend Andrew Charters is asking for your help."

191

He squinted at her. "You're a sweet girl, Sandy, but that's not all you are. What are you thinking?"

"What am I thinking?" She smiled and sat back. She made Andrew flinch away when she tried to touch his shoulder, and settled for pantomiming a tap in the air between her palm and his body. "Even if I wasn't thinking anything else, that's enough of a reason. Andrew needs you."

Denver frowned and said again, "What are you thinking, Sandy?"

"I'll go with you," she said. "As a member of the press."

"*The Kirby Grizzly*? Seriously?"

"For starters. But a story like this? Don't you think it'll get picked up? Can you imagine how good it would be for Andrew's family?"

He snorted a laugh. "And for one Sandy Graves, former big-city reporter, not coincidentally."

Andrew sat in his chair, legs jumping, and watched them volley.

"Sure," she said. "I smell a story. Shit, it's probably the biggest story of my life, and that, as you know, is saying something." She lowered her voice. "But I'm serious, Denver. It's just the right thing to do."

He rolled his eyes. "The right thing to do is pick up the phone and have them come and get him."

"No," Andrew's eyes were wide. "Don't want to go with them. Don't trust 'em! Want to go *to* them. Need to be able to leave if I want. Need you to take me. You...only trust *you*. Won't go otherwise. Gotta go...but...won't go." He was hyperventilating.

"Easy, Andy," Denver said. "Easy." To Sandy, he said,

"Even if we did...you can see it makes sense to wait until after Declaration Day, right? At least?"

She shook her head. "I can think of no better time."

"You're thinking about headlines!"

"No!" She looked away when she denied it. "Mostly, I'm thinking about the boy. You saw him on that show."

Andrew said, "Show?"

"He was on a television show," she said. "He looked so..."

"Sandy..." Denver's voice carried a warning.

She stopped. "He looked like a boy who could use his father." She looked hard at Denver. "Right?"

"We gotta go," Andrew said. "You gotta take me. We gotta go."

Denver deflated. "Aw, hell. You're being unreasonable. Both of you!"

"We gotta go," Sandy said. Her smile was thin.

"Aw, hell," Denver said again.

Andrew looked at them both. He sensed Sandy was some kind of ally, and settled his gaze on her. "We can go?"

She looked at Denver, who nodded, then back at Andrew.

"Yes, Andrew," she said. She looked back at Denver. "First thing tomorrow?"

When he nodded again, she turned back to Andrew and wrinkled her nose.

"Meanwhile, Andrew, we're burning your clothes. You're taking a bath, or six. And I'm going to see about that horrible hair of yours..."

Andrew paled beneath his ratty beard and the layers of grime on his face.

"A bath…?"

Byron Teslowski
Five

Byron found Haze playing *Star Castles* in the game room off the cafeteria. Despite what sounded like angry pieces of machinery leaking from her Walkman earphones, she turned around and faced him before he figured out how to announce his presence.

She smiled when she saw his surprise. She clicked the stop button on the portable cassette player, pulled off her headphones, and said, "Body heat. I could feel you coming."

"Whoa. That's pretty cool."

She shrugged, but her smile didn't fade completely. "Eh. It's only good when someone's right up on me. Not all that useful."

"That's the sort of thing Doc Mazmanian could probably help with. If you wanted."

Haze's eyebrows rose. "Oh, so I can join the team? No thanks."

Byron shook his head. "I don't know what you have against the SCET." He felt a little hypocritical as soon as he said it.

She looked at him. "Let's get a pop or something. Walk with me."

They started toward the cafeteria. Byron laughed. "A what?"

"What, what?"

"'Let's go get a' what? What did you say?"

"A pop," she repeated. "A...what, a soda, a cola, an orange drink or something."

"You're not from around here, are you?"

"Newsflash, doofus. Neither are you."

They helped themselves to fountain drinks in the cafeteria. "You got me there."

Haze led them out of the cafeteria and along the walkway connecting the Institute buildings. The air was a little brisk. Byron kind of wished he'd grabbed a hot chocolate instead of a cold drink.

"Chilly," he said.

"Is it?"

He remembered Haze generated her own heat. "Trust me."

"I didn't feel like sitting around," Haze said. "You mind?"

"Nah. We can walk. It'll give me a chance to try something—I wanna see if I can, like, adapt to the temperature."

Haze rolled her eyes. "Always on, eh, soldier boy?"

"Not even," he said. "No one asked me to try it; I just, like, thought I'd see."

"Asked, told, whatever."

He glared at her. "What's your problem?"

She sipped at her drinking straw, eyes ahead. "No problem, dude. It's cool."

They walked a few yards in silence before Haze said, "Anyway. How was your clubhouse meeting?"

"A trip," Byron said. "They're worried people are gonna, like, start shit on Declaration Day."

She tilted her head. "Makes sense. Celebrating Declaration Day is stupid, given how pissed off so many people are about us. Can't blame 'em for wanting to shove it up our asses."

Byron didn't want that to make sense to him. It made things a little too confusing. Better to have clear teams, shirts and skins, Sovereign and human, right and wrong. He felt like he was playing devil's advocate, but hell, he was committed, right?

"Haven't they been fucking with us for a while, though? We can't let them just do whatever, right?"

Haze laughed. "Seriously, Byron. Before you came here, weren't you, like, some high-school football hero, or something? Tell me all about how the humans totally beat you down, dude. I can't wait."

She was doing it again—making him feel stupid. "Well...not, like, me, like, specifically. But Donner says—"

"Donner says!" She chuffed. "Yeah, yeah. Another rich white guy who probably hasn't dealt with anything worse than a parking ticket his whole fucking life. Gimme a break."

"Maybe, but...look, right before I came here, people were totally after me. This guy, this doctor dude, he totally wanted to lock me up and, like, fuckin' experiment on me and shit."

Haze sobered. "Yeah, okay." She nodded. "I grok. You went through some shit. You're national news, after all, you and your buddy." She stopped walking and looked at him. "You get it, though, right? Why they're afraid of us?"

Byron's mouth twisted. "Yeah. It's...shitty. But...yeah."

"So...us making a big deal out of Declaration Day, it's like rubbing their noses in it, y'know?" She grimaced. "It's all ego."

"Maybe. I don't know." Byron looked at her. "But no matter what, we can't just, I don't know, let people try to hurt

197

us."

A ripple of heat came off her, and she sneered. "Let 'em try."

"Easy for you to say, right? You're, what, Standard?"

"I don't know. I keep blowing off the tests."

Byron rolled his eyes. "Whatever. Point is, you can take care of yourself. Not everybody can." He pointed vaguely in the direction of the Visitors' Center. "Plus, what about all the regular people who work for the Institute?"

"What about them? If I was a Norm, I'd totally call in sick on Friday. Not worth it."

"They won't have to. We'll be there." Byron paused. "Well, not, like, me...but Kelso and that Schulmann guy, plus Croy...they'll be watching out for everybody."

Haze's lips turned down, and she shook her head. "They're just gonna make it worse."

"Why?"

"Seriously?"

"Yeah, seriously!"

Haze took a deep breath and looked off to her left, at nothing, for a second or two. "Check this out: let's say there's a big demonstration, anti-Sovereign yahoos on one side and a bunch of us on the other side."

Byron nodded. "That's pretty much what's gonna go down."

"Yeah. It's totally predictable. Plus, our side's gonna have a bunch of newbies. You've seen 'em coming in; half of them don't even speak English. That's gonna make it even worse."

Byron hadn't thought of that, but it made sense. "Okay. Sure. Whatever...the SCET..."

"Hold on." She held up a hand. "I'm not done."

"Sorry."

"So they get all preachy at each other, and maybe throw some rocks or whatever. Normal demonstration, the cops are there to keep the two sides apart, right? Nobody really wants to get arrested or get their head bashed in, mostly, so it never really gets out of hand."

"I guess." Byron thought he had her. "But—that's just it! When one of the cops is a dude like Kelso...fuck, who'd want to mess around with him?"

She shook her head violently. "No, no, no, no. Byron, dude: the cops aren't on anybody's side. Your new buddies aren't cops, man. They're not neutral."

He laughed, but it sounded a little weak to his own ears. "They're the Sovereign Conduct Enforcement Team Alpha," he said. "They're supposed to enforce our conduct—make sure we're on the straight and narrow. Not take the place of regular police. People know that."

She clicked her tongue. "Dude, not even you really believe that."

Byron remembered how eager Schulmann and Kelso sounded to have a chance to defend Sovereigns from Normals.

"It's..." He saw triumph rising in her expression. Damn, it made him mad. He let that anger push down his uncertainty down.

"It's what we're for, Haze. Fuck. Why do you have to assume the SCET's gonna get all fucked up?"

"Because they can, Byron. Absolute power, blah blah blah."

He frowned. "What? You're not even making sense."

She looked mildly disgusted with him. "Read a book, dude. Fuck." She started walking fast back toward the apartment building. "Forget it. Forget it."

He trotted to catch up with her. "Wait up. Jesus."

She kept walking.

"Haze. C'mon."

She stopped and turned to face him.

"Y'know...I bet if we'd been at the same school..." Her eyes narrowed. "I bet you totally wouldn't have even talked to me."

She was totally right. He couldn't deny it.

She must have seen it on his face. "Yeah. Thought so. You were a jock, after all, right? Fucking jock. I know exactly how it would have gone down."

"You don't," he said.

"Bullshit," she snapped. "You're a jock, here, too, you know that, right? SCET, *semper fi, honorifice perficite proprio actio*...you're the jocks of Sovereign high school."

Byron shook his head. "You're fucking crazy. Why does that have to mean it's automatically bad?"

"Because people who *can* do shitty things eventually *do* shitty things," Haze said. "Tell me you never did, when you could. Tell me you're some perfect exception, Byron letterman jacket jock hero Teslowski."

Byron thought of all the fucked-up things he'd done to Nate Charters over the years. Goddamn it, he didn't want her to be right. She was too fucking sure of herself.

Besides, he'd *learned*. He'd totally grown up. He'd changed. She had no fucking idea.

No fucking idea.

"You're a fucking bitch." He moved past her, brushing her shoulder just a little, and strode for the apartment build-ing.

Her heat lingered on his shoulder, through his jacket.

Marc Teslowski
Nine

Traffic thickened on the narrow mountain road as Marc and Ray neared the Donner Institute for Sovereign Studies Visitors Center. Half a mile or so before the gate, they were effectively parked on the road. Ray peered ahead through the windshield, then looked at Marc.

"You okay with walking some?"

"Sure."

Ray let a little space grow between his car and the back bumper of the pickup truck ahead of them. When there was just enough room, he cut the wheel to the right and pulled onto the dusty shoulder of the road.

Ray cut the engine. Marc got out of the car and looked up and down the road. The cars stretched as far down the mountain as he could see. All coming to the Institute?

How many of the people in those cars…weren't people?

Ray came around the front of his car and gestured up the road. "C'mon. It's not far."

As they walked, it became clear that Ray hadn't been the first to make the side of the road their parking lot. Before long, they were in a loose queue of people making their way to the Visitors Center.

Marc overheard accents and languages he couldn't place. Ray caught it and squinted thoughtfully.

"The human family, like I said." Ray nodded to a bedraggled young man in hiking boots and Dolfin shorts with a heavy backpack on his shoulders who looked like he might have walked all the way up the mountain. "Come from all over."

Marc's skin crawled despite the light sweat he was building up. "Seems to me, if people come here from far away, they're not who you think they are, Ray. I don't know."

Ray glanced around. "Sure, there's some devils in this bunch. There must be. But it's just numbers, Marc. Just numbers. We outnumber them a thousandfold. Won't be any different here."

Marc felt like he should keep his voice down. "Yeah, but why'd regular people make the trip? Why now?"

"Same reason as the freaks." Ray pointed ahead.

Marc heard the crowd's murmur as he followed Ray's gesture and saw the people gathered by the entrance to the Visitors Center.

Two clusters of people faced off, the road into the Center forming a convenient divide between them. A third group, the Donner Institute uniformed security force with which Marc was already acquainted, hung near the closed gate to the parking lot. Marc thought the traitorous bastards looked pretty damn nervous. Served them right.

"Be cool," Ray muttered to Marc as they threaded the needle down the driveway to the gate.

Neither group of demonstrators was organized enough to be chanting or shouting slogans, but some of the people on the left had homemade signs. Marc saw one that read "Go Back to Hell" and another that demanded someone "Wipe Donner's Shit Off Montana."

That meant the group on the right must be full of freaks.

He surreptitiously looked as he and Ray walked past. The group, about fifty or so strong, was dirty and sullen and mostly quiet, and they all looked pretty much just like the group on the left.

A pop, like the sound of a pressure hose being removed from the valve stem of a car tire, made Marc jump just a little. A weird, yellowish ball of light rose up out of the crowd on the right to float above their heads.

It looked like a dirty soap bubble made of piss or weak cat puke, only...shimmering. The crowd on the left—the *people* on the left—were surprised into silence.

Marc felt very exposed.

The bubble of light popped soundlessly. Marc flinched. He heard gasps and groans from the human demonstrators and laughter from the presumed Sovereigns and their sympathizers.

Dim streamers, like the tails from washed-out fireworks, drifted through the air and faded away. When the last of them was gone, the spell was broken and the shouting resumed, more urgent and angry than before.

Marc and Ray faced the security guards. They stared back through mirror-lens sunglasses.

"Invitation?"

Marc scowled. Ray guffawed.

"Invitation? We want to talk to someone inside, son. We're visitors. For the..." He winked at Marc. "For the Visitors Center. Right?"

The security guard turned his head to take in Ray and Marc in turn. He spoke to Marc.

"I'm afraid the Visitors Center is closed today unless you have an invitation."

Ray grinned. "An invitation from who, now, son?"

The security guard kept his tongue. He probably understood he was being baited.

Marc stewed. "I don't need an invitation. My son is in there."

Another of the guard said easily, "Then you must have an invitation. Once we see that, I'm sure there won't be a problem, sir."

Marc couldn't tell, what with the sunglasses and all, but he was pretty sure this jackass had been one of the guards he'd dealt with yesterday.

"You son of a—"

"Marc." Ray touched his shoulder and drew him back, gently but firmly. "Hold on a minute. Look."

A blue van moved through the parking lot. Before it turned to head for the gate, Marc saw KECI stenciled on the side doors.

The security guards gave just enough ground to let another of their number open the gate wide enough for the van to slip slowly through. "This is going to turn out just fine," Ray said. "Hold on."

"They're leaving," Marc said.

The anti-Sovereign demonstrators organized themselves enough to chant "Ah-bom-meh-NAY-shun! Out OF the NAY-shun!"

"Oh, I doubt it," Ray said.

Sure enough, the van stopped. A woman in a peach pantsuit bounced out holding a microphone, followed by a man lugging a camera and another man holding a fuzzy microphone on a stick.

"Oh, fuck," Marc moaned. "I'm not gonna be on TV again."

"This is different." Ray held on to Marc's shoulder. "This is different." He nudged Marc to face the reporter more directly.

Marc saw recognition on her face. He watched her say something to her little crew before the cameraman hefted the camera onto his shoulder and the guy with the boom mic slapped on a big pair of headphones. They moved toward him, the woman taking point, literally leading the way with the smaller microphone in her hand.

"Are we good?" she said to the others.

"We're hot," said the cameraman.

Ray snickered. "Now we're cooking with gas, Marc. Yes sir."

The woman was on Marc. "Lori Parapetti, KECI, Montana's News Channel. Marc Teslowski, what brings you to the entrance of the Donner Institute for Sovereign Studies two days before the Declaration Day festivities? Are you with the protesters?"

Marc recognized the formation of the camera and sound guy from his experiences with far too many roving-reporter ambushes in the last eleven months. If he wasn't actually on television right this instant, he would be by six o'clock.

There was no escape.

"I'm here to see my son. That's all."

"Has Byron Teslowski broken his silence and invited you to visit him on the Institute grounds? That's pretty big news!"

She shoved the microphone in his face. The yellow foam pop protector on the end was stained from her lipstick.

"I don't need a damn invitation," Marc said. "He's my son."

"Tell 'er, Marc," Ray said.

Parapetti shifted her attention to him. "Mister Greene, you're the editor and publisher of a white-supremacy newspaper, isn't that right? Are you and Marc Teslowski friends?"

Ray smiled, at her and for the camera. "*The Good Human* is a *Homo sapiens* supremacy newsletter, and if there's anything wrong with that, we're in a heap of trouble, and twenty-five-thousand patriotic subscribers might be a little miffed, Ms. Parapetti." He put his arm around Marc, who cringed a little by reflex. "And hell yes, I'm proud to call this hero of humanity standing next to me my friend."

Parapetti shifted back to Marc. "Mister Teslowski, are you at all disturbed by the views represented by Mister Greene's publication and the alleged militia supporting his cause, given that your son is a Sovereign?"

Marc's neck felt hot. "I'm sick of people assuming my boy is one of those freaks. He was kidnapped. The Sovereigns are holding him against his will. Everyone knows that."

"Isn't it true the Sovereign have made no demands connected with the release of Byron Teslowski?" Parapetti rolled the questions out in a well-practiced tone. "Why are they allegedly holding him if they haven't made any demands?"

Marc had a trick with reporters who pissed him off, which so far meant every reporter he'd ever met. He imagined her getting fucked in the ass while she asked her questions. Not by him. Just fucked in the ass in general.

It helped him feel like he was in a better position than them, made him feel like he was just a little bit superior. It worked quickly.

"I don't know why," he snapped. "You'd have a better

chance of asking them than I would. But so long as I'm his father and he's a minor, he belongs with me. With his mother and me. It's that simple."

She flipped again. "Mister Greene, isn't it true that your publication advocates the genocide of the Sovereign people?"

Ray's jovial expression cooled a touch.

"Ms. Parapetti, you just used what they call an oxymoron."

"Very clever, Mister Greene. Our viewers will note you didn't deny it. Let's just say for the sake of argument that Mister Teslowski's son actually was a Sovereign. Would you support, as your publication has, that Byron Teslowski, and I quote, be 'hanged at the crossroads with his own guts for a noose,' unquote?"

Marc jerked his shoulder out from under Ray's clenching hand. What the fuck?

Ray's face was red. "You city reporters, you think you can twist things around, make good people look like monsters?" Marc saw Parapetti blink when spray from Ray's mouth struck her face, but she didn't flinch beyond that.

Ray stabbed a finger at the Sovereign demonstrators and their supporters. "There's your monsters, woman! Why ain't you asking them anything, with that devil tongue of yours, in that…that harlot's mouth?"

Ray strode back toward the road. He brought up his hand and extended his middle finger for Parapetti and his crew to see.

Marc followed him automatically. The man might be crazy, but he was his ride, and Marc's stuff was at his house.

Ray didn't say anything until they got back in the car.

He started the engine and drove up the shoulder as far as he could before parked cars forced him to inch back into traffic, which was still awful.

"Marc, you listen to me," he growled. "I swear on the grave of my dead wife: the next time me or mine come to that devil's nest, Doctor motherfucking William Karl Satan Beelzebub Donner himself will know it."

He rolled down his window, stuck his head out, and screamed at the car he was trying to cut in front of.

"You wanna let me in, jackass?"

Marc looked at Ray.

"That thing she said. You said that about my boy?"

Ray pulled his head back in. He kept his focus on the car in front of him. "What? No, goddamn it. She put words in my mouth. You've said it yourself, Marc. Your boy ain't no Sovereign." He leaned on the horn. "C'mon!"

Marc nodded slowly. "Right."

From The Journal Of Nate Charters
Eleven

Our plan was to scare the shit out of Eric Finn.

At the very least, we'd send a message that someone was out to get him. In the beginning, it wouldn't matter if he knew who it was or not. That could come later.

Jason's folks were gone at least until the weekend, so he felt free to continue using the car. He drove me to the parking lot of Sunrise Import Shop late Wednesday afternoon, where we sat in the parking lot and ate Slim Jims until I spotted Eric Finn leaving work.

"There he is." I tapped Jason's shoulder.

"What a loser," Jason said. Finn got into an old black Mustang that looked like it had come off the assembly line the day before yesterday. "Fuck, nice car, though."

Finn pulled out of the parking lot. Jason started the Bonneville and followed him.

"Not too close." I slouched in the seat. I didn't want him to see that Nate Charters, the freaky kid from the tabloids, was in the car behind him. He might make a connection I didn't want made just yet.

"I got it," Jason said with a touch of impatience. "Fuckin' A Team, dude."

"Fuckin' A Team."

Finn headed down El Toro Boulevard. Jason let a car get between us.

"Don't lose him," I said.

"Yeah, right," Jason said. "I'm gonna lose sight of that."

He had a point. Finn's classic car stood out. Turned heads, even.

"Hey, he's turning into Argyle's," Jason said. "What should I do?"

"Uh..." I slouched down even farther in the seat and pulled my hoodie down over my eyes. "Go in. Get behind him."

"In the takeout line? I'll have to order!"

"So?"

"So do you have any money?"

I didn't want to move my head or draw any attention to myself on the off chance that Eric Finn would choose that very moment to glance in his rear view mirror. "Don't you?"

"Don't you?"

I groaned. "Dude! Your parents left town for a week or whatever, and they didn't, like, leave you any fucking money? Seriously?"

Jason giggled. "Nah, dude. I've got money. But you totally owe me."

"Jesus! Fine!"

We were at the menu board. The intercom crackled.

"Welcome to Argyle's. Can I get you an order of potato cheese cakes today?"

Jason lowered his voice and said to me, "Dude, what do you want?"

I went on automatic. "Argyle Deluxe, with Pony Dip. Twisty fries. Um...an orange soda."

Jason frowned. "I'm keeping track."

"Good for you."

Jason ordered. Up ahead, not even twenty feet away, Eric Finn got his food and pulled out.

"Shit! We're gonna lose him!"

Jason pulled us up to the takeout window. A bored-looking girl reached out her hand to take his money.

He looked at me instead. "What should I do?"

Finn was waiting at the driveway for traffic to clear so he could merge in. It could happen at any moment.

"Fuck! Let's just go!"

Jason glanced at the cashier. "Sorry! Not my fault!" He drove through just as Finn merged into traffic.

"Can you get him?"

Jason watched the traffic. "Hang on, dude!"

With a rebel yell, he peeled out into the lane. The Bonneville fishtailed for a split second, and my heart lurched. I realized I had a pretty tight grip on the armrest and forced myself to relax before my extraordinarily thick, sharp fingernails made a mess of the vinyl.

We survived. Finn put two cars between us.

Jason beat a rat-a-tat on the steering wheel with his palms and bounced a little in his seat. He grinned widely. "Heh! We got him." He looked at me with a face bright with glee. "This is fun, yeah?"

"Yeah." It kinda was. "But dude, we have to catch up with him. We need to figure out what we're gonna do."

Jason peered ahead. "He's going to Laguna Canyon."

I sat up a little in the seat. "That's good, yeah? Fewer chances to lose him."

"Yeah."

We were headed west, more or less, but the staggered hills of Laguna Canyon kept the setting sun out of our eyes, mostly. Before long, Laguna Canyon Road would be in twilight.

I'd be able to see just fine—my eyes soaked up light like those fancy paper towels the giant lumberjack hawked on TV soaked up water. I wasn't sure about Jason, though.

"Hey, are you okay to drive at night?"

"Pshah. Why wouldn't I be?"

I shrugged. "I don't know. Just checking."

"Chill out." Jason was still grinning. He switched on the radio, but we were already too deep in to the canyon, and it was staticky. "Poop." He shut it off.

I noticed we now just had a single car separating us from Finn. "Hey, we're catching up. Don't let him know we're following him."

"I thought we wanted him to know someone was after him?"

"I don't know. I'm not sure what we should do. I want to freak him out, but...is it a good idea for him to know it's us?"

"Dude! We're making justice, here, remember? Don't wuss out!"

I glared at him. "I'm not!" I turned back to the road ahead.

We were directly behind Finn's Ford.

"What happened to the other car?"

"They turned off, back at the art school."

"Well...put a little space between us, maybe."

Jason saluted. "*Jawohl, capitan.*"

Jason slowed down a touch. I saw that there were no cars ahead of Finn for a good ways.

Finn gunned it.

"The fuck?" Jason said.

"Go!"

Jason dropped his foot, and the Bonneville lurched forward, closing the distance between us.

Finn braked, hard. My heightened senses registered it a microsecond before Jason. We both yelped. Jason braked and glanced in his rearview mirror. Thankfully, we had a good deal of space on the road behind us, too.

"The fuck," Jason said again.

"He knows," I said. "He must know. Fuck."

Finn gave his brakes a tap and accelerated again. Jason glanced at me.

"What do I do? Should I let him go?"

Let him go?

I felt a wave of heat move up my back. The muscles of my shoulders bunched. I sat all the way up in my seat and yanked the hood off my head.

"No fucking way."

Jason nodded rapidly. "Yeah. Heh. Yeah." He closed the distance between the two cars once again, this time leaving enough room to deal with any more funny stuff.

Finn turned on his right turn signal and slowed down.

"He's gonna turn," Jason said needlessly.

"What's up there?" I saw, though. The next place to turn off the road was the vacant gravel lot used for parking during the summer arts festival.

"Oh." I got it. "Yeah, he's totally on to us."

Jason's face was hard. "Looks like we're gonna make some justice right here."

I took a deep breath, let it out, did it again. My legs jumped. My fingers ached. I curled and uncurled them, scraping my fingernails against my palms.

The parking lot was a little higher than the road. Driving by, you couldn't really see it. No one would be able to see us. And no one else would really have a reason to join our cars up there.

Gravel crunched under the Bonneville's tires as Jason navigated up the driveway and into the lot.

Finn was already parked. His headlights threw off my night vision, overwhelming my light-sensitive eyes.

Jason stopped and put on the parking brake. He squinted ahead. "He just got out of his car." He looked at me. "You good? Fueled up?"

My nostrils were flared so much, my upper lip pulled into a sneer. I pulled fast breath in and out of my nose and let my mouth hang open, the better to process scents. I didn't really have much control over any of that. It was all part of the artificial augmentations I'd inherited from dear old dad.

Right now, though, I wanted it. I needed it. I needed the reminder that I was what I was.

I'd fought monsters. I was bad ass. I was.

"I'm good," I said. "Let's go."

We got out of the car. Finn stepped out of the glare of his car's headlights, still a good twenty feet away. One good leap, for me.

His voice was calm with just a hint of disgust. "Hey, fuckers. Are you sure, totally sure, that you little shits know what you're doing?"

I didn't expect him to get the first word in. It threw me off. Jason glanced at me and picked up the slack.

"Dude, you tried to make me rear-end you. What the hell?"

Finn's lips twisted. "Right. You've been following me, kid." He looked at me. "I know who you are."

He knew I was Lina's boyfriend? This was not going the way I'd imagined it.

"You're the Sovereign kid," he said.

I usually corrected that assumption since I didn't particularly enjoy being lumped in with those guys. Right now, though, it didn't seem like the smart thing to do. I'd ride it.

"Good for you." My voice hadn't cracked for a while by then, but I was inexplicably terrified it would happen now. I was tense, nervous; my breathing wouldn't calm down. "You watch TV."

This was the guy. Right here, this was the guy who had tried to rape Lina.

He didn't seem intimidated. "Why are you here, Sovereign kid? What's the deal? Little joyride?" He stepped to his right, putting a little distance between us. More importantly, he was no longer directly in front of his headlights. I pivoted as well.

"Justice," I said.

He regarded me. "We've never met...Nick? Right?"

"I thought you said knew me?"

He scowled, spread his arms, let them drop. "I know who you are. Everybody does, kid. Doesn't mean I actually give a shit." He looked at Jason and back to me. "Now. Tell me why you and your boyfriend here were following me in that piece of shit Bonneville."

"I told you."

He lowered his voice and adopted an exaggerated somber expression to intone, "Justice..." He dropped the look and laughed. "Very impressive, Sovereign boy. Only, like I said, we've never met. What's your damage?"

"Laugh if you want," I said. "If you know about me, you know what I can do."

He laughed again. "Nick, the thing is, you don't know what *I* can do. Because we've never met. So maybe you should just get back in your little fagmobile and lay off, yeah?" He lowered his head and raised his eyebrows. "Hell, come to think of it, you don't want to tell me why you bothered with your lame *Simon & Simon* routine, I'm outta here." He turned back to his car. "Later!"

"Stop," I said.

He turned around. "Are you trying to tell me what to do? Seriously?"

"If you leave, I go to the police next."

"Fuck, go, then, man. Do as thou wilt." He smiled slightly and shook his head. "This is boring."

If he left…if he got in his car and drove away…I'd be right back where I was when I first saw him. If he left, that'd be one more asshole in the world, getting away with shit they should suffer for. Getting away with hurting people. With fucking with our lives.

Right then, this guy was Brenhurst and everyone at Tyndale Labs. Everyone at PrenticeCambrian. Every asshole who'd hassled me in school. I couldn't do a damn thing about them.

But *this* guy. Eric Finn was right here, right in front of me.

The idea of him leaving, of him thinking there wasn't a damn fucking important reason I'd called him out, of him thinking this was just some teenaged prank…

That was no way to make justice. No way. He had to stay.

I said, "Lina Porter."

He stopped. Our eyes met. His lips twitched.

"Ancient history."

"Not how I see it," I said. "It's unfinished business."

He feigned confusion. "What is?"

"What you did to her."

He tilted his head and did smile then. His eyes narrowed. "I think maybe you don't have your story straight, buddy. I didn't do anything to her."

I should have expected him to deny it, but hearing it come out of his mouth pissed me off. I stepped toward him, bent slightly at the waist, my arms out from my sides.

"You fucking tried to rape her, you piece of shit!"

He didn't back away when I advanced. His scent, under a mask of engine grease and deodorant, was as relaxed as his body language.

He looked to the sky, grinning. "Is that what she told you? Really?"

"Not just her," I said.

"Oh, sure," he said easily. "They'd stick together, that tribe. Tight little group. Everybody knows each other. Really well." He leered. "You probably know how it is if you know Lina."

He was dancing around it. That was worse than just flat-out admitting it.

"You know what you did."

I took another step toward him. We were about ten feet

apart now. I could be at his throat in an easy leap.

My fingers clenched.

He shifted a little, so his side faced me. "Nick, my boy, you're all worked up over nothing." His voice was low. If he was trying to sound dangerous to me...well, he really didn't have any idea who I was after all.

"I don't think so."

He licked his lips and nodded. "I get it. I do. You're the boyfriend, right? She's not going with that Meunetti dude anymore?" He laughed again. "Jesus. That guy has some bad hair, but she picked you? She's made some seriously bad choices since...well, you know..."

I didn't know I was going to leap.

Nails first, teeth bared, growling, that's what I did.

He slipped to the side, and I flew past to land with my feet sinking into the gravel. I whirled around, half-expecting him to be right there, but other than getting out of my way, he hadn't moved.

"This is going to be an interesting experience," he said. "I'm not bored anymore."

Jason said, "You're gonna get 'interesting,' all right, asshole."

Finn looked at Jason. "Hey, you know what? I forgot you were here."

"Jason," I said, "I'm good."

"I got your back, dude."

Finn said, "Jason, 'dude,' you really better listen to your freak boyfriend." He said to me, "You're a, whatever you are, and that's cool. I think you Sovereigns are great. But you do not want to fuck with me, Nick. Okay?"

"You tried to rape my girlfriend, asshole"

Finn adopted some sort of martial arts pose. "'Rape,' 'tried'…all a matter of interpretation, Nick. One version of the truth. Who was there? Were you?"

Why was he so fucking calm? I couldn't take it. He acted like he held all the cards, like he had the power, but he was just a fucking Norm, just a human. He didn't have shit.

"I'm gonna fucking kick your ass."

"I guess you think you have to try," he said. "C'mon, then." He waved his hand at me like he was fucking Bruce Lee or something. "C'mon!"

This wasn't like fighting Brenhurst's augmented agents at the cabin, or even like my brief scrap with Byron Teslowski. For the first time, I wanted it. I wanted to get in with him, feel his skin parting under my fingernails… I wanted him bleeding, and scared, and damn fucking sorry he'd ever even looked at my girl.

I leapt again.

Again, he slipped to the side.

My feet hit the ground earlier this time, though, and my sensorium—the collective impressions of my hearing, my sense of smell, and my hypersensitive vision—placed him behind me and to my right, so I lashed out behind me, pivoting in the gravel as I did.

He grabbed my wrist and used my own momentum to put me off balance. While I was still scrambling, he punched me in the ribs, fast and hard.

It hurt, but it was more the shock of the contact that freaked me out. He wasn't fast in the way Byron Teslowski had turned out to be that painful day we figured out he was a

Sovereign, but Finn was fucking fast for a human.

I found my feet and swiped at him. He knocked my arms away, but I saw him flinch at the contact. Fucking right, asshole. I'm strong.

Strong and stupid. Before I could get my guard up, he punched me in the stomach, probably as hard as he could. It hurt, a lot, a kind of stinging that spread into a sickening ache as the impact traveled through my abdomen muscles.

I backed off a couple of steps.

"I warned you, Nick," Finn said. "You're gonna get hurt for real if you don't stand down. Right now."

I was having a little trouble getting enough air in my lungs. "You'll…get tired…"

"Not soon enough," he said. "I'm not kidding. I know how to fight. You, you're fast and strong, but I'm here to tell you: none of that makes a difference. You're going to get the shit kicked out of you, and all because your girlfriend made up a little story, got your hackles up."

"You're a fucking liar!"

He shook his head. "You didn't know her, man. She wanted to try everything." He showed his teeth. "Such a little rebel child. Anything to piss off her daddy. "

Something, not words, came out of my throat. I dove for him again. This time he tried to kick me, but fuck if he wasn't right about this: I am fast.

Faster than he thought. I was inside of the arc of his kick before he could do anything about it, and just like that, he was down, and I was on him.

He tried to hold on to me, in a clinch, or whatever the wrestlers call it. He was right about my strength, too. Yeah, he was taller and older and maybe even heavier than me, but my muscles are simply not the same as his, or yours. They just work better.

I twisted out of his grip and pretty much by luck avoided having my balls mashed by his leg. He started to punch at my ribs and kidneys, but he didn't have a lot of room to get anything good in.

He kept moving his head back and forth. I slapped him across the face. I drew blood, three dark lines right across his cheek.

His eyes squeezed tight, and his sweat broadcast alarm when the pain hit him, then he opened his eyes and got serious. He tried to head-butt me, just like in the movies, but only succeeded in kind of brushing against my face with his cheek when I moved.

He had stubble on his face. Feeling it scrape against my skin was repulsive. I suddenly hated that I was so close to him, in such close contact. Without deliberate thought, I drew back.

He took advantage of the space to kick out with more desperation than control, and that gave him the chance he needed to twist out from under me.

Where was he going to go? Nowhere. But I still didn't want him to get back on his feet or have a chance to get control of himself.

I caught him on the back of the neck, right along his ducktail. My fingers slipped in greasy hair product. I tightened my grip. Blood slid down his neck from where my nails broke the skin.

I heard Jason yell, "Punch him, Nate. Punch him!"

He didn't sound like he was urging me on. He sounded worried.

I got it. If I kept using my nails, I could do some real damage. Dangerous stuff. His jugular vein was millimeters away from my thumb.

I rolled him over and punched him in the stomach as hard as I could. His eyes bulged. A rush of breath came from his gaping mouth, along with a spray of spit. He tried to curl up.

I fucking pummeled that fucker. His arms, his face, his head, whatever. Wherever my fists ended up, I didn't care. It was all pain. It was all justice.

Eric Finn was getting what he deserved.

I didn't see him. Not like you're seeing these words. I was running on all cylinders then, my whole sensorium driven by the slippery, sharp heat of blood. The sound of flesh on flesh. The stomach-turning crunch of cartilage. Of bone. The spray of saliva. The breath. The tears.

If I'd been more in my own head, Jason wouldn't have been able to pull me back. He yanked on my shoulder, and we both tumbled. I growled, crazy, and made a sloppy, blind grab for him, but Jason either got lucky or had good instincts because he had scrambled away.

"Dude, enough!"

The red haze cleared from my eyes a little. I wiped the sleeve of my hoodie across my face and that took care of the rest of it. My sleeve was wet.

My hands throbbed. Some of the blood there was from my knuckles.

"Enough," Jason said again. "Fuck!"

I held my hand out, nodded. I got to my feet, swayed, took a step, got steady.

Eric Finn was fucked.

He was curled up, fetal, shaking. The three cuts on his face had split open where I'd hit him again and again. Those were scars he would wear for a long time.

His lips…his eyes… You've heard the phrase, "a bloody pulp." Right? It's like a cliché.

I made that happen.

To a person.

On purpose.

I gagged. My gorge rose, and I forced it down, hot and sick. I was breathing shallow and fast. Something like a groan or a sob came out of my mouth. Snot ran onto my upper lip, warm and slick on my tongue.

"We gotta go," Jason said. "We gotta go. Is he…fuck!"

I walked over to Finn, who was still curled tight on his side. The eye I could see was nearly swollen shut, but I could feel him looking at me.

He put words together. His lips were fucked up, and I had to have broken some of his teeth, but I think I heard him right.

What he said was, "Thank you."

What he said next was, "I gave her what she wanted."

From The Journal Of Nate Charters
Twelve

I got into the car. Jason got us out of there.

He drove us back toward El Toro. I sat in the passenger seat and shook.

My hands hurt. My stomach felt like it was gnawing on my other organs with a slow grind of acidic teeth. There were a couple of Slim Jims left, but the thought of eating anything, no matter how much my spent metabolism told me I needed it, made me dizzy with nausea.

Jason pulled into a gas station, near a pay phone. He opened the door and turned to me before he got out. "Don't...don't move, man. Don't. Okay?"

I nodded.

The fluorescent lights of the gas station were so bright. I closed my eyes against the glare, but that wasn't good: a movie of red and black and heat and pain played against the inside of my eyelids. I couldn't stand it.

I settled for just keeping my head down and staring at the floor of the car.

There were specks of blood on my shoes.

I heard Jason drop coins into the phone and press three buttons. Breathlessly, he anonymously called in a badly beaten man in the festival parking lot on Laguna Canyon Road, then hung up. I heard his coins falling into the coin-return slot, since you didn't have to pay to call 911, but he didn't seem to care. He got back in the car and put us back on the road.

"Someone will get him," he said. "He'll be fine."

"Good." The sound of my voice seemed very, very far

away from my ears. That was crazy. I had really, really good ears. Right now, they felt like conch shells were strapped to the sides of my head. "Good."

Jason hunched forward and hovered over the steering wheel while he drove. He kept his eyes on the road. "Man. I knew about it, but…fuck, Nate." He shook his head. "I didn't know you were gonna…"

"I didn't either," I said. The roaring was starting to quiet down some. "I swear. I was just gonna freak him out. I didn't know we were gonna fight. Not like that."

"He's more badass than we thought he'd be," Jason said, "not that it did him any fucking good." His voice didn't have any of the enthusiasm he'd expressed on the drive out. "What happened to you, man?"

"He…I just…"

I didn't know.

"I don't know."

I felt like I didn't know much of anything, really. Situation normal for the boy freak.

Why had Finn seemed so…guiltless?

Jason took his eyes off the road long enough to look quickly at me. His face was pale beneath his teen beard. "Jesus fuck, look at you. You're a fuckin' mess, dude. How're you gonna get past your mom?"

"Garage door, right to my room, or right to the shower. Do it all the time."

What did Finn mean, what he said, right before I left him back there? How could he even think of fucking with me, when I'd just kicked the shit out him? Fuck, I was pretty sure I was in shock, and I wasn't the one bleeding all over the gravel.

How could I find out what he meant?

"Let's go to Lina's first," I said.

"Bogus idea, dude."

"Yeah." I nodded. "C'mon. I should see her. It's been since Friday. We should talk."

"I don't know about that. Seriously, dude, you look like you just walked out of a Wes Craven movie. Scary shit. Seriously."

I sighed, and it damn near turned into a sob. I clamped my mouth shut and looked out the window, away from Jason. I took a few deep breaths. I was so tired. I'd burned through just about everything I had in that fight. It was like Kirby Lake all over again.

Only this time, I'd played the part of my father. At least Eric Finn's guts were still on the inside of his body.

I shuddered. My mouth filled with saliva, a threatening precursor to puking whatever bile was left in my gut. I swallowed and took a few more deep breaths.

"She's seen worse," I finally said.

Jason shook his head. "You shouldn't see her."

"Gotta."

"What are you gonna tell her?" His voice went up, volume and pitch. "She'll know, one look at you. She'll know what went down."

"I know." I closed my eyes, snapped on the fight, opened them up again. "We have to talk. I have to ask her about some stuff."

"Oh, no. Get out. You—you're not buying that shit, are you? Dude, the fucker was trying to psych you out, man. It's all part of his bullshit!" He glanced at me again. "You don't have to ask Lina anything, Nate. Fuck."

I closed my eyes; looked at the ceiling of the car; opened my eyes. "Are you gonna take me? 'Cause I'm just gonna get on my bike and go there anyway if you take me home." I laughed; it was pitiful. I looked at him. "You're seriously gonna make me ride my bike after all of this?"

Jason expelled a long breath and licked his lips. "She's not gonna like it."

"You'll take me, though. Right?"

He nodded without looking at me. We didn't say anything else until he parked at the curb in front of her house, when I asked him to go get her. The way I looked, if her folks or brother answered the door, all hell would break loose.

I waited in the car, watching. Lina answered the door herself. She was dressed in gray sweats and a Care Bears T-shirt, probably pretty much ready to relax before bed and cute as hell.

It was terrifying to see her.

As she followed Jason down her lawn, I stepped out of the car.

Lina saw me, stopped, and actually took a step back. Her mouth fell open.

"What…did they come after you? Is it them?"

The fear poured off of her. I didn't understand.

And then I did. She thought this was to do with the people who'd caused us grief last year, the people who came after us in Kirby Lake with augmented killers and who continued to come after my mother and me with lawyers.

It threw me, how freaked out she was.

"No. No, no, nothing like that," I said quickly. "I'm okay. It wasn't them. It was…"

Her relief came and went. "Then what the hell, Nate? You look horrible! You're…bloody!"

"Lina…" My legs shook. I think the term is "wobbled," and right then, I clearly and fundamentally understood what that meant. My arms felt like rubber. I couldn't tell if I was dangerously fatigued or just scared to say anything else to her.

But I had to. Tonight was all about "had to."

"I saw him. I saw Eric Finn."

"You what?"

"I saw him."

Her face turned hard. She kept her focus on my body.

Her words came out just louder than breath. Plenty loud for me.

"Is he all right?"

I felt like my legs might stop working. I reached back and braced myself with a hand on the roof of the car.

"Is…he…*all right*?" I repeated.

The stone in her face was breaking apart under the force of her anger. "Yes! You're standing here, Nate; I know you're fine. I know what you can do, and I know you're fine; you're…" She indicated me with a thrust of her right hand, quick and sharp. "You're here. So what about Eric? Is he all right, or are you in deep fucking shit?"

She used his first name. "He's gonna be okay. We called…Jason called…"

Her eyes widened, and her mouth opened and closed. She glanced at Jason and back to me. "Called? As in, 'called 911'?" She shook her head slowly. "Did you actually fight him, Nathan? Did you actually pick a fucking fight with him? You?"

I didn't say anything. Shame wrestled with indignation at feeling shame. I was silent a beat too long, apparently.

She took a step toward me.

"Answer me!"

She was so angry. Why was she so angry? Why was this going like this? What was happening?

Why was she so angry at me?

"Yeah. We fought." She jerked away with a grunt. I pushed through. "I didn't pick a fight with him, Lina. He pushed me. He's…he's an asshole!"

"No shit, you…idiot!" Her hands were clenched, her arms stiff at her sides. "So you thought you could just…fuck!" She grimaced at the bloody smears on my sweatshirt. "Did you fucking cut him?"

"No, I…" Something clicked off in my head. I shut my mouth and looked away from her; took a harsh, hard breath.

"Lina, why do you care? The guy tried to rape you!" I sniffed. I wasn't crying, not exactly. Things were just so intense, I felt like I was saturated. Things were bound to leak, if I didn't flat out collapse in a flood first. "Didn't he?"

She flared again. "What do you mean, 'didn't he?' You've obviously got the whole fucking story—who told you? How'd you find him? Never mind; it doesn't fucking matter. What the fuck do you mean, 'didn't he?'"

You know how you feel when you're running really fast, but you don't keep your body straight enough? Your center of gravity's all off, and your momentum starts to pull your head closer and closer to the ground. All of a sudden: wham, you're doing a shoulder roll on the pavement, full tilt.

That's how my head felt. That's what my thoughts were like. My feelings. I couldn't stop. I was going to hit the ground, and I couldn't stop.

"What were you like back then, anyway?" I said. "Why would you even be with a guy like that?"

Full tilt. No way to stop.

Wham.

Her jaw dropped and her eyes went wide. For a split second, her face went slack, like all of the muscles had just given up, or couldn't organize themselves.

It didn't take long for the hurt and anger and betrayal to take over, and that's when Lina—*my* Lina—cracked and fell away from her. I saw it in her face, in the way her eyes reflec- ted or, I guess, didn't reflect anything at all when she looked at me.

"God, Nate. You must be right. I must have been crazy. What was I thinking?" She was right in front of me then, right up in my face. I could smell the Lina scent, but just barely, all but lost under adrenaline and rage. Her eyes were rimmed and glistening, but the tears refused to fall past her lower lids. Refused to let go.

"Lina..."

"No, I know! What kind of a little slutty cunt was I, right? Jesus, he's like, what, fifty years older than me, right? All sly and slick and shit! Why would I do that? Why would I do him?"

Do him? "You didn't..." No. She was pissed. She was trying to hurt me.

"Didn't I? Are you sure? How do you fucking know,

Nate? Who was I? Huh? Who was I? Maybe I did! Maybe he didn't have to fucking drug my sorry ass to get me to fuck him, huh? Huh? What do you think, Nate?"

"Stop it," I said. My tears were not as strong as hers. They fell down my cheeks. She couldn't be serious. She couldn't be.

She pushed me, both arms, palms flat on my chest. My back was against the car, hard against me.

"Why should I," she growled. "Why should I stop? You didn't! You went right ahead and did whatever you wanted, Nate. Right? Who gives a fuck what I want? Right?" She pushed me again. "God! You asshole!"

"Stop it!"

She pushed me again. "Fuck you!"

I pushed her back.

She stumbled a few steps before her balance failed. She sat down fast and hard on the grass of her front yard.

That was the same moment her father came through the front door.

"What the hell is this? Nate?"

I looked at Lina, on the ground. Her head was turned to the side, looking at nothing.

Graham Porter came down the steps of their porch and crouched behind his daughter. He put his hands on his shoulders.

He looked angry. Sure.

But the thing that sent me down the street, running away in the true Charters tradition as fast as my exhausted but still allegedly better-than-human legs could take me? The thing that had me practically choking on my snot and tears as

I put streets between me and Lina and Jason and him?
The other thing I saw on his face.
The disappointment.

From The Journal Of Nate Charters
Thirteen

I didn't get far.

For one thing, I just couldn't run for long. My augmented reflexes and strength, as well as, no doubt, the energy required to process the information from my extra-sensitive senses, are paid for with a fast metabolism. After the fight with Eric Finn and the stress fighting with Lina, I didn't have the energy.

For another, Jason found me. He pulled the Bonneville over, opened the passenger-side door from the inside, and nodded to me when I got in.

He didn't say a word until we got to my house.

"You all right?"

"Nope."

His eyebrows jumped, and he nodded.

I needed to know my options. "When do your parents come back?"

"Tomorrow afternoon."

"Can I call you tomorrow morning, if I need to?"

The look on his face told me I was pushing the limits of our friendship. I'd asked him a lot tonight.

"Yeah." He didn't look at me.

"Thanks," I said. I dragged myself out of the car.

After Jason drove off, I stood in the driveway. I wasn't sure what to do.

The front door opened. My mother said, "I thought I heard a car. Are you coming in?"

I turned toward her and got another shocked reaction from my haggard, bloody appearance. She recovered quickly, though. She pursed her lips, glanced up and down the street in as much as she could see it from where she stood, and waved her hand.

"Get in the house."

I slipped past her and fell on the couch. She closed the door and turned around. She shook her head. "Is anyone... Nathan, is anyone seriously hurt?"

"No one's dead," I muttered.

"Then get yourself off of the couch; you're filthy. Take a shower. Eat something. Or the other way around; I don't care. When you're done, we'll talk."

She sat down on the loveseat and directed her attention to the television. It was clear she was pissed, but my mother could be almost offensively pragmatic sometimes.

So I ate half a package of pastrami, most of a block of cheddar, a few pieces of bread, and a handful of pickles. I washed it down with hard swallows of milk right from the carton. If she was going to ignore me until I did what she said, I was fine with doing things she wouldn't approve of for the sake of taking care of myself.

Not an unusual state of affairs for us, really. But not one that had worked out all that well so far, either.

Eating and showering gave me time to stabilize and think. By the time I was fueled and clean, I had an idea of what I needed to do. It sucked that I'd need her help for it.

I presented myself to her in the living room.

"Okay," I said.

She got up, turned off the television, and sat back down on the loveseat. She pointed to the couch. "Sit down."

I sat down.

"What's going on, Nathan? Who did you hurt?"

That put me off, right out of the gate. Bad enough when Lina had done it.

Aw, fuck. Lina. What kind of conversation was she having with her parents tonight? How much did her dad hear?

"Are you going to tell me, or will I find out when the police arrive?"

I wondered if they would. Would Finn report this and risk incriminating himself? What was the statute of limitations on attempted rape?

"I got into a fight," I said. "Why don't you ask me how I am?"

"Because you're you," she said flatly. "With who, and why?"

"A guy named Eric Finn tried to rape Lina, a year or so before we met. I found out about it."

She stared at me with the mixture of disgust and anger she had practiced so often in the last year or so.

"So you decided to fight him."

"No," I said. "It's not like that. And did you hear me? The guy tried to rape Lina."

"I heard you. I'm concerned about tonight, right now. Who..." She sighed. "I can't believe I'm asking it, but who started it?"

"I—I'm not sure. He said some stuff. I...I lost my temper."

She regarded me. "Your temper."

"What?"

"I'm still not used to you having one," she said. "Before...you were a different kid, Nathan. A good kid."

This wasn't going so hot.

"Before." I tried to keep the irritation out of my voice; like it or not, I needed her on my side right now. "Before I knew the truth, you mean."

She shrugged.

"So you fought with this boy. And he lost. How badly is he hurt, Nathan? What can I expect to be dealing with, here?"

"You?"

She leaned forward. "Yes, me, Nate. It's me who'll have to deal with his parents. They'll probably sue, but I guess they can get in line, right? They might press charges. Do you know how serious this is?"

"Do I know—?" No, this was not going well at all. "First of all, you won't be hearing from his parents. Eric Finn isn't a kid, mom. He's, I don't know, like twenty, twenty-one."

Her eyes narrowed, but she didn't say anything, so I kept going.

"If he says anything about me, I say something about him trying to rape Lina. He'd be stupid to do it."

"Does Lina intend to press charges? You have to tell me everything about it, Nate, so I know where we stand."

"I don't know."

"Well, what has she said? Hell, what do her parents have to say?"

"I don't know!"

She studied me for a moment. "Oh. You had a fight."

"She just told me about this whole thing a few days ago," I admitted. "She told me to let it go."

"You couldn't."

"Hell no! What was I supposed to do?"

"Off the top of my head, not pick a fight with the guy." Her voice got an edge. "They won't protect you, you know."

She meant the Sovereign.

"That's not why I did it."

"No," she said. "You did it because you could, I bet." A bit of anxiety mixed with the hard anger on her face. "You have to be better than this, Nathan."

She looked down. "Tomorrow morning, we'll call Drake Ottman and fill him in. Hopefully, we can talk to him before the police come around." She looked up. "If they do."

She scratched the sides of her head with her hands. "We'll have to figure out how this plays into everything else. Once Brenhurst's people get hold of this, we're going to be at a big disadvantage..."

"No." She was so concerned with the legal shit, she wasn't even paying attention to me. "Mom. No."

"No, what?"

"No," I said again. "You...you're right. I need to..." I faltered.

"What?"

"I need to figure this out," I said. "I've been feeling...I don't know. Less in control, I guess. I've been so angry... It's like it's always just, right there, waiting for something to happen, waiting to come out."

"What do you mean?"

I dropped my head, hands on my knees. I probably looked a lot like she had just a minute before. That familial similarity wasn't something I was all that happy about just then, so I moved my hands to the couch cushions. Anything to put some difference between us.

"I mean I think I'm losing it," I said. "I think—I think I'm getting to be more like him."

She scowled. "Like your father."

"Yeah."

"I don't know."

I grabbed a lungful of air and shot it out through pursed lips. It was time to spring my plan on her.

"I want to find him. I think I need his help."

"Andrew's help?" She frowned and laughed. "I don't think so."

"Why not? He's been dealing with this for a long time, right? I think he could tell me, give me some tips. Make sure I don't lose it."

She shook her head. "He's crazy, Nathan. Do you understand? He's not well." Her mouth was a thin line. Her nostrils flared. "He's probably dangerous. Even if we knew where he was."

"We could start with Denver," I said. "He helps him sometimes, right? He might know—"

"Absolutely not."

I stood up. "You can't say that!"

She kept her seat and looked up at me. Her eyes were like cold metal.

"The answer is no."

I bounced on the balls of my feet while we looked at each other. My breath came in short bursts. God, I wanted to cry. I couldn't wait to go to bed so I could do exactly that.

This first.

"You owe me," I said.

Her eyes flashed. "Careful, Nathan."

"I didn't ask for any of this," I said. "None of it. And you...you lied to me about all of it." My voice went up in pitch and volume. "All of it!"

"I'm not doing this with you again," she said.

"Tough! You lied about my dad, you lied about me, to me... If Brenhurst hadn't forced me and Byron out of town, you'd probably still be lying about it.

"You totally *do* owe me, Mom." I held out my hands. "I just want your help finding him. That's all."

She had caught on something. "Forced you? That's a pretty self-serving way for you to think of it, isn't it? No one forced you to sneak away, Nathan."

"He was going to do shit to Byron! He was on to us!"

"You should have come to me," she said. "If you had, everything could have been avoided." Her face darkened. Was she thinking about her own kidnapping by Brenhurst and his pet monsters? "Nothing needed to happen the way it did. It happened that way because of what *you* did."

"Oh, okay." I realized I was having the third fight of the night. It was almost funny. "Sure. So if I'd come to you with Byron that night, you would have made it all better, right? You would have told me the truth then?" I laughed. "Sure. Right."

She didn't answer immediately. She just looked at me, like I was some weird thing standing in her living room.

Well, fuck.

I was.

That was the whole fucking thing.

Finally, she said, "We are not going to look for your

father. He is out of his mind, Nathan. Don't you understand that? He's not a…person anymore." Her face relaxed into something a little more imploring. "He's of no use to you, Nathan. You have to depend on yourself."

"That's been a great plan so far," I said.

She acted like she hadn't heard me. "Or the Sovereigns. They've offered to take you in." She was thinking fast. "Byron's already there. If you accepted their…asylum…the police couldn't touch you."

I couldn't believe my inhumanly sensitive ears.

"What? Now you want me to run to them? Are you kidding me, Mom?"

"Obviously I'd hoped to settle all of this in court, make them pay for what they did to you, and yes, Nathan, what they did to your father." She raised her eyebrows and her hands in an expressive shrug. "Whatever you did to this idiot tonight has shot that to hell. You have to accept that. We're lucky if we make it through the night without a knock on the door."

I shook my head.

"Finn's not going to talk." Not tonight, anyway. They'd have to give him something for the pain while they cleaned him up.

I had tonight. I had tomorrow morning.

She seemed to read my thoughts.

"How badly did you hurt him, Nathan? Tell me."

"I didn't use my claws," I said. "Jason stopped me."

"Jason was there?" That triggered a new flare of angry astonishment.

I nodded. "Yep."

She bit her lip, closed her eyes, and rubbed her temples. "Another family dragged into our shit." She opened her eyes and shook her head. "Frank Talbot is such a bastard, too...." She looked back at me. "So you didn't use your claws. I'm asking again: how badly is he hurt?"

"He's beat up," I said. "Pretty badly. That's why I don't think he'll talk tonight. They'll have to, like, sedate him."

She had that my-son-is-a-stranger look on her face again.

"I don't know what to do with you any more, Nathan. I don't."

I'd been pissed off at my mother for nearly a year. Our relationship had suffered, big time. Finding out your only parent has been lying about your origins as the mutant son of your artificially augmented, insane father...pretty much keeping you in the dark your entire life, that'll do it.

But I tell you what, it never didn't suck to see that look on her face.

"Just, like, help me, Mom. I don't like what's been happening. With me and my stuff. I don't."

"Andrew Charters can't help you," she said.

I shook my head, hard. "I know it's a long shot, Mom. If it wasn't for this...I couldn't care less about him." I wished that was true. "And fine, I don't know if he can do anything for me. But he's the only one on the entire planet who has any idea what this is like!"

There was some sympathy in her voice now. "You don't know that. The people at the Institute—"

"Fuck them! Do you seriously trust them?" I knew she didn't.

"Honestly, Nathan, I don't know. But they've been help-ing us, all along." When I opened my mouth, she held up her hand. "Whether it's more to serve them than us, I don't know...but they've been helping us. Why not find out?"

I realized that this wasn't going to go anywhere. She was going to continue trying to play parent, only her idea of par-enting was now apparently pushing my problems off on the fucking Sovereigns. I was pretty sure their number-one con-cern was how my particular case could help them, not so much how they could help me.

I already felt like I was their puppet in the whole legal thing with PrenticeCambrian and the government and the Teslowskis. My mother wanted to actually put me someplace where they could literally pull my strings any way they wanted.

Parent of the Year, second year running.

I was on my own.

It was a calming realization, in a way.

"Can I think about it?"

"Sleep on it," she said. "I can see you're dead on your feet; one of us will sleep tonight. Tomorrow morning, assum-ing you're right about...things...we'll have a chance to work out a plan."

She lowered her head and kept her eyes on me. "The plan will not include finding your father, Nathan. I hope you understand why."

I sighed. "Fine, Mom." I turned to walk toward the hall-way, and my bedroom. "Maybe if I could talk to Byron."

"Maybe it can be arranged." She was already sounding more relaxed.

I nodded.

"Nathan," she said, "I understand you're worried. God knows, after what you've told me tonight, I'm worried too. We have to be so careful, though. You understand what's at stake, I know you do."

I didn't give a fuck what was at stake, beyond figuring out my own shit.

"Yeah," I said. "Yeah, I do." I took a step back. "I'm gonna go to bed."

She nodded and looked away. "All right. Try not to worry. We'll figure something out."

I waited a beat, just to test her. She'd stopped wishing me good night a few months after she'd stopped saying she loved me.

That was fine.

Her silence helped me.

From The Journal Of Nate Charters
Fourteen

The police didn't come to our door in the middle of the night. If they came by Thursday morning, I wasn't around to find out. I called Jason and woke him up at four a.m.; by four-thirty, I had snuck out of the house and met him at the Gas 'n' Sip down the street.

The heat was on in the Bonneville. It felt good.

"Dude." Jason looked tired. "This is it for a while."

I felt like I should, I don't know, clasp him on the shoulder in a manly fashion or give him a hug or something. That wasn't our style, so much, so I settled for a somber nod. "I know. Thanks."

He shrugged it off, dropped the car into gear, and popped the parking brake. "So this time I get to go to Kirby Lake."

"This time isn't like the last time."

"Guess so," he said. "So, you think your mom's friend is just gonna be cool with you showing up on his door? Won't he just call her to come get you?"

"Probably." I looked out the window, feeling glum. The last time I'd made this trip, Lina had been driving. Things had been shitty then, too, but at least she was with me.

"So why bother?"

"I'm counting on Denver being on my side. After all, he's been watching out for my dad all these years. He even kept the fact of my dad being alive from my mom."

"What good's that going to do if your mom just ends up scooping you up?"

I scowled. This wasn't a great time for Jason to start

being all reasonable. "Even if she does, I'm hoping my being up there, like, already, will, like, force the issue. Y'know?"

"Oh."

Jason got up on the freeway. I turned on the radio. He drove, I changed the station when commercials came on or the morning DJs got to be too lame. Miles passed like that.

We were in the foothills, starting to climb up the 330, when I had to ask, "So...uh...what happened after I... y'know. Left. Last night."

After I ran away.

Jason grimaced. "Not a whole lot. Lina's dad scooped her up and got her inside. She gave me a pretty nasty look."

"She didn't say anything?"

"Nope."

"Okay."

I felt like Jason's "I told you so" was a cartoon anvil floating in the air above my head and I had just until the Merry Melodies music cue before the thing squashed me, accordion style.

He didn't say it. He drove, and made a little show of drumming along with the radio with his fingers on the steering wheel.

So I said it.

"You called it, huh?"

"Hm?"

"You told me I shouldn't see her. You called it."

He coughed a laugh. "Well, duh, dude."

"Yeah."

"You let that guy get to you," he said.

"I guess."

He glanced at me quickly. "What, you're still freaking out? You still think she, what, faked the whole thing?"

That was crazy. "No! I mean, shit, there were witnesses and stuff. Everybody knows what happened."

"Then, dude, what's your problem?" He looked fed up. "Why are you fucking this up?"

I looked away from him. "I lost it."

"Fuckin' A. I wish I'd never pushed you to go after that guy. If I'd known you were gonna fuckin' whale on him like that..."

"Dude, I didn't even know! He pushed me!"

"And you couldn't just walk away?"

"That's pretty funny, coming from you." Jason was well known for acting so batshit crazy, he'd been seen intimidated linebackers.

He shook his head. "Different, dude. When's the last time you remember me actually getting into a fight?"

Well, fuck me.

"I can't remember."

"It was freshman year," he said. "Norman Raley—remember him?"

His whole family moved away after his mother killed herself right before our sophomore year.

"Yep."

"That kid was so fucked up, he wouldn't back down. I didn't have a choice." Jason frowned. "Still kicked his ass." He didn't look like he relished the memory.

"I didn't have a choice, either," I said.

He laughed again. "Oh, c'mon. Norman Raley jumped me and started throwing punches. That rockabilly faggot...all

he did was, what, say you were worse than Car or some shit."
He looked at me sideways. "You totally had a choice, dude.
Don't even."

"That's why I need to find my dad," I mumbled.

"You think you're going crazy. Right." Jason sighed.
"Seriously?"

"I don't know," I said. "I just…more and more, I just get
so…angry. And it's like I can't see straight. I can't think. I
just wanna…lash out."

I looked at my hands. My knuckles were bruised; they
hurt, but that wouldn't last much longer. I healed fast,
another benefit from my share of dad's augmented genes.

"The way I am," I said, "it's not good. I could do…worse
things than I did to Eric Finn."

Jason looked thoughtful. "Your dad—he totally smoked
one of those dudes with his bare feet, right?"

Ripped out an augmented PrenticeCambrian agent's
guts with his dirty toenails while the guy held him off the
ground by his wrists, to be exact.

"Yep."

I could still call up the way it had smelled.

"So…fuck, dude, what if your dad's worse now? What if
he's all-the-way nuts?"

Worse, the memory of the smell didn't seem nearly so
bad as it used to. Sometimes, I revisited the memory like it
wasn't even a full-on horror show.

Sometimes, the memory of the smell of that guy's blood
and guts and raw shit falling out of his body made my mouth
water a little.

I shuddered.

"If my dad's all-the-way nuts," I said, "then I'm fucked. I'll do whatever my mom wants. I'll go live with the fucking Sovereigns."

"With that Byron dude."

"Yeah."

"That guy was a pussy," Jason said.

I had to laugh. "You caught him at a bad time."

He laughed, too. "Fucker was up your ass since grade school, but he finds out he's a Sovereign and it's all, 'Oh, Nate, let's be friends, and hey, can you save me from the crazy mad-scientist guy?'" Jason snorted. "I don't care what he can do. Dude's a pussy."

I let it go. I wasn't sure if Byron had done the right thing for himself. I just knew it wasn't the right thing for me.

I'd spent my whole life wishing I could be a normal kid. Just because I now knew there was no chance of that didn't mean I wanted to throw in with people who insisted on being treated differently. That was nuts.

We got to Kirby Lake, which is about a mile up in the mountains east of Los Angeles, around eight o'clock. There was snow on the curbs and street corners.

"It's gonna be cold out there." I had my sweatshirt and a jacket, but for shoes I'd just thrown on my high top sneakers. They were canvas; I'd have to watch I didn't get them wet.

"Took forever to get up here," Jason groused. "Which way to this guy's house?"

I told him, and he got us there, a woodsy street where the houses were nearly obscured by the trees around and between them.

I didn't see Denver's van in his driveway. Just some old

junky sportscar. I knew that couldn't be his.

"Shit."

"What?"

"I don't think he's home."

"Oh."

I thought about it. "Hold on."

I got out of the car. It was even colder than I'd expected. Snow on the ground, a mile above sea level—I should be a weatherman.

I knocked on the front door. I noticed a fence of painted wood between his house and the one to the right; it looked new and out of place. The big luxury car in the driveway next door looked new, too.

I knew that my dad sometimes hung out at Denver's in the colder months. I hoped the rich new neighbors hadn't spooked him off.

I knocked again.

Nothing.

There was no one home.

Where would Denver Colorado go, first thing in the morning?

I walked back to the car and got in.

"He's not home. Let's hang out."

Jason huffed. "Dude, I can't."

"Just a few minutes."

"No. It took, like, way longer to get up here than I thought it would. My parents are coming home today, remember? I have to get back before they do." He blinked. "Fuck, I have to get back before they call to tell me they're at the airport."

"When's that?"

"Like, eleven-thirty."

"Oh."

Given the morning traffic Jason would hit, that wasn't a lot of time.

"Nate. Dude," he said. "You should just come back with me."

"Huh? No way!"

"Look, man. We came up here; dude's not home. It's a sign. You should just...play it like your mom wants to."

I stared at him. "What'd you do with my friend?"

He shook his head. "Seriously, dude. I mean...last night...all the trouble you're already in...you said it yourself: this guy will probably call your mother as soon as he sees you anyway, right?"

"But I'll have—"

"Just come home, Nate."

I didn't need hypersenses to know that Jason was concerned about me. Worried, even. It warmed me.

But to go back now, when Denver Colorado was probably just out buying donuts or something...worse, to have to face my mother when she figured out I had skipped out and come here, just like last time...to have to eat crow and put myself in her hands...

No way.

"I'll have all that time," I said, "from when he calls her until she gets here. I can, like, plead my case, or whatever."

He shook his head. "I gotta go."

"I gotta stay."

He looked exasperated. "Dude, I can't just leave you up

here!"

I shook my head. "It's cool, Jase. Seriously. You've gone above and beyond. Go."

He looked miserable. "I gotta."

"It's cool."

"What are you gonna do?"

"I'll hang out. I'll wait. Denver will show up; I'll surprise him, piss him off, we'll have a few laughs, shoot some hoops, whatever, my mom'll come up, we'll go to dinner..." I grinned at him. "It'll be great."

"You should come with me."

Now I did clasp him on the shoulder. It was as awkward as I'd guessed, and I let go quickly. "Nope." I got out of the car. "Thanks, dude. I owe you fifty billion favors."

"Fuckin' right you do." He looked up at Denver's house, then back at me. "Be careful. You have change to call your mom, just in case your guy doesn't come around?"

I nodded. "I learned my lesson from yesterday."

That made him laugh, but there wasn't much joy in it. "Like hell."

"Oh, hey, I get it. Nice one. Subtle." I tapped the roof. "I'll call you when I get back."

"All right. Late."

"Late." I shut the passenger door. Jason pulled out and was lost from sight pretty quickly. The Bonneville's exhaust made my nose run.

Plus, it was fucking cold.

From The Journal Of Nate Charters
Fifteen

I hung out at Denver's for about twenty minutes. Whenever I heard a car coming, I turned my back on the road and acted like I had just knocked on the door. I didn't want anyone to wonder why the funny-looking teenager was hanging around the crippled sculptor's house, and hey, by the way, didn't he look like that freaky Nate Charters from *The Weekly World News?*

I started to think Denver wasn't coming back any time soon.

It was going to look kinda weird if any of those passing cars came back the other way and still saw me there.

I sniffed, and my nostrils cleared for a breath or two. The air was cold across my sinuses.

It carried a message, too.

It was him.

My father. He'd been here.

I wanted to slap myself on the forehead. He'd been here. Right there, pretty much right where I'd been loitering.

How long ago?

I didn't have a reliable frame of reference for my dad's scent. It was like my own, in a way, but more pungent, riper. If I had a better idea of how much stronger, I might be able to guess how long ago he'd been there. As it was, though, I didn't even want to guess. The olfactory messages were too vague, confusing.

But he had been there.

On a whim, I slipped around the left side of the house. I found Denver's trashcans under an overhang of wooden planks coming off the roof.

I glanced toward the street. Nothing. My ears didn't detect any traffic. The few fir trees between the street and my position might obscure me, too.

I took the metal lid off one of the trashcans. It was almost full inside, but right on top was a white trash bag, the right size for, like, a kitchen trashcan.

I'd taken out the trash enough times to recognize the bag was the same brand that my mother bought. It seemed fresh; it was still a little puffy from captured air from when it had been tied shut.

The FBI went through people's trash to find counterfeiters and killers and stuff. Would I be able to learn anything from Denver Colorado's trash?

I really hated trash. Because of my sniffer.

Whatever. I untied the bag.

Yep. Smelled like old garbage. I gagged and flinched automatically.

The thing with my crazy senses, though, is that once I've experienced the, I don't know, the big picture—the "mighty brush" version of things—if I concentrate a little, I can kind of separate things out. Sort of like putting each of the sounds, or in this case scents, in their own little boxes in my brain, so I could get past the really strong stuff and focus on sorting out the rest.

I scrunched up my face, took a couple of big breaths through my mouth, and turned back to the trash.

Bam.

Ratty, filthy, shitty old clothes under some scraps that looked like the crap you scrape off your dinner plate. A flannel shirt. A pair of dark blue slacks, like what a workman (or Eric Finn, said a dark part of my brain) would wear. A torn-up, frayed cable-knit sweater.

It all totally reeked of my dad.

These were my dad's clothes. Or, I guess, they had been.

This was just like a cop show. I giggled a little, putting the "crime scene" together in my head. Andrew Charters had been here, recently, and when he left, he was either naked or dressed in new clothes…or at the very least, different clothes from the ones he'd had on when he arrived.

That meant something.

What?

I deflated a little. Really, all it had to mean was that every now and then, Denver probably picked up some dis-cards at the Goodwill or wherever, and my dad swapped them for the clothes he'd worn sleeping in the woods for the last however long.

So this "evidence" told me my dad, wherever he was, didn't look as homeless as he probably usually did.

That didn't really help me for shit.

Fuck, but those clothes were filthy. I didn't really want to touch them, but I felt like it would be stupid to not invest-igate a little more of the trash.

I snuck back toward the front of the house and found a fallen branch about as long as my forearm. Perfect.

I stripped the leaves off, which left a sappy, green smell on my hands that, given the circumstances, I could hardly mind. Back at the trashcan, I poked through the clothes and moved them to one side.

Under the shirt was a semi-transparent plastic produce

bag like you get at the grocery store. It was full of hair. Knotted, clumpy, long, salt-and-pepper hair.

"Holy…"

I forgot about how gross everything was and snatched the bag out of the trash can with my bare hands. I yanked it open. My father's scent hit me like heat from an open oven.

I coughed. My throat clenched up. It wasn't a terrible smell—it was too familiar, too much like me to be flat-out offensive—but it was so strong! My eyes watered.

I remembered the one and only time I'd seen my father, a little less than a year ago, not more than a few blocks from where I was standing, at my grandmother's cabin. He'd had a beard that looked like it had jumped off of Grizzly Adams, rolled around in a pigsty, and then latched onto my dad's face. His hair had been long and tangled, all, what's it called, dreadlocks, like a reggae guy.

All that hair. It was mostly in the bag in my hand now.

Denver Colorado had given my dad a haircut.

And bought him clothes.

That probably didn't happen too often, based on how the guy had looked when I saw him last year.

Why had it happened…when? Yesterday?

The fresh trash bag cinched it. My dad had been here yesterday.

I put the hair bag back in the trash and put the lid back on the can, thinking.

Where were they, now? When were they coming back?

I sighed. I couldn't wait here forever. It was almost nine o'clock. By now, my mother was up, and pissed. She may have called Denver already. She may be on her way up here—

she knew I wanted to find my dad, and where else but here would I go?

I was lousy at running away. I kept going to the same place. But hell, that was where the action was always going to be, apparently.

Point was, I couldn't just stand around outside Denver Colorado's house. Someone would notice. There was no *not* noticing me.

Frowning, I threw my sweatshirt hood over my head and, lacking any other direction, walked back to the front of the house.

Once again, I noticed the funky new wooden fence between Denver's place and his neighbor's. It needed about three winter freezes before it didn't stick out like a sore thumb.

I stuck out like a sore thumb, too.

Nine o'clock. No Denver, no Andrew Charters, and my mother was probably on her way here right now, driving like the devil. Maybe she'd catch the same traffic Jason was worried about, but she'd be here eventually.

Maybe they were in town? If my dad had fresh clothes, a shave, a haircut, he'd look like anybody. He didn't share my unusual features. Maybe they were just having breakfast?

I didn't really want to be noticed, but with my hood up, maybe I could just skirt through town. It wasn't far. It was kind of on the way to my grandmother's empty cabin, too, and I had a key.

The more I hung around Denver's place, the more paranoid I got. He and my dad had to be around. Close. It was just a matter of finding them.

I had a plan. Walk through town. If I didn't see them, go to the cabin, let myself in, call Denver's house. If he wasn't there, leave a message. Wait.

Either he'd call, or my mother would show up. My mother was going to show up eventually. And it would be warm, or warmer, at the cabin.

I had a plan. Okay.

I started up the street, head down, past new-fence neighbor's house.

A door opened. A woman's voice called out.

"Hey. You waiting for somebody?"

From The Journal Of Nate Charters
Sixteen

I very nearly ignored the woman. My hood was up; I had a good stride going. I could have kept on walking.

I should have.

It might sound strange, but when she called to me, I got the exact same feeling in my gut and up my spine that I did when my mother caught me doing something I shouldn't. A hands-in-the-cookie-jar jolt that stopped me cold.

I looked to the left, keeping my head down as much as I could. The woman standing in the open door of the house next to Denver's place didn't look like anyone's mother.

She was older, sure...maybe in her thirties, I guess. She was tall, and slender. She wore those stupid furry suede boots girls like and a black turtleneck tucked into blue jeans. Her hair was dark brown, straight, and just touched her shoulders. Her eyes were very dark, and her face had lots of angles, like the Nagel painting on the cover of *Rio*, but, I don't know... harder. Not in a bad way, though.

She grinned before she said, "I didn't mean to scare you. I just noticed you hanging around Denver's place."

"Um, yeah." I kept my head down. "He's a family friend."

She crossed her arms across her chest. "A family friend, huh? You sure you're not just casing his place? Shouldn't you be in school, anyway?"

Despite what she said, she didn't sound suspicious. I wished I could catch her scent, but the air wasn't cooperating with me. It sounded like she was having some fun with me.

"No," I said.

"No, what?"

Huh?

"No...ma'am?"

Her laugh was throaty. "Wow. No, I mean...oh, hell, never mind." She brought one hand up to cradle her jaw and cheek. Her fingers were long and thin, like Lina's. "I think he took off."

"Yeah. His van's not there. Thanks."

"You live around here, 'family friend' of Denver's? I don't think I've seen you at his place before."

"Just visiting." The way she talked, it sounded like she knew Denver. Were they friends? Had he talked about me? Did she recognize me?

"You're not from Kirby Lake? Family have a cabin up here, or something?"

I nodded. "Yeah. I'm just gonna head back there...I'll call Denver and leave him a message, catch up with him later."

She nodded with a thoughtful pout. "Well...he probably won't be gone long. He hardly ever goes down the hill—I bet he's just at the Pantry House, getting some breakfast." She stepped to the side and propped the door open with an out-stretched arm. "If you want, you can use my phone and wait here for a while. Beats walking, at least until the day heats up a little. It's cold."

I could have said no, thanks, and walked on. And do you know why I didn't?

Because I was not quite seventeen years old and a hot older woman who was home alone asked me to come into her house.

That's why.

I'd read enough *Penthouse Forum* magazines Mel pilfered from his dad to understand what could happen in a situation like this, even if I wasn't so naive as to think spontaneous sex with a lonely older woman was what was actually about to happen.

Still. The whole situation was too damn inviting.

Besides, it made sense. No point in walking all the way to the cabin if Denver came back (with my dad!) a few minutes after I left.

As for worrying about being recognized, well, if she knew Denver, I could assume she already knew about me. That guy loved to talk.

"Well...okay," I said. "Thanks."

"Come on in."

She didn't put a whole lot of effort into getting out of the way when I came through the doorway. We got really close. I smelled her shampoo.

I hated myself a little.

From The Journal Of Nate Charters
Seventeen

For someone like me—which is to say, me, and maybe my father—houses smell like the people who live in them painted the air with layer after layer of day after day of their presence. It's not a bad thing, usually, but it's certainly distinctive.

I remember talking to Lina about it, one time. She said it must be like the way your house smells when you come back after a vacation, only more.

This house smelled like furniture. Leather and dust and wood. New furniture, at that. Eventually, furniture smells mostly like the people who use it, and this stuff still smelled a little like department store.

One thing I could tell, though: the woman didn't live here alone. There was a man.

The living room had a leather couch, a glass coffee table, and one of those big console televisions that weigh about a ton and a half.

She closed the door. My eyes adjusted instantly to the dim interior. She held out her hand.

"My name's Evelyn."

I shook her hand. "I'm Nate."

I saw expected hint of recognition in the way she tilted her head. "Nate…?" She glanced at the top of my head. "Take off your hood, Nate." She grinned. "Show some manners."

Here we go. What the hell. I pulled the hood off and watched her expression as she took in my big eyes and the odd bone and muscle structure in my face. She seemed bemused by the leopard spots Crystal Dubois's mom had dyed into my short, sandy-brown hair.

"I thought so," she said. "You're *that* Nate. Friend of the family, just like you said."

She didn't sound freaked out. More interested than anything else. It gave me some stupid confidence. "Yep. Boy freak, at your service."

As soon as I said it, I could feel a blush threaten my cheeks. At your service? What would she think I meant by that?

But she was walking through the living room and gesturing toward the kitchen. "Phone's in there, Nate. Help yourself. I'll be right back."

She went down the hall and through a door. I called "thanks" after her, went into the kitchen, and found the phone.

I kept a thin, tiny address book in my front pocket. I pulled it out, found Denver's number, and dialed it.

His answering machine picked up and played a warbly recording.

"This is Denver Colorado. If you're calling about a piece you commissioned, it's not ready. If you're calling about commissioning a piece, it's probably going to take a while because you just heard I have to do that other one, and it's late. If you still need to leave a message, you know what to do and when to do it."

Beep.

"Hey, um, Denver. It's Nate Charters. I'm...um, well, I'm actually right here at your next-door neighbor's house. Surprise. I really need to see you. I think you're with my dad, and I really, really need to see him, so that's, um, that's good.

I hope he's still there. With you. Uh, when you get back."

I recognized that I was rambling.

"Anyway, I don't know the number here, but I'll be looking out for your van, and I'll just come over, I guess. I wanted to leave this message so you wouldn't be too shocked. Maybe you can give my dad a heads-up, too. Okay. Thanks. Bye."

I hung up and wished I could get a do-over on that message. But whatever. Good enough.

From somewhere in the back of the house, Evelyn hollered, "Make yourself at home. I'll be out in a sec."

"Okay!"

Other than a roll of paper towels, the kitchen counters were empty. I tried one of the cabinets.

It was empty.

Next one over had a stack of paper plates, a box of plastic utensils, and two stacks of Styrofoam cups.

That was sure weird.

I opened the refrigerator. Evelyn had said to make myself at home, after all.

A carton of milk. A loaf of bread, which I didn't get. Who puts bread in the fridge? Four bottles of some beer I didn't recognize. An open package of sliced ham. A bottle of ketchup. Two Chinese food takeout containers with those thin metal handles.

That was it.

I closed the refrigerator door and glanced around the place. The bare counter tops, the furniture that still smelled new... I stepped back into the living room and noticed that the glass coffee table didn't have a smudge or fingerprint on it. It didn't have any cleaning residue on it, either; I would have smelled that shit.

My mother's a real-estate agent, so I've seen those model homes they set up with the fake books and old magazines in the bathroom and silk flowers and whatever. These people didn't even bother with that.

I didn't like it.

I thought maybe I should just go.

I turned toward the hallways and saw Evelyn coming toward me. Her arms were straight out in front of her, and she held a gun with both hands.

From The Journal Of Nate Charters
Eighteen

The hole at the end of the barrel of the gun in her hands lined up with a spot just to the left of my breastbone. That hole didn't waver as she walked down the hall. It was like the rest of her was anchored to the end of the gun.

I froze.

She stopped about eight feet away from me. Her eyes were bright. She had the slightest smile on her face.

"Too good to be true," she said.

It was hard to take my eyes off of the hole at the end of the barrel of the handgun. I remember thinking that I hadn't even made it a whole year without someone pointing a gun at me. The last time it happened had been less than a mile away from where I stood at that moment. Just down the street, more or less.

I figured that couldn't be a coincidence.

"What's going on?" I was surprised to hear my voice come out of my mouth in a ragged whisper. It was like the rules of being held at gunpoint were the same as being in a library or church. I wanted to clear my throat, but I was too scared to make too much noise, too sharp a sound. The last thing I wanted was for her to be shocked into doing something by reflex.

"You, Nathan Charters," she said around that half-smile, "are what we call a target of opportunity. It's my lucky day."

She didn't move.

So I didn't move.

"I don't...I don't understand."

She chuckled. "I bet you can figure it out. I'm told you're

a pretty smart little monster."

The things I knew blazed through my head in a fuzzy collage of impressions. A vague picture formed, outlined by a certainty that I blurted out.

"Brenhurst. You're with Brenhurst."

Her smile stretched to three-quarters. The hole at the end of the gun never budged from the spot on my chest.

"I wouldn't say that. But the same guy signs our paychecks. Good guess."

I felt like the air in the room pushed on me from all sides. My peripheral vision blurred out; all I could see was the woman and the gun.

"So you were…you were just, what, waiting for me?"

"God, you teenagers think you're just the center of the universe, don't you?" She shook her head. The hole at the end of the gun didn't move. "You're a bonus. Make sense?"

All of a sudden, it did. She and the mystery man that wasn't here worked for PrenticeCambrian, the mega-corporation that owned Tyndale Labs.

Tyndale Labs was where Lester Brenhurst said he worked when he tried to get his hands on me and Byron Teslowski last year. Supposedly Tyndale Labs had been researching exceptionally physically talented young people to help make better prosthetic devices, but Byron smelled a rat, and so did my mother when Brenhurst set his sights on me.

When Brenhurst bullshitting my mother didn't work, and when Jason and I (with Lina's help) made sure Byron got away, Brenhurst came after us, up here in Kirby Lake. No longer trying to act like everything was on the up-and-up, Brenhurst brought a couple of bruisers with horns growing out of their bodies to help collect us all.

No one had counted on my crazy, augmented dad showing up at the big confrontation at my grandmother's secluded
cabin. Hell, I hadn't even known my father was alive, let
alone that he'd been made into a nutty animal-man by some
experiments back in the Sixties—experiments apparently
headed up by the very same Lester Brenhurst.

When the police made the scene, my dad was gone
again, and Byron was bleeding out. One of Brenhurst's monsters had been killed when my dad ripped his guts out. The
other had been killed by Brenhurst by some kind of weird
poison that was supposed, and failed, to also hurt my dad.

Brenhurst himself had some nice deep cuts on his face
courtesy of yours truly. Last time I saw him in court, he was
using makeup to cover the scars.

Now Byron was at the Donner Institute for Sovereign
Studies, safe under the wing of William Karl Donner, the
most powerful metahuman out there. Me and mine were safe
in the public eye, or so I thought, at the center of the legal
tangle that grew out of the whole mess. And my dad was...

"You were looking for my dad," I said to her.

"Oh, we found him." I imagined the worst, and it must
have shown on my face. She added, "My partner's on his tail
while you and I are having our little visit. Don't worry. Nothing's happened to you dear old dad."

I pretty much heard the "yet" as if she'd said it out loud.

The whole world funneled down to the woman and her
gun. You could have smashed cymbals behind my head or set
off a stink bomb, and I wouldn't have noticed. If you've ever
gone through that fake hyper-alert phase of being drunk, it

was like that, only not fake. And, like, fifty times more intense.

"What are you going to do with us?"

She shook her head slightly. "Let's focus on you. Like I said, you're a target of opportunity, the long-odds reason I stuck around while my partner chases down your daddy. So I'm going to run down a couple of options for you, and you tell me what you think. Okay?"

When she said to focus on me, I read it as writing off my father as dead.

And it was easy to interpret "a couple of options" as none at all.

Yet again, it struck me how much of my life was determined by the decisions and motives of other people.

It hit me, for the millionth time, that most of those people didn't give a shit about me.

At best.

At worst, they wanted me in the ground.

Somebody told me once that fear and anger are pretty much different degrees of the same emotion. I could feel the needle moving into the red.

I had my voice back.

"Okay."

"Option number one: I put handcuffs on you, we go out to my car, and I turn you over to my employers."

"What happens then?"

She head-shrugged. "I don't know."

The gun didn't waver. How could she hold it so still for so long? Was she augmented in some way, like Brenhurst's assassins and my father?

"What's the other one?"

"I shoot you, take you out to my car, and I turn you over to my employers."

Just like I thought. No real choice at all.

The needle was pegged. There was no more room in me for fear. Distantly, I realized I was trembling.

"Easy, there," she said.

My chest heaved as my open mouth took in lungfuls of air. On the exhales, I said, "First. One."

"That's what I'd do," she said. "And really, you should calm down. I'm told they'd rather have you alive, so you're probably going to be all right."

She thought I was scared or crying or panicking or something. Like a blubbering child.

She shifted the grip on the gun to her right hand so she could reach behind her hip with her left hand. Probably to get the handcuffs.

The hole at the end of the barrel of the gun finally moved.

I leapt.

My left hand closed around her right forearm, and the gun went off. I felt the recoil through her skin, up into my arm. The sound was agony. The left side of my head vibrated with a high-pitched whining noise.

She couldn't do anything with her right arm; I was too strong. She hit me again and again with her left fist, all over my head and face and shoulders, while my momentum tumbled her back onto the carpet.

I managed to get her flailing left arm by the wrist. I had her pinned.

Her face was inches below mine. Her expression was one of perfect calm.

She bashed me just above the bridge of my nose with her forehead. Just like in the fucking movies.

I saw stars. I lost my grip on her left arm. Nothing could make me let go of the other one.

I couldn't see from the pain. Half of my head was filled the haywire noises my shocked left eardrum transmitted to my brain. I felt her twisting, hitting.

She got a knee between my legs, fast.

Sickening pain twisted up my guts. The gun went off again.

Blind, half-deaf, unsure of even where the gun was pointing, I lashed out with my right arm. I connected with skin. I slashed back and forth, crying, desperate.

My hand and arm and neck and face felt hot and wet.

My vision cleared.

Her face was close enough to kiss. She stared at me with a different kind of calm.

Her body relaxed. The ragged mess of her throat bubbled with blood. Each pulse was weaker than the last.

She didn't dare die because of me. I could *not* kill someone. It was something that just could not happen.

I tried applying pressure to her neck to slow the bleeding. My fingers slipped in the blood and sunk into her flesh.

Her whole neck was a jagged, flayed wound.

"No no no no no no no…"

I tried using my whole hand. I pushed my palms hard on the pulpy flaps of her neck. Her head lolled back when my fingertips pushed the base of her jaw.

The blood no longer flowed. If she had breathed her last, I hadn't heard it.

She was gone.

From The Journal Of Nate Charters
Nineteen

It really happened.

I killed someone. With my bare hands.

I killed someone.

Her eyes were open. Staring at the ceiling. Whatever moisture there had already dehydrated, leaving them dull. Flat. Hard.

I followed her (dead) gaze up. The ceiling was just as dry and flat as her eyes.

I understood why people closed the eyes of the dead in movies and whatever. It wasn't a sign of respect or some symbolic gesture that the person was at rest.

It was so people wouldn't have to look at them. Because it was horrible. It was the future.

Blank, staring, nothingness.

I finally turned away. Finally turned my own excellent, inhumanly sharp, unique eyes that would disappear completely from all of everything when I eventually died...so that I wasn't staring at the cold gray things on her face.

Instead, I found myself looking at my hands.

So much better.

Not.

My hands were bloody. Cold. Sticky. Clammy. Worse, the smell filled up my brain with actual, fresh essence of dead woman.

She was all over my hands.

I had just a moment of horrible, helpless realization before the gagging hit, and no warning at all when my stomach rebelled entirely and hot vomit erupted from my mouth and nose.

I doubled over. My instinct was to grab my stomach, but even through the burning pain of acid tearing up my throat, I stopped before I got the blood on my hands all over my sweatshirt.

My knees gave way, and that too-new carpet got bloody handprints when I broke my fall, me puking all the way down.

At least I couldn't smell anything for the moment. Just my own guts.

Violent retching gave way to tearful gasping before too long. I stared at the blood and puke soaking into the rug until the trembling in my arms—more like seizures along my muscles—got me scared that I might just collapse into the mess beneath my face.

I pushed myself into a roll and ended up on my side on the cold kitchen floor. The view from down there, plus the fact that I was absolutely wrung out, forced some calm on me for the moment.

Calm enough to think.

Which was bad.

This day here in Kirby Lake was all part of an inevitable progression. This had to happen eventually. How could it not?

It started last year with Byron. He had only wanted to talk. He was scared: worried about Brenhurst's plans for him, worried over what he might be, and he turned to the one kid in town who just might be able to sympathize.

Except I was also the kid Byron had picked on for years, and I was full of a double dose of confidence thanks to my first date with Lina (Lina! Damn it!) and the Sovereign news and what it might mean for me.

He came to me for help. I jumped him. He fought back, better than he should have been able. That was our first clue he might be a Sovereign. I cut him, lightly, across the belly.

That was the first time.

A week or so later, a little swipe across Lester Brenhurst's hatchet face. That one, it felt kind of good.

Then, a year...a whole year...of feeling like the part of me that liked flesh under my fingernails was growing under my own skin, like I would eventually shed my self-control and let it all just happen. That the...whatever I was...maybe *deserved* to be...

Me.

Then the thing with Lina. Which led to knowing about Eric Finn.

Fucking Eric Finn. Dude got off easy.

Over there in the living room, getting cold on the carpet...that could have been you, Finn.

Every time I exhaled, shallow and fast, curled up on the linoleum, I made a little noise. Keening, it's called.

I sounded crazy to my own ears. Even to the left one, which no longer felt like it was mostly stuffed with cotton and broadcasting a high-frequency heartbeat.

I wasn't going to be half deaf. Yay me.

Carefully, slowly, I got myself upright. My legs felt like tubes of water.

That woman. She had to happen. It was just a matter of time. The thing inside me had been threatening. She brought it out.

What if I'd just allowed myself to be handcuffed? Taken to wherever she was going to take me? I could have found out what this whole fucking shit has been about, all these months, really, for real.

I leaned hard on the kitchen counter.

Yeah. They would have told me the whole deal, right before they killed me, because that's how that works, right?

The whole question wasn't worth asking. When she threatened me, the thing inside came out. It doesn't like to be caged. It doesn't like to be refused.

She fixed it. That thing is me, now.

Hello, me. You are one fucked-up piece of shit.

"I'd like that glass of water now, Evelyn."

Oh, that was no good. My voice. I barely recognized it.

Rather than dwell on that, I ran the kitchen tap, squirted some dishwashing soap into my palms, and rubbed my hands furiously under water that was hot as I could bear. The sink didn't run red nearly as long as I thought it would.

Just like that, my hands were clean.

"Sure," I said out loud, just to try it out. "It's just that easy. You're soaking in it."

It's not like I sounded like my crazy dad or anything. Just shaken up. Totally to be expected.

Because.

I had just killed someone.

With my hands.

I stared at them. The knuckles were almost healed from my fight with Eric Finn. I didn't look too closely under the fingernails. I knew what was there.

I wondered if there was a nail file in their bathroom.

Because it matters if there are pieces of a dead person's skin under my fingernails. Right now my nose was full of bile and puke and a little hint of soap, but before too long, I'd smell that shit on my fingers, and I didn't want it.

I didn't want it.

To get to the bathroom, I'd have to go down the hall.

To go down the hall, I'd have to walk past her.

I did it. There was no way not to walk on bloody carpet. It was soaked through. My shoes made squishing noises.

I looked at them. They were, big surprise, a bloody mess. I realized my fucking socks were probably wet.

Not just wet. Be clear. Bloody. From all the blood that came out of the dead woman's body. The woman I killed. That one.

I was in the hall.

There were two rooms on the right. On the left, the bathroom and, father down, what was probably the master bedroom.

Can you hear the sound a television makes right before the picture comes on? Kind of an electric crackle-hiss? Or is that just me (and probably my dad)?

My hearing was coming back just fine, because I heard that, then. Only, lots. Coming from the back bedroom.

The bathroom would wait. Just like the too-new furniture and the paper plates in the kitchen, that electric buzzy hum didn't make sense, somehow.

I squitched down the hall and into the master bedroom.

There was no bed there.

The room was full of televisions.

From The Journal Of Nate Charters
Twenty

Three folding tables were set up along the far wall of the master bedroom, where the headboard might have been if there had been a bed. The tables held a bunch of black and silver boxes with glowing LED lights and displays, all connected with a mess of cables.

The televisions, three rows of them, were mounted along the wall above the tables. Only they weren't really televisions. Each square of black glass had a little glowing green light, but no channel switcher or volume knob.

I was reminded of the pictures of the mission-control room at NASA, but smaller. That meant those weren't televisions at all. They were monitors.

Two small office chairs waited in front of the table. I would have leapt at the chance to sit down, but my body was so low on fuel I settled for falling into one of them. It creaked a little. Its casters rolled on the thick plastic mat between them at the carpet before I planted my feet. I left red smears on the plastic.

I examined the array of electronics boxes on the table. I couldn't make heads or tails of some of them.

Some of the others, though, were pretty obviously some kind of video-cassette players.

What the hell was all this?

I noticed one long box with a set of A/B switches not unlike the ones on the amplifier Alex, Carson Meunetti's guitar player, used.

I turned everything to A and flipped a chrome toggle.

The monitors fuzzed to life.

I fiddled with switches and buttons. Pictures in black and white popped up on screens on the wall.

They were all from Denver Colorado's place. The tree line at the edge of his backyard. His back porch. His front porch. The rooms of his house, even the bathroom. A shot of the roof, even. The inside of his garage workshop.

I didn't realize I was looking at live camera feeds until I noticed the wind chimes hanging above Denver's back porch shift in the breeze at the same time as I faintly heard them outside.

What the hell?

These people had cameras all over Denver Colorado's house. How was that even possible? And what the hell for?

How, that was a mystery. But the why-for was easy. The woman—

(her name is Evelyn, my nasty subconscious burst out, and you killed her.)

—the woman and her partner had been watching Denver's house for who knows how long, waiting for my dad to show up.

Which he had done, and left again, apparently with Denver, for who knows where. With the woman's partner following.

Holy fuck.

Were the cameras all over my house? Is that why (Evelyn) had stayed behind? Had they been waiting for me?

That didn't feel exactly right. She seemed genuinely surprised when I showed up.

Didn't mean they hadn't been spying on me. That was... gross.

I played with more buttons. The things I thought were video-cassette players, Betamaxes or whatever, didn't actually have any cassettes in them. They played recordings all the same once I figured them out.

I watched the silent screens.

The images were strange, as if they were made up of hundreds of little boxes that constantly rearranged themselves to form a kind of mosaic, or coordinated collection, I guess, of pictures. The movies were somehow blurry and jagged at the same time, and they made my eyes ache.

I watched, though.

I saw my father, grizzled, hairy and filthy, come into the yard from the woods. Him and Denver talking. A woman about Denver or my mother's age—who was that?

On another screen, my father sitting down for sandwiches just like plain folks. Some kind of discussion.

I saw my dad in the bathroom, stripping bare-ass naked. Under the layers of rotten clothing, his body was all lean muscle. Given his long, tangled dreadlocks and beard, I was surprised to see he had almost no body hair. That was weird.

He put his clothes into a garbage bag, opened the bathroom door just wide enough for the bag, and thrust it out. On a different screen, the mysterious woman took it and carried it out to the trash.

My dad took a long time figuring out how to draw a bath. While he was working out all of that, Denver Colorado and the woman had a pretty spirited conversation in a bedroom.

I found the fast-forward. The screens jumped and sped.

I hit play when I realized I was seeing my dad getting a

haircut and a shave. The woman was doing it: big drastic chops with the scissors on his scalp and over most of his beard, a straight razor on his face for the last of it. He looked like he would bolt at any moment.

I watched, fascinated. He didn't bolt.

So many questions. It was frustrating to see it all happening but not hear a thing. What was this all for?

Clean-shaven, with a close haircut, in clean clothes he must have borrowed from Denver, my father was nearly unrecognizable. Only his eyes, still wide and half-scared and always moving, betrayed him as the same person.

I fast-forwarded again, but eventually everyone went to bed, my father curled up on the floor on a pile of blankets he pulled off Denver's couch.

I stopped the "tape" and thought about what I'd seen. My dad shows up at Denver's, he gets all cleaned up by Denver's friend, or girlfriend, maybe, then the next morning they're all nowhere to be found, and one of the PrenticeCambrian fuckers goes after them.

Did they know the guy was after them?

It shouldn't have taken that long to hit me, but looking back, I guess I can be forgiven for being a little dense, given my morning.

My dad was in some very serious danger, and he probably didn't even know it.

I had to figure out where they were all going. Somehow, I had to catch up with them before…Evelyn's…partner did.

If I could find them, if we could get to the partner…I couldn't give the thought any more form than that, but it drove an urgency into my body that gave me a sudden burst of energy.

If I could figure this out. If I could find my dad. If I could stop the partner from doing whatever it was they had planned. Maybe...maybe, somehow, everything would work out.

I shot out of the chair, out of the bedroom, and down the hall. I had to get back to Denver's.

The body stopped me.

She was so very, completely, absolutely dead.

It had happened. This thing had happened.

I closed my eyes. I just couldn't look anymore. I let the rest of my sensorium guide me until she was behind me and I was at the front door.

If I could figure this out, maybe everything would work out.

Yeah. But she'd still be dead. And I'd still be the person who killed her.

From The Journal Of Nate Charters
Twenty One

I felt like every housewife and kid home sick from school in Kirby Lake could see me leave that house and slink next door to Denver's. The skin on the back of my neck crawled. I couldn't stand up straight; anything more than a crouch felt like I was painting a bull's-eye on my back.

There was a dead woman back there. How was it possible the whole world didn't know it?

If they did, they hadn't had time to come running just yet. I made it around to the back of Denver's house undetected, so far as I could tell.

I didn't know how to get in. I didn't have a key. He was like family, but that didn't mean he trusted me with coming and going as I pleased.

I decided shit was too important to fuck around. I took advantage of what little energy I had left in me and kicked the door in.

The sound surprised me; it was very loud in the quiet of the neighborhood. I slipped inside the dim kitchen right away.

Bath or not, my father's pungent animal scent was all over the inside of Denver's house. I was probably the only person who would notice, but man, it was strong. I half expected to see him come around the corner.

The house was not quite silent in the way that only empty houses could be. I didn't have anything to worry about, as far as that went, at least.

I had to figure out where my dad, Denver, and the mystery woman went. But first...

Standing in the kitchen with my energy reserves pretty much entirely drained from the awful business of the morning, I couldn't resist opening the fridge. I wouldn't be able to do a thing if I didn't get some food in me.

I tore a few slices of butter-top bread out of its plastic bag and shoved them in my mouth. Apparently keeping bread in the fridge wasn't so weird after all. While I chewed, I found a nearly empty tube of Braunschweiger wrapped in plastic wrap. I tossed the wrap aside and squeezed what was left of the sandwich spread into my mouth.

Denver had a half-gallon of milk. I gulped from the carton. I also ate a few slices of Swiss cheese, let pickle relish fall out of the bottle and into my mouth, and crunched down two handfuls of baby carrots.

I made a mess. I felt better.

Okay.

Now what?

I wandered out of the kitchen, hoping my gaze would fall on something useful. Instead, moving past the dining table, I was struck by a powerful sense of déjà vu.

I had just seen a view very much like the angle from one of the strange surveillance tapes next door.

I spun in a slow circle. Where in the hell were the cameras hidden? Were they watching me, taping me right now?

So creepy.

"Fuck it," I said to myself. There was no time to care. Wherever my dad was, the PrenticeCambrian guy was getting closer. I had to find them.

I stepped into the living room. I saw Denver's old rotary phone on an end table, right next to a small, lined spiral notepad.

I hunkered down to take a look. There were a lot of white paper scraps stuck in the metal spiral holding the thing together, as if a bunch of pages had been torn out. I flipped the cover back.

The very first page had some numbers scrawled on it. Was this something?

18, 15, 90, 93…

Oh, yeah. This was something. I knew it.

My love of maps was about to pay off. Over the last year, staring at the interwoven red and blue and black lines of the giant National Geographic map of the United States on my bedroom wall, I'd become pretty familiar with one particular potential "elsewhere."

My father was on his way to Missoula, Montana.

To the Donner Institute for Sovereign Studies.

From The Journal Of Nate Charters
Twenty Two

With the food in me and my new knowledge, I had a fire under my ass. One way or another, I would retrace their route. Maybe I'd hitchhike. Maybe I'd have to get a bus, or something.

Whatever. I couldn't do it without money, and I couldn't do it in the clothes I was wearing. The woman's blood was all over me.

I found Denver's bedroom, stripped off my bloody sweatshirt, and raided his closet.

The old man's flannel shirts didn't fit too badly. His upper body was built up from decades of pushing himself around in his wheelchair. My chest and shoulders were freakishly broad just because I was a freak. It worked, especially once I rolled up the sleeves.

My jeans and shoes had some blood on them, but wearing Denver's pants was out of the question—they were too small. If our upper bodies were similarly unusual, our lower halves were different as could be for the same reasons, kind of.

I'd have to get by with a fresh shirt and hope people didn't realize what the other stains really were. Good enough. Clothes, done.

I'd need money. Denver had an empty bottled-water jug about a third full of coins, and I considered raiding that, but it would take a ridiculous amount of change to get me across three or four states. That would never work.

I tried to think like someone who would hide a bunch of money in my house. I looked under the mattress. I looked under the cushions of the couch in the living room. I remembered a movie I'd seen and looked in the tank behind the toilet. All of this was pretty much in a mad rush. I felt the clock ticking.

Denver didn't have any money.

With a sigh of resignation, I realized who might. With another slouchy dash, I returned to the house next door.

The fancy car, of course, was still in their driveway.

I could take it. Somewhere in their house were the keys. I didn't have a license beyond my learner's permit, but shit, what was one more petty crime?

I had another thing to keep an eye out for in the house. Money and car keys.

I went back in like I lived there and stopped just inside the door.

She was still there.

Cold, on the floor.

There was no goddamned time to be a baby about it. She had tried to kill me, or might have. Now her partner was going to do the same damn thing to my dad, and he was the only person who could help me with my shit.

Fuck it.

Thin bravery aside, I still ended up doing a tiptoe dance around the body.

Once she was safely behind me, I turned my attention to the question of where I would stash my spending money if I was a couple of badass killers staking out a house.

I returned to the surveillance room. I opened the closet (empty) and glanced around and behind the assorted video recording boxes, but there was no secret hidey-hole of cash there.

The next room was the woman's, if the lacy things in a dresser drawer were any indication. It made me feel a little strange, but I rifled through them. My mother kept fifty dollars in her bra drawer, after all.

This one didn't. I couldn't even find a purse.

Next up was the partner's room. Definitely a guy. If his underwear drawer hadn't clued me in, the pictures I found would have done the job.

They were under the bed in a shoebox I felt certain would be stuffed with hundred-dollar bills. The pictures made my stomach clench.

They were all of the woman. Evelyn. All of them had the same blocky quality of the surveillance videos, and it was pretty clear from the way she stood that she had no idea the photos were being shot.

In one, she was half-undressed, naked from the waist up. I didn't want to think it, didn't want to feel it, but seeing her in that snapshot, totally at ease, in the privacy of her bedroom, getting dressed or undressed...no idea her partner was taking secret dirty pictures of her, a whole box of them...

She looked...vulnerable. Soft. And I'm sorry, I couldn't help thinking it. She was hot.

This was the person I killed.

The person in this picture was dead on the floor in the living room down the hall. Because of me.

I felt like crying. I shoved the picture back in the box, slammed the lid in place, and put the thing back under the bed instead.

There was no damn money in the bedrooms, and no car

keys. Fine.

I went into the kitchen. It wasn't until I was there that I realized it was getting easier to walk past the woman's body. I didn't like that. It should always be difficult. Always. Forever.

As I suspected, the kitchen drawers and cabinets were empty or nearly so. I already knew what was in the fridge. I tried the freezer compartment.

Two long, wrapped packages of white paper sat on the frosty metal mesh shelf. It looked like they might be pieces of fish.

I grabbed one and knew right away that it wasn't frozen fish. I unwrapped it with rising anticipation and found a loose bundle of fifty-dollar bills.

"Holy fuck," I breathed. I grinned and started counting it, but I realized the exact amount wasn't important. What mattered was that it was a shitload of money. I shoved it in my front left jeans pocket.

I tore open the other package. No fifties there.

That bundle was of hundreds.

Into my front right jeans pocket that went.

I had the money I needed. Where the fuck were the car keys?

I made another circuit through the house, but after a minute or two I knew I was just avoiding the obvious. After all, where did I keep my own house keys?

In my pocket, that's where.

I would have to search the woman.

Evelyn. "Her name is Evelyn, Nate."

I bent down next to her, my back to her face. It made it a little easier, but there was still the blood in the carpet squishing under my shoes, the awful pallor of her skin, the sheer...weight of her body.

I looked at her jeans. They were tight on her hips. The pocket on her left side had a kind of keys-shaped lumpiness to it.

I had to reach into the tight jeans of a dead woman, my fingertips just a few layers of cloth away from the bare skin of her thigh, just a few inches away from her crotch, to get those keys.

It made me think of being with Lina. I hated it. I hated myself. I felt like some kind of necrophiliac. I mean, not that I wanted to do something to the body, nothing fucked-up like that...but the whole things was just...

It was bad.

I had the keys.

The phone rang.

I straightened up fast, my heart in my throat, my skin flushing.

The phone rang three more times while I stared at it. A click, and the answering machine picked up. I heard Evelyn's voice, curt and short, instruct the caller to leave a message. The machine beeped.

I held my breath.

"It's Uldare. Lou. Obviously." The voice on the machine laughed. He sounded a little nervous. "You there? C'mon. Goddamn it. Okay. I'm in...Baker, I think. Baker, Barstow, you know, it doesn't matter. Based on the gizmo, I'm not too far behind the target. Engaging as planned shouldn't be an issue. Let the big guy know if he calls. I'll make contact again after the package is delivered." He laughed. "'The package is delivered.' What a crock. Okay, talk to you later, Ev."

Click.

After touching the body, I really, really, really wanted to wash my hands. But that was the guy—that was the partner! Lou.

And if he was in Baker, he had a pretty damn big head start, and that meant my dad was even farther away.

I had to go. Time to see if I could drive well enough to keep from attracting the attention of the highway patrol. In my stolen car.

Andrew Charters
Five

They'd been on the road for nearly three hours since stopping in Baker for gas and snacks. Andrew had taken a pass on getting out of the van then. Even though he looked more normal than any time in the last fifteen years with his fresh haircut and shave and Denver's clean clothes, internally Andrew still struggled to hang on to his slippery humanity. Exposing himself to the busy humanity, the oily smells, and the jarring sounds of cars and trucks coming and going at a gas station was a little too much, too soon.

But by the time they approached the border of Nevada and Arizona, Andrew felt like anything was preferable to the interior of Denver's van.

"Need a break!"

Denver looked over his shoulder from the front passenger seat. "Need to stretch your legs, buddy? Squeeze out the bladder?"

Sandy harrumphed from the driver's seat. "Denver."

"What?" He laughed. "Oh, I'm so sorry! There's a lady present!"

"You'll watch your step, mister," she said with a smile in her voice, "if you want anything to do with this lady in the near future."

"Yes, ma'am."

Andrew couldn't really follow their banter. The best he could do was catch whiffs of their pheromones in the close air of the van. Their attraction was cloying and increasingly irritating.

"Need a break!" he said again.

Sandy said, "He's not the only one. Let's fill the tank and stretch our legs."

"If you'll pardon the expression," Denver said.

"Get over yourself," Sandy said.

Denver chuckled. "One of these days. Hey, don't stop in Mesquite. Might be easier on Andy if we go somewhere a little less busy."

"Good idea."

Sandy pulled off Interstate 15 at Old Highway 91 and eased the van up to the pumps of a truck stop / travel center.

When she turned the engine off, the sudden absence of noise, vibration, and the smell of exhaust made Andrew realize just how tight and tense he'd become. He sighed and clawed for the latch of the back doors.

Sandy was already there. "Can you help me with Denver's chair, Andrew?"

He looked over her shoulder at the expanse of pavement and sandy earth. The horizon was reassuringly far away. The air was warm, almost hot. Andrew thought it would be nice to just run...

Sandy stared at him. "Hey, there, Andrew."

There wasn't really enough cover in the terrain to suit him, anyway.

"Yeah," he said to Sandy. "I'll help." He turned to the wheelchair, mounted on its ramp contraption. "Uh..."

Sandy climbed into the van. "Here." With her help, they got the chair out of the van and onto the pavement. Andrew couldn't have repeated the steps twenty seconds later.

"Gonna...stretch," he said to Sandy.

She wheeled the chair around to Denver's side of the

van. "Stick around, all right, Andrew?"

He grunted an acknowledgment and stepped away from the van. There was a hint of breeze; it felt strange to feel wind without it passing through his tangled hair and beard.

The air brought the scents of his surroundings into his sensorium: motor oil, ammonia, asphalt, warm tire rubber, sweet engine coolant, stomach-clenching gasoline... cooking grease, weird fast-food meat...sweaty, tired humans...a dog?

Andrew grinned. Dogs hated him. He confused them. Maybe they even resented him, since he registered as more animal than man to them, but he walked around and went where he pleased like the things that held the leashes and filled the food bowls.

It wasn't a nice thing, but he never could resist messing with a dog when he had the chance. Maybe it made him feel a little less like an animal. Maybe he was just an asshole.

He laughed and inhaled deeply through his nose while keeping his mouth just slightly open and his tongue moist. Information flowed in.

One of those big, white, blocky house-trucks was parked near the edge of the lot. Andrew loped toward it.

The dog, tied with a length of rope to its collar, trotted into sight from the far side of the recreational vehicle. It started barking as soon as it saw him.

Andrew laughed again. The names of dog breeds were lost to him, but it was one of the big ones, easily three feet at the shoulders and probably a couple hundred pounds. It was also all tied up.

"Sucker." He laughed and stopped a leap away from the thing.

The dog's muscles flexed under its tawny fur as it bunched itself. Its hackles bristled. When it leapt and was yanked with a jerk at the end of its tether, the RV rocked on its chassis.

Andrew crouched on the pavement, his arms wide and his fingers hooked, nails ready. Grinning, he bared his teeth and growled. He stomped the ground in Denver's slightly-too-large boots, and his feet jostled uncomfortably within.

The mild pain of his feet was ruining his fun. Had to lose the shoes. He straightened up and pulled each one off with his feet.

The dog never stopped barking and pulling on his make-shift leash.

The side door of the recreational vehicle swung open and slapped against the siding. A slender man with gray hair and a neat beard stepped out.

"What the hell is…"

He caught Andrew a little off-balance in the middle of yanking Denver's socks off his feet. Automatically, Andrew dropped into a low, three-point crouch, balanced on his toes and the fingers of his left hand and ready to leap. He pulled his lips back from his teeth and growled.

The sight of a barefoot but otherwise clean-cut middle-aged man in crisp new blue jeans and a bright red-and-black checkered flannel shirt growling in a very convincing impersonation of a rabid animal gave the man pause, but not for long. He stepped away from the RV, well within Andrew's striking range.

"The hell is wrong with you, messing with my dog like that?" He turned to the beast, who barked on and on.

"Massive, shut up! Jesus!"

Andrew shifted his balance so that he could keep both prey in sight. He could smell the dog's intent to rip out his throat if he could just break his leash. There was a good chance that rope wouldn't hold.

The surprise appearance of the dog's owner was almost enough to push Andrew over to his more bestial nature. He was ready. Neither of these creatures was threatening enough to trigger the instinct to flee. It was fight, all the way.

Andrew, cooped up in Denver's house all night and in the van all day, wanted it. It had been over a year since he'd cut into a human; a dog, even longer.

Maybe he'd just pick one and go for it.

And then there were three. A little boy, maybe six years old, appeared in the open doorway of the RV. His dark eyes popped.

"Daddy?"

And then there were four. The mother, even more of a meatless stick than the father. "Dan, what—?"

The dog barked on. The RV shook.

The kid hollered, "Mommy!" and started bawling.

Andrew decided on the dog. Those people were no challenge at all. No meat, no risk.

He barked a challenge. The animal seemed to realize the human was crazier than it was. It recoiled and whined, its head low.

Andrew tensed to leap.

"Andy! Lay the hell off, right now!"

Denver's voice and familiar scent cut through Andrew's

hunter focus like a knife in the belly. He jerked up and back, nearly colliding with Denver in his chair.

"Get off of me, you idiot!"

Denver shoved him hard. It was enough to make Andrew stumble and nearly fall. The sudden vulnerability, coupled with Denver's no-bullshit attitude, fully shattered Andrew's animal persona.

He saw Sandy stride past. The dog resumed barking, but Andrew made out Sandy offering strident apologies to the family.

Denver wheeled into his field of vision. "Get back to the van, Andrew. Now."

Andrew ran back to the van the fastest way he knew how: on all fours. He leapt through the open back doors and closed them behind him.

Inside the otherwise silent interior of the van, he could still hear the dog, whining now, confused and worked up.

Andrew sat on the wheelwell and shook. He felt frustrated and ashamed to the point of pain.

A door opened, and Denver lifted himself up and into the driver's seat. Sandy opened the back doors and got the wheelchair secured without asking for Andrew's help.

"We have to go," Denver said. "Right now. Come on."

"All set." Sandy climbed into the back, shut the doors, and went up to the front passenger seat.

"Have to go," Andrew nodded. "Gotta get to Montana. Please go."

They had to be able to help him there. They had to be able to do something about this.

They had to.

Andrew noticed his feet were bare. He had no idea what had happened to Denver's shoes.

From The Journal Of Nate Charters
Twenty Three

I'd never been so far away from home in my life, but after three hours of desert and no good stations on the radio, the experience kind of lost its novelty.

The car was some kind of classy Oldsmobile with all the extras. I'm pretty sure it had cruise control, but I never could figure out how to use it. At least it was an automatic. Otherwise, this whole plan would have been screwed—more screwed—from the start. My mother never taught me how to drive a stick.

I had Denver Colorado's directions, along with the name and address of a hotel in Provo, Utah, he'd written in his little notebook. I had about fifty bucks' worth of gas-station food and drink to keep me going: lots of health-food energy bars and nuts and stuff. Every now and then, I pulled over to the shoulder and took a piss. By the time I'd traveled through Las freaking Vegas, I think I passed my behind-the-wheel test a few times over.

I had a lot of time to think. That's why I kept changing the station on the radio. I heard a lot of country music and a lot of gospel. There was a station playing rock most of the way through California and almost to Vegas, but it faded out eventually.

I didn't *want* to think. I didn't want to dwell on what had happened in Kirby Lake. What I'd done. Who knew, by now. What would happen. It was hundreds of miles in the past, and at least at the moment, it was entirely out of my control anyway.

So I kept my eye on the road, got really good with the

radio and the air conditioning but not so good with the cruise control, and focused on the destination. When my mind wandered, I coaxed my thoughts in the direction of what was next.

Finding my dad. Warning him about "Lou" from PrenticeCambrian. Joining him on the road to the Donner Institute. Maybe even seeing Byron Teslowski.

Everything else, like the woman who'd tried to kill me, Lina, Eric Finn, my mom—I tucked away in a little box in my head that might as well be locked in the trunk.

Yeah, it knocked around a little, back there. I turned up the radio when it did.

My legs started to get a little jumpy right before I reached the Arizona border, which was pretty good timing for stretching my legs, since I'd need gas before long, too. I considered stopping somewhere in Mesquite, but it looked a little too...populated. I was, don't forget, a national celebrity. Of a sort. And even if my face hadn't been rendered on supermarket tabloids in gorgeous airbrushed black-and-white for the last several months, once you saw me, you remembered me.

All things considered, it was better if I didn't get seen by too many folks. I'd managed to skip the busier gas stations so far; it made sense to skip Mesquite.

I crossed from Nevada to Arizona and saw signs for a truck stop just north of the freeway. That would have to do— the gas tank wouldn't allow for much else, and I didn't know when the next place might come along. I took the exit and pulled in to the self-serve gas pumps.

I got out of the car, arched my back, and inhaled deeply.

Who knew when I'd get another chance to take in the scents of wherever-in-the-hell I was?

Sure, there were all the usual gas-station odors, all tangy and sweet and vaguely nauseating, but above that, outside of that, sneaking in on the wind, was the smell of the *place*. This was the northwest corner of Arizona, a stretch of freeway maybe thirty miles long, and now I knew how it smelled.

I smiled at the novelty of it all, the idea that I was on the same road that started all the way back in southern California, that I was in freaking Arizona, pumping gas in a truck stop, Arizona wind sending Arizona scents into my brain.

Then the guilt hit. I shouldn't be enjoying myself. I was at a truck stop in Arizona less than twenty-four hours after I'd hurt the guy who'd tried to rape my girlfriend. Less than a day after I'd fucked up my relationship with Lina but good, thanks to that.

Just a few hours after I'd killed someone with my bare hands.

It was self-defense. It was. But I did it. I did it.

Standing there next to the big Olds, I damn near started to bawl. I was in *so much trouble*, that wasn't even enough of a word. I wasn't even the same person I was the day before yesterday.

My brain wanted to keep going down that road, but I couldn't let it. I had to keep it together. I had to fuel up and get going.

The 15 to the 90 to the 93. A Super 8 motel somewhere in Provo. The 15 to the 90 to the 93. A Super 8 motel.

Then my dad. And then…who knew what.

I sighed hard. I wiped my eyes on the sleeve of Denver

Colorado's shirt. I glanced around, self-conscious, but no one paid any attention to me. That was good.

I went into the station to pay for my gas. The guy who took my money gave me a long look.

"You just pump and get going, all right?" He had a sour look on his long face.

"Ah…yeah. That's the plan."

"Had enough trouble around here today," he volunteered. "I don't know what you're doing out here, but we've had enough trouble here."

"I'm just…"

The guy stared hard. I could feel the eyes of a few other people in the place on me, too. A woman scooped up her little girl and they hustled out. The man with them glared at me.

"I'm not…I'm not here to make trouble," I said. "I'm just buying some gas, all right?"

The attendant nodded sharply. "We already called the cops on you people once today. I don't care what the rules are; I'll call the cops. Watch me."

You people.

"I don't even know what you're talking about." I was tired, to the bone, to the soul, but this kind of shit bugged the hell out of me. "What people, anyway?"

"All you Sovereigns, rolling through here on the way to your big party or whatever. Last guy terrorized a whole family; tried to go after their dog." He squinted at me. "You know him?"

Shit. I probably did. "Ah…what…happened?"

"Big freakout." He put emphasis on "freak" and backed

it up with challenge in his eyes. He had no fear on his scent. "But I guess you all aren't so hot." He scoffed and looked superior, like I was automatically part of the Sovereign club and so must be personally put in my place for whatever had gone down. "Guy got scared off by a dude in a wheelchair."

Well, that pretty much cinched it. Mother *fucker.*

I got out of there. I filled the tank. I had three dollars and twenty cents of change coming to me. I didn't go back to collect. It wasn't my money, anyway.

I got back on the road. As I drove, my imagination made up a steady flow of little movies about what kind of "freakout" my dad put on when he had passed through there.

Going after a family. Going after their dog.

The last time I saw my father, he'd been a mostly crazy, bloodthirsty wild man. Did I think he'd be any different just because he'd apparently had a haircut and a bath?

Did I seriously think he'd be able to help me at all? That he'd even need *my* help, assuming this Lou guy got to him before I did?

"Fuck, fuck, fuck!"

I put Arizona behind me and slipped into Utah wondering what the hell I was doing.

From The Journal Of Nate Charters
Twenty Four

Another three hours and change on the road, and I found the place. The clock on the dash said six-twelve, but I hadn't moved it back an hour to account for the fact that I was in a different time zone. It seemed way too light out for being almost a quarter after six.

Funny what you remember.

I pulled into the parking lot and drove around the back of the Super 8 motel. The motel was on my right. The left side of the lot ended near the start of a low hillside.

Through the windshield of the Olds, I saw Denver's white Econoline van right away, and pretty much right after that, what do you know, a motel room door opened, and here comes Denver himself, in his wheelchair, pushed by the gray-haired lady I recognized from the weird videos.

And hello…next out, all crouched and nervous, came my dad.

I did it. I found him.

I didn't know if I should honk, or park and come over to them totally casual, or what. I grinned like a kid at Christmas.

Then a section of doorframe right next to my dad's head exploded.

From The Journal Of Nate Charters
Twenty Five

My dad leapt back into the room so fast it was like he'd dis-appeared. The lady, ducking low, hustled Denver behind the van.

I slammed on the parking break and got out of the car.

A little puff of disintegrated stucco blew off the wall of the motel just beyond the door frame From my left, some-where on that hillside, came a very faint, sharp *pft* and a louder noise like a crack.

My sensitive olfactory nerve registered, almost as faintly, the tangy, smoky smell of gunpowder.

I put the two together. Whoever was shooting was on that hillside, hidden from sight.

Who could that be but Lou from PrenticeCambrian, Lou from the answering machine...Lou with the dirty pic-tures of his roommate?

Lou. Shooting at my dad. Well, fuck that.

I ran across the parking lot toward the chain-link fence marking the base of the hill. I'll never be as fast as my dad, but I'm pretty damn quick, especially in a sprint. Even so, I kept expecting the guy to turn his gun on me.

He fired again, all right, but he was still aiming for my dad. I wished I could spare a glance toward the motel, but my sensorium had done its work.

I knew where Lou was.

A second leap, and I was on the edge of a concrete drainage ditch running horizontally along the hillside.

A third leap, and I was on his back.

I don't want to make it sound like I'm some kind of

action hero. That's not how it was. Not even.

It'll probably take you longer to read all this than the time that passed from when I got out of the car to when I reached the guy.

Also, I'd just spent several hundred miles and pretty much the entire day thinking about what would happen when I saw my dad. The idea that one of these PrenticeCambrian assholes would kill him before that could happen was so far off the table, it was, like, ridiculous. Offensive, even.

My head went like this: hey, my dad! Hey, someone's trying to kill him! Fuck that! Make it stop!

Adrenaline kicked in. My crazy augmented muscles got me where I needed to be. I even got my hands on the barrel of the rifle and managed to yank it out of the shooter's grasp.

I didn't expect it to be so hot. I tossed it away by reflex.

While I was doing that, the guy twisted around and kneed me in the nuts.

Another heartbeat, and I was on my back in the drainage ditch. I hit the back of my head on the concrete and saw stars even as he got on top of me and started pounding me with his fists.

He was heavy. Like, overweight-heavy. But he was really strong, and he knew just where to land those punches on my chest and gut and sides.

Pain was everywhere and kept coming. I felt pinned by the sloping sides of the ditch.

I finally got my arms between him and me. I pushed; he got off of me.

In the scrambling moment it took for me to get off my back and onto my hands and knees, fire wracking me all up and down my torso, barely able to draw a decent breath, he was up and ready.

He'd also managed to pull a pretty big knife. I didn't know shit about such things and still don't, but it sure seemed to me like he knew how to use it. And planned to.

I couldn't get to my feet. I was freaking out.

"She's dead," I barked to buy some time. "She's dead!"

"What?"

"I killed her, all right?" Something in me insisted I say her name. "Evelyn. She's dead."

His face, which had been red from our struggle, paled a notch. His small eyes widened. His mouth dropped open.

I recognized his reaction as a vulnerability. The wild part of me took over in that thin slice of time. Pain flew out of me in a red rush that seemed to close around my head and narrow my vision down to nothing but this man who had just turned into prey.

I knocked him back, and we played our previous scene with the roles reversed. He lost his grip on the knife. I got on him and started to punch and kick with zero finesse, not that I really had any to display. I sucked at fighting, this was clear, but my augmented strength and speed and reflexes made up for it.

I was crying.

I don't know why I didn't use my fingernails on him. That would have been it, right then and there, and I would have had another death on my hands in every sense of the word.

I've given that a lot of thought. Things would have turned out very differently if I'd just hooked my hands and given him a couple of slashes across his throat in that mossy, cold, wet gutter. That would have been it.

Instead, I hit him and screamed at him and cried like a crazy person. He did his best to fight back, but I was too fast, too strong, too out of my head. Pretty quickly, it was all he could do to curl into a fetal position and cover his soft parts.

Something very strong gripped my shoulders, pulled me off the guy, and spun me around.

I found myself staring through my tears at my father's face.

"Stop," he said. "Stop it now."

From The Journal Of Nate Charters
Twenty Six

The last time I'd seen my father in the flesh, his hair had been a long, dreadlocked, filthy mess tangled with an equally long, dreadlocked, filthy mess of a beard. His clothes had been layers of rags. He'd stunk like a mildewed pile of feral old socks and trash bin meat.

The man who stood over me on the hillside next to the Super 8 motel bore a scent that was something like my own, something like the warm, vaguely comforting smell of a dog just a few days past its bath…with just a hint of soap. Not rangy or unpleasant at all.

His hair was gray and closely cropped. His bare face was pale and surprisingly smooth.

I knew him by his eyes, though. Green and vibrant, red-rimmed and wide. Half, or more than half, crazy.

He looked past me to where his would-be assassin lay curled up and groaning on the damp concrete of the drainage ditch.

"Didn't remember you as much of a fighter."

I looked at the guy named Lou and fought the black urge to keep going on him. At the same time, I was almost giddy to see he was still breathing.

"Sorry," I said.

"What for?"

My father crouched down on the balls of his feet, wrists on his bent knees. He sniffed at the killer, who looked at him with one swollen, bright eye full of fear and tried to curl into an even tighter ball.

My dad grabbed him by an ear and lifted his head off

the ground. "Wonder...should I finish?"

"No!" The thought of seeing another death, of seeing my father kill, of hearing the sounds and smelling the blood and shit and terror...it was terrible to consider. "No! I...I think we should, like, question him. Besides...I thought you didn't want me to hurt him anymore?"

"Didn't want *you* to do it," he specified. "Still wanna *do* it. Tried to shoot me!"

From the parking lot, I heard Denver's voice. "Nate? Jesus Christ, what the hell are you doing here?"

I turned and looked down the slope at Denver and his friend. "I...I came to find you guys. To, um...go with you."

Andrew straightened up and stood over the assassin guy. "How'd you do that?"

The woman with Denver scowled. "There'll be plenty of time to catch up later. We have to go."

I noticed more than a few people watching us from their motel room windows. Some were trying to be careful about it, peeking around curtains. Others just gawked. It was easy to guess that someone had called the cops.

"We should take him with us," I said in a rush. "He's some kind of spy or something. For the people behind the whole thing...the same company as Brenhurst." I looked from Denver to my dad and back to Denver again. "I totally think we should take him with us to the Institute."

From the ditch, Lou coughed. It was a wet, painful sound. He sobbed, "Evelyn!"

Chills ran down my back. "We can't leave him!" He'd talk to the cops if we did. And they'd know to check the house in Kirby Lake. And I'd be fucked.

My dad nudged him in a rough way that wasn't exactly a kick. "Should finish him."

Denver leaned forward, his hands tight on the arms of his wheelchair. "Are you nuts? You can't just kill people, Andrew! Come down, both of you." He shook his head and muttered, "Damn kid. Damn kid," but if he was hoping I wouldn't hear him, that was just stupid.

"We have to go right now," Denver's friend said again.

My dad's head tilted, and his eyes widened even more than usual. "Yep. Gotta go."

I heard it a second later. Sirens. Far away, but coming closer, fast. That settled it. We'd have to leave the Prentice-Cambrian assassin there to be found by the cops.

"Get in the damn van!" Denver started to wheel himself away from his friend.

She grabbed the chair. "We can't take the van! The hotel has the license number." She shot me a no-nonsense look. "How'd you get here?"

I pointed to the Olds, which was right where I left it, the front door hanging open and the engine running. "Right there."

Denver looked pissed but resigned. He didn't waste any time wheeling over to the car. "Open the trunk and throw the chair in. One of you will have to put me in the car. Who's driving?"

I started to reply, but his friend cut me off with a tone not too different from how my mother sounded when she wasn't interested in my opinion, only the results she wanted.

"I am. Nate, open the trunk and give me the keys."

I did it. I was well-trained.

323

It irritated me all to hell. But I did it.

My dad carried Denver to the shotgun seat. We got out of there.

From The Journal Of Nate Charters
Twenty Seven

Denver's friend was named Sandy. She got us out of the parking lot of the Super 8 and back on the 15 headed north without running into the cops.

The atmosphere in the car was pretty tense for a while. For the first half-hour or so, Sandy's observation that the Olds "beat the shit out of that old van" and Denver's grouchy "that was *my* old van, and leaving it was a mistake" were the only things anyone said.

I sat on the wide back seat, leaning against the door. It felt strange not to be driving. With Sandy driving, Denver sitting next to her, and me in the back, I had the odd sensation this was what most kids experienced the whole time they grew up: two parents in the front and you in the back. Not me, though.

My whole life, I'd been told my father had died in a laboratory experiment back when I was a baby. In truth, he'd been driven out of his mind after undergoing something called the "augmentation regimen." It altered his physiology to be more like a hunting animal than a human being. Before long, he shook off his handlers and lived like a hobo, or a hermit, or whatever, for the next fifteen years or so.

Now he was a few feet away from me, on the far side of the car, staring out the closed window at the darkness and the lights.

Somebody had to say something. I voted for me.

"So…what do you think will happen to that Lou guy?"

I saw Denver and Sandy look at each other. My father, still staring out the window, grumbled, "Shouldn't be here."

"Who?"

"You," he snapped.

I waited for more. A mile went by. I got tired of waiting.

"I knew that guy was coming for you," I said.

"Could have handled it."

I didn't understand why I was getting attitude from the crazy man.

"Really."

He looked at me. "You shouldn't be here."

"I..." Frustration welled up in me, and with it, to my horror, tears. "I fucking saved your life!"

"Could have handled it." Broken record.

"You hid in the room!" It took deliberate effort to keep my voice steady. I would not lose it. I didn't even understand why I was so worked up...unless you count the twelve hours on the road, the fighting off armed killers, seeing my father again, and so on and so forth. "You have no fucking idea... what I did to get—!"

He turned to the window again.

From the front, Denver said, "Nate, how in the heck did you find us, anyway?"

"I came to Kirby Lake looking for this asshole." No reaction from my father. "I..." How much to tell? It would all come out eventually. I wasn't ready. "I figured out where you guys went."

"How?"

"Just kind of...put it together. I saw his hair and old clothes in the trash—"

"You went through my trash?"

"Yeah. Sorry. I guess." I took a breath. "I knew he'd been

there, and now you were all gone—well, I didn't know about you, Sandy," little lie, "but I, um, like, waited around, and kind of just put it all together."

Denver looked over his shoulder at me. "You put it all together."

I nodded.

"How'd you manage that, exactly?"

"I...saw your notes. With the freeways and the motel."

His voice had a little iron in it this time. "How, again?"

What the hell.

"I kinda broke into your house."

Who really cared, now?

Denver squinted at me, scowling, before turning back to face the front of the car.

"Well, that's great," he said. "Are you wearing my shirt, by the way?"

"Yeah."

"I don't even want to know why."

I saw Sandy glance at me through the rearview mirror. "Nate."

"Yeah?"

"Whose car is this?"

Fuck.

"Denver's next-door neighbor's."

"Yep. Thought so," Denver said. "How'd you get the keys?"

I felt tight in my throat and all wobbly in my stomach. "Can I not say right now? I'd rather not say right now."

My father surprised me with a painful slap on my leg. I jerked.

"Hey!"

He watched my face. His crazy eyes seemed less nuts and very serious. Quietly, he said, "Whose blood?"

Of course. He would have seen it on my pants. He could certainly smell it. I'd blocked it out hours ago.

The urge to break down hit me again. I bit my lip.

"Can I really not say right now?"

He kept staring at me. Every couple of seconds, he tilted his head to the left or the right. Like a curious dog. His nostrils twitched.

He leaned toward me. I didn't have anywhere to go. I could feel his breath on my ear.

"Evelyn." He must have heard the name, back on the hillside. "Right?"

He pulled away and went back to studying my face.

I nodded once. I had to blink; the tears were there, but I was doing a really bang-up job of not bawling.

Denver said, "Blood?"

"Wait, Denver." My father's rasp was a little less crazy. I remembered what I'd heard him say, last year, after the big fight outside my grandmother's cabin. That his grip on his sanity comes and goes. Sure seemed like this was a different guy right then.

To me, he said, "I didn't want that to happen. Should have been there."

I laughed on reflex and immediately had to sniff hard when snot threatened to bubble out of my nose. "Just missed you, I guess."

"Should have been there."

I'd been around my dad maybe an hour and a half, in

total, my entire life, so it's not surprising I'd never seen the expression on his face I saw then.

He looked very sad. My chest hurt for him.

"I...lately..." I wiped my nose on my sleeve. "Lately, I've kinda...not been myself. The stuff...the parts like you...it's been stronger. I thought if I could talk to you..."

I sighed. "That's why I was in Kirby Lake. I figured I'd talk to Denver and see if he knew where you were, or if he could help me find you."

My dad sat back a little. He laughed. I heard Denver chuckle briefly, too.

"What?"

"S'why I went to Denver," my dad said. "Why we're going to Donner."

I shook my head. "I don't get it. Sorry..."

"Wanted to help you," he said. He looked down—suddenly bashful? I was captivated. "Wanted to...get a grip. First."

Denver filled in the blanks. "He got a bug up his butt that he should be in your life more. But to do that, he'd have to come in from the cold, as they say in the John LeCarre books. You know what I mean?"

"Yeah."

"So he talked us into taking him to see Donner's people, to see if they could help him get his...nature...under control. Make sense?"

I looked at Andrew Charters. He glanced at me, then back at the dark floor of the car. A tentative smile twitched on his lips.

"Yep," I said. I laughed a little; I didn't know what else

to do with the feelings flowing and shifting and slipping around in my head. I sniffed again; I was still crying a little.

I felt like I should do something, but I couldn't quite bring myself to hug the guy. We weren't there just yet.

I shoved his shoulder.

"Thanks, and stuff," I said.

Marc Teslowski
Ten

Marc barely saw Ray around the house on Thursday. The place was crazy with Ray's follow-ons running around preparing for a big party at the ranch that night, a windup for when they joined the protesters at the Institute on Friday.

Marc stayed out of the way. No one asked him to help with the preparations, and everyone he ran into made it clear they thought of him as an honored guest, and that he should just put his feet up. Still, all the activity made him uncomfortable, and not just because he wasn't helping with anything.

Whether they were just doing regular chores around the house, coming back from "down the hill" with kegs of beer, boxes of chips, bags of ice, and loads of other party supplies, or having impromptu planning sessions in the hallways about their plans for Declaration Day rabble-rousing, all of Ray's family and followers seemed lit up like Bible thumpers knocking on the door on Sunday morning.

It was damn disturbing. Marc felt like he was a bystander in Jonestown, the night before the Kool-Aid got passed around.

Marc had reasons to hate the Sovereigns. Real-life, personal, firsthand reasons. They'd insulted him by taking Byron, taken a swipe at his balls by maybe taking advantage of his son's normal teenage rebellious tendencies...all probably because of Byron's involvement with the Charters kid.

Marc had never figured that part out, but who knew how the freaks thought, or what kind of plans their leader had in his head? It sure as hell made more sense than the bullshit idea that Byron was actually one of them.

But Greene and his people…their hate, it was like religion or something. The people running around the house today, and the new ones coming in, they all had a light in their eyes that was just a little too nutty.

It wasn't personal for them. It was bigger than personal.

And that was *crazy*.

A few times through the day, Marc considered picking up a phone and getting himself a taxi back down to Missoula. He could call Jeri, have her wire some money. He was pretty sure she'd started her own bank account a while back, on the sly. He hadn't given a shit, so long as she was quick to give up whatever she'd stashed away whenever he decided to ask for it.

Now might just be the time.

On the other hand, he wanted to be at the Institute tomorrow. He figured all the confusion of the celebration and speeches and yelling back and forth would give him his best chance to slip through the Visitors Center and, hell, just walk up the road to the damn place. Start knocking on doors.

And if Greene had something balls-out crazy planned—something dangerous—the same basic plan applied. Marc would rather be in a position to get Byron out of there than hear about it all on the news the next day.

So he'd ride it out with the weird, culty, "speciesist" crazies. At least they'd saved him a few days of hotel and rental-car fees.

Marc took a nap, walked around the grounds and watched the place get transformed for the night's festivities, helped himself to a beer or two, and watched a little television. When the sun went down, he wandered out and joined the first of the revelers.

Almost immediately, someone put a beer in his left hand and a plate loaded with a hot dog and some potato salad in his right. There was backslapping. People wanted to shake his hand and get their picture taken with him.

Crazy fuckers.

A country-and-western band—not one of those toe-step-kick faggoty urban cowboy outfits; these guys had a little southern rock in their sound—started up on a bandstand that hadn't been there when Ray had given him the tour the day before. Marc stood around and listened to them for a bit, then moved from group to group, accepting beers (and the occasional shot) when they were offered.

After a few hours, Marc had a pretty good buzz. He made sure to visit the guys manning a row of smokers and barbeque grills so he could keep a little bit of food in him, and every third beer, he downed a plastic bottle of water. The buzz was good, a party was a party, but he didn't want to get shitfaced. There was work to do tomorrow.

It was some time after nine o'clock when he heard a ruckus swell up out of a cluster of rednecks near the house. Somebody let out a rebel yell, and there were a lot of whoops and hollers. Somebody started up a chant of "Speech, speech!" and the rest of the crowd took it up.

"What the fuck now?" Intrigued and amused, Marc hung near the back of the crowd and waited for something to happen.

Ray Greene climbed up on a picnic table in the middle of the crowd and the chanting dissolved into cheers, applause, and shrill whistles. Grinning, Greene let them go for a few seconds before he raised his arms.

"All right, all right!" The crowd calmed down. Marc noticed more people gathering; he was no longer on the outskirts of the audience but right in the middle of it.

"All right," Greene said again. "I hadn't planned on saying anything…but you folks, all you beautiful people—all you beautiful human beings—how can I say no to all of you?"

Someone off to Marc's left shouted, "Humanity!" The crowd whooped it up in a quick swell as Greene nodded.

"Damn right. Humanity…and we're the best of it, right here. I'm damn privileged to see so many of us in one place, gathered as we are to celebrate our purity so that, united in our resolve and fellowship, tomorrow we'll be ready to show that devil's nest we will not go quietly into extinction!"

Marc looked around at the men and women gallivanting around him and wondered how many would actually show up for protesting after they woke up hungover.

"In fact," Greene went on, "in fact…some of you out there—I see your faces, I recognize you from snapshots in your cards and letters—some of you have taken the battle for human supremacy personally. Some of you have met the enemy, right up close…" He raised a fist and shook it. "…and you gave 'em what-for!"

Applause erupted. Marc saw some people exchange high-fives and backslaps. Boots stomped the dirt.

"Speaking of that very thing…" Greene scanned the crowd. "Where's Scott Pond? Where the hell is he?" Greene grinned wickedly. "Don't tell me you're not out there, Scotty; I paid for your damn plane ticket!"

Laughter rippled. A hand shot up from the crowd. "Over here, Ray!"

Ray swept his arm in a wide gesture. "Get up here, Scotty! Get up here! Get him up here!"

The crowd got crazy, stomping and clapping. Scott Pond found himself lifted up and crowd-surfed to the picnic table, where he found his feet next to Greene.

Greene shook his hand. Pond got into the spirit of things and pumped his fist in the air and whooped.

The crowd settled down as Greene resumed speaking.

"Scotty's been a big supporter; a great long-distance friend of *The Good Human* from the beginning. I'm so pleased he'll be by my side tomorrow morning...and I tell you what, it was a bit of providence that Scott flew into town today."

Greene paused and scanned the faces in the crowd. "Do you want to know why, my friends?"

An obligatory sweep of applause.

"Well, fine. I'll tell you. Arby and I drove down to meet Scotty today—I'd get Arby up here, too, but he's taking care of another...heh...very special guest we have here tonight—you'll find out about that later. They're the guest of honor!"

Marc thought maybe Greene was talking about him, but he hadn't seen Arby all day, and anyway, Marc wasn't a big deal to the speciesists after he'd been palling around with them all night.

"Anyway...Arby and I meet Scott, and we're driving back from the airport along Reserve Street, talking 'bout how much fun we're gonna have tonight and what's on the plate for tomorrow and such and like...and we see her. A woman."

Greene winked. Hoots and catcalls came from the

crowd. He waved his hands and shook his head. "Nah, c'mon! I'm a widower, friends! Besides…I should have said: something that almost, mind you, almost, looked like it might *pass* for a woman!"

Hisses and boos.

"That's right. You got it; smart bunch, you bet." Greene nodded slowly. "It was a Sovereign, right there in broad daylight, bound for the devil's nest, and…wrap your heads around this one, my friends: it was hitchhiking!"

A quieter wave of commentary from the crowd at that. They were hooked.

"So, hell, we did what any decent human being would do. We pulled over and offered that thing a ride."

Marc heard more than a few lecherous asides from here and there. Greene let a wry grin flow across his lips as he shook his head.

"Nope, nope…even if I wasn't a widower and Scott here wasn't married and Arby…well, wasn't so damn shy…believe you me, friends, no one would think of having relations with this creature.

"It was so pale, its skin was almost blue, with all the veins running like, I don't know, maybe like a roadmap, underneath, plain as day. It didn't have no lips—and I don't mean they were thin, I mean it when I say it didn't have no lips, period. Just a slit for a mouth.

"It had the devil's mark, too, my friends. Plain as day. The thing's eyes—the pupils were like what you see looking at a snake."

Greene shivered theatrically. "Damn disturbing. Inhuman. But we saw an opportunity there with it. So we swallowed our natural revulsion, faked big good-ol'-boy smiles, and got it in the car." He laughed. "Arby had a hard time of it, with it back there with him in the back seat. He didn't like that one bit."

Greene put his arm around his guest. "Scotty, why don't you tell a little bit. I need a drink." He looked out at the crowd. "Does anyone know where a man can find a drink around here?"

People fell over themselves to get a beer in Greene's hands while Pond coughed into his hand, smiled a little nervously, and took up the story.

"Well...so, we get it in the car, and everyone makes sure to act friendly and interested and sympathetic while it gives us a sob story...comes from some little town in Wisconsin, no one likes it, parents won't talk to it, boo-hoo-hoo.

"I won't speak for Mister Greene—"

"Call me Ray, you son of a bitch," Ray interjected. The crowd laughed. Ray pounded about half his beer.

Pond grinned. "All right, all right! So I won't speak for Ray or Arby, but I was a little worried about what kind of trickery it might have up its sleeve, what its Sovereign ability was.

"We didn't need to worry about it, after all. It said it didn't know if it could do anything...that it just started changing one day and couldn't take it anymore, poor albino, snake-eyed freak, and that's why it was headed for the devil's nest: to see if they could tell it what kind of curse it carried."

Ray drained the last of his beer, belched, and picked up their tale. "We drove on up the mountain, only we took 200, right—all you out-of-towners, it's the local's way to get out to these parts—telling it we knew a shortcut. Not a lie," Ray smiled slowly, "but I bet you can guess it didn't turn out to be no shortcut for that thing, either."

The crowd went crazy. Marc, who was not a small man, got pushed around like he was at one of those punker dance parties he saw on the news. He stepped back and let the crowd push in front of him.

He kept his eyes on Ray Greene. Greene let the crowd boil for half a minute or so while he stood there, open-mouthed, chest heaving. His face was dark. The beer was hitting him.

He held up his hands. The crowd quieted down immediately, but Greene still raised his voice to tent-revival-pulpit volume.

"I got two questions for you, friends! Are you ready to answer two questions?"

The crowd yelled in the affirmative.

"Question number one! What's the color of devil blood? Who can tell me?" He didn't wait for a response. "Devils run red! Red as you or I—that's why they're devils! Now—how many of those damn monsters are crawling around God's dominion with us? How many Sovereign?"

A lot of voices offered up the standard answer: six thousand. Greene shook his head. Spittle flew from his lips.

"Hell with that! Not as of today! Five thousand, nine-hundred, ninety-nine, my friends! Five thousand, nine-hundred, ninety-nine! And we ain't done! *We ain't done!*"

Scott Pond raised both fists above his head and howled in triumph. The crowd—which it seemed to Marc had swelled to include pretty much everyone at the ranch that night, more than two hundred people—exploded.

There it was, Marc thought. There's the damn Kool-Aid.

From The Journal Of Nate Charters
Twenty Eight

Sandy put miles of Idaho behind us while I brought them up to speed. Mostly. I didn't mention what I'd done to the woman, Evelyn. My father knew the gist if not the details, but he didn't press for more.

There was some discussion of stopping somewhere and putting me on a plane back to California, or at least calling my mother and letting her know where I was.

I sure as hell wasn't ready to go back yet, not after coming so far and going through so much. Not getting to Missoula was just not an option. If me and Sandy took shifts, we could be at the Donner Institute for Sovereign Studies by morning. Why not just call her from there?

I was surprised Sandy agreed with this. "It's what makes the most sense, all things considered."

Denver said, "What do you think Uldare will tell the cops?"

"Maybe nothing," Sandy said. "Think about it."

Denver muttered, "We're all going to jail."

Sandy slapped him lightly on the shoulder. "I'm not so sure." She said to me, "Tell me more about the cameras."

"Uh…well, I didn't really see any cameras. That's the weird thing. They were definitely filming Denver's place, inside and out. But I never saw a camera."

Denver said, "Sure, but would you know what to look for?"

It was a fair question. "I don't know. And I didn't really, like, have time to look too hard, either."

"Doesn't really matter," Sandy said. "The fact is, the

evidence is there in that house…all that recording equipment, that man's message on the answering machine…"

The woman's gun.

Her body.

I focused on Sandy's voice. "This is really big. Really big."

Denver grinned. "Your reporter's instinct kicking in?"

"Reporter?" I asked.

Denver said, "Sandy works for *The Kirby Grizzly*…but before that, she was big-time."

"I had my moments." It sounded to me like she wanted a few more. "And yes, any fool could see there's something there."

Denver feigned offense. "Hey!"

"Look at it. PrenticeCambrian has two hitmen staking out your house, have you under illegal surveillance, all just in case Andrew Charters shows up. All while, they're neck-deep in a legal battle with his son and ex-wife? Please!"

"Okay," Denver nodded. "It's big. It's movie-of-the-week stuff, at the very least."

"Screw that," Sandy said. "It's Pulitzer stuff."

I liked her.

"This is why we have to get Nate and Andy to the Institute," she said. "Getting Andrew help is one thing, but Donner's people need to know about this. And they've offered both of them sanctuary in the past…"

"Not staying there!" my dad barked.

"Not permanently," I said in what I hoped was a soothing voice. "But I can't think of anywhere safer right now. Can you?"

My father laughed, I think. It was a wet, nasty sound. He stabbed a thumb toward the window. "Sure. Out there." He slumped a little. "Won't run. Sticking it out. Can still help."

I nodded. "I think so."

We were all quiet for a little while. I found myself thinking about everything I knew so far and how little it all made any sense.

"Like, who are those people, anyway?"

"Who?" Denver said.

"Brenhurst. Tyndale Labs. PrenticeCambrian." I looked at my dad. "What's the deal with all of this stuff? I mean, like, really."

He scrunched up his face and seemed to put a lot of effort into thinking. I watched memories play off his face. I smelled fear, and anger, and frustration, play out of his pores.

"Not sure," he finally said.

That was a little exasperating. "Are you sure you're not sure?"

He looked irritated, then gave it another go for another little bit. He huffed and shook his head vigorously.

"Big stuff."

Denver said, "That's about all you're gonna get, Nate. You know as much as we do."

"Sure," I said. "Project: Rancher. Changing people into fake Sovereigns. My dad, brilliant scientist, being crazy or stupid enough—no offense—to be a test subject."

"Or principled enough," Denver said quietly.

My father hacked another burst of laughter. "Stupid." He looked out the window.

"Anyway." I didn't want things to get too weird for everybody, so I plowed through. "Obviously they're still at it, if those guys with the big horns sticking out of their skin at the cabin last year are any indication, right? But...why?"

Sandy said, "Maybe they saw things coming."

"What things?"

"The Sovereigns."

I blinked. That made sense, sort of. I tried my dad again. "Ringing any bells?"

"Bigger," he said.

"What's bigger?"

He shrugged. "Bigger thing coming."

"Bigger than Donner and the Sovereign?"

He scowled. "Dunno. Thinking about it...it's like catching a scent...wind changes...gone." He looked depressed about the whole thing.

Sandy said, "Well. There's another thing we can ask about when we get to Missoula." She shifted in her seat. "Nate, do you think you can sleep?"

I was exhausted. "Like, five minutes ago."

"Good. Try to. I'll need you to spell me in a while, if you're up for it."

"Okay. Totally."

What with the cozy warm darkness of the car and the rhythmic road noise, I was out in seconds.

Thursday was finally over.

Marc Teslowski
Eleven

Marc didn't need to hear any more. He wandered away from the gathered crowd with deliberate casualness.

With his back to the throng, Marc flashed back to his football days. The ball's been snapped, you're looking for your man, defense is doing their job...but you can't be sure somebody didn't break through out of your line of sight. You can't be sure you're not gonna get slammed with a helmet in your kidneys from out of your blind spot...

Nobody seemed to give a damn that he'd left. The more ground he put between him and them, the more relaxed he felt.

Sixty-some acres, Ray had said. Plenty of space to clear his head and get some fresh air.

Alone with his thoughts, Marc's head rang loudest with: These people scare the shit out of me.

Did they really kill that girl, or was it just a made-up thing to get the crowd going? How'd they know for sure she was a Sovereign? What if she was just a regular albino? Sure, there was the thing about the eyes, but what if that was just bullshit?

Marc had been pissing about the Sovereigns for most of a year, but he'd never thought about killing anybody. He wanted his son back, whether the Sovereign were holding Byron against his will or the boy was just biding time to get back at his pop. It didn't matter what the reasons were, just that he get things back the way they were, get control of his family, make sure Byron and Jeri and the whole damn world, for that matter, knew he was nobody's fool.

He didn't want to kill anybody to make it happen. That was taking things a little too far.

"Jesus fuck," Marc sighed. He put his arms behind his head and stretched, tilting his neck back. Light-gray clouds blotted out the stars and reflected the half-moon.

It was nice out here. Marc turned most of a circle, breathing the chill, dry air and trying to figure out if he'd manage to get any sleep tonight.

He stopped when he saw the birds.

They circled over the old barn, a flock like a thick cloud, black against the actual clouds in the sky, turning and swooping, never leaving the barn.

Marc didn't know how things went on a farm or a ranch or whatever, but he'd seen crows circling over roadkill out in Trimpe Canyon and figured that's what this was. Something must have died over there.

Marc started for the barn. Maybe it was a coyote. He'd never seen a coyote in real life. Even if this one was dead, it might be neat.

Closer to the barn, he could see them now, flitting by above him. The whirling flock was actually made up of all kinds of birds. It was too dark to name them, and he was no damn bird watcher anyway, but Marc for sure saw crows or ravens and little tiny sparrowish ones, and an owl or two, and some that might be hawks.

They didn't make any noise. No hoots, no chirps, no cawing...nothing. Just the soft percussion of their wings pushing at the air.

What the fuck was that all about? It almost made Marc want to go back to the crazies. It sounded like they were shooting guns off now.

Marc made it to the barn. Dirty windows in the big doors glowed from inside with a yellowish light. He leaned against the padlocked latch and felt the doors give on their hinges under his weight just a little.

He watched the birds. He felt the breeze from hundreds of pairs of wings. Droppings fell like rain, and Marc was glad for the overhanging roof above him. He pushed a little closer to the door.

A crow—he thought it was a crow—dove for his head. He yelped and ducked.

A soft smack above him, and another crow, or the same one, slapped to the ground at his feet. Its neck was broken.

An owl came for him, thick talons outstretched, just in time for Marc to flinch to his hands and knees. He felt the tips of its wings tousle his hair. Those wings didn't make any sound at all.

One hand partially shielding his face, Marc looked up and saw the owl furiously battering the window with its wings and scratching at the frame with its claws before pivoting and flying off.

They came faster after that. A few more made for him, but never hit. Marc started to feel like they weren't trying to hit him at all. He was a big, easy, stationary target, and they kept missing, after all. It was more like they were trying to keep him down.

The birds were much more interested in the windows. Suicidally interested. They fell around him, two and five and now a dozen, finches and jays and ravens and other varieties, with soft thumps that made Marc a little queasy.

He kept his head low and wondered, crazily, if Alfred Hitchcock and Alan Fundt were going to come out of the darkness with a camera.

A crash of glass. The shards fell on and around him. Marc curved his body in the old duck-and-cover and hoped he didn't get cut up.

Then something big, all stinking feathers and hard claws and beak, ten or fifteen pounds of dead weight, slammed onto his back.

Marc hollered and scrambled away, arms waving.

The thing tumbled from him and flopped, twitching, bloody, and dying, on the ground.

Fuck if it wasn't a goddamned bald eagle.

Smaller birds streamed in through the broken window. With Marc away from the door, big ones, the owls and ravens and hawks, converged on the door itself.

Feathers flew and blood sprayed like mist. They attacked the door, inside and out, and didn't seem to care they tore into each other in their frenzy.

Marc couldn't look away.

Even as they died, slamming into and tearing at the wood, ripping past the shards of glass in the windows frames, they still made no sound.

The door latch hit the dirt with a muffled clang. The surviving birds rejoined the circling flock above the barn.

Marc couldn't ignore the facts. The goddamned birds just broke into the barn.

He shivered. Not because of the thin-air mountain chill. Because he was freaked the fuck out.

The birds inside the barn burst through the doors in a

rush to join their pals above. Marc damn near had a heart attack.

They left the doors slightly ajar. The light inside painted a rectangle across the field of broken birds piled on the ground at the front of the barn.

Marc's heart rate slowed to sledgehammer pace. He caught his breath.

Those birds had gone to an awful lot of trouble. He had to see what was in the damn barn.

Marc slipped through the doors.

Eddie Schwippe swayed a few feet above wet, rusty hay strewn on the floor of the barn. His arms stretched over his lolling head. Heavy bull rope looked like it had been tied and duct-taped around his wrists and looped over a beam that extended from the hayloft.

Schwippe's naked, bony torso was roadmapped with cuts and blossomed with red and purple bruises. His left nipple was a glistening red hole.

His face was black with caked blood. His right eye was swollen shut. His enormous nose twisted to the right. His lips were cracked, practically exploded over his broken teeth, and slack.

Ray Greene's guest of honor.

Son of a bitch.

Marc crossed the barn. "Hey." He whispered and didn't know why. "Hey."

Schwippe's chest moved. He was alive.

"Hey." Marc examined the rope; it was too high for him to reach. He'd have to get up on the hayloft and untie it from there.

A storm of feathers and black eyes rushed through the open door. Like some twisted, nightmare version of a Disney cartoon, the birds roosted around the beam holding the roof and stabbed at it with their beaks.

Marc took the hint. He was ready when the rope frayed and snapped. He lowered Eddie Schwippe to the bloody hay as carefully as he could.

Schwippe's lips moved, cuts and cracks seeping as he tried to speak. Marc couldn't make it out.

The birds tore out of the barn again. Marc squinted when bright light illuminated their wings as they crowded through half-open doors.

Headlights.

He stood up, balled his fists, and put himself between Eddie Schwippe and the barn doors.

Marc Teslowski was no friend to Sovereigns. But he'd be no kind of man at all if he let any more harm come to the poor fool lying on the ground at his feet.

Marc Teslowski
Twelve

Car doors opened and shut. Ray Greene's son Arby and the kid with the flag tattoo on his hand—Drake—came through the door.

Drake carried a shotgun.

Arby's surprise was plain on his face. "Mister Teslowski. Dang, sir. Didn't expect to find you here."

The suspicion on Drake's face was just as clear. "What happened to the Sovereign?"

Marc ran some plays through his head, real quick.

"Somebody roughed him up pretty good," he said. He tried to smile, but it felt sloppy and cold on his face.

"Hell, yeah," Drake said. "But last I saw it, it was tied up."

"Birds cut him loose."

"Birds?" It seemed to Marc that Arby wanted to give him the benefit of the doubt.

"Yeah. That's what made me come over here. All the birds, circling over the barn."

Drake and Arby looked at each other. Drake squinted at Marc.

"How'd you get in here, anyway?"

Marc shrugged. "Birds, like I said."

"Those dead ones?" Drake gestured generally behind him with the shotgun. "What birds?"

Arby scratched the side of his head. "I don't see no more birds, Mister Teslowski. Beggin' your pardon, sir, but you probably shouldn't have been out here, sir."

"No shit," Marc said lightly. "Damn things nearly

pecked my eyes out."

Drake was getting angry. "Goddamn it. What birds?"

Marc heard the rush of wings through the roof. The light from the headlights flickered and was eclipsed.

"Those birds."

They poured into the barn and swarmed around Arby and Drake, who stumbled and floundered, swiping the air and trying to protect their faces and their eyes.

This time, the flock didn't keep quiet. Their cries were deafening.

Time to go.

Marc picked up Eddie Schwippe and made for the door. The birds parted for him; they formed a wall of talons and beaks and obscuring wings as he passed the flailing species-ists.

Drake and Arby hadn't bothered to turn off the ignition or lock the doors. Marc got the back passenger door opened and worried Schwippe onto the back seat.

He heard a shotgun blast, followed by a short scream that was almost lost in the screeching of the flock. He flinched hard, automatically, before he realized he hadn't been hit.

He ran around to the driver's side of the car. He reached for the car door latch and just felt the cold metal on his fingertips when Drake slammed into him.

They hit the ground rolling. Drake's bare arms were slick with bird shit and blood. It made it hard to get a grip on him.

At least he didn't have the gun.

Drake's flag-draped hands wrapped around Marc's neck.

The kid's face was pocked and cut and bloody. One of his eyebrows was loose, and the top of his right ear was mostly missing.

Strong hands. Marc felt the edges of his vision getting dim.

But both *his* hands were free. He used them to pound on Drake's sides, but that didn't give the kid enough grief to let go.

Marc got smarter. He grabbed that bloody ear and twisted as hard as he could.

That did it. Drake howled and loosened his grip.

"Off of me!" Marc pushed him hard and rolled away. Panting, he got to his feet.

The birds, a black, undulating ball of noise and rage, found Drake.

Marc scrambled into the car. His throat hurt like hell. He found and disengaged the brake and dropped his foot on the gas pedal. The back end of the car fishtailed in the dirt for a couple seconds before the tires found some traction.

Marc had to go past the main house to get to the only road off the ranch that he knew. The revelers either hadn't been alerted or just gathered something wasn't right when he flew past pushing eighty miles per hour.

The exit of the ranch was blocked by a long wooden gate.

Marc made a sound that was equal parts groan and scream and leaned into the steering wheel. He drove through the gate. The sound of wood and metal grinding and breaking was very loud inside the car. The impact vibrated through him.

He was on the road.

After the sound of the birds, the screaming, and the collision of the gate, the comparative calm of the car's engine and the wheels on the road made his ears ring.

From the back seat, Eddie Schwippe croaked, "Action... hero..."

Marc laughed, then winced. Fucking kid nearly crushed his larynx back there.

Marc Teslowski
Thirteen

Marc aimed the car for the Donner Institute for Sovereign Studies.

What choice did he have? Eddie Schwippe was beat to hell. Marc bet they'd let him through the gates if he showed up with a Sovereign in very damn serious need of medical attention.

He grimaced as he focused hard on the slice of the mountain road in the arc of the headlights. He couldn't deny that Schwippe might not have been trussed up in Ray Greene's barn for the last few days if Marc had done something when he and the scarecrow Sovereign first arrived in Missoula.

Marc thought about the albino girl.

"You are one lucky son of a bitch," he muttered to the prone form lying on the back seat.

Marc was surprised to hear some movement back there, and a soft groan.

"Thanks…"

Marc didn't need to hear that. Didn't want to hear that.

"Just go to sleep. Let me drive, for chrissake."

If Schwippe said something else, the words were drowned out by a loud and rhythmic clanking coming from somewhere under the hood. The engine seized seconds later.

"Fuck!"

Apparently driving a car through a wooden fence at full speed and getting away without any serious damage wasn't something that happened in real life. Marc brought the car over to the shoulder of the road in a controlled coast. He turned off the headlights.

"Schwippe. I take it back. Wake up."

Marc turned and saw his passenger sit up slowly, moaning all the way. "We stopped."

"Yeah. We're fucked."

"Where…where were we going?"

Marc's lip curled. "Donner Institute." Not how he'd planned it. "Figure you need the help of your own kind."

Schwippe blinked the eye that wasn't swollen shut. His whole face bunched slowly; the wince extended down to his shoulders, and the whole move looked like it hurt. He exhaled sharply and took a moment.

"How…" Another moment. "How close are we?"

"Too damn far." Marc frowned. "And I don't know if anyone's after us."

Schwippe carefully wrapped his thin arms around his battered chest. "Probably…pretty cold out there."

"Sure. But it'll stay warm in the car for a while, I guess."

Schwippe raised his head. "I think…we can't stay in the car. I think we can make it. To the Institute." He tried to lick his cracked lips. He cringed and gasped. "I think we have to."

Marc figured it probably wasn't safe to just sit on the side of the road in one of Greene's cars and wait for the crazy rednecks to show up with their guns. But…

"You're crazy. How're we gonna get there? You can't travel."

"Oh, I'll travel." He closed his eyes for a moment; opened them. "Given the alternative…there's no alternative. Right?" He tried to smile.

"You think you can walk all that way? We're talking

miles."

"With your help. Besides…it's closer…as the crow flies."

Marc shook his head. "You're punch-drunk. I can't just set off hiking through the mountains in the middle of the night and find the place. What're you thinking?"

"What are you thinking? We'll have help."

Schwippe looked past Marc, out the windshield. Marc turned around and jumped.

An owl stood on the hood of the car. It blinked patiently and preened.

"Jesus," Marc said. "Seriously?"

"Oh, yeah. Listen." He tried to lean forward. It didn't go so well. He tried to sigh, and it turned into a little grunt. "You did something good, Marc Teslowski. You saved me. You saved a Sovereign."

Marc looked away from Eddie's one good, big, black eye. "Wasn't thinking about it like that."

"My…" A grunt and flinch. "My point. So let's…push the irony a little more and have my Sovereign ability save us both."

"So you can make birds do whatever you want?" It was fucking creepy.

"Oh, hell. No. I…communicate with them, sort of." He shifted his weight. "Just so happens they think I'm a pretty nice guy, I guess. They go along with my suggestions."

Marc shook his head. "More than that. They died for you."

Schwippe blinked hard. "Yes. They did." His laugh was thin and short. "Who knew? Up until tonight, I have to admit," he coughed, "I thought my Sovereign so-called ability was pretty weak."

His expression hardened. "Not anymore."

Marc didn't have anything to say about that. They sat in silence for a couple of minutes until Marc decided they should get going if they were really going to do this. There was another problem, though.

"Even if your pal out there can guide us," he said, "and I don't break an ankle on the way…it's too cold. I can let you wear my jacket, but…"

"I was thinking about that. I have a hunch. I bet if you look in the trunk, there'll be a blanket or something. It'll be better than nothing."

"What makes you so sure?"

"Those lunatics have a militia in the mountains of Montana. They probably have…stockpiles of freeze-dried food…" Schwippe did his cough and flinch thing again. "…in the basement. They'll have an emergency kit in the trunk. I think."

Marc popped the trunk, got out, and looked. Schwippe was right.

Byron Teslowski
Six

Byron jerked awake. Wisps of his last dream dissipated in seconds and left him feeling confused and, for no reason he could figure out, a little sad.

Someone was knocking—no, someone was pounding—on his apartment door. He sat up in the bed.

"Hold on!" He slipped out of bed. "Coming..." He checked the clock; it was twenty after six in the morning.

Byron opened the door. "Jon? What's up? I thought..."

Jon Schulmann looked like he'd been sick. "Need you now."

"What's going on?"

"Nothing good."

Schulmann waited in the doorway while Byron quickly dressed.

"You're not going to tell me what? Is it my dad again?"

"I sure hope not."

Byron locked up. Schulmann was already walking down the hall. Byron trotted to catch up with him.

"What's that supposed to mean? Dude!"

"You want to hear it from Croy." He shook his head. "And I don't want to talk about it."

Byron just met this guy day before yesterday, and he thought he was kind of a jerk, but this morning he seemed different. Worse.

They left the building, and Schulmann led the way to a golf cart. Byron was surprised to see Haze leaning against it.

They hadn't said a word to each other since Wednesday. She didn't exactly jump up and give him a hug. "You hear about it?"

Schulmann broke in before Byron could respond. "Please get away from the cart. He'll be briefed by Mr. Croy."

Fuck that.

"No, Haze. Jon won't tell me. What the hell's going on?"

Haze gave Schulmann a dirty look, then said to Byron, "They killed one of us."

"Aw, what? Who? When?"

Schulmann got behind the wheel of the electric cart. "Get in, Byron. This is SCET business."

Byron sat down in the cart but kept one trainer on the pavement. He looked at Haze. "How'd you hear?"

"Couple of guys I met, they work the infirmary night shift. Saw her brought in. Everybody on graveyard knows by now. It's all they're talking about in the cafeteria."

Schulmann said, "We're going, Byron."

Byron pointed his thumb at the back bench of the cart. "You want to come?"

"Yep." Haze climbed aboard. Schulmann rolled his eyes but kept his mouth shut.

Croy, Dr. Mazmanian, and Ed Kelso were ready for them inside the barracks. Croy wore field fatigues. Kelso wore a nightshirt big enough to serve as the mainsail of a clipper ship, reminding Byron that the giant was the only person who actually slept here.

Byron wasn't all that happy to see Derek Fontino there as well. He'd managed to avoid the DOD liaison all day yesterday, and no doubt the guy still wanted to meet with him. But this morning Fontino barely registered his presence.

If Fontino was unwelcome, the presence of the fifth man was flat-out surprising. It was William Donner's actual personal biographer, the newspaper guy, Ewing Kass. In comparison to Fontino's crisp suit, Kass looked like he'd slept in his white dress shirt and chinos, or like he hadn't slept at all. Still, for him to be there...he was almost Donner's proxy.

Doc Mazmanian raised an eyebrow when he saw Haze.

"Ah...we were thinking this was going to be a little more just for SCET and Institute staff, Haze. Sorry...you can take the cart back if you want."

"And you can waste time trying to get me on it, Vic," she looked pointedly at Schulmann, "or you can get on with it. I want to know what happened last night."

Schulmann rolled his eyes again. Mazmanian glanced at Croy, who hadn't moved and didn't respond to the drama. No surprise there. Mazmanian smiled slightly.

"Well, I guess we'll get on with it, then."

Croy seemed to take that as his cue.

"Her name was Yvette Schwenck. Her body was recovered in a ditch on Highway 200, one third of a mile west of Garnet Range Road."

Vic Mazmanian said, "I believe she was thrown from a car." His voice was low and not quite emotionless, but it just didn't come naturally to him like it did with Croy. "She was killed when they drove back to run her over."

Schulmann asked, "Who did it?"

Croy said, "That's not known at this time."

Ed Kelso's voice was like a rock grinder. "At what time will it be known, then?"

Croy didn't answer that directly. "We know of one other

Sovereign expected at the Institute before today who has not arrived. We must assume he met a similar fate. We have also received reports from new arrivals this week of harassment from members of the local speciesist militia group."

Ewing Kass spoke up. "Rayford Greene's people."

Croy didn't respond; everyone knew Croy never responded to things he considered obvious, so maybe the comment was meant for the rest of them.

"Hey," Byron said, "that's the guy you guys were talking about Wednesday."

"That guy's the asshole your dear old dad's been hanging out with, too," Schulmann said.

Byron found himself more than a little bugged by Jon today. "Look, my dad's a fuckwit, and a total asshole...but he wouldn't kill somebody. He's all bark."

Mostly.

Fontino stood with his legs slightly apart. He cupped an elbow in one hand and thoughtfully covered his mouth with the other. Byron thought he looked like a male model in a department store catalog.

"You think the Schwenck killing is a message."

"I cannot speculate," Croy said. "It is reasonable to assume that the local militia is involved. Possibly responsible. It is a given that group will be represented at the Visitors Center today. Provoked, violent engagement during Declaration Day festivities is expected."

"Figured as much," Kelso said.

"I have revised the agenda. We will not wait for an incident. The SCET will be onsite all day. I want you all back here and ready to deploy by 0830. Byron, you will accompany Mister Kelso and Mister Schulmann."

"I will?"

Doc Mazmanian said, "You got fitted for your uniform yesterday, right?"

"Yeah."

"Okay, then."

Haze said, "Mister Croy." Byron almost forgot she was there.

"Yes."

"Who called it in?"

"Can you be more specific?"

"Sure I can. How did we know where to find the girl's body?"

"Doctor Donner sensed her death."

That gave everyone in the room a little pause, except for Ewing Kass, who bowed his head, and Derek Fontino, who, Byron noticed, focused very hard on Spencer Croy.

Haze seemed really tense. "Wait a minute. You said there was 'one other' Sovereign who was expected but hasn't show up yet, right?"

"Correct."

"Back when I got here, I just, y'know, walked up to the gate. Did these two Sovereigns, like, call ahead, or something? Make an appointment?"

"Not to my knowledge."

"Then...how—?"

Croy anticipated her question. "Doctor Donner was aware of them."

Byron saw Haze's eyes narrow and her face tighten. "I'm going with you guys."

Schulmann shook his head. "No way. Sorry. You're not trained."

"I'm a Sovereign individual, by your boss's made-up laws and by rules of the Compromise." She strode up to Schulmann and got in his face. "You wanna stop me?"

Byron felt the heat coming off of Haze from ten feet away. He saw beads of sweat pop on Schulmann's face.

"You really want to play firefly with me, girl?" Schulmann said.

"You think I'm gonna wait for you to run and get your little suit?" Haze said.

Kelso said, "Zing!" Schulmann reddened from more than the heat.

Doc Mazmanian said, "Seriously? This is not the day for this kind of bickering."

Croy turned to Byron. "Mister Teslowski will vouch for Ms. Edgars. Or not."

Byron realized Haze had never told him her last name. "I—why me?"

"Works for me," Doc Mazmanian said. "You know Haze better than anyone here."

Croy just looked at him, waiting.

Byron assumed this was another on-the-spot test he didn't understand. It was stupid.

"Like she said. Who's gonna stop her?"

It wasn't really a glowing endorsement. Haze's sarcastic half-smile let him know she knew it, too.

"Settled," Croy said. "Oh-eight-thirty."

Schulmann immediately went to the golf cart and puttered off, back to the apartments. Byron yelled after him,

"That's cool, Jon! We'll walk!" Quieter, he said, "Dick."

Haze went with Byron. Alone with her, he couldn't put their fight out of his head.

"I'm surprised you want to come with us."

"I have my reasons," she said. "Don't think I'm joining up or anything."

"I know." Byron shook his head. "That girl. It's totally fucked."

"Uh-huh." She moved stiff and fast, practically power-walking.

"It got to you, huh?"

"They knew she was coming, Byron. Donner *himself* knew she was coming, and no one went to pick her up and make sure she got here. What is wrong with these people?"

Byron thought about it. "That is fucked-up," he agreed.

She hawked and spat as they walked. "Something is, all right." They reached the apartments. "I don't have a stupid uniform, thank god. I'll wait here."

"Okay."

"Happy fucking Declaration Day," she growled. "And hurry up, because I cannot fucking wait to start burning shit."

From The Journal Of Nate Charters
Twenty Nine

Less than a mile short of our destination, every vehicle crawling northbound on the two lane mountain road leading to the Donner Institute for Sovereign Studies collectively surrendered. The road was a parking lot.

"Looks like we walk from here," I said.

"This is gonna be a bitch," Denver groused. "Shoulder's not paved."

Sandy said, "Don't fuss, Denver. We'll wheel you right up the road. No one's moving; it won't matter."

Andrew growled quietly. "Lots of people. Lots."

That was for sure. Having left their cars behind, people streamed the last little way to the Visitors Center in clusters. It was as if we'd parked in the farthest lot from the gate of Disneyland…except I didn't see any little kids anywhere.

Probably for the best.

I exhaled. "We'll be all right. Right?"

"Sure." I had the feeling Denver's upbeat tone was strictly for Andrew's benefit. He knew better. If *I* could smell traces of anxiety on our sweat, we must have reeked to my father.

Sandy opened her door. "Come on, men. History beckons, etcetera, etcetera."

I got out of the car. The morning air was crisp and cold, refreshing after the last two slow hours in the car. It was hard to savor, though. I felt a little exposed just standing next to the car and found myself scanning the woodsy hillside and the faces of the people trudging past.

"Help me out, Nate?" Sandy called from the back end of

the car.

"Right." I helped her get the wheelchair out of the trunk and Denver into it, not that he needed a whole lot of help. Only Andrew remained in the car.

"Time to go," I said through his window.

He looked at me, then stared straight ahead. I thought we were going to have a problem, but he tapped on the window, so I took that as a signal to open his door for him. In his on-again, off-again state, he'd probably forgotten how to do it himself.

Andrew got out of the car and maintained a low crouch. His nostrils twitched busily. "Sovereigns..."

"What? How do you know? Where?" I looked around.

"There. There...there...all around." He pointed at various people, mixed in with the throngs making their way up the road. "Smell 'em. You can't?"

I couldn't. Or could I? Maybe it was just a matter of knowing how to filter it out. I'd ask him about it later, when we were safely at the Institute. Might be a handy trick.

Each of the people my dad pointed out looked like tired, road-dirty, haggard travelers. Just like us, in other words.

"Wild."

In fact, I thought we probably stood out. Guy in a wheelchair. Me with my double-take features. I wondered how long it would be before I was recognized. It gave me the willies, like the feeling someone's standing behind you.

"Let's get going, you guys."

"I'll lead the way," Denver said. I quickly saw the sense in that. People instinctively cleared a path for a guy in a wheelchair. The rest of us followed close behind, with

Andrew right after Denver and Sandy bringing up the rear.

We made it about ten minutes before a ripple of excited noise from down the road made us stop and look behind us.

"Duck." My dad's warning was so calm, it almost didn't register with me.

A shirtless, flying man buzzed us. The buffeting air from his powerful, flapping wings smelled like body odor. He climbed about fifty feet, laughing, and leveled off for the rest of his flight to the Institute.

My tongue dried out, which cued me in that I'd been staring after him with my mouth hanging open. I closed it.

The last time I had seen that guy, a Sovereign whose name I would later learn was Gary Chancellor, it had been on grainy news-copter video footage on TV, one year ago tonight.

It felt like a lifetime. That night, I'd been dragged to my grandmother's empty summer cabin in Kirby Lake by my paranoid mother, who had been freaked out by Donner and what his declaration might mean to the world and to her "special little guy." Lina and I had just met. I had no idea Byron Teslowski was anything more than a schoolyard bully.

Now I was maybe just hours away from meeting Donner himself. Byron was there, right now, at the Institute, far as I knew.

And Lina and I were probably totally over.

When we finally got to the Institute, I almost wanted to meet Chancellor more than anybody. Seeing the flying man was like bookends on either side of the last year.

We watched him do loops in the air. I heard distant cheers.

"I wonder if we can catch up to that guy...?"

Andrew frowned and wrinkled his nose. "Stinks."

Sandy said, "Even I could smell his backdraft. I wonder if his wings have sweat glands? Like big radiators?"

"Already taking notes, eh?" Denver said with affection.

"Of course!"

As someone with a hyperactive metabolism to fuel my augmented abilities, I had an idea of what she was talking about. "You mean he burns hot...because it takes so much energy to fly?"

She winked at me. "Bright boy."

We walked on, using the literal aerobatics of Chancellor as a marker. We could hear the white noise of a crowd somewhere ahead. We were really close.

I think I was the first one to see the thrown rock hit Chancellor and the flying man's head snap back. His back arched, his wings faltered, and he fluttered dangerously close to the ground before he got it together and shakily gained altitude. I lost sight of him somewhere beyond peak of the hill ahead.

The attack had a bad effect on the crowd. Shouts swelled into screams of shock and fear...and very quickly, rage. Things were going to get nasty.

I looked at Andrew, Sandy, and Denver. "We have to... Come on!"

Andrew narrowed his eyes and bared his teeth. I saw a moment of regret and frustration cross Sandy's face before she put a hand on Denver's shoulder.

"You two go. Find out what happened."

I slapped my dad's shoulder. "Come on! Let's go!"

I got to the top of the hill and stopped. About fifty yards away were the gates of the Donner Institute for Sovereign Studies Visitors Center.

About fifty feet away, a line of cops were having a very difficult time keeping two angry mobs from tearing each other apart. There was no sign of the flying man.

Someone screamed, "Look!"

I didn't know they were talking about me until the first rock bounced off the pavement at my feet. It left a chalky streak on the asphalt.

While I stared at it, the second rock hit me right below my left clavicle.

From the Journal of Nate Charters
Thirty

The mob on the right must have seen someone in the mob on the left throw the stone. They must have seen get hit. Just like the anti-Sovereign gang on the left had already figured out, folks in the pro-Sovereign gang on the right started recognizing me.

I heard my name screamed from many different mouths on both sides, and then it got crazy.

Ever hear of a slam pit? It's when a people in the audience at a punk-rock show start jostling and shoving each other. It's not really *American Bandstand*-style dancing. More like human pinball. It probably looks violent and crazy to an outsider, but there's a logic and a flow and a friendly etiquette to the whole thing. No one wants to hurt or be hurt.

This was the biggest, most crowded slam pit I'd ever been in, except there was nothing friendly about it. The two sides rushed each other, tentatively at first and then with blind abandon. I found myself in the middle of it, standing back to back with my dad.

I didn't feel particularly endangered. I knew if I watched out for myself, stayed alert, and worked toward the edges, I'd get out of the human storm with nothing worse than a few bruises.

My crazy, half-feral dad with the razor sharp fingernails and the metahuman strength and speed was another matter. I wasn't scared for him. I was very worried for the people around us. These poor fools, friendly or otherwise, were in the deadliest situation of their lives, and they didn't even know it.

"Andrew," I screamed. "Dad! Hold it together! No killing! No killing!"

The roar from my dad's throat sent a shiver through me. Some of the people pressing against us recoiled automatically. I could smell their fear slicing through the tang of adrenaline.

"No slashing," I yelled. "Push them away—head for the gate!"

I did just that, shoving hard against the shoulders of the person closest to me. I'm not as strong as my dad, but I'm stronger than most everyone else I might meet. The effect was human bowling pins. I used the sudden space to get us closer to the gate of the Visitors Center.

My dad didn't say anything, exactly, unless you count his grunts and growls and weird guttural barks as a response. But I didn't hear screams of agony around us or smell any fresh arterial blood, either. So long as the level of chaos didn't get any worse, I started to think we'd get through this without a Charters killing anyone.

The odds collapsed when I saw a tube trailing smoke bounce off the skull of a woman who had her tiny fist headed for my face.

She dropped like someone cut her strings. Smoke billowed. My eyes filled with tears, and the inside of my nose felt like it was melting.

I grabbed my dad's shirt. "Jump," I coughed.

We leapt over the heads of the crowd. I got a split-second glimpse of the Visitors Center gate and a van with people leaping out, and what looked like a huge statue of a man just beyond it, before I landed.

Some people saw me and cleared away. I still ended up

plowing awkwardly into one poor guy.

My dad jumped again immediately. The guy I landed on must have been on my side; he touched my arm and gave me a quick thumbs-up before pushing past me to jump back in the fray.

Just like in the slam pit, I thought. Except for the tear gas.

I jumped again and landed stumbling into chain-link. The gate was just ahead.

A skinny, scowling red-haired girl stepped out of the van, followed by none other than Byron Teslowski. He held in one hand what looked like a one of those helmets bicyclists sometimes wore. He slid the door closed behind him.

As soon as it latched, the van pulled back into the Visitors Center parking lot and the gate closed. Byron looked at the riot in front of him and strapped the helmet to his head.

It was surreal to see him there. I realized in a flash that we'd been surrounded by violence the last time we'd been together, too.

"Byron!"

He turned toward me. I saw the shock of recognition on his face, then he pointed toward the crowd with one hand and held up the index finger of the other as if to say, "Hang on, I just have to take care of this little mob-riot thing, and I'll be right with you."

I had about a heartbeat to be amused by the craziness of it all before the statue moved.

It wasn't a statue. It was a fifteen-foot-tall giant in what looked like slabs of gray body armor.

Behind me, I heard my father's alarmed hiss. I was glad

I knew where he was, that he wasn't still in the crowd.

Between the tear gas, which we'd managed to get upwind of, and the shocking, impossible presence of the giant, the mob was literally too choked up or freaked out to do much more rioting.

The cadre of state troopers got interested in maintaining order again and moved in with batons and lots of those plastic zip-tie handcuff things. I hung by the fence with my dad and tried to look harmless while I kept an eye out for Denver and Sandy.

I almost didn't recognize Spencer Croy in fatigues since every time I'd met him he'd been in a business suit. He seemed to be in charge of Byron's group, which apparently consisted of the giant, the red-haired punky-looking chick, and what I would have sworn was a life-size, real-life version of that robot space-knight toy but was in fact, I would learn, Byron's teammate Jon Schulmann in the special suit that protected him from his own Sovereign abilities.

Croy seemed to be directing his team to specific individuals who were then ushered through the gates of the Visitors Center by Byron or one of his pals. Everyone else was being arrested.

I finally saw Denver and Sandy. A couple of cops were hassling them.

I turned to Andrew. "Can you wait right here? I need to get Denver and Sandy."

My dad seemed preoccupied with watching Spencer Croy. He grunted. I took that to mean he wouldn't wander off.

I walked toward Denver and Sandy. "Hey, officers?

They're...um...I, they're with me. They're not protestors."

One of the cops pointed his baton at me.

"Get on your knees and put your hands behind your head, now."

"No, I'm not..."

Byron intervened. "Hey, you guys...these people, they're under Sovereign protection. Oh!" He pointed at my dad. "And that one by the gate, too. Thanks."

The police lost interest in us immediately. I shook Byron's hand.

"You...you seem...different, man."

He laughed and took off his bicycle helmet. "Dude, you have no idea." He looked me over and raised an eyebrow when he got to my dye job. "What's with the leopard spots?"

"It's just a thing. I don't know if you ever met Denver Colorado...and this is his friend Sandy."

Denver said, "Interesting to finally meet you, Byron."

"You too, sir."

Sandy shook his hand. "Are you part of the Sovereign Conduct Enforcement Team I've heard about, Byron?"

Byron looked a little bashful. "Yes ma'am. It's...I guess it's my first day."

Sandy smiled. "Well, I guess it could have been worse, right? I'd love to interview everyone on your team."

Byron looked cautious. "Oh, well...uh, I don't, like, handle any of that. I don't even know who you'd talk to. Maybe Mister Kass or this other guy, Fontino. But we'll totally figure that out for you."

I nudged his arm. "Hey, you remember my dad?"

"So that is your dad, by the fence!" He shook his head. "I

figured he was with you 'cause I saw you guys standing together, but, dude…talk about changed."

"Shave and a haircut. Come on; you should meet him, too, officially."

He shook his head and laughed as we walked over to the fence. "Dude, can you even believe we're here, now?"

"You wouldn't believe what it's taken to get here."

Byron looked at me. "I wanna hear about—"

"Help us!"

We stopped and turned around to see a burly guy with a flattop stumbling down the hill, one meaty arm supporting a tall scarecrow of a man wrapped in a blanket and beat to shit.

Byron gaped.

"Dad…?"

Byron Teslowski
Seven

Spencer Croy responded first. "Haze. The van. First-aid kit."

She looked confused. "How will I know—"

Ed Kelso boomed, "White box, red cross! Jeez!"

Byron saw a flash of embarrassment quickly masked by irritation on Haze's face before she bolted for the van.

Marc Teslowski eased his burden to the ground before sitting heavily next to him.

"Dude," Nate Charters breathed. "That's your dad."

"I…" Byron took a step forward and stopped. "What's he—"

"Go find out! I'm gonna check on Andrew."

Byron had spent the last year rebuilding his life, making one that didn't include his dad breathing down his neck every second of every day, pushing him…but now, the guy was here. Even crazier, it looked like he'd rescued someone.

If this was a movie, Byron thought, I'd run over there. Hug him and stuff.

But this was the guy who practically sold him out to Lester Brenhurst last year.

Byron chose to walk.

He and Haze got to Marc and the beat-up guy pretty much the same time. Byron's dad looked up at him, a tired grin on his filthy face.

"You've filled out," he said.

The last thing Byron expected was for his dad to be happy to see him. "What are you doing here?"

Spencer Croy took the medical kit from Haze. "Mister Teslowski, are you injured?"

"No."

"Please give us a little room, then, please."

"Ah…right." Marc started to stand up. The guy he'd brought with him grabbed his arm.

"See you around, Marc Teslowski."

Marc nodded. "You'll be all right, Eddie." He got to his feet and stepped away from Croy and two Visitors Center employees who had come to help.

"Dad," Byron said again, "What are you doing here?"

It took Marc a couple seconds to look away from the guy he'd called Eddie and turn to Byron. His face had welts and cuts all over, and his eyes were exhausted.

"Came to see you," he said.

"Did you…walk? Who's that guy? Is…is mom here?"

"Your mother's back home. That's Eddie." He laughed. "I only walked the last few miles."

Byron didn't know how to feel or what to think. "What happened to him?"

"He got mixed up with a bad crowd," Marc said. "Good thing I did, too." He sighed, tired, and looked at the arrested protestors.

They were seated cross-legged on the side of the road, their hands zip-tied behind their backs, as the state troopers processed them. Marc squinted, then scowled. "Son of a *bitch*!"

Byron's dad power-walked to the line and yanked one of the protestors, an older man with silver hair, to his feet. Marc followed quickly.

Marc yelled in the man's face. "Greene! You son of a bitch. You piece of shit…" He raised his fist.

Two state troopers rushed over, hands on their holstered service weapons. "Sir! Stop!"

Byron found himself standing between the cops and his dad. It was a scary place to be, bulletproof or not. "Hold on, hold on. Dad, put him down. Come on!"

"This is the piece of shit who set this whole thing up," Marc said. He pushed Greene to the ground as much as let him go. "This is Ray Greene. He killed a girl. He had Eddie beat up. Probably woulda done worse, too."

Greene looked up at Marc. "Well. You're a disappointment, aren't you, Marc?" He smiled. "Mostly. Still glad I got to buy you that beer." His smile widened.

Marc Teslowski spat in his face. Byron wanted to know when aliens had replaced his father.

One of the cops pulled his weapon. "Step away, sir. You won't get another warning."

"Dad."

Marc backed away a couple of paces. "Scum."

Spencer Croy walked up like he owned the place. Byron figured that was close enough to true.

"Officers, I am Spencer Croy of the Donner Institute for Sovereign Studies and a recognized, authorized representative of William Donner. I'm invoking my Sovereign right to immediate extradition of Ray Greene under EO 12512."

Byron thought that was probably the most he'd ever heard Mister Croy say at any one time. It had the ring of something official; maybe he *had* to say it like that.

The cops looked confused. "What the hell does that mean?"

"This man murdered a Sovereign," Croy said. "He will

face Sovereign justice."

The trooper who had been ready to draw on Byron's dad looked uncertain. "We're not on Sovereign territory, here, Mister Croy. I'm not so sure about this."

Three security guards from the Visitors Center stood behind Croy. Jon Schulmann, his gleaming protective suit creaking like chrome-painted latex, stood nearby. Ed Kelso lumbered over as well, his footfalls sending vibrations up Byron's calves and his shadow blocking the morning sun.

"Call it in," Croy suggested.

Haze came up and bumped Byron on the shoulder. "This your old man?"

"Uh...yeah."

She smirked and looked Marc up and down, lingering on his gut. "You like the beer, huh?"

"What?"

Haze tapped Byron's flat stomach with the back of her hand and said to him, "Keep up on your sit-ups, soldier boy. Otherwise, there's your future."

"Jesus, Haze..."

Byron expected his dad to spew a load of venom on her. Marc just shook his head and turned back to glare at Ray Greene.

Haze had a cold twinkle in her eyes and a playful smile on her lips. She opened her mouth to contribute more to the exchange.

If Haze said anything, Byron didn't hear it. He was distracted by the crack of a rifle and the sight of Nate Charters bounding across the road and up the hillside, screaming all the way.

From The Journal Of Nate Charters
Thirty One

I started to jog back to where my dad stood near the Visitors Center gate, but after the mob scene and all that driving, going any faster than a walk felt like an awful lot of work. I wasn't sure what the rest of the day held in store, but I hoped a whole lot of breakfast was somewhere on the agenda.

Andrew seemed like he was on full alert, sniffing the air, glancing around. I waved to get his attention as I closed the rest of the space between us.

"Did you see that? That's Byron's dad. Byron's dad is here!"

I was maybe six feet away from him. He looked at me.

My father said, "Hey," as if he'd just seen something unusual or interesting or a little confusing or surprising.

He fell back against the fence. A red mist filled the air where he'd stood. The front of his shirt turned dark and wet.

I heard a pop.

I heard screaming.

I was screaming.

I knew my father was dead.

From The Journal Of Nate Charters
Thirty Two

Another pop. I moved. Another pop. My sensorium did the work, found the source.

Later, they cleaned gravel and dirt out of the bloody palms of my hands. That's how I know I dropped to all fours and bounded, leaping and running, to close the distance to the person who shot my father.

I saw Byron hauling ass along with me. He'd sure gotten fast. I lost sight of him when he jerked abruptly and slowed down, an eye-blink before I heard two more pops.

The killer started to move his fat ass up the hillside. He tried to keep to cover behind fir trees. Between his weight, hanging on to the rifle, and the beating I'd given him just a few hours before, he was much too slow.

Of course it was Lou Uldare.

I landed on his back. He exhaled and went flat. I grabbed the hand holding the rifle and ripped the gun from his grip.

I threw the gun wildly, just to get the thing away from him. Two of his fingers went with it. He screamed.

I wanted to rip into his bloody hand. With my teeth. Instead, I flipped him over and, having learned my lesson, drove my knee into his groin.

I wrapped my hands around his hot, bloated, meaty throat and squeezed.

No more holding back.

No more feeling bad about what I was, or what I could do, or what it meant.

"Is this what you wanted?"

I think that's what I said to him. Screamed, probably.

I know that's what I was thinking.

I wasn't talking to him, so much. I wasn't asking him anything.

I think I was asking god.

You know I was born with a tail and fur all over my body? They removed the tail, and I shed the fur before I'd filled up my first dozen diapers. Still, there it was: fucked from moment the doctor spanked my ass.

Every stranger to ever cross my path has looked at me with surprise or fear or revulsion or my absolute favorite, pity. I've lived with adults treating me like I must be retarded because of the big eyes and weird head and the short hair. My own mother loved to refer to me as her "special" guy.

I was alone, everywhere, with everyone.

I thought maybe Donner's Declaration would change all that, but no. I'm not even a Sovereign. No such luck. I can't even rate being a real metahuman. I'm the unexpected off-spring of a failed military experiment.

I thought Lina would change that, too, but no. Not in any way that really mattered.

Project: Rancher outcome: one crazy, uncontrollable animal man and the freakish sport he made in turn, and left behind.

If the intended result was to make a killing machine, a gun loaded with teeth and nails and inhuman strength and speed and rage, rage, rage…that's what I would be.

There was no point in pretending I was anything else.

I thought my progression had peaked with Evelyn. I didn't mean to kill her. I lashed out at her in self-defense and fear. She was stupid enough to point the gun at her own head. I didn't want it. I didn't like it.

I was wrong.

The progression would end in the dirt and pine needles on a hillside in Montana. It would end when I dug my fingers into Lou Uldare's throat and pulled meat away until I could see that motherfucker's spinal chord.

His face was purple. I relaxed my grip so that he could pull in a few ragged, painful swallows of air.

He shat himself then, too. It smelled like surrender. It smelled great.

"This is what you get," I said to him.

I caught Byron's scent. All I could see was Uldare and black and red in my peripheral vision, but I knew he was there.

"Nate! Lay off!"

I pulled my right hand back and curled it into a stiff claw.

Uldare wept. A bubble of bloody snot grew on his nostril. He was a destroyed person.

"This is what you get."

I hoped the blood would shower me when I ripped the first gibbet of flesh from his throat.

Instead, I felt hands under my arms. I was pulled away, and up. I hit the ground on my right shoulder, and the air rushed from my lungs.

I wanted to roar with frustration. I could barely catch a breath.

I saw Uldare twist onto his belly and try to slink off.

No. He wasn't getting away. Not again.

Byron reached down, grabbed Uldare by the collar, and tossed him. He hit the pavement twenty feet down the hill, feet first. One of his ankles bent. He went down.

I could still get to him. One leap, and I could be on him. I could still finish the fucker.

I got to my feet.

"Nate."

Byron put his hand on my chest.

"You'll lose that," I rasped.

"No. Nate. They're working on him. Look."

He grabbed my right shoulder, hard, and pain shot down my arm and my back. I was helpless. He twisted me and pointed. "Look. Your dad's still alive."

From The Journal Of Nate Charters
Thirty Three

I was told they gave Denver and Sandy access to one of the empty apartments to get cleaned up and rest. Byron and his friend Haze took me to the cafeteria and let me refuel my spent metabolism with a plate full of everything ready to eat in the place.

While I stuffed my face more out of necessity than with any sense of enthusiasm, Byron and Haze tried distracting me from the fact that doctors were operating on my father.

"This place is a trip," Byron said. "It's, like, almost totally self-...you know...they can do everything right here."

Haze grinned and looked sideways at Byron. "Self-sufficient?"

"Right." Byron nodded. "The cafeteria; there's an arcade —"

Haze raised her hand. "High score, *Star Castles*, right here."

Byron glanced at her and smiled, then turned back to me. "We even get cable in our apartments...heck, we get our own apartments! That's pretty cool."

"Beats living with your dad, huh?"

Byron shrugged, threw up his hands and blew air through his lips. "Dude, I don't even know what to make of my dad. He's been harassing this place since I got here; he's trying to sue you guys...then he shows up on Declaration Day with some guy they tell me he saved from certain death, or whatever?" He shook his head. "Who is that? Not the dad I remember, that's for fucking sure."

Haze picked up one of my leftover toast crusts and gave

me an inquiring look. "Where is he, anyway?" I don't like the crust, so I nodded, and she popped it in her mouth.

Byron's laugh was thick with disbelief. "Actually meeting with Doctor Donner. Can you believe that?"

I remembered Marc Teslowski boasting on live television that he would snap Donner in half if he got in the same room with him. Whatever they were talking about, I bet it wasn't going like that. I chuckled. "I…it's pretty funny."

"It's a trip, dude."

There was a crack in our conversation just wide enough for me to start obsessing about my own dad. Haze filled it up.

"So, Nate. Byron tells me you once almost kicked his ass."

My eyes met Byron's. We both smiled slightly.

"It was more like a draw," I said. "And it was totally my fault."

"Damn right, dude." Byron looked at Haze and pointed at me. "It's, like, two days after the Declaration, and I'm freaking out, putting everything together in my head, and it's totally making me crazy. I figured the only guy I could talk about it with is Nate."

"Except," I said, "that's the same guy you'd been picking on for, I don't know, forever? I wasn't in the mood."

Haze clicked her tongue and regarded Byron with narrowed eyes. "I knew it. You're an asshole."

Byron didn't look happy, remembering it. "I was." He looked at me. "I was." He shook his head slowly. "A whole fuckin' lot has happened since then, man."

It struck me how much more grown-up Byron seemed. I wondered if I seemed that way to him. I know I felt eight hundred years old.

"It's been a year," I agreed.

Haze looked over my shoulder. I turned to see Spencer Croy walking toward our table.

"Nathan, come with me." He turned for the door.

I got to my feet and to his side quickly. My stomach played rock tumbler with the mountain of food I'd just eaten.

"Is it my dad? Is he out of—?"

We passed through the doors of the cafeteria and into the early-afternoon sunlight. Croy stopped and faced me.

"Andrew Charters did not survive his injuries."

"What?"

I heard him. But I didn't get it. It was my first time. Stupid; weird, what happens when you get news like that. My head felt empty. My ears filled with a sort of rushing sound.

I couldn't feel my body.

"But...he's..."

Croy put his hand on my shoulder and applied some pressure. I put one foot in front of the other and moved where he directed me.

"Would you like to see him?"

Those words drove an icepick of *real* into the glacier I felt around me. It was hard to breath. I opened my mouth, but nothing came out.

I just nodded.

Croy took me into the Institute infirmary, down a hall, through a door...I have no idea where we went. If we were there right now and you asked me to retrace my steps, I couldn't do it.

Croy guided, my legs moved, and we were there, in front

of a door. It had a little glass window reinforced with dia-
monds of thin wire. Through that window was a shape under
a sheet. I looked away, fast.

Another body.

My father's body.

"Take all the time you need." Croy pushed the door
open for me.

I plodded through.

His face was uncovered. His eyes were closed. His skin
was not right.

He smelled like chemical things. Residual odors from
the operating room, maybe. Anesthesia gas. I don't know.

His smell was *missing*. The musty, feral, adrenaline-in-
fused signature that was just a few molecules and several decades' worth of living different than my own…it wasn't there.

He wasn't there.

He'd come all that way. Got a haircut and a bath and
fresh clothes. Sat in a car for hundreds of miles. Got as far as
the gate.

And now he wasn't there. Wasn't anywhere.

That was really, really unfair.

There was a metal stool near the table where they'd laid
him out. I slumped onto it.

It was really, really unfair.

That's what brought the tears out of me. I hope that
makes sense. I hope you get that.

Because, see, we didn't really know each other. When
you get right down to it, most of the time I'd even known he
was alive, I'd been kinda pissed at him. It was only when I
figured out I was kind of losing it, kind of getting to be more

like him, that I thought maybe he might be able to help me get a grip on...me.

He left. Then he was there, and he left again. I had figured he *owed* it to me to help, in a way. I was his responsibility. I was his creation, you get right down to it. It's his fault I'm the way I am.

I wanted him to do something about it.

How could I know, until we'd sat in the back seat of poor stupid dead Evelyn's car, that he wanted to do something about it, too?

Now he was gone. The same fuckers who made him managed to finish him, after all those years.

I was, right then, beyond being angry. The fact of my father's dead body, inches away from me in that, cold, sterile, silent room...it was too far from all the things that brought us to that place. It was bigger.

It was tragic, is what it was. Right out of the dictionary: tragic.

And it made me cry. Hard. From my chest. From my gut. From my heart.

I howled in that room. I threw things around. I exhausted myself, felt a little self-conscious, and then I'd see his face and start all over again.

It was a whole new kind of crazy for me.

It hurt. So much.

I don't know how long I was in there. After I'd been mostly quiet for a while, Spencer Croy opened the door.

"We have somewhere you can rest."

I looked at my dad's face, half-expecting that it would set me off again. I only shuddered.

That was it, then. That was it. I was done.

I let Croy walk me to an apartment, somewhere in the same building that held the cafeteria. We passed people. We rode in an elevator. He held another door open for me. I walked through and found myself in what pretty much looked like a big hotel room.

There was a bed. I fell on it. I thought I would cry more, but I didn't.

I slept.

When I woke up, the light through the window felt like late afternoon. I was thirsty. I was hungry. My face hurt.

I wanted to know what they had done with Lou Uldare.

From The Journal Of Nate Charters
Thirty Four

I was awake less than five minutes when Byron called on the room phone.

"Nate...I'm...I'm sorry."

"Thanks."

A beat of awkward silence. Awkward for me, at least. I was still sleepy; I hadn't finished processing things.

"Uh," Byron said, "Listen, do you think you're up for being around people? Doctor Donner is going to, like, talk to the people who...I mean, the guy from that militia and the guy who..."

The guy who killed my father.

"Fuck yes."

"Okay. Good. I'll come get you in, like, half an hour, okay?"

"Okay. Hey, Byron?"

"Yeah?"

"Thanks. I really want to be there."

"Dude," Byron chuckled. "Donner wants you there. This is, like, a big deal. Bad news for those pieces of shit, too, I bet."

"Even better," I said. "Half an hour?"

"Half an hour."

"I'll be ready. Later."

"Later."

I hung up, took off my filthy clothes, took a very hot shower, and put my filthy clothes back on.

Evelyn's bloodstains on my jeans didn't bother me anymore. I hoped I'd have a chance to tell Uldare what they were. Maybe he'd cry like a little baby again.

Byron showed up and took me into a building I was told was the nerve center of the Institute, where Donner and Croy and all the other Sovereign bigwigs had their offices. We got into an elevator in the lobby, and Byron pressed B8. We went down.

When the doors opened, we stepped into a nearly featureless, wide corridor with a tile floor and the dropped-ceiling/fluorescent-lighting combination like you'd see in a classroom or my lawyer's office. Totally normal; totally plain vanilla.

I sniffed. The air was almost sterile, too. It made me a little uncomfortable.

"I feel like I'm in a James Bond movie," I said.

"I've never been down here," Byron said. "I don't think this gets used a whole lot. So far. Come on."

He led me down the corridor until we came to a steel door with I-01 stenciled on it. He faltered.

"I...I'm not sure if we're supposed to just, like, go in, or knock, or what."

I shrugged. "You'd know better than me."

He shook his head. "Dude, every other day something happens around here that makes me feel like the new guy. I don't know."

An older guy with a narrow, lined face opened the door and decided for us. "Byron. Hi, Nathan. I'm Ewing Kass. Come on in."

The room was almost as plain as the hallway. White cinderblock walls. No windows, of course, since we were apparently eight floors below ground. About a dozen plain gray metal folding chairs set up in three rows, but nobody was sitting in them. Everyone was standing near them—Byron's dad, Sandy, Denver (okay, he was sitting, but in his own wheelchair), and Spencer Croy—looking at the two people in the middle of the room.

One of them was an old man with thick, slicked-back white hair. The other one was Lou Uldare. They'd been dressed in white coveralls. They had handcuffs on their wrists and shackles on their ankles. Uldare had a cast on his left leg and a thick bandage on his hand.

Seeing Uldare was not good for me. Heat spread under my skin, out from my chest, and up my neck. My breath went all fast and shallow.

The last man in the room, who had been standing apart from everyone else, came toward me with his hand extended.

I'd seen him on television.

"Nathan, I'm William Donner. It's an honor to meet you. I'm sorry it had to be under these circumstances."

I shook his hand, which was dry and firm and smooth. He smelled vaguely of cedar and more than a little like spearmint. I think he'd been chewing gum. He wore black dress slacks and a pale-yellow dress shirt with the sleeves rolled up. I caught a whiff of the polish on his shoes.

"Hi," I said.

He released my hand and nodded. "Please join everyone else." He looked right through Uldare and the other prisoner to Denver and everybody. "If you all would take a seat, please. Ewing, are you ready?" His tone was all business.

Kass held up a little tape recorder. "Yeah."

I went over and sat in the first row in the seat closest to

the door. Denver was in his chair on my left, Sandy directly behind him in the next row, Byron on my right, and his dad next to him. Spencer Croy remained standing just behind the first row of chairs. Ewing Kass leaned against the wall near the door, tape recorder in hand.

Denver put a hand on my shoulder and squeezed. He looked tired, sad, and very serious. I didn't know what to say to him or if I even should say anything. I just nodded.

Donner stood near the door. "You two," he said to the prisoners, "stand with your backs against that wall. Keep two feet between you."

The white-haired guy glowered. "What's the point of this, Donner? You know what you're going to do. Why bother with this...kangaroo court?"

"Mister Greene. Mister Uldare. Do what I've asked you to do."

I jumped a little in my chair. Donner's voice was fucking scary. It scraped on my bones.

Uldare said, "Come on, Greene. Keep your dignity." He shuffled to the wall.

Greene frowned and followed suit.

Donner regarded them. "This isn't a kangaroo court." He looked at us. "This isn't any kind of court." And back to his prisoners. "There isn't going to be any kind of trial. That's not what this is."

Denver shifted his shoulders next to me. A frown creased his forehead.

Greene's eyes were bright. "Like I said, then. Do what you're gonna do."

Donner said, "Good. Let's start with you."

Greene paled.

Donner smirked. "You're here to answer my questions, in the company of the people you've done wrong."

Greene's glance flicked to Byron's dad, then back to Donner. "I'm at war with you, you unholy, abominable freak. Don't you know that? There's not a damn thing I wouldn't do in the service of my species."

Greene's anxiety made him sweat. The air was a little thick for me in the closeness of the room.

Donner, on the other hand, broadcast level calm in every way my sensorium could receive. It was creepy.

"In the service of your species?" His eyebrows drew together. "Mister Greene...I misspoke. There are two people you did wrong that aren't here to witness your...testimony. Eddie Schwippe is resting in our infirmary, no thanks to you and all thanks to Mister Teslowski." Donner smiled very briefly at Byron's dad, who looked deeply troubled and confused.

"The other..." Donner sighed. His lip curled. "You, Rayford Greene...you gave us reason to use our morgue for the very first time."

He stepped close to Greene, who, I was not really surprised to see, shrank back against the wall.

Uldare didn't move, despite Donner's proximity. I wished he would. I wanted him to try something. Anything, even with the handcuffs and shackles and cast and missing fingers. Anything.

"Tell me you killed Yvette Schwenck, Greene," Donner whispered. "Say it out loud."

Greene tried to suppress a shudder, but I noticed it, and

I bet Donner did, too. Greene straightened up a little, looked Donner in the eye.

"Well, now, Mister Donner." His voice had the slightest tremor to it. "It was my boy who pushed the bitch out of the car." Despite the fact that he smelled like terror, Greene held his head up.

"But it was my distinct pleasure to smear the bitch all over the road. Yes, sir."

Uldare laughed. Fucker *laughed*. My legs twitched with the urge to destroy him.

Donner took two big steps back away from Greene. His face was dark. "I wonder if it felt like this?"

Greene's whole body spasmed. He made a croaking sound, kind of like, "Urk!" and doubled over, retching, jerking.

He collapsed onto his side. His eyes were wide open and blank with pain. Blood and puke shot from his gaping mouth.

"Jesus!" Marc Teslowski pushed himself back in his chair. The metal legs screeched on the floor.

Behind me, Sandy gasped. Denver said, "Goddamn it."

Byron gripped the sides of his seat and stared at Greene.

Ewing Kass said in an even voice, "Will…"

Spencer Croy didn't so much as blink.

Donner didn't acknowledge Kass. He looked at us. "This is not a court. I said that."

Sandy said, "You didn't say it would be a chamber of horrors. What the hell is the matter with you?"

"Ms. Graves, if this is troubling to you, I'll have Byron escort you to an apartment, where you're welcome to…maybe watch some television? Every room has one of those Atari machines. Maybe you'd like to play *Pong*?"

Donner was too scary-fascinating to look away from him to Sandy. She didn't say a word.

Donner smiled quickly. "I know you came here looking for a story. Take notes, if you like."

Denver cleared his throat. "What did you do to him?"

"Mister Greene's abdominal muscles contracted quickly and severely," Donner said. "If I'm right, the result is muscular tearing and, hopefully, rupturing in his internal organs."

Greene jerked and whined. Red drool dribbled from his lips.

"I think I'm right," Donner said. He bent his legs, set his palms on his knees, and regarded Greene. "This might be a little bit of what that poor girl felt before you finished her off, you piece of shit."

He stood up and kicked Greene in the face with sudden and precise violence.

"And that's a little something like what you and your band did to Mister Schwippe. *Feel* it."

I had been worried about my augmentation messing with my sanity, my self-control. My dad, he had lived the last third of his life like that.

It didn't seem like Donner was losing it. Everything I knew told me he actually in perfect control. One hundred percent.

I wondered if that meant he was crazy.

I still wonder.

Knowing all he knows...with all he's seen...how could he be right in the head?

Donner turned to Lou Uldare. I leaned forward in my seat. Crazy or not, Donner was doing god's work now, far as I was concerned.

"Lou Uldare. The man who made us use our morgue the second time, and took a boy's father from him. You're known to us, Mister Uldare."

Uldare didn't seem too worked up over Greene's punishment. "That means I'm doing my job."

"That's what we're going to talk about," Donner said. "You're going to tell us all about PrenticeCambrian and your master, Mister Quince, and, ideally, his masters. You're going to talk about how you helped Mister Greene's organization, and how they helped you.

"Oh…and you're going to help us understand, in detail, how young Mister Charters fits into it all, and why you assassinated his father."

Donner turned his head toward me. The compassion on his face, the empathy I saw there…my eyes filled up. I blinked and my cheeks got wet. I didn't care.

The corners of his lips twitched. "I'm sure we'll learn a great deal."

He turned back to Uldare.

"Do you understand?"

Uldare smiled. "Fuck you, Donner. You crazy freak."

Donner didn't flinch. "I don't usually bother with threats, Mister Uldare. After all, you, of all people, know what I can do. I imagine my jacket is quite thick, back at the home office."

"I'm not inclined to discuss the topics you suggested," Uldare said. "You loony fuck."

"Reconsider," Donner suggested.

Uldare shook his head. His forehead was slick with sweat. "I'm a company man, Willy. Besides," he smiled, "as soon as I feel you begin to manipulate me like you did that old fool...bad things happen."

Uldare looked at Marc Teslowski. Byron's dad squirmed in his chair.

Byron said, "Dad?"

Donner paced away from Uldare, shaking his head. "This is not how I wanted to spend this day." He pivoted on his heel.

"Seriously, Uldare. Do you think we don't know about the nanomech explosives you had Greene slip Marc Teslowski?"

From The Journal Of Nate Charters
Thirty Five

I couldn't believe it. "What? He what?"

Uldare shrugged. "It doesn't matter what you knew or know. I'm telling you that if you fuck with me, we'll learn, very quickly, just how much energy a human body stores. Ought to be more than enough to rid the world of one room full of vermin and their friends." He glanced down at Ray Greene writhing on the floor. "This whole thing was worth it to get Teslowski in the room with you."

Byron turned toward his dad. "Did...did you know? Is that why—?"

Before Teslowski could respond, William Donner said, "Remain calm, please."

I wasn't calm. I knew the score. I understood what nanomechs are. I'd seen a guy dissolve from the inside out, just fall apart, last year at the battle of Kirby Lake, thanks to those little machines. I knew Project: Ranger used nanomechs to add the augmentations to my dad. Maybe that's how they did the camera thing at Denver's house, too.

Now they'd somehow turned Marc Teslowski into a living bomb?

Fuck that. I got up and grabbed Uldare by the throat. My fingers just naturally went right back to the bruises I'd put on his neck a few hours before. My fingerprints.

"You don't even try it! You turn it off!"

"You can't do anything else to me, boy," Uldare said. "I'm already dead. But as soon as I go...so do all of you."

"Turn it off!" I wanted to squeeze, to finish this monster, to pay violence back with violence. "Kill my father with a *gun?* With a gun? Fucking coward!"

"That's why they pay me the big bucks."

That was enough. Fuck it. I didn't care, at that moment, about anything other than wiping this shitstain off the face of the earth. So what if it killed me. So what if Marc Teslowski got blown up—that guy had always been an abusive, bullying piece of shit, anyway.

I didn't care.

Byron did, though. "Nate, come on! Chill! My dad!"

His dad. Worthless fuck that Marc Teslowski was, Byron still had a dad.

I glared at Byron. "That's not fair!"

It worked, though. Pulled me back from the ledge. I eased my grip. Slightly.

"Call it off," I said to Uldare.

"Can't. I live, or every one of you freaks and freak-lovers dies. Looks like you get to choose, Nathan."

William Donner said, "Nate, let him go. This is point-less."

"No! He doesn't have the fucking right to do this! Play with us! Fuck him!"

Donner stepped over Ray Greene and stood next to me. "We've been deactivating PrenticeCambrian nanomech since 1980, starting with the kill switch in your father. We cleaned Mister Teslowski while you were eating breakfast."

Uldare said, "You what?"

Marc Teslowski said, "Fuck you, lard-ass."

Byron's laugh was a high, nervous chirp. "You knew?"

"Will asked me to play along. Sorry, son."

Marc Teslowski was on a first-name basis with William

Donner? What?

Donner said to me, "You can kill him, Nate. No one else will come to any harm as a result. But I really hope you don't."

I looked at Uldare. His eyes had a lot more fear in them than a minute ago. I wished his eyes didn't show anything at all, just blank, glassy vacancy.

"Why not? Why shouldn't I? He deserves it. You know he does. And it's what I'm fucking made for. It's what they made me for."

Denver Colorado spoke up. "You don't have to be that, Nathan. It's not what Andrew wanted for you."

"Shut up!"

Donner's voice was calm. "We need him alive, Nathan. We need him to talk...and I want you to understand, he *will* talk. And when he does...all the people who hurt you, and your father, and your mother, and Byron, too...they'll all be exposed. Your legal troubles will be over. You'll be free to live your life."

I squeezed Uldare's throat a little tighter. The bruises on his face—marks I'd put there—darkened. His eyes bulged.

"It doesn't matter," I said. "I need to...I need to feel him die!"

Donner said, "Nathan, look at my face."

I had to.

"Do you think your father was this monster's first victim? Do you know how long I've been waiting to have him at my mercy? Tell me you really don't think I intend to show him that I have none."

I saw it again.

I don't know what drove him to it, but I think when William Donner killed, he did it for vengeance. And I'm telling you: he relished it. The guy was one damaged piece of work. He made me feel about as dangerous as Don Knotts.

I believed him.

"Okay," I said. "It's fine. Don't worry. I won't kill Uldare."

Donner nodded slowly. "I appreciate that. It's for the best. For now."

"He still has to pay."

I made the devil sign with my free hand: a fist with the pinkie and index finger extended.

When I killed Evelyn, it was out of desperation. I've wanted to kill out of rage, out of frustration.

But I understood a little something about the need for vengeance, too.

Uldare's right eye got my pinkie. His left eye got my index.

He didn't have time to close them.

There was a split second of resistance before a hot, sticky fluid covered my fingers.

We both screamed.

For different reasons.

Byron Teslowski
Eight

Byron really needed her to be there, but he still stood outside her door for a good minute before he got up the nerve to knock.

Haze opened the door blinking. She wore a big white tee shirt. Her feet were bare.

She rubbed her eyes. "Hey. What time is it?"

"Sorry," he said. "It's, like, late. It's not Friday anymore. I just couldn't sleep."

"So you thought you'd make sure I didn't?" He could tell she was kidding. He was pretty sure, anyway. "Come in. What's up?"

"You were right," he said. "I'm sorry."

She frowned like she was confused, but she smiled, too. "I like the sound of that...and also, huh? What about?"

"I...what you said. On Wednesday." He opted to look at his shoes. "If we'd, like, gone to the same school. I totally wouldn't have talked to you."

"Is that the thing you're also sorry about?"

"I'm sorry I called you a fucking bitch."

She wrinkled her nose. "Hah. I *am* a fucking bitch, Byron. I kick ass at it." She smiled. "Apology accepted."

Byron was surprised at just how intensely relieved he felt right then. He laughed nervously. "Good. Cool. So we're cool."

"You can be cool. I'm hot. Yuk-yuk."

"Nice one." Byron sighed hard. "Fuck, Haze. This has been a shitty day."

"Your friend's dad getting killed?"

"That, yeah, but…Donner brought me, and my dad, and Nate, and his dad's two friends…he brought us all into this… I don't know, meeting, or, what, like an interrogation room, with the dude who shot Nate's dad, and that leader of those crazy people. Ewing Kass and Spencer were there, too. It was a trip."

"What happened?"

Byron ran a hand through his spiky blonde hair. "Nate… I'm kinda scared for him. He's so fucked-up right now, what with his dad getting killed and stuff. We were in there, and this Lou Uldare guy, the dude who shot his dad, right? He threatens us, and Nate, like, just jumps him.

"Right there in front of Spencer, and Donner. Just gets up in his shit and threatens to rip his throat out."

"Fucker deserves it, you ask me," Haze said.

"Donner talked him down; I guess they want to grill the guy for whatever they can get about our enemies. So Nate—check this out—Nate fucking pops the dude's eyes out. With his fingers."

Haze's own eyes opened wide. "That's…hardcore. *Jesus.*"

Byron's chest tightened. He sucked on his bottom lip. "It was gross. And fucked, dude. But…I don't know…it was sad, too. Nate made this noise…like he was angry and kicking ass, and totally, like, bummed out. All at the same time." He shook his head. "Dude's fucked-up. Way more than I ever was about this shit."

Haze took a seat at her little kitchen table. "Sit," she said.

Byron did.

Haze said, "So…it freaked you out? To see this kid you

used to, I don't know, give wedgies to or something, do something like that?"

"He freaked me out yesterday morning when he went for Uldare in the first place, right after his dad was shot," Byron said. "If I hadn't pulled him off the guy, that would have been it. He was ready to kill him. With his bare hands."

Haze raised her eyebrows. "I repeat my question."

"The answer is, hell, yeah. I hope we can help him get that shit under control." Byron shook his head. "That was hard to watch. But Donner...I don't know about that guy."

Haze raised her hands. "Hello? Finally!"

"He's a cold son of a bitch. Totally willing to, like, torture Uldare and the other dude. I mean, I never really spent any time with him before...we got introduced when Spencer first brought me here, but that was different."

"He didn't shake your hand in between stretching someone on the rack, you mean?"

Byron didn't laugh. "He wasn't the dude you see on TV. Mister politician, mister freedom fighter." Byron pursed his lips and shook his head. "*That* guy was totally not in the room tonight."

"It's like I said. Power corrupts. Nobody's more powerful than Donner."

Byron frowned. "I don't even know if he's like that, though. I mean, he can do anything, right? How can he be, like, corrupted?" He shook his head, thinking. "No, I just...I don't...I didn't think everybody'd be so fuckin' violent, you know?"

Haze smiled and laughed, but her eyes were sympathetic. "Oh, Byron. You joined the SCET. You had to know

411

that was a full-contact kind of thing."

"No, that's not what I mean. I get that we're gonna have…situations. Like this morning, with those protestors." He inclined his head toward her. "It was totally cool of you to come with us, by the way, even if I was, like, blown away that you wanted to."

She looked away. "That was for Yvette." She shrugged. "Besides, I didn't really do anything. Ed Kelso blocks out the sun, and everybody settles right down. He's fifteen feet of psychological warfare." Byron laughed. "But go on."

"I get that there's gonna be shit to deal with. That things could get rough," Byron said. "I'm cool with that; I think it's, like, necessary if a Sovereign is, like, breaking the law or whatever."

"You stopped Nate from killing that dude."

"Exactly. I just figured I had to…like it was the right thing to do, even though Uldare's totally a killer. It wouldn't be right, and…I don't know…it totally *wouldn't* be right for Nate to do that. He'd be sorry. I know he would."

Haze's "Maybe" was neutral. "So what's your damage?"

"It just freaked me out to see Donner doing what he did to the militia guy…and not doing anything to directly stop Nate from fucking poking a dude's eyes out." He sighed. "I don't know."

"You coming to your senses?"

"I just…it's more complicated that I thought. The whole thing—being a Sovereign. It's like life is more complicated." He breathed a laugh. "I mean, a year ago, one of the reasons I took Spencer up on his offer was because I couldn't handle the idea of going back home. Because of my dad. I…I ditched out, totally left my mom and my friends and everything…because I couldn't stand being around that guy once I, like, knew what I knew. And I didn't know *shit*, y'know?"

She nodded.

"Then he shows up here, and he's a hero of the Sovereigns and totally, like, still that guy, I think, but…I don't know. Better?"

"People change."

"He's a pretty old dog, Haze. It's weird. It's a trip." Byron sat back, stretched his back, stared at the ceiling. "I don't know what to think. About all this stuff."

"Do you need to have it all figured out?" She laughed. "Right now? 'Cause I don't know about that, dude."

"Nah." He laughed and leaned forward. He rested his elbows on the table and looked at his hands.

"Here's the thing, all right? All night, after the fucking shit that went down with Donner and everybody, I've been just, like, walking around and thinking. And the thing is…I know I'm not so good at seeing some stuff."

He looked up at her, then back at his hands. "You are, though. You called a lot of it."

"I've seen it before," she said.

"Well, I guess I'm sorry if you have…and glad, too, 'cause you can point it out for me when I'm all gung-ho and shit." He looked up at her. "Anyway. I don't want us to be angry at each other."

"Dude, I accepted your apology."

"I know…I know."

"Okay."

"Okay."

Byron felt better. But now it was him and her, late at night, alone in her apartment again, and she was wearing a T-shirt and maybe nothing else. He started wondering things.

She stood up. "Okay!" She walked out of sight. He could hear her rustling around.

She came back with his hair dryer. "I'm done with this. Thanks."

He stood up and took it from her. "You're welcome."

They stood there.

"Good night, Byron." She lifted her hand and swiveled it left and right, a tight little parade wave. "I want to go back to sleep."

"Okay." He felt a lot better than when he'd arrived. He smiled. "Yeah. Me, too."

"Okay. Good night." She moved him to the door. "I'll see you at...you know. The thing tomorrow."

That was a buzz-kill. "Yeah."

He hadn't wanted to think about it. Now he'd get about five hours of sleep before the Donner Institute for Sovereign Studies had its first funeral.

From The Journal Of Nate Charters
Thirty Six

Around eight o'clock Saturday morning, an employee of the Donner Institute for Sovereign Studies dropped by and invited me to visit their commissary. She gave me a voucher good for anything I wanted to buy.

The unspoken intention was that I not have to show up at my father's funeral wearing the same damn clothes I'd first put on Thursday morning. Made sense to me.

After the stunt I pulled on Uldare, I got the very strong impression Denver and Sandy weren't all that keen on hanging out with me for a while. And Byron didn't answer his phone.

These things also made sense to me.

So I went alone.

There was a time I'd preferred being alone. The way things were going, I thought maybe it was a good idea for me to get used to it again.

The commissary looked a lot like a K-Mart, which was jarring and strange to me. These Sovereigns wanted to be held separate and apart from the rest of humanity, but I guess they still want all the same stuff, presented in a familiar way, as the rest of us.

I found jeans and a button-down shirt and socks, all black, and a pack of boxers. Picked up some black creepers, too, even thought they were a knock-off brand. Another surprise.

I wandered around the aisles and realized that as long as the Sovereigns were buying, I might as well get enough clothes for a couple of days. I got another pair of jeans, a pack of socks, and a couple of flannel shirts.

I looked at jackets. Would I need a jacket? How long was I going to be in Montana?

I finally couldn't hide from the fact I was stalling. Plus, the funeral wouldn't wait for me. Or maybe it would, but that would make me a whole different kind of asshole than some people probably already thought I was.

I paid. The guy at the checkout was actually very nice. He expressed his condolences. I went to the apartment, got cleaned up, and dressed for the funeral.

I had about an hour to kill. I spent some of it sitting on the edge of the bed, trying really hard to think about nothing.

I cried a little. Not about my dad. Not exactly. More out of exhaustion, I think.

I went to the cafeteria. The place was practically empty, which struck me as odd until I remembered that pretty much everybody at the Institute was going the same place I was.

There would be a huge crowd to see him off, but from what I'd seen, my dad got real nervous around people. I wondered if he'd been like that, but, you know, less so, before the augmentation regimen.

If there was an afterlife, which Andrew Charters was there? The scientist, or the feral homeless wild man?

I got a double-decker cheeseburger and a big pile of chili fries and a corner table.

I had almost finished eating when my mother walked up.

"Nathan…"

The intellectual part of my brain knew her being there should have been a big surprise, but my emotions were so blunted and worn out, I simply waited until my brain reconciled her presence with the surroundings.

She looked like she needed to hug her son. So I stood up.

It was only once we were embracing that I started to feel something. I didn't like where that was headed. I pulled away from her.

"How'd you get here?"

She studied me as she spoke. "The Institute called me about...Andrew. They arranged everything. A car, a plane, a ride from the airport." She touched my cheek, and I didn't even want to pull away. Maybe I was just too tired to care. "I feel like it was ten minutes ago that I was sitting home angry and worried about you."

There was pressure behind my eyes. I blinked once or twice and hoped for the best. "I told you I had to see him. I told you I needed help."

"I'm not here to fight with you, Nathan." She sounded pretty tired, herself. She looked at her watch. "Are you ready? It's time to go."

"Okay."

There weren't any golf carts available outside the cafeteria, and it would have been pretty lame to go to a funeral riding on a golf cart, anyway. We walked. We didn't say anything to each other.

It was so strange that my mother was there.

She had a right to be. But it was so strange.

I didn't know exactly where this thing was going to happen, but that didn't matter. All we had to do was follow everybody else out across a wide meadow to a square of fresh sod next to a big three-story house.

It was the house William Donner grew up in. He'd had it moved here, apparently, and his uncle still lived there. I saw that on a documentary.

I wondered how the uncle felt about having a tiny cemetery for a side yard.

The sky was a little cloudy. It was a little chilly. I should have bought that jacket.

There were rows of folding chairs, the same kind as in the scene of my latest rage-out, set up before a lectern.

Two coffins. Two rectangular holes in the ground.

The chairs were mostly filled up. Lots of other people milled around. The giant guy stood toward the back. He wore a black suit, the biggest black suit ever made for anyone, ever.

Ewing Kass spotted my mother and me. He showed us to our seats, right in the middle of the front row. Denver, Sandy, Byron, his girlfriend, and his dad were already there, seated.

The skinny guy Marc Teslowski rescued from the speciesists was seated next to him. He caught my eye with his all-black ones and nodded in that somber, respectful way people do. He looked a lot better than the last time I'd seen him.

Sovereign doctors could work wonders, I guess. Just not miracles.

Far as I know, the woman named Yvette Schwenck was not represented by friends or family. Fortunately, about five hundred loved ones she'd never met turned out to honor her.

That was sad.

"Oh, damn," my mother said quietly. It was mostly a sigh.

I took her hand. She squeezed it and held on.

Doctor William Karl Donner, the most powerful Sovereign known, self-proclaimed steward of the most dangerous minority group on the planet, came out of the house and walked across the lawn to the lectern. The ends of his pant legs got damp from the wet grass.

Other than that, he was perfectly groomed. His suit was very dark gray and, while I don't know a thing about such things, looked very expensive. He had a dark-red handkerchief folded in the breast pocket of his jacket. His tie was black. His shirt was a little lighter than the jacket.

Understand that I don't really care what people wear, most of the time. It made an impression on me then because I knew what he and I had both been doing the night before.

No one would see this guy, who, no kidding, looked practically presidential, and think, "I bet he tortured an old man a few hours ago, and liked it."

Except for most of the people in the front row.

We knew.

It could be said that this wasn't the time or place for judgment. And even if it was, who the hell was I to cast stones?

I'm thinking about it now, though. So I wrote it down.

He didn't appear to have a speech prepared. He looked out at us all, pausing briefly to make eye contact with Denver, my mother, and me, and got to it.

"Today, as we begin the second year under our Declaration of Sovereignty and freedom from oppression, it is with deep regret that we gather together to honor two that have fallen. And, it is with great admiration and respect that we recognize that one of those we honor today was not a Sovereign.

"Andrew Robert Charters was a human being with an extraordinary mind and a loving heart, made more than human by the hand of man. He should have been a Sovereign. I name him one today."

Extraordinary mind? Sure. From what I understand, my dad was one of the scientists that made the augmentation regimen possible. The fact that he used it on himself makes no sense, but, whatever.

Loving heart? How in the fuck would Donner know? I looked at my mother to see her reaction to all of this, but she was staring at nothing, apparently deep in thought. I couldn't tell if she'd heard any of it.

And posthumously declaring Andrew Charters a Sovereign? That was bullshit. Sorry. My dad wanted to have as little to do with the Sovereigns as possible. The only reason he was even here was because of me.

"Andrew stood up to the forces that, even two decades ago, had gathered to persecute the people I would one day declare Sovereign. In his defiance, he made a choice that changed him forever. A choice that his brave son carries as legacy."

I felt people's eyes on me. I didn't like being a celebrity among Sovereigns any more than I did anywhere else. I was irritated.

"Finally, even though Andrew Charters never asked for the life he lived, he rose to that challenge and, in the end, sacrificed himself in the struggle against the same antagonists that made him the unique person he was.

"May he rest well."

The bullshit was just too thick.

My father was not a Sovereign hero, and fuck Donner for turning his death into an excuse to spout his particular brand of bullshit. The only thing my dad had in common with this band of freaks was that he wanted to be left alone. Donner wouldn't even let him have that in death.

Also: my dad didn't sacrifice himself for shit. He was standing around trying not to freak out, and Lou Uldare shot him in the chest. To death. The end.

I had enough. I got up and walked back to my apartment.

From The Journal Of Nate Charters
Thirty Seven

By the time I got back to my room, I felt kind of stupid. Yeah, Donner was a jackass, but the people at the Institute, the normal Sovereigns, had all been totally cool to me. I worried they'd be offended by my stomping off in the middle of their beloved leader's speech.

Turned out it was no big deal. None of those people knew me or my dad. Later, my mother told me later everyone assumed I was too broken-up to stick around.

"I almost went with you." She was never one to suffer through politicians' lies and propaganda.

Of course, that was pretty much why I'd been so pissed off at her for the past year. She'd lied to me about my dad my whole life. Way to model grown-up behavior, mom.

After everything else that had happened in the past few days, all of that didn't matter too much to me anymore. It was just one more example of how the world was. I was too tired to make a big deal of it. I decided to adjust my expectations. Move on.

When she asked to go with me while Doctor Mazmanian and his team ran their tests and drew my blood and scraped my skin and put me through their machines and what not, I didn't really care. Having some company didn't suck.

But when Mazmanian called me in late Sunday afternoon to give me the results, I told her to please wait outside.

I liked Mazmanian. He wasn't a Sovereign, so that was points in his favor right off the bat. He was also super down to earth and funny in the way that people who try too hard to be funny are, if that makes sense. He reminded me of my friend Mel, if Mel had a big bald spot and a bushy mustache.

I went into his office and closed the door behind me.

Mazmanian sat behind his desk. He had a white lab coat on, with a stethoscope draped around his neck, like a TV doctor. He grinned. "Sorry about all the poking and prodding today. Sit down, sit down."

I sat down. "It's okay. It's the whole reason I wanted to come here."

Unspoken: people died so I could sit here and hear this news.

His eyes narrowed. He blinked and nodded. I think he got it.

"Well. Let's see if I can get you your money's worth." He flipped through a file folder on his desk. "Here's the deal."

"Yeah?"

"You don't have to worry about ending up like your dad."

I wanted to be relieved, but it sounded a little too simple. "But...how do you know?"

He tapped the file. "The results. Plus, I know stuff." He smiled. "I'll make you a copy of all this, then you go off and get a few doctorates so you can understand it, too. Sound good?"

"C'mon..."

He held up his hand. "I'm just being an ass. The movie-of-the-week version is that Andrew Charters had greatness thrust upon him, and you...you were born great."

He picked up a pen and bounced the point on the desk a couple times. He looked thoughtful.

"No disrespect to your dad, but his mind simply couldn't handle the input it received. Not without repurposing important parts to pick up the slack."

I nodded. "Like the sane parts."

"Like the rational parts. Sure. But you...I mean, you know this; you're custom-built, and you were from the beginning, from conception, cell by cell. You don't have a problem with your...what did you call it, earlier today? Your sensorium?"

I shook my head. "Yeah. I know. That part...I like it."

"No reason why you shouldn't. I like being ambidextrous. It's just who we are."

"But I get so *angry*," I said. "I mean, like, literally seeing-red angry...and when that happens, all I want to do is... you know..."

"Get rage-y. Yeah. I know."

"Like him."

Mazmanian smiled and shook his head. "Not like him. Trust me."

"Well, then...what's going on with me? Why do I get like that? I mean, it's...people...I've..."

"Easy, champ. I'm getting to that. You're probably not going to like it."

That focused me but quick.

"Okay. Just tell me."

"Nate," he said, "you're a teenager."

"So?"

"So, that's it." He shrugged. "You're a teenager. Like any teenager, you've got hormones pumping through your brain like never before in your life. Everything's intense. Right?"

"I don't know."

He chuckled. "I guess you wouldn't. You have no frame of reference. Trust me on this."

I shook my head. "But I'm, like, you know." This guy did a full physical on me—and I mean full—a few hours ago, but I still felt a little embarrassed. "I'm, um, fully developed, and stuff."

"Sure, mostly. You're not done growing—I'm betting you've got another inch to go. Your bones, your musculature…even though you're already stronger than most grown men, I don't think you're done there, either." He smiled. "Things are still finding their level with you, Nathan. Hence, the intense anger. Intense everything."

It sunk in.

"So…I'm not crazy. And I'm not gonna get crazy."

"Not because of your genetics, no." He closed the file. "What you are, though, is a kid going through normal puberty with a full range of metahuman, potentially danger-ous abilities."

He scratched his nose and casually pointed at me. "It's like you're learning how to shoot, but you're knocking down bottles and cans with a howitzer instead of a BB gun." He seemed pleased with that, then looked more serious.

"You want to watch that. Until things level out."

I felt really heavy. I knew I'd cry if I wasn't careful.

"Too late," I said.

His mouth turned down and he nodded. "I know. I heard. You know you could have sanctuary here, until that's all worked out. Those people, that woman…they were all committing about a million crimes."

"Yeah." I stood up and held out my hand. "Thank you, Doctor."

He stood up and we shook. "Get what you came for?"

"I guess so. Thanks again."

I left him in his office and found my mother.

"Well?"

"I know what I needed to know," I said. "And what has to happen next."

And then, bang: there it was. I broke down, hard. She put her arms around me, and for the first time in a long time, I let her be my mother.

After a while, when I could make a noise that wasn't keening or sobbing, I choked out, "I need to go home, Mom."

Byron Teslowski
Nine

Byron, Haze, and Marc took a slow walk around the grounds of the Institute Sunday afternoon before a driver would take Marc down to the airport.

It was a tour, of sorts, and it made it easy for the two men to keep their conversation at a safe, superficial level. It helped having Haze there as a buffer.

They almost reached the courtyard in front of the apartment building, nearly completing a full circuit, and the conversation had wound down to a not-quite comfortable silence.

Marc broke it. "So. I guess you like it here. Have all along, huh?"

Byron glanced at Haze, who raised her eyebrows and gave him what he took to be an encouraging shrug.

"I guess so," Byron said carefully. "I mean, it's kind of like being away for college. Some stuff sucks." He still wasn't sure how he felt about the motives of his fellow Sovereigns. Especially the ones in charge. "Some stuff's really cool."

Marc looked straight ahead as they walked. He grinned slightly. "Gets you away from your old man for a while, at least, right?"

A single, loud, laugh burst from Byron. He stopped walking. His dad and Haze took a few more steps, stopped, and looked back.

His dad's grin was not quite a smile now. "What?"

"Fuck, Dad." Byron remembered a time when he would have been terrified to use that kind of language with him. Things had changed. "Way to, like, oversimplify things."

They looked at each other. Byron's dad laughed a little.

"That's what I thought."

They resumed their walk, Byron and Haze a little way behind Marc.

Haze elbowed Byron and mouthed, "Do it."

Byron took a deep breath and matched pace with his father.

"So, uh, I was, like, thinking…maybe in a couple of weeks, y'know, if things are mellow here and everything…I was thinking I might come down for a visit."

Byron saw the corner of Marc's mouth twitch. Marc kept his eyes on the path. "Your mother, she'd like that."

"Yeah. Okay." He sucked on his lips to keep his own expression as close to neutral as his dad's. "Cool."

They reached the courtyard.

Byron's dad turned to him. He looked him up and down.

"Looks like you turned out all right, Byron," he said.

Byron felt Haze slip her hand into his. He grabbed hold. Her fingers were warm. His chest felt like it would burst.

"Likewise, Dad."

From The Journal Of Nate Charters
Thirty Eight

It was my idea to meet in a public place on Tuesday. It was Lina's idea that it be Romita Park. I felt lucky she'd agreed to meet at all.

Everything else was set. The only thing left to do was talk to Lina.

I walked to the park after telling my mother to give it forty-five minutes before she came to get me. I asked her to park by the curb and honk.

Lina's car was already there.

My hands shook. I couldn't quell the ache in my chest no matter how many deep breaths I took. There was nothing left to do but walk up the slope and into the park.

She was half-sitting, half-leaning on a molded-plastic picnic table near the monkey bars. She wore her old denim jacket over her Japan T-shirt, which was tucked into a tartan miniskirt. Eighteen-hole Doc Martens on her feet. Black leggings.

It was almost exactly what she'd worn on our first date. She had to have planned it.

I didn't know what it meant.

She saw me coming. Her left hand rose and fell.

"Hey."

"Hey."

I stopped a few paces away when the breeze delivered her perfect Lina scent to my nostrils.

"Wow."

She frowned. "What?"

She smelled so good.

I was going to miss her.

"It's good to see you," I said.

I wasn't sure if we were supposed to hug. She didn't make a move in that direction, so I crossed my arms on my cheat, decided that looked too much like I was all closed off, and settled for hanging my thumbs off the belt tabs of my jeans.

She nodded. "Are you okay?"

"I dunno. Now, or in general, or—?"

"In general," she said. "Now. I don't know."

I shrugged. "I'm getting there, I think. Planning to be?" My mouth twisted, rueful. "What about you?"

"Fine." She lifted herself to fully sit on the top of the picnic table and patted the plastic next to her. "You can sit here. It's…I'm not mad at you."

I sat down. The plastic was cold through my jeans, but that was nothing compared to how awkward and weird it felt being next to her. The last time we were this close, we were screaming at each other, and I pushed her, and she fell.

"You should be," I said. "I'm really, really sorry, Lina. You have no idea how sorry I am."

"Okay. I know."

The apology didn't make anything different. I still felt like there was a million miles in the inches between us.

I didn't know what to say. I stared at the ground.

I fretted that it would be a long wait for my mother to get there if neither one of us said another word. But Lina said, "You were there? When your dad…"

"Yeah."

"I'm really sorry, too, Nate. I can't even…I can't think

what it would be like to lose my dad."

I just nodded. Graham Porter, important and wealthy man, was a world away from Andrew Charters. I knew she knew that. But for a moment, once again, I didn't know what to say.

I settled on redirecting things a little.

"You and your dad still getting along?"

"Really good," she said. "Really good."

A crisis will sure bring a family together. I'd brought the Porters more than a few. "I bet he's pretty done with me."

She tilted her head to one side and raised her eyebrows. "Well, you probably don't want to drop by anytime soon."

I wouldn't be.

"Okay," I said. "Makes sense."

She sighed suddenly. "Nate, why'd you do it?"

"You mean Eric Finn?"

She looked at me. "Yes, Eric Finn."

"Sorry. The last few days...you don't know. I had to narrow it down."

Her shoulders dropped and she scowled. "I saw that you were there, at the Institute. I don't even want to know how that went."

I nodded. "I'm not really ready to tell you about it," I said.

"Okay. Tell me about Eric Finn."

I shrugged. "It's stupid."

"I already know that. It was the stupidest thing you've ever done, even stupider than Kirby Lake last year, and I was stupid enough to go along with that one."

She shook her head, looking at me. "It broke us, Nate.

You get that, right? You know that?" Her face flushed. She swiped her jacket sleeve across her eyes. "It broke us."

I'd known we were done. I didn't see how it could be any other way, especially since I'd made my mind up on what to do.

Hearing it from her, though, that was terrible. My throat jumped. I felt my own tears brimming.

"I know." My voice broke.

She raised hers. "So tell me!"

"I did! I'm not kidding! It was stupid." I sniffed. "It was childish and insecure, and I was jealous and—"

"Jealous of him? Why?"

I looked at her. I'd figured this out, mostly. I think I understood. Telling her, right then, with her close enough to kiss, knowing there'd be no more kissing, no more anything…I couldn't open my mouth.

I had to, though. That was part of my deal with myself.

"It's hard," I said by way of beginning.

"Try."

"I am." I breathed. "Okay. Yeah. Jealous. I felt like if you were with a guy like that, an older guy, all…like he is…"

"I don't know what that means, Nate."

"Looking like he does." Once that was out there, the rest was a little easier. "I couldn't figure out why you were with me. Why you'd want to be with a guy like me."

"You mean a guy who looks like you."

"Partly, yeah."

She closed her eyes and inclined her head. "Jesus. So you hunted him down and almost beat him to death. That's great. That's great."

"No! I—no!" I didn't want her to think I was a monster. I couldn't handle that. "No...I did that because...look, I just didn't get it, okay? I don't understand why you would let him get away with what happened."

She opened her eyes. She turned her head slowly toward me.

"Are you crazy, Nate? I'm...I'm serious."

"No." I sighed heavily. "Turns out I'm just immature. And stupid. Like I said."

"You said 'don't understand.' You don't understand. Not 'didn't.'"

I nodded.

She looked like she was going to cry again. "Fuck, Nate, don't you see how much that sucks?"

"I...yeah..."

"No! I can tell, you don't get it! You still don't get it! It's not about you understanding what's going on in my head. You're just supposed to trust me! You're just supposed to want to do what...what I ask you to do, as my friend! As my boyfriend!"

She choked on a sob and sniffed hard. "After everything, Nate...you know what I've been going through, after Kirby Lake. You knew."

There was nothing for me to argue against. This, right here, if I had to be honest, was why I'd come here. I just nodded.

"I know."

"And you still did that! God!"

"I know. I know. It was wrong. I'm sorry. I've learned better. I get it better, now. I do."

"Oh, you get it now? After, what, a week, now you have your shit together?" She looked disgusted. "It doesn't work that way, Nate. I'm sorry. You don't get off that easily."

"I know that. Believe me."

I drew my leg up onto the table so I could sit facing her.

"Lina, I thought I was losing my mind. From the...from my dad's stuff. I thought it was making me..." I shook my head. "You know. Stupid."

She wiped her eyes and looked sideways at me. "You've been acting kinda shitty, Nate. For a while. So?"

"So I was wrong. There's nothing wrong with me. Not like that."

"So...I don't get it. What's your excuse?"

I took her hands. She looked down quickly, but she didn't pull away. She looked at me.

"That's my point. There's no excuse. I've been stupid."

I thought of the woman, whose full name, I learned before I left the Institute, was Evelyn Tamara Hill.

She was thirty-three.

I thought of Lou Uldare. Of Eric Finn.

"Worse, I think I let myself be stupid...because I thought I was, like, sick or going crazy or turning into my dad.

"But I wasn't. I'm not."

She was quiet for a bit before she said, "How do you know?"

"The Institute."

She nodded.

She looked at our hands again.

"I'm scared for you, Nate."

"Me too, Lina. And thanks. That's, you know, better than scared *of* me."

She laughed weakly. "Dude. I don't care how badass you are. You know I can take you."

It felt strange to laugh.

"Nathan?"

"Yeah."

"Pushing me, like that? Knocking me down? You...you get why that was about the worst thing you could possibly do, right?"

I saw Evelyn's mangled throat in my mind and started to cry. Lina let me. She released one of my hands so I could pull some tissues out of my back pocket and blow my nose.

"I do," I said.

A car horn honked.

Too soon. Too soon.

"Time to go," I whispered.

"Where are you going?"

I disengaged my other hand from hers and stood up. "It's time to pay the price," I said, then shook my head and laughed. "Jeez, it sounds all stupid and melodramatic like that."

Lina smiled. "That's us," she said.

I grinned weakly. "Well, that's just lame." I felt like a burden had been lifted, and the lightness was a whole new kind of heavy. "I gotta do the right thing. No more running off."

"Brave men run," she reminded me.

"Ugh," I said. "You know what? I used to be pissed at my dad over that. I thought it was just his half-crazy brain, riffing on a stupid line from a stupid movie and passing it off as some kind of, like, wild hobo wisdom."

I thought of my dad as he was on our trip, clean and trimmed and just this side of sane. I was glad I got to see him like that.

"Maybe it was, when he wrote it. I don't know, you know?"

Lina nodded.

"But here's how I'm gonna take it from here on out," I said. "Brave men run...not away, or to fight another day, or whatever."

I saw that she understood. "No," she said. "Not that."

"I gotta run toward the trouble," I nodded. "My trouble." I shrugged. "It's a stretch. Work with me."

"That sounds like a good thing," she said. "But...what does it mean, for real?"

My mother honked the horn again from somewhere down on the street.

"That's my ride," I said. I opened my arms. "Can we hug, Lina?"

She stood up, but didn't come to me. "What are you doing, Nate?"

"Turning myself in."

Her eyes widened. "For Eric Finn?"

"And...stuff. Stuff I...I can't talk about with you, not right now. In a while. If...you want." I half smiled. "If you'll visit?"

She looked sad. It was a sad thing.

But there was something else in Lina's eyes that made that new heaviness in my chest ease off just a little. Something like understanding. And pride.

She stepped forward.

I put my arms around my best friend and breathed her in, breath after breath after breath after breath.

the end

September 7, 2012 ~ January 31, 2013

Long Beach, California

Afterword

This book exists because my community of friends, readers, and fans came together and said they wanted it. The following people even put money down to make it happen:

Elizabeth F. Nalagan • Joel Gerhold • Rachel Steele • Thom Byrne • Brian Hunt • Bruce "Icepick" Press • Michael C. Dougherty • Dee Morgan • Seth Nicholas Johnson • Keri Orstad • Jeffrey A. Benson • Rick Jones • Stephen Jacob • Robin Hudson • Dan Campbell • The Grailpack • Scott Roche • Earl Newton • Eric Baumwell • James Ballard • James Durham • Mur Lafferty • Joe Mieczkowski • Laura A. Burns • Andrew Delaney • Matt McRoberts • Julie Press • Paul Fischer • Kendall P. Bullen • Theodore Minick • Dave Rayburn • Charles Eugene Anderson • Jonathan Hickel • Al Crowley • Joshua Messinger • C. A. Sizemore • Richard Sutton • Christopher Weible • Mark • Phillips • Eric Scott Elliott • Jim Waters • CJ Marsicano • David Sobkowiak • Matthew Blocker • R.W.W. Greene • Justin R. Macumber • Dr. Francis T. O'Donovan • Kurt Hines • Mark Gibson • Sherry D. Ramsey • Jeffery E Doherty • Susan Jones • Grant Baciocco • Dave Pitts • Jared Congiardo • Josh Wolff • Pon3zer Brkmn • Chris Moody • Mark Jeffrey • David Fisk • Samantha Brandt • Dwight Dunlop • Ray Slakinski • Mark Harris • Charles Sheehan-Miles • Buddy Brannan • Troy Clem III • Robert J. Noble • Nuchtchas & The Clockwork Doctor • Brandon Campbell • Jim Ryan • Steven Saus • Derek from Monster Kid Radio • Kris Johnson • Ryan Harron • Chris Rickard • Lianne Burwell • Nicholas Ahlhelm • Andrea Gideon • Tony Mast • Robert J. Peterson • Rick Stringer • Peter Ellis • Cher Reese • Dave Robison • Thomas Pryce • John Archdeacon • Brian McKelvey • Marc Jordan Paxton • Aws Al-Najjar • Hugh J. O'Donnell • Dave Wiener • Erik Ackerman • Angie & Joe Morency • Cyber Cowboy • Stephanie Harvey • Jarrett Lennon Kaufman • m. • Jason Ramboz • C David Dent • Jeffrey • Asher • Jon Tollerton • Alan White • Jeff Schultz • Glenn Seiler • Kevin Crosby • Jason Newland • Yvette Schwenck • David P Mackler • Shawn Thorpe • Seth "Palms Daddy" Harwood • David M Robb • Tim O'Donnell • Patrick M. Monaghan • Stephen • Mrs. Marie Krieger • Anita M. King • C E Dorsett • Kent Perry • Angela Greene • Bruce Lerner • Pearce Kilgour • Doug Rapson • P.G. Holyfield • Terry Mixon • Cedric Speleers • Elisha L Griego • Mary Ellen Warren • Charles Brown • J. Marcus Xavier • Nicole Feldringer • JJ • Jerry Harrington • Scott C. Leeds • Dharma Kelleher • Javier Garza • Shawn St Pierre • Spants • James Husum • Steve Bickle • Jeff Xilon • Jim Lewinson • Linton Bowers • Brion Humphrey • Aura • Scott E. Pond • Meason Kolkhorst • Kira Mandel • Justin Holdridge • Ed Garbacz • Richard Read • Susan Z • nulloperations • Nicole Gugliucci • M.J. Brudenell • Daniel Monson • Biscuit • Tabitha Grace Smith "TABZ" • William L. Ross

Thanks, everyone!

About the Author

Matthew Wayne Selznick is an author and creator living in Long Beach, California with the best gal in the world and too many pets.

Pilgrimage—A Novel of the Sovereign Era is his second book. You can find more about him and his storyworlds at his website, http://www.mattselznick.com. Or, subscribe to his free e-mail newsletter: http://bit.ly/subscribemws.

More by Matthew Wayne Selznick

The Sovereign Era
Brave Men Run—A Novel of the Sovereign Era
Pilgrimage—A Novel of the Sovereign Era
"The World Revolves Around You"
The Sovereign Era: Year One (editor)
Paramount (forthcoming)

Daikaiju Universe
"Reggie Vs. Kaiju Storm Chimera Wolf"
"Reggie Vs. Kaiju Dragon Squidbat" (forthcoming)

Protector
"Cloak"

Non-Fiction
Worldbuilding For Writers, Gamers, and Other Creatives Volume One: Star, Planet, Moon
Reading The Amazing Spider-Man *Volume One* (forthcoming)
Crowdfunding For Indie Authors (forthcoming)

Before You Go...

I want to say thank you, very much, for buying this book. As an independent author and creator, your patronage means a great deal to me. Your purchase quite literally helps keep a roof over my head and food on the table.

Would you do me two final favors?

First: if you found any typos, continuity errors, or other apparent mistakes, would you let me know? Please e-mail mwsmedia@gmail.com with the details. If applicable, we'll fix things very quickly.

Second: I'd love it if you'd write an honest and thorough review of this book on Amazon.com, Barnesandnoble.com, Goodreads.com, your own blog, or wherever you'd like. Reviews help sell books, and I really value them. Don't have time for a review? How about a quick note on Facebook, Twitter, or the social network you prefer?

Thank you, very much!

Sincerely,
Matthew Wayne Selznick

www.ingramcontent.com/pod-product-compliance
Lightning Source LLC
Chambersburg PA
CBHW071218250626
47163CB00001B/32